All The Good Things Around Us

An Anthology of African Short Stories

All The Good Things Around Us

An Anthology of African Short Stories

Foreword by Wole Soyinka

Edited by Ivor Agyeman-Duah

ayebia

An Adinkra symbol
meaning *Ntesie matemasie*
A symbol of knowledge
and wisdom

Table of Contents

TABLE OF CONTENTS

TABLE OF CONTENTS

About the Editor

Ivor Agyeman-Duah, Director of the Centre for Intellectual Renewal in Ghana, was special advisor from 2009 to 2014 to the Ghanaian President, John Agyekum Kufuor on international development cooperation including work with the World Food Programme in Kenya and Ethiopia and also with the Geneva-based Interpeace. He had previously worked in the diplomatic service as Head of Public Affairs at Ghana's Embassy in Washington, DC and later as Culture and Communication Advisor at the Ghana High Commission in London. He is co-author of two appraisal and advocacy anthologies, *Assessing George W. Bush's Africa Policy* (2009) and *Assessing Barack Obama's Africa Policy* (2014) for the Washington, DC-based African Studies and Research Forum. He is also editor and co-author of: *Pilgrims of the Night: Development Challenges and Opportunities in Africa* (2010), *Africa: A Miner's Canary Into the Twenty-First Century-Essays on Economic Governance* (2013) and *An Economic History of Ghana* (2007).

He serves as Development Policy Advisor to The Lumina Foundation in Lagos, which awards The Wole Soyinka Prize for Literature in Africa and was the 2014-15 Chair of the Literature Jury of the Millennium Excellence Foundation. Agyeman-Duah was part of the production team for the BBC and PBS' – *Into Africa* and *Wonders of the African World* presented by Henry Louis Gates, Jr. He wrote and produced the acclaimed television documentary, *Yaa Asantewaa: The Heroism of an African Queen* and its sequel, *The Return of a King to Seychelles*. He has also co-edited, with Peggy Appiah and Kwame Anthony Appiah, *Bu Me Be: Proverbs of the*

Akans (2007) and with Ogochukwu Promise *Essays in Honour of Wole Soyinka at 80* (2014).

Agyeman-Duah has received fifteen awards, fellowships and grants from around the world including: the Distinguished Friend of Oxford Award from the University of Oxford, Member of the Order of Volta, Republic of Ghana, Fellow of the Phi Beta Delta International Society of the College of Arts and Letters, California State University, Pomona, US State Department International Visitor, the Commonwealth's Thomson Foundation award, among others.

Agyeman-Duah has held fellowships at the W.E.B. Du Bois Institute for African and African American Research at Harvard University and been a Hilary and Trinity Resident Scholar at Exeter College, Oxford. From 2014 to 2015 he was a Research Associate at the African Studies Centre, Oxford. He holds graduate degrees from the London School of Economics and Political Science from the School of Oriental and African Studies, University of London and the University of Wales.

About the Book

"Humanity is the business of writers," was the editor of this anthology, Ivor Agyeman-Duah's response to the literary critic, jurist and Publisher, Margaret Busby's question: "what brings together these distinguished writers?" in a collection that is obviously comprehensive and multi-thematic.

This collection comprises twenty-eight stories in varying degrees of diversity and complexity from coastal and regional locations. From West Africa – Nigeria, Ivory Coast and Ghana to the East African coast from Kenya's Mombasa through the Indian Ocean Rim of Seychelles and further down to Zimbabwe, Zambia Malawi and other countries. These are stories recounting the joys of life even if sometimes they include painful experiences. Themes addressed include love, marriage, the joys of motherhood and fatherhood, family murder in anticipation of an inheritance in Kumasi, the dangers of Oshodi in Lagos, stories from Maiduguri and Northern Nigeria under Islamic crusaders and paradise regained in a family life in the Astove island of Seychelles. But there are also stories across the Atlantic: African migration experiences as in shared pride in Harlem after Obama's presidential victory and the participation of Nigerian-American soldiers in the Syrian war.

The authors are globally recognised and have between them won the following prizes: the Booker Foundation, the MacArthur Fellowship, others have been awarded the Commonwealth Writers Prize for Africa, the BBC Literary Prize, the Hurston/ Wright Legacy Award, the NOMA Award, the Orange Prize, the Caine Prize for African Writing, the Wole Soyinka Prize for Literature in Africa and the Macmillan Writers' Prize for Africa. They include: Ama Ata Aidoo, Chimamanda Ngozi Adichie, Tsitsi Dangarembga, Sefi Atta, Yvonne Owuor, Taiye Selasi, Monica Arac de Nyeko, Ellen Banda-Aaku, Tope Folarin and Chika Unigwe. Other nationally and internationally acclaimed writers include: Ogochukwu Promise of Nigeria, Martin Egblewogbe and Yaba Badoe of Ghana, Benjamin Sehene the Rwandese writer based in Paris, the Malawian prominent writer, Shadreck Chikoti, the South African Bridget Pitt as well as the Nigerian-Canadian, Irehobhude O. Iyioha, all of whom are cosmopolitan writers of complex plots and creators of memorable characters.

Foreword

On reflection of post-independence, I sometimes referred to my generation as the "wasted generation" and by that I was referring in fact to the aspirations and the achievements of our collective. The vision was there, the enthusiasm was there, as was confidence. I sometimes referred to ourselves as the "renaissance people" because we felt there was absolutely no limit to the potential for rebirth of the African continent, and in some kind of false mythical, romantic way, we felt we were the generation to produce this. I often refer to us as the "wasted generation" because of that disparity between vision, aspiration and achievement.

Notwithstanding that, on the cultural field, there has been a real, genuine and sustaining explosion of creativity in all the fields – music, the arts, the plastic arts, but literature most vibrantly. Literature and culture were at the forefront of decolonization and the African Writers Series, for instance, was able to bring out quite a few remarkable gems of literature which normally would have just atrophied for lack of indigenous publishing enterprise. And that indigenous publishing enterprise, despite its setbacks from time to time, has brought up quite a number of inspiring writers in the younger generation.

There have also been economic reverses on the African continent, we must not forget, which affected publishing. Writing cannot hope to escape the general economic malaise which has overtaken many of these nations, and so we must recognize the fact that, yes, there will be ups and downs in the dissemination of literature in Africa.

But I wouldn't say there has been a transition in writing of my generation compared to the current one, a good number of them in this anthology. I think the literature has been on a very normal developmental curve, like everything else. Foreign publishers recognize that African literature is not just a quota system. This has been improved by the numerous prizes – national and international such as the Commonwealth Writers' Prize for Africa, Macmillan Writer's Prize, the BBC, the Caine Prize and others awarded to Africans. You look at the young crop of female writers in particular, especially in the novel, and it is really remarkable. And the young generation of writers also stationed outside: Ben Okri, Chris Abani, Ifi Amadiume, Sefi Atta, Chimamanda Ngozi Adichie and others.

Some ask what accounts for this, especially the women dominance, as it is again reflected in this collection, because, they say, it wasn't the case in the 60s and 70s. My answer has been that, it's not a shift, it just shows that women constantly get marginalised, whether in politics, social development, or literature but that, they have been there all the time; that's what we are all learning. If you look at the tradition of the griot, for instance, you'll find that in some of those countries where the griot culture is deeply entrenched, there have also been prominent female griots who are more aggressive. I hope I don't exaggerate here but, according to my direct experience, especially when I was doing my research in theatre, which also meant of course the epic, music and the others, I realised the female in our traditional society has always been more or less at par with male productivity. So maybe what we are witnessing in this collection is a return to that cycle of equilibrium.

Wole Soyinka
Nobel Laureate in Literature, 1986.

Prologue:
As Clouds Pass Above Our Heads

As clouds pass above our heads
So time passes through our lives.
Where does it go,
And when it passes,
What do we have to show?
We can plant deeds in time
As gardeners plant roses.
We can plant thoughts, or good words too
Especially if they are noble and true.
Time is an act of consciousness:
One of the greatest forces
Of the material world.
We ought to use time
Like emperors of the mind:
Do magic things that the future,
Surprised, will find.
We could change our life today
And seek out a higher way.
The Buddha sat beneath a tree
And from all illusion became free.
And as we travel on this life that is a sea
We can glimpse eternity.
We can join that growing fight
To stop our world being plunged into night.
We can wake to the power of our voice
Change the world with the power of our choice.

But there is nothing we can do
If we don't begin to think anew.
We are not much more than what we think;
In our minds we swim or sink.
If there is one secret I'd like to share
It's that we are what we dream
Or what we fear.
So dream a good dream today
And keep it going in every way.
Let each moment of our life
Somehow help the good fight
Or help spread some light.
The wise say life is a dream;
And soon the dream is done.
But what you did in the dream
Is all that counts beneath the sun.
The dream is real, and the real is a dream
Each one of us is a powerful being.
Wake up to what you are,
You are a sun, you are a star.
Wake up to what you can be.
Search, search for a new destiny

Ben Okri

Introduction

A good number of this collection's anthologists are of the early post-independent and current generation of African writers and Africanists. They also constitute a futuristic African literati. They are by a good measure wtiting from varying geographical locations and judging by the finesse of their individual crafts may be regarded as among some of the the best in contemporary writing. This is a generation who are confident in writing about their contemporary experiences while simultaneously drawing on traditional literary sources which they cannot completely escape because a people's culture manifests in the settings of their beings: from architectural tastes and fashion to other attitudes, these observations are not completely oblivious of the folkloric past.

They may be cosmopolitan or global in their ordinary lives living as they do in Europe, United States and other parts of the world and particularly as they might not necessarily have African citizenships even though they have a claim to an African heritage but revert to Africa in many ways as their stories here demonstrate. Their parents' narratives of migration, their own love on visits and through cultivated knowledge. Those who were not born in Europe and the United States have had reasons for migration whether on temporary or semi-permanent basis. Their migration helps to bridge the gap of our divided humanity of Africa and the rest while they simultaneously acquire multiple identities by becoming global citizens.

It is tempting to find a parallel in the Japanese-European cultural experience after World War II. Could this be the benefits of Diaspora patriotism or contempt from afar? If there has ever

1

been a consistency of hope in Africa's post-colonial journey, it has been (as the Nobel Laureate Wole Soyinka says in his Foreword), in the arts and cultural fields. From the literature as defined by the Achebes, Soyinkas, Armahs, Nwapas, Bâs, Heads and from the ancient royal songs and ballads of the griots and the contemporary Afro-beat music of protest lyrics and Hip Life, Africa has a different and sometimes unsettling story to tell.

These twenty-eight stories from twenty-three African writers are set in over forty-eight cities, towns and villages in Africa and beyond with a foray into Western Europe and the United States. These stories cannot be generalised into the so-called "Africa Rising" narrative, whose potency has always been exceptional.

Migrations. Sojourns. Travels. In a way, the generation that some of this collection's writers looked up to when they were growing up also had reasons to indulge themselves and they too wrote about their own experiences. For some, it meant decades away from home because of the threat of persecution in their homelands and for others, a life of living in two worlds. But neither their temporary nor permanent absences extinguished their creative yearning for Africa. Achebe began and ended his career: *Things Falls Apart* and *There Was a Country* with Igboland on his mind. Soyinka's *Death and the King's Horseman* and *Alapata Apata* are Yoruba-centred narratives. Ama Ata Aidoo's *The Dilemma of a Ghost* was written in her twenties when appreciation for the consequences of the Trans-Atlantic Slave Trade and the cultural identities involving Africa and the United States were little discussed. Ngugi wa Thiong'o's thoughts for a quarter of a century on Gikuyu language usage and advocacy for writing in African languages were developed in Europe and the United States. Away from home.

To the present. Taiye Selasi's Euro-American upbringing and education has served her well in her representation of her double Ghanaian and Nigerian heritage in *Ghana Must Go*, a *New York Times* bestselling novel of love and migration with a plethora of Ghanaian and Nigerian glossary terminologies and idioms. If that outcome is an incident of geographical birth and fitting into other acquired identities from one's indigenous background then that may be said to be becoming the norm in today's "small" world made possible by migration and current advances in the new technologies of the internet generation. This is demonstrated in the Rwandan Faustin Kagame's recently translated story *Exchanging the Crown Someday for Exile* (Chapter Nineteen) or the metamorphosis of that monarchical era into modernity.

So where is home and what are the sources of inspiration for African writing? What cord is it that pulls these strings for a recognition of one's heritage even in absentia? A prayerful Yoruba statement might have the answer in its plea: "May their shadows never shrink!"

One is motivated to bring together these beautiful stories from across Africa and beyond in other to help further broaden the literary landscape in new writing. International literary prizes from the Commonwealth Writers Prize, BBC, Orange Prize, NOMA Award and Wole Soyinka Prize to the Caine Prize for African Writing could and have illuminated the career paths of some of the writers in this collection. But admittedly, not all writers win awards for many reasons including the issue of the language barrier and writing locations nor should they write because of awards. Invitation for this anthology was purposely to create a communion of known and hidden talents. There is also no restriction on the categories of the traditional versus the contemporary to themes which when combined with the former may have a way of limiting creativity and might be tantamount to censorship. The inspiration behind these stories are universal: love, marriage, the joys of motherhood, death – both natural and those designed by terrorists, inheritance conflicts between immediate and distant families, challenges of double or triple identity in changing times and in war and post-war situations as witnessed in Yvonne Owuor's "These Fragments" and Irehobhude Iyioha's "It is Something that Happens to Other People."

Out of the twenty-eight stories, however, only three have previously been published, otherwise, they were written specially for this anthology. Incidentally, the editor has travelled to twenty-five African countries and the settings of many of these stories. Some contributors were invited during visits to these destinations and others on a formal request. One, the Anglo-Ghanaian novelist,

Peggy Appiah, died a decade ago. She mostly wrote traditional stories for children. I had the privilege of working with her and her philosopher son, Kwame Anthony Appiah on some of her writings among them; *Bu Me Be: Proverbs of the Akans*. She left me *The Skull in the Garden* years before she passed on and said that: "It should be published someday."

The source of Appiah's artistic inspiration (if it could ever be de-constructed from the normative discussed above) from the 1950s when she lived in Kumasi, has also been a major source of inspiration to others as well: in her case, the art and meaning of Ashanti goldweights and folklore and other interests including geographic rock formation and art in the Yoruba city of Abeokuta, stories of Igbo proverbs, sculpture interpretation, the idyllic topography of the Seychelles, paintings of the historical Monomatapa ruins in Zimbabwe, the "Half of a Yellow Sun" flag of Biafra, which is but an artistic notation of sovereign yearning in that secessionist movement, of other events triggered by the thirst for freedom such as the Mau Mau Uprising in Kenya which influenced most of the writings in the 60s and 70s with re-currence for generations to come.

The arts could be nostalgic of the past, renewal for the present and future life incarnations, depending on the intention of the artist. This collection is offered in that spirit.

Ivor Agyeman-Duah
Mahe, Seychelles
January 2016

CHAPTER ONE

Rebellion

Ama Ata Aidoo

Like all others, the games people play are always complicated and endless, anyway you look at it: left, right, up, down, or centre. It's not just that you can play any single game forever, but there always are so many of them. And new ones are getting invented all the time.

"Ma, we are here, o!"

I noticed the "we" and my heart sank. I had had them at close intervals, and whether it was due to that fact or not, from when they were babies, my three daughters always and ferociously competed with one another over everything: my attention, and my affections especially. They fought one another relentlessly with envy, jealousy, greed and the rest of the deadly sins. Then one day, when they were all in their teens, it dawned on me that there were times they actually cooperated with one another in the form of ganging up to torment me.

My children competed with one another for and over everything. Toys, books, school grades, girlfriends and later, boyfriends and retrospectively or anticipatorily, even their weddings: dates for, size of gowns and the catering too. In the end, and to my utter delight and the delight of the extended family, we had ended up with fourteen grandchildren from the three of them. Doreen, *aka* Nana Efua, the oldest. She had had three: two boys and one girl. Rosemary, *aka* Dede, the middle one. She must have secretly decided to up the game on her big sister. So she bore three boys and one girl. When the third and youngest set about it, she first begat five children, all girls. Then unable to deal with not getting a boy at all, not to mention some pressure from her husband, she had two more children in quick succession in a rather desperate attempt to remedy the situation. Equals, seven daughters. Her name? Miriam, *aka* Mansa.

How could I not what? Of course, they all knew I always thought that having three children is the most elegantly sensible thing to do if that's possible and convenient for you. If those children are also gender-mixed, that's a wonderful detail. But these days, why should anybody's daughter go through the horrors of another pregnancy just so she can have a boy or a girl? Meanwhile, have you tried and succeeded in stopping any young women from doing anything foolish or even dangerous, just because their mother said they shouldn't? In fact, I'm absolutely convinced that even Doreen stopped at three, not because she thought I would approve. No, that's exactly what *she* wanted.

Or was Mansa mad? Not really. Unless we admit that much of the time, the reasons we women give ourselves for making children, one or any number, are quite crazy.

"Come in."

They did. And for the millionth time, I literally gasped. There they were, each one of them a picture of health and beauty. The three together a composition so incredibly wholesome, I found myself wondering if they were all born by me, and if so, how had I managed such a feat. In early middle age, obviously settled in their lives as professional women, all suitably and comfortably married with children, smug.

Their father? A very long story. Put simply, he had obviously loved me long enough to give me the gift of his gorgeous genes towards the production of my wonderful daughters. Then he had skipped town for greener pastures. Or to continue his goodwill mission among womenfolk.

"Ma, how are you?"

"Me? I'm fine. And seeing you lot is like a booster shot."

"Uh-uh, booster shot ei?!... That's our cool Mama... You are so, so contemp. You kill us." They said, sounding almost

6

rehearsed. In fact, it had been unconsciously rehearsed a thousand times. The teasing and eventual torture had started. And my poor almost battered antennae managed to raise themselves up one more time. It was on my lips to ask them what's so youthful about a term like "booster shot'? But I didn't. What good would it have done anyway?

"We came to beg you to go and visit your son-in-law."

"Which one?"

"Koffs," said one. As in Kofi, of course.

"Oh Ma." The other two said this with a great deal of disapproval. As far as they were concerned I should have remembered which of the two sons-in-law named Kofi they were referring to, since the relevant wife might have called me earlier to give me the info on which husband had been taken ill.

"What's wrong with him?"

"When we called you last week, we told you…" We are clearly beginning to whine.

"U-huh?"

"He is ill"

"Where is he?"

"Millennium Central Hospital."

"He collapsed at work. And they took him there."

"U-huh?"

"… The doctors diagnosed a mild stroke."

"U-huh?"

"Ma, stop saying u-huh, u-huh, and please listen." Looks like the scolding has started in earnest.

"Koffs is on admission at the Millennium Central," one slightly raised voice said. Clearly, it was agreed that I hadn't heard them the first time they had mentioned the hospital.

"S-s-so?" I couldn't bite my tongue in time.

"Ma, what do you mean by 'so'?" The cry of horror was genuine, in unison again, and ear-splitting.

"He seems to be doing quite well…"

"How do you know?" That was asked with "that's-why-people-think-all-old-women-are-witches or batty-and-we-think-that-you-are-getting-to-be-both-unfortunately" in the background. My poor children and their poor generation. How can they claim to be Christian or whatever and still believe in witches, and "powers and principalities", as they and their friends put it? Here it comes, the feeling of failure. Watch it.

"... after all one of the eminent senior doctors there is his father, no?"

Nearly sixty years after Independence, *na be whomyouknow*. Still. Of course, I didn't say any of that aloud. Wouldn't have done to sound critical of any processes and procedures through which my own son-in-law might be rescued from the jaws of debilitation and possible death.

"Are you coming with us to go and see him?"

"No."

"No?"

"What"?!

"Why must I?"

"Why must you? But Ma, how can you even ask such a question?"

"Because he is only my son-in-law."

"Only'? "

"I mean... What I mean is that he is the husband of one of you..."

"You mean that you don't even remember which one of us is married to Koffs?"

"But two of you are married to young men called Kofi, and I can't always assume that I know which one you are talking about."

"Ma-h"!

"They are both family anyway!"

"You must come with us to visit him."

"Or go there later by yourself."

"You must show family solidarity..."

"... and proper concern as an in-law..."

"... otherwise it will look bad..."

"... very bad."

"To whom?"

"What do you mean by 'to whom?' How about his family"?

"And the neighbours?"

"You know you are popular..."

"Lots of people know you."

"And when they hear of what you did…"

"Or didn't do…"

"It will sound bad."

"Very bad."

"It wont look good… at all…"

"At all!"

"At all!!"

"At all!!!"

I don't know whether it was real, or an illusion. The last thing I remember was the three of them picking me up from the chair, and me fearing they were then going to throw me down and… and crack my skull, and break all the other bones in my body. I think I screamed at them to put me down. I don't think anyone heard me…

I must be awake. This must be a hospital room. I know because it is very clean, very bright, and very calm in a particular kind of way. Those three are still here, each of them cooing and gently fussing, and each of them genuinely – or trying to look more distressed than the other two. There are other people around me. They look like nurses and doctors. Two of them look familiar. The husband and son of one of the girls? Am talking, but it doesn't seem like anyone is hearing me. Ah, well, who cares? Am just going to shut up, shut my eyes, and maybe never bother to open any of them again. Then what peace…

CHAPTER TWO

Unsuitable Ties

Sefi Atta

She would rather not be here tonight. For her, a dinner party at a hotel – especially a five-star hotel like this in London – is research work. She might notice a seating-card design, a flower arrangement or some other catering idea she can use when she returns to Lagos. She will study the menu from *hors d'oeuvres* to desserts. As for the company, she knows what to expect, rich Nigerians, all connected to each other.

The hotel, Greek Revival style, is in Knightsbridge. It is cold for May, so she and her husband, Akin, wear coats, which they leave at the cloakroom near the lobby. The cloakroom attendant hands her a ticket and she puts it in her clutch bag. She is conscious of her heels clip-clopping along the marble-floored corridor that leads to the bar. At the entrance of the bar, a waiter lifts a silver tray with flutes of champagne and Buck's Fizz. She goes for the champagne, as does Akin. They thank the waiter, a woman.

The bar resembles a candle-lit library in a stately home. It has shelves of old, leather-bound books and maroon patterned wallpaper. Cocktails are at 7pm, dinner is at 7.45pm, followed by dancing. Carriages are at 1a.m. The dress code is black tie. Akin has decided that means he can get away with wearing a tie that is black.

She took the time and trouble to go from their flat in West Kensington to Kensington High Street to buy a new dress the day before. It was typical of Akin to forget he needed a bow tie

10

until the last moment, yet he was the one who insisted that she come.

Other guests are on time. All are appropriately turned out, a few in colourful traditional Nigerian wear. She and Akin return their smiles and waves as they approach their host, Saheed Balogun.

"How now, my brother?" Saheed asks.

"Hey," Akin says, shaking Saheed's hand.

"Saheed," she says, with a nod.

Saheed looks as if he has only just recognised her. "Yemisi! Long time no see!"

She winces involuntarily as he hugs her. She has become used to seeing his face under newspaper headlines since his fraud investigation began a month ago. He was also recently listed in an online magazine as one of Nigeria's top ten billionaires. He is remarkably slight in person and sports a grey goatee. His bow tie is not quite as symmetrical after he hugs her. She was not expecting him to welcome her that way. Feeling hijacked, she looks around the bar and asks, "Where is Funke?"

"She's taking care of last-minute seating arrangements," Saheed says.

Yemisi grimaces. Nigerians don't always RSVP and sometimes show up with extra guests. Funke is Saheed's wife. Yemisi might call her an old friend, though she is more accurately someone Yemisi socialised with when they were both law undergrads. Funke was at the University of Lagos while she was at University College London. Their paths often crossed in Lagos and London. For reasons she can't explain, she doesn't mind Funke, but she absolutely cannot stand Saheed.

She leaves Akin with him. She had told Akin she intended to stay as far away from Saheed as possible. That was the condition on which she came.

The Baloguns' dinner party is one in a series of fiftieth birthday parties that she and Akin have attended outside Nigeria, given by Nigerians. There have been several in London and destination parties elsewhere. One in Cape Town, another in Dubai, and yet another, much talked about and blogged about, on the French Riviera, which they missed. At the end of May, Funke is having a more intimate party in St Kitts. They will skip that as well. On Funke's actual birthday, which is at the end of June, she will finish with a masked ball in Lagos, in the Civic Centre Grand Banquet Hall. Saheed is flying in a seventies American funk band for that. Why such a blatant display of wealth when he is being investigated by the Economic and Financial Crimes Commission, Yemisi cannot understand.

She circulates, champagne flute in one hand, clutch bag in the other, greeting friends, curtseying to elders and laughing. She is astonished at her capacity to look as if she is enjoying herself. She can't believe the people who have shown up, despite Saheed's investigation – legal people, church people. There is a former state attorney general she attended law school with, and a Pentecostal church pastor she had a crush on in her teens one summer in Lagos when they took tennis lessons at Ikoyi Club. Funke is a member of the pastor's church. Saheed is Muslim, but he attends church services now and then. Through Funke, the pastor apparently receives a fee for praying for Saheed's business, and ten per cent of his profits.

Yemisi doesn't have any clients in the bar. She usually gets work through her connections with the banking crowd in Lagos. Akin has a private equity firm and his clients are senators, governors and government ministers, former and incumbent. Only to her would he admit they are a bunch of thieves. His wealthiest clients, like Saheed, are in the petroleum industry. He sometimes refers to them as oil money.

A waiter approaches her with a tray of vol-au-vents and she tucks her bag under her arm. She chooses one with chicken and mushroom filling and thanks him. Most of the waiters are English, but some look as if they are from other countries in Europe. They are friendly yet unobtrusive and poised without being snooty. They go about their business as if they're with their regular clientele. They've probably been briefed on how to handle the Nigerian function. She thinks of her waiters back home, who would be timid around Nigerians like these. She often tells them they are working, not asking for favours, but they ignore her or laugh at her.

The vol-au-vent is perfectly light. She is eating it when Oyinda and her husband, Oliver, walk in.

"Hello, darling," Oyinda says.

"Sorry," Yemisi mumbles. "My... mouth... is... full."

She dabs the corner of her mouth with her napkin in a mock-ladylike manner.

Oyinda is in a short, black dress and her hair is cropped and natural. She wears no make-up, as usual, but her nails are painted lilac.

She points at Akin. "I see we're not the only ones wearing unsuitable ties."

"It was a struggle," Yemisi says.

"Mine thinks bow ties are silly," Oyinda says.

"Bow ties *are* silly," Oliver says.

His English accent makes him sound ruder. He is blond with thick-rimmed glasses and an overly serious expression. His suit and tie are mod. Yemisi remembers when Nigerians, out of laziness, described him as "that punk rocker guy." She has never known if Oyinda drifted away from other Nigerians, or if it was the other way around, because she married Oliver.

"How are your parents coping with retirement?" Oyinda asks.

"Quite well," Yemisi says. "And yours?"

"Oh, my mother's still working. Yes, she's still going strong. She's not as active as she used to be, but she will attend a conference when she can. My father, on the other hand..." Oyinda pulls a face. "He's busy golfing or doing whatever else he does. What about your kids? They must be out of their teens now."

"My daughter is," Yemisi says. "My son's eighteen."

She and Oyinda met when they were thirteen. There were not many Nigerian students in English boarding schools back then. Her school was in Canterbury, Kent, and Oyinda's was somewhere in Dorset. Their parents made them go to the cinema together during an Easter holiday in London. Oyinda was one of those students who just never returned to Nigeria. She is a paediatrician now, and a Fellow of the Royal College of Paediatrics and Child Health. Oliver is a photographer, and brilliant, apparently. They have no children. They ski and hike together. Their last trip was a sponsored climb up Kilimanjaro to raise money for a medical cause that benefited African children.

"How's Lagos treating you these days?" Oyinda asks.

"You don't want to know," Yemisi says.

"Go on," Oyinda urges. "Tell me."

Yemisi rambles on about her life on Lekki Peninsula. Armed robberies are rare, the main streets are fairly clean, but the side streets get waterlogged during the rainy season. The traffic is getting worse there was a petrol shortage before she travelled and still no regular electricity. She had to buy a new electricity generator for her catering kitchen because her old one broke down.

Oyinda exclaims, "Oh no," over and over, her voice getting higher, until it drops in a confession: "That's why I can't live there."

"We're luckier than most," Yemisi says. "And at least we get to escape once in a while."

She can't complain further. She and Akin live in a serviced estate, so they have constant electricity and running water. Their home is a four-bedroom house with boys' quarters, where their house help stays during the week. Their drivers live elsewhere.

Oyinda widens her eyes. "Did you read the article in which Saheed was mentioned?"

"What article?"

"The one about the one percentile in Lagos."

"Oh, that."

Oyinda shakes her head. "So embarrassing. So, so embarrassing."

"Yes, it was."

For a moment Yemisi thought Oyinda was referring to Saheed's EFCC investigation. Nigeria itself has been in the international news of late, and not in flattering ways. There was the article about the one percentile in Lagos, which appeared in an American newspaper, followed by another in a British glossy magazine about spoiled, rich Nigerian students in London. Two Christmases ago there was the underwear bomber, who was ridiculed back home for being privileged, above all else. For years there have been reports on Boko Haram attacks in Northern Nigeria, and this January there was the Occupy Nigeria movement.

"It was a hatchet job," Oyinda says. "I mean, some of us work hard for a living. We're not all flying around in private jets and lounging on yachts."

"I know, I know," Yemisi says.

She would say the article lacked perspective, but foreign press coverage of Nigeria often does. She dismissed the article. It wasn't worth her energy to take umbrage as a Nigerian who lived overseas might.

"Mind you," Oyinda whispers, "some of this lot here…"

Yemisi blinks slowly. She gossips only at home. Oyinda has a reputation for gossiping anywhere and without discretion.

She can see why Oyinda thinks she is part of the one percentile in Lagos, even though Oyinda doesn't live there. Oyinda would think she belongs because she comes from what Yemisi's mother would call "a good family," based there. Fathers' illustrious careers count, mothers' less so. Oyinda's father was a First Republic health minister and one of the top gynecologists in Lagos of his time. He was also notorious for having affairs with his nurses, for which Oyinda has never forgiven him. But Lagos has since changed. Talking about backgrounds will only get laughs. All it takes to belong to the one percentile is money. The Baloguns belong by virtue of the billions of naira Saheed receives from the government as fuel-subsidy payments to import petroleum products. The EFCC investigation is to determine if his company actually does import petroleum products or if it exists solely to collect the subsidy payments.

"This party must be costing a fortune," Oyinda says.

Yemisi raises her hand. "I'm not saying a word."

People trust her as if she were a doctor. She and Akin could easily be mistaken for being part of the one percentile in Lagos, but she would say they live off them, by providing services, that they have to be useful to belong, and they also have to be loyal.

Oliver finally smiles, though conspiratorially. Perhaps he takes a while to warm up in company, as she does. Or perhaps he feels outnumbered. So far he is the only foreign guest. Whatever the reason, Yemisi has seen his photos of their Kilimanjaro trip on

Facebook, and Oyinda, the only African besides their guide, was smiling away.

She excuses herself, trying to figure out how Oyinda knows the Baloguns. They are definitely not Oyinda's friends, but she would come to their party anyway, out of homesickness or curiosity. They would invite Oyinda because she is the sort of Nigerian they admire. Her mother, a public-health specialist, is a descendant of Lagos royalty. Her mother's father was a lawyer, her paternal grandfather was a politician, and his father was a publisher. She has generations of family history on both sides, recorded history, which is uncommon. The Baloguns would approve of her as a guest. They don't have social functions; they have social agendas.

Akin is still with Saheed. He leans in to listen to whatever Saheed is saying. Yemisi can tell from his discreet expression that they are discussing business. Could Saheed possibly be trying to invest more money with him at a time like this? She would have to find out. She would have to put a stop to that.

A waiter approaches her with a tray of canapés and she again tucks her bag under her arm. She chooses one with smoked salmon and cream cheese, eats it and finishes her champagne.

She met Akin at Cambridge. They got their master's degrees in law there. They gave up law for banking when the banking sector was privatised in the eighties. Akin joined a commercial bank in Lagos where everyone went by their first names. She joined a merchant bank as a company secretary. They got married after Akin was appointed managing director. She left banking before he did to start her catering business; their children were in primary school and she could no longer cope with her long working hours. Akin's parents were retired high court judges. They lived in Lagos, so they would sometimes babysit. She was never comfortable with relying on his parents. Her parents lived in the federal capital, Abuja. Her father was a retired diplomat and her mother, who throughout her father's career had hosted cocktail parties and dinner parties in Bonn, Paris and London, on a Nigerian budget, would describe herself as a housewife.

She and Akin were children of civil servants whose net worth shrank during the Structural Adjustment Programme of the eighties, so they had to be ambitious. She has her father to thank for not turning out like other diplomats' children, who ended up shell-shocked in Nigeria after their fathers retired from the service, going on about the lives they used to have overseas. Whenever she asked her father for money, no matter how little, he would reply, "You think I'm rich?" She credits her mother for getting her into catering. As a girl, she would sulk whenever her mother called her to help in the kitchen. Her brothers never had to help. Her mother, worried Yemisi would turn out to be a useless wife, encouraged her to take a cordon bleu cookery course during her father's posting to London, which she unexpectedly enjoyed. That was when she realised she didn't actually hate cooking; she just wanted to get paid for it.

Akin earns more than she does. He always has. Their daughter is a junior at the University of Pennsylvania, studying economics. Their son wants to go to Imperial College London to study engineering. With foreign-student fees to pay, and a house in Lagos and flat in London to maintain, what else is Akin supposed to do but keep the money coming?

He is talking to Saheed now and she is sure he is making a pitch. After twenty-two years of marriage, she is past arguing about matters they can't resolve. There was a time they argued about his habit of procrastinating, his reluctance to do his small share of chores at home and his presumption that he was in charge of their children's education. These days, they have more than enough help at home and they are lucky if their children listen to them. Akin still procrastinates, but he has that pitiful look good men develop when they've been nagged too long, not that different from the expression of a knackered horse. She is trying to be a nicer wife now, so she gives him breaks, but this is one quarrel they revisit as they go from one function to the next: his financial dealings with dubious clients like Saheed.

"Happy birthday to you," she sings, as Funke walks into the bar with Biola.

Funke feigns shyness. "None of that, please!"

"I beg you," Yemisi says to Biola. "Let me hug the celebrant first. I'll get to you next."

She hugs Funke and tells her she looks radiant because she can't think of a more suitable word. Funke is in a gold-lamé maxi dress, which must be custom-made. She is all diamonds from her décolletage up. She has a long hair weave and a thick layer of bronze eye-shadow that suggests she hired a make-up artist and dictated exactly how she wanted to look. She is pretty –much prettier without make-up.

"I've lost weight, haven't I ?" Funke asks, posing.

"You never needed to," Yemisi says.

Funke often claims she is on a diet, though her appetite secretly remains healthy. Twice a year she disappears to a health spa in Spain for liquid detoxes and colonic irrigations. She bleaches her skin. That she can't hide. She also claims her complexion is the same as it has always been, but she was much darker before.

Metallic fabrics must be in. Biola is in a pewter-coloured dress. Her black-pearl earrings match her dress, her short bob wig is flattering and her make-up colours are neutral. She is naturally skinny, but may have had Botox work on her forehead. Yemisi suspects she deliberately tones down her appearance to make Funke look as if she is trying too hard.

"The lovely Mrs. Lawal," she says, hugging Biola tighter than she hugged Funke to make up for temporarily bypassing her. Biola is a family friend. Their mothers were childhood friends. Their fathers are diehard Metropolitan Club men: any talk of allowing women to become members rubs them up the wrong way.

"How are Auntie and Uncle?" Biola asks.

"Very well," Yemisi says. "How's Chairman?"

"Chairman's fine," Biola says.

Everyone calls Biola's father Chairman. Biola's father calls himself an industrialist, to set himself apart from ordinary businessmen in Lagos. He has never manufactured a single product. He is chairman of several companies he acquired shares in before they became old and established.

Yemisi doesn't ask after Biola's stepmother. Biola's mother died when Biola was just ten and Chairman remarried – a glamorous Liberian divorcee, whom Biola refused to obey. Biola called her "the refugee" behind her back. When their rows got too much for

Chairman, he sent Biola off to Le Rosey in Switzerland and gave her whatever she wanted to compensate for abandoning her. By the age of thirteen she was shopping on Bond Street. Chairman's only rule was that she study and pass her exams. Her stepmother hoped she might fail. Biola got into the London School of Economics to study law. After she graduated, she returned to Lagos for law school.

"So," Biola says, accusingly. "We only meet in London these days."

"Where else?" Yemisi says.

"You're a real socialite caterer, are you?"

"If you really mean I cater for socialites like you? Yes."

Biola laughs. She can't help but put another woman down, even in the course of saying hello.

The last place they met was in Lagos. They were at a barbecue on New Year's Day at Funke's house. Funke had waiters walking up and down with trays of jerk chicken, shrimp kebab and grilled tilapia. There were bottles of Moët rosé dripping on every table. Yemisi asked Funke who her caterer was and Funke said, "I flew in a chef from Senegal."

Biola arrived late that day with her ladies-in-waiting, a group of women who started the Birkin-bag trend in Lagos. Funke was also one of them. Yemisi would never cater for any of them. They would be too demanding. They would try to bully discounts out of her. They would never bother to return her phone calls or texts. If she persisted in trying to contact them, they would refer her to their personal assistants. They could end up mistreating her waiters, which would drive her up the wall. After the job was done, they would pay her in their own sweet time.

She looks forward to seeing Biola and Funke at functions anyway, knowing they will entertain her. She is particularly amused when they carry on as if Lagos and London are neighbouring cities. "I'm going to London next week," Biola might say. "After which I come back to Lagos for a day, then I'm off again." Lagos is a mere six hours away by plane. They travel first class or business class.

The code of loyalty applies to them as well. Biola is married to Tunji Lawal, a senator who took a ten-billion-naira bank loan he never repaid. The EFCC investigated him, too. Funke said any rumours of financial impropriety on his part were a political vendetta. The EFCC eventually dropped their investigation. Funke again stood by Biola when Tunji's affair with a Lagos publicist was exposed. There were lewd text messages, which were quoted in the tabloids. There was a sex tape, which was posted online. Funke said the footage wasn't clear. The whole scandal made Yemisi more sympathetic towards Biola, who is now involved in eradicating poverty in Africa. She is invited around the world to give speeches. She is photographed with international celebrities and posts her photos on Facebook to spite her enemies.

Tunji is in Nigeria, attending a senators' forum. He is with the People's Democratic Party and still hopes to be president. Biola probably wouldn't mind being first lady, but meanwhile won't associate with the new crop of Third Republic politicians Tunji mixes with. She calls them bush people.

"Love your dress," Biola says. "Whose is it?"

"Who knows?" Yemisi says.

It is a pastel-blue maxi dress she bought on sale.

"She always looks good," Biola says to Funke.

"Where did you get it?" Funke asks.

"High Street Ken," Yemisi says.

"The colour suits her," Biola says to Funke.

Yemisi wonders if her dress is worthy of this much attention or if it is just their inquisitive nature that gets the better of them. Perhaps they are mocking her, she thinks in amusement.

"It looks like a lawn van," Funke says.

"It doesn't look anything like a Lanvin," Biola says.

"It does. It looks like a lawn van dress I have."

"Lanvin is understated. You, my dear, are never understated."

"Have you seen their latest collection?"

"Excuse me," Yemisi says.

She hurries as if someone is calling her. There is only so much she can take when Funke and Biola begin to spar. Funke is the challenger here and Biola is the undefeated and undisputed champion.

Biola has always been the champ. Funke may have had her

moments of local glory: a fashion show, she is there in the front row; a Nollywood film premiere, she is on the red carpet as a producer. She is named in best-dressed lists. But only recently has she had international recognition, for building a world-class boutique hotel in Lagos. Saheed hired an American PR company to cover the opening and flew in the architect who designed the hotel, a Somali, highly celebrated in London. Saheed's billionaire status is most likely another PR stunt. Yet Biola wins every time because she gets Funke to up the ante. Biola has been making women feel small since she was a girl: her stepmother, her stepmother's friends, her friends' disapproving mothers. For her, this is sport.

Yemisi heads for the other end of the bar. She rarely sees either of them these days. She hears about them. Funke is considered a social climber and Biola an outright fraud. People get furious about her photos with international celebrities. Yemisi just wishes she could pull the celebrities aside and say, as her mother would, "Know the calibre of Nigerian you fraternise with."

They will pose with any African for a photo op. The gossip about Funke and Biola so far only puts her in awe of their ability to withstand it, though she imagines that, in private, they are just as brutal about people who talk about them.

The bar empties a little after 7.45pm. Yemisi guesses there are about a hundred guests in all. Oliver is no longer the only foreign guest. She passes a couple of men who sound German or Austrian. They must be Saheed's business partners.

On the pilgrimage to the dining room, she sidles up to Akin and whispers, "What were you and Saheed talking about?"

"When?" Akin asks.

"Keep your voice down, please."

"My voice is down."

"Lower it."

"Is this low enough?"

"For God's sake."

She walks ahead of Akin as he watches her with a bemused expression. His whispers are loud. Everyone around them will hear what he is saying.

Perhaps he has sold his soul to Saheed. Perhaps this is the man she married. Her clients are no different from his. She had one who bankrupted a finance house using an expense account before fleeing the country. She had another, a lovely woman, who would send her flowers after every catering job. The woman was frogmarched out of a bank when she was caught doing illegal foreign-exchange deals. But Yemisi no longer caters for them.

She remembers when Saheed's became the name to drop in Lagos. She asked Akin how Saheed made his money and Akin said, "Why are you asking me?" Then Saheed became Akin's client and Akin told her how and she said, "Here we go again." There was oil in Nigeria, plenty of oil. In a normal country, there would probably be no need to import petroleum products. But the refineries in Nigeria didn't work, so the bulk of the oil was exported overseas and people like Saheed were in business.

She and Akin believed Saheed's business was bona fide back then, so she wasn't surprised Saheed had made his money overnight. She was just put off by how much he spent. When Akin told her Saheed was thinking of buying a yacht, she said she hoped Saheed could swim. When Akin mentioned that Saheed travelled to Monaco to watch the Grand Prix, she said if Saheed was interested in watching drivers trying to kill everyone in their way he should have stayed in Lagos. Akin called her a snob. She didn't deny that. She got her snobbery from her mother. "He's so nouveau," she said. "We're all nouveau," Akin said.

The dining room has a marble fireplace, above which is a gilt-framed mirror. There are crystal chandeliers and period paintings of horses. The tables are beautifully set, but so far nothing inspires her. The designs are old and staid. Her clients want cutting-edge modern. She finds her name on the seating chart. She is on the same table as Funke and Biola. *Shit*, she thinks.

Akin is on Saheed's table. She doesn't want to be separated from him. Why would Funke switch seats with him? Why would Funke want to be on a different table from Saheed? Her clients in general want to sit next to their spouses, even when they're not in the mood to speak to them. They don't mind being miserable as they eat. After dinner, women will gather together, so will men, separately.

She usually avoids getting involved in planning her clients' seating arrangements because of the sheer drudgery of considering the relationships between people at any given table in Lagos, their alliances, rivalries and politics. She finds her way to Funke's table, which is nearest to the dance floor. Funke has probably done the best she can with her last-minute seating arrangements but, on Saheed's table, Funke has Saheed's business partner, Mustapha, next to the pastor who blames emirs like Mustapha's father for Boko Haram attacks. If Mustapha's father had his way, Nigeria would be an Islamic country. He lobbied for the right to adopt sharia law in Northern Nigeria. Mustapha prefers to play polo there. He founded the first polo-cum-country club in his home state. Saheed, a one-leg-in-one-leg-out Muslim, courted his friendship for years, inviting him to the polo club in Lagos whenever he was in town. The club veterans made fun of Saheed behind his back. He had only just started taking riding lessons. He barely knew how to mount a horse. They said he would never succeed in aligning himself with a Northern aristocrat like Mustapha. But he did. He and Mustapha teamed up to invest in an Islamic banking scheme. How they separated Islam from banking, God only knew.

On the elders' table, Funke has her father, Professor Akande, a hardcore Yoruba secessionist who believes the South West of Nigeria would be better off as a country in its own right, next to a chief who sits on the board of Saheed's company. The chief is from the South-South region of Nigeria and is too financially shrewd to be a secessionist. He understands what secessionists don't, that it makes more sense to do business with Nigerians from ethnic groups he can't stand, than to demand the partitioning of Nigeria. Still, as an elderly statesman of the South-South, he attends meetings in his home state to discuss how Nigeria's oil, which is drilled there and has polluted the land, doesn't benefit his people. He assures his people that any concerns they have will be fully addressed whenever the president decides to convene a national conference.

Yemisi remembers her father saying there were no divisions amongst rich Nigerians, but they created divisions so poor Nigerians could kill each other off. She has had moments of panic at parties in Lagos, when she imagines a suicide bomber gatecrashing, followed by a bloody aftermath with food and blood splattered everywhere, followed by a thought that terrifies her so much she immediately suppresses it: *one bomb at a party like this and half of Nigeria's problems would disappear.*

She finds her seating card on the table. She is next to Funke and Biola. She is beginning to think Funke switched seats so their husbands could discuss business without interference. She and Funke are the only wives separated from their husbands on the table. Oyinda and Oliver are together across from them. Akin is right next to Saheed on Saheed's table. She imagines herself running over there and yelling, "What is wrong with you? How could you even consider doing business with him at a time like this? Have you no shame?"

The menu distracts her for a while. The first course is salad with goat cheese or lobster bisque. She goes for the bisque, which turns out to be bland. The main meal is chicken breast in a béchamel-based sauce with steamed vegetables. Her clients are usually not keen on white meat or any meat mixed with dairy. They don't appreciate *al dente* vegetables. Or vegetarian meals. The vegetarian meal is a risotto. Oliver is the only one who has requested it.

She is not a food or wine connoisseur, or a conversationalist. Her favourite way to pass time at dinner parties is to listen to other people talking. She avoids looking at them to decode their conversations. Her father taught her how to: he fancied himself as an expert on espionage.

"That country is useless. Useless, I tell you."

Biola complaining to Funke about mobile-phone services in Nigeria. Yemisi has heard Nigerians call Nigeria a useless country for more trivial problems, a bad pedicure, a shirt button lost at the dry cleaner's. She calls Nigeria a useless country whenever she gets stuck in traffic.

"They don't practise medicine there. They practise business. Any doctor who wants to practise medicine has left the country and the newly qualified ones are just badly trained…"

A man telling Oyinda why she is better off practising paediatrics in England. His mother was misdiagnosed with malaria in Nigeria, when she had pancreatitis. He is managing director of a cable-television company. Yemisi holds him personally responsible for the latest trend of theme parties in Lagos. Because of E! Entertainment Television and other such networks, her clients want menus to match their themes. They ask for cupcakes and cakepops.

For a moment, she panics over her parents. She must call them in the morning to find out if her mother has had her blood pressure tested, and if her father has seen a doctor about his lower back pain.

"She carries herself well. She dresses conservatively. What I like most about her is that she is not trying to upstage her husband. She came into that family knowing her place."

Funke talking about Prince William and Kate and making them sound awfully Nigerian.

What is it with clothes? Yemisi thinks. What is it with Nigerians and clothes? It's not as if there is a designer in Paris, looking at his collection and saying, "*C'est parfait pour mes clientes Nigériennes!*"

"I still don't understand the fuss about Pippa."

Biola, doing what she does best.

"Of course I'm against free education!"

The same man who said newly qualified Nigerian doctors were badly trained.

"How can anyone be against free education?"

Oyinda, who laughs even though she's outraged.

"Don't mind him. He's talking rubbish."

The man's wife. Her bluntness is unusual. She may be upset with him over an unrelated matter. She is an interior decorator – a real one, not just an attractive woman who has an eye for colour and knows how to put a room together. These days, in Lagos, any woman who can put a meal together can call herself a caterer.

"Free education ruined the school system in Lagos. We used to have good schools before they opened them up to the masses. I went to Saint Greg's. People like us can't send our sons to Saint Greg's anymore."

The man, ignoring his wife.

"I suppose that's one way of looking at it."

Oyinda, disagreeing.

"Don't mind him. He doesn't know what he's talking about."

His wife, refusing to be ignored.

"Did anyone read that article about the Lagos elite?"

Oyinda.

"What article?"

Funke.

"Saheed was mentioned."

Oyinda, soliciting gossip.

"Not that article again."

Funke, pretending to be embarrassed.

"They were just upper-middle-class Nigerians. You can't compare them to the global elite."

Biola, an authority on class since her early schooling in Switzerland.

"It made us look bad to the rest of the world, though. We don't all live lavishly."

Oyinda, who still doesn't realise she is not part of the one percentile in Lagos.

"Anyone can live lavishly in Nigeria if they have money. That doesn't mean they have class."

Biola, taking a jab.

"Some elite Nigerians do."

Funke, blocking.

Elite at what? Yemisi thinks. Shopping? What does class mean in Nigeria anyway? Nigerians call themselves upper middle class if they manage to buy a house on a mortgage. Akin once called her high class because she made *spaghetti allaputtanesca*. English classes cause confusion. American percentiles are better suited to Nigeria. Besides, who in the world would take seriously an article about people who are of no consequence to anyone but themselves?

"It was shocking to me, actually."

Oliver.

"Really? Why?"

Biola, attempting to bully him.

"That people can be so excessive in the midst of so much poverty."

Oliver, with First World indignation.

"There's poverty in Europe. That's why half of Europe is here."

Biola, with Third World defensiveness.

"Not the kind of poverty you have in Africa, surely."

Oliver, laughing cautiously.

"You look like a world traveller. Which African countries have you been to?"

Biola, condescendingly.

"Oyinda and I went on holiday to Kenya. We hiked up Kilimanjaro for charity."

Oliver, humbly.

"He took photos."

Funke, bored with the conversation. She is an intelligent woman. She may not be as intelligent as Biola, but she practised law for many years, which was more than Biola did. Biola had a one-year stint at her uncle's firm, then she worked for her father, which amounted to attending boardroom meetings on his behalf. The problem with Funke was that as soon as Saheed made money, she had new concerns. She got involved with a group of women who had similar concerns. Now, if a conversation isn't about their concerns, she is not interested. Biola has to stay on top of issues outside their circle to run her foundation.

"Kenya is very different from Nigeria, economically."

Biola, professorially.

"Yes, I know Nigeria is oil rich, but there is that gap between the rich and the poor, isn't there?"

Oliver, earnestly.

"There is, there is."

Oyinda, who sounds as if she's rocking back and forth.

Yemisi has heard Nigerians refer to themselves as poor because they can't afford to send their children to schools abroad. She would say her house help and catering staff are poor. If they stopped working for a month, they might starve, unless they were prepared to beg. Yet they might say beggars on the streets are poor. She gives leftover food to her catering staff after jobs. She pays her house help's hospital bills. Akin thinks they take advantage of her. "They're always sick," he once said. He is polite to them because he is a polite person, but he doesn't trust them. He has the usual anxieties about theft and that other unspoken fear, that no matter how well he treats them, come a revolution, they would turn around and slit his throat.

"I imagine that affluent Nigerians are sufficiently well-placed to do something about the economic divide."

Oliver, who doesn't know the calibre of Nigerian he is fraternising with. He thinks he can shift their consciences. He cannot. He thinks they're capitalists. Poor Nigerians are the capitalists. They have to be. They don't depend on the government for deals; they don't get to dip their hands in state treasuries or commit bank fraud; they don't even get to smell oil money.

"I think every Nigerian should do what they can. I run a foundation. I'm an advocate for the eradication of poverty in Nigeria. I've been invited to the UN to give a talk. It may not be as arduous as a trek up Kilimanjaro, but it's a start."

Biola.

Knockout, Yemisi thinks.

The dessert options are chocolate gateau or tiramisu. She goes for the gateau, which has a glutinous filling that sticks to the roof of her mouth.

After dinner, Funke's mother stands up to lead the room in a prayer. A dignified woman in a vintage *asooke* outfit with matching stole and head tie, she seems unlikely to tolerate extravagance. "Lord," she says, "we ask that You grant Funke wisdom and humility with age."

Saheed makes the toast between pauses, as guests respond to him.

"She is the love of my life."

"Ah!"

"I am forever indebted to her."

"Ah!"

"And to my in-laws, Professor and Mrs. Akande."

Where are his parents? Yemisi wonders. He flies everyone else around the globe. Why couldn't he fly them here? All she's ever heard about Saheed's parents is that they live in their hometown.

The guests stand up to clink glasses. They sing "For She's a Jolly Good Fellow" and sit down.

"Well," Oyinda says afterwards, "that was more like an anniversary toast. You know, I'd much prefer to celebrate my twenty-fifth wedding anniversary than my fiftieth birthday."

Oyinda knows full well that given a choice, Nigerian women will celebrate their birthdays before any wedding anniversary.

"It's envy," Biola says, out of nowhere. "It's all envy at the end of the day."

"Yes," Funke murmurs."It is."

Yemisi can't decide if they are talking about Oyinda or Oliver. Then she guesses from Funke's sober expression that Biola may have been referring to someone else. She reconsiders a rumour, which she initially ignored, that Saheed has several girlfriends in Lagos he is supporting financially, including one who has a son by him. That could explain why Funke is not sitting with him.

The DJ, who has been setting up his equipment on the dance floor, begins to play Afro hip-hop music. Oyinda and Oliver get up to dance, followed by Funke and Biola and other couples on their table. Women take over the dance floor. Akin won't dance in public. He thinks it emasculates him. Yemisi, a self-confessed lousy dancer, stays in her chair and watches. Oyinda and Oliver do a calypso dance as Funke and Biola point at each other and sing, "I'm hot and you're not," to a D'banj song.

The men on Saheed's table finally disperse and head for the dance floor to join their wives. Only then does Akin remember her. He smiles as he approaches her, sits in the chair next to hers and then frowns.

"What's wrong?" he asks.

"Nothing," she says.

"Sure?"

"Sure."

"Having a good time?"

"Yeah."

He rubs her knee. They watch other couples on the dance floor. Funke is dancing with Saheed, side by side rather than face to face.

"What were you and Saheed talking about?"

"He wanted my advice."

"On?"

"Some business idea."

"I knew it! That's why they separated us!"

"Who separated us? Why?"

She softens her voice. He might retreat back to Saheed's table.

"What business idea?"

"He wants to invest in a country club."

"Where?"

"Somewhere off Lekki Expressway, past our estate. Mustapha is involved."

"Are you involved?"

"You think I'm stupid?"

"It's not about being stupid."

"What is it about?"

What is it about? she thinks. Saheed has not been charged. The EFCC may never even charge him. This is his chance to play country clubs with Mustapha.

"Are you sure you're all right?" Akin asks, narrowing his eyes.

"Why do you keep asking?"

"I mean, I thought it worked out well that we were on separate tables. You said you wanted to stay as far away as possible."

"I know, I know."

She has also said he shouldn't take her literally.

He laughs. "Or are we still on the matter of my choice of tie?"

She smiles. "Of course not."

CHAPTER THREE

Dead Leaves on the Beautiful River

Ivor Agyeman-Duah

David sat in his living room chair still unbelieving of the television footage. He had argued several times how puzzling and senseless it was that people took to drinking in times of happiness and sorrow. But there he was, a bottle of Nederburg red wine almost gone. He was a leading African American sociologist of Urban Poverty. His wife Sarah from Alabama was just recovering from a suspected malaria infection from her one week visit as head of the African American Community Development in Boston to the Democratic Republic of Congo. They had gone to help build an orphanage in the post-war central African country.

"I am glad to be part of this," David said, as Sarah walked intermittently between the kitchen where she was preparing dinner and the living room where her eyes would focus on the television footage on this day of days.

"Hello Chicago," the new global political star, his awaited hour upon the world stage, greeted. "If there is anyone out there who still doubts that America is a place where all things are possible, who still wonders if the dreams of our founders are alive in our time, who still questions the power of our democracy, tonight is your answer."

David's sobbing had turned into rolling tears. Sarah had put off the gas cooker by then and was holding David's hand as they listened to the man of the moment: "But tonight, because of what we did on this day, in this election, at this defining moment, change has come to America and the road ahead will be long, our climb will be steep. We may not get there in one year, or even in one term but America, I have never been more hopeful than I am tonight that we will get there…"

"I never expected that this day would come in my lifetime," David interspersed still. When the CNN camera focused on a sobbing Oprah Winfrey, David wondered what was going through the mind of this woman from a once poor background of southern Mississippi, a sojourner in Milwaukee, whose forebears left the rural south and migrated to the north of the new world in search of better living conditions in the 1950s. When the camera shifted to Jesse Jackson, standing and weeping not far from Oprah, David told Sarah that, the cameraman was a historian. "Jesse Jackson stood very close to Martin Luther King at the Lorraine Motel and was full of smiles whilst King was pensive, just hours before he was assassinated. Today, Jackson is weeping for the struggles and humiliation that descendants of slaves lived with and for which King paid the price. But he is gone…" David started to weep some more as silent tears fell down Sarah's cheeks.

Stories of Martin Luther King still remind Sarah of her eighty-year-old grandmother living in Alabama who took part in the African American bus boycotts in Montgomery of which King was a front-liner. She had managed against all odds and shaken hands with him as they all sang, "*We Shall Overcome Some Day.*"

"The journey has been long," David said as he wiped his tears. As a leading sociologist, he had supported Hillary Clinton as a democratic intellectual, knowing very well that Obama would not get anywhere in the Democratic Party primaries as another black politician. The speeches had been brilliant and *Dreams of My Father* had been a compelling argument. It was when Obama won the Iowa caucus that David felt that this candidate was different and so as someone with influence, he decided there and then to support him, more in reverence for the toils and tribulations of the forebears who crossed the Atlantic by force to work on the plantation economies in the new world – those who did so in rural Ohio, those who came from the west coast of Africa, especially, Senegal into the Carolinas and taught America how to grow rice.

David, now sober after the speech, asked Sarah to buy two tickets online so they could travel to Harlem together to see how the events played out in two days time.

"Yes, we will go. I have never appreciated fully the negro-spirituals of Paul Robeson, never given much spiritual interpretation to: *Go Tell it on the Mountain*," he said to Sarah as hand-in-hand husband and wife climbed the stairs, dinner forgotten; no mission in sight even as they went to the bedroom of this two million dollar mansion he had bought.

They had previously lived in New Haven in Connecticut in their childless marriage of fifteen years where David was a professor at Yale, before they moved into Cambridge, Massachusetts. David had gotten himself into trouble over a two-year affair with a blond white woman called Monica. Sarah had suspected the relationship but had always felt handicapped with how far she could exercise control in her marriage in the absence of a child. As David's attitude and character had not changed, Sarah's parents and even her eighty-year-old grandmother in Montgomery had urged her to adopt patience and always remember her modest background.

Monica who had served as an assistant professor at the university by the fact of the relationship has always seen herself as not only better placed in terms of education to "that Southern woman you call a wife," a reference spoken to the face of David, who became furious and that strained the relationship for days. "This relationship should have nothing, no reference whatsoever to my wife," he had told her. But Monica is blond, has an Ivy League PhD compared to the University of Alabama bachelor's degree of the stable competitor and the fact that many African American men once successful have been accused, perhaps unfairly, of marrying white women for career progression or as a mark of their new class status.

The result of David's inability to terminate the relationship was the resultant pregnancy. Sarah had wept bitterly when David came home one evening, sobered and in a sorrowful voice disclosed to her that Monica was pregnant for him, a situation which Monica wanted the whole world to know. He had wanted Sarah to be aware before she got it from the gossip machine. With the pregnancy as ammunition, Monica's anticipation had been the usurpation of the marriage. David paid all the bills associated with the pregnancy and ensured that mother and unborn child were in a healthy state, but Monica's target was beyond that. When, after giving birth to a boy and two years into that, he showed no inclination towards achieving that, she went to the media with all sorts of stories to tarnish his professional career including an accusation of grade inflation for black students.

It revived the discussion about why some successful black people go in for blond white women. David was battered because he had given sociological reasons to class behaviour in urban communities on prime time television whenever the need arose. But virtually all the accusations including grade inflation fell flat apart from the fact of pregnancy and subsequent childbirth.

Boston was to give them a new life after they had taken time off to visit Sarah's family in Alabama which David observed still lacked sufficient street lights compared to nearby Georgia State.

It was a bright mid-day when they finally got to their hotel, Hotel Harlem in East Harlem on 115th Street and 1st Avenue, after three and half hours of driving. Just after having lunch, they left to walk on the streets and to the informal markets nearby. It had always been a pilgrimage space. These streets of Harlem that have seen great renaissance in history, the outpouring of literary works, art, music, architecture. It had been on these streets, in these slums that you find slavery architecture-wooden cabin structures and historical poverty that people remember most. As David was explaining to Sarah in their walk-about, the erected big screens were re-playing Obama's speech in Chicago after his declaration as the Democratic Party nominee and a president elect, a man wearing a dirty bear black cap and a cardigan with a coat on top of it, approached them in a zigzag movement with outstretched arms.

"Can you give me some change, brother, even a dollar change?" David would normally have walked on but got stalked as this man, pretending not to take the walking-on as an answer, continued, "I never thought I would see this day in my life. If I knew that such progress was possible, I would have led a better life." That was striking! For whilst he has to some extent a similar background with this apparent drug addict, he realized that not all would have the same perspectives, same thinking but the remorse at least of acknowledging Obama's reality of hope was something he also thought impossible days ago. David gave him $20.

Just after this gesture and as he turned to continue their walk, David saw Caroline, Monica's younger sister who had lived for some years with her boyfriend off Harlem-Way and who had first introduced him and Monica to the best hotel around the area, Hotel Harlem. She pretended not to see David and with a face suddenly straightened, passed by him.

"Brother, God bless you," this beggar-friend said in receipt of the money ." But brother, can I give you this gift?," simultaneously running back to a table of their first encounter and bending down to retrieve an art work: an C18th painting: a cabin situated on a plantation, perhaps somewhere in New Orleans or North Carolina with three black women, one of them washing items, the other with a baby sitting, and the third one peeling vegetables. There is a nearby chariot, a presumed farm manger and hens parading around the compound – one painting, too many stories!

"Thank you so much," David said as he held this exotic painting in his hands and to Sarah's view.

"It is interesting that this man wanted just a dollar but he now has $20 and even given you perhaps someone's stolen painting worth hundreds or thousands of dollars," Sarah said with a mocking voice as they continued walking. But the man was not done yet. "You say you are a university professor," he began again, at which point David and Sarah stopped walking even though they found the stench coming from their new friend unbearable probably from days of no showering. But where they stopped walking was also the site of a makeshift bookshop the seller shouting the prices of his items: "Every book for a dollar, every book for a dollar!" It was one makeshift shop in a long chain in this informal lane market. The items and book titles were intriguing: a coffee-size colour photo book of Obama and family and T-shirts, Richard Wright's *Native Son*, Harriet Wilson's *Our Nig Or Sketches from the Life of a Free Black*, Baldwin's *Notes of a Native Son, Go Tell It on the*

Mountain and from the maestro Du Bois, *The Souls of Black Folks* and many more.

"Now tell me," their friend said, pointing to the titles, "Are these titles relevant anymore; these are protest literature overthrown by Obama's hope message. Are they dead leaves on a beautiful river?... Is it the end of a history of all the tribulations of our saints and heroes come to an end?"

These were very perceptive questions and even Sarah's dislike for this guy did not prevent her from recognizing this. "These are intelligent questions we all need to seek answers to," David responsed and added, "It's difficult to know now as it is still early days yet." To which the friend responded, "Have a good day, brother!"

But the barrage of rhetoric and philosophical musings from a suspected drug addict had stunned David. He turned to Sarah and said, "In the midst of hope, of maiden history, this guy still cannot tell whether it is sunrise or sunset on us. I cannot tell either. But at least he knows that when a leaf falls in a season, it is weak or dead and that even if it falls on a beautiful river as a metaphor for Obama's victory, it is of little value. Renaissance has not left Harlem. It still has a spirit even its simpletons, so-called dregs of its environs."

The short journey back to Hotel Harlem had created so many things on their minds. When David finally collected their room key from the reception after a few pleasantries, he was informed of a visitor in the nearby Waiting Room.

"A visitor in this hotel? I have no appointment with anybody," he said in response. But Sarah had retorted that maybe some media people saw "you walking around the shops or somewhere near and have tracked you here in want of an interview."

"Well, I did not come here for that," David replied as they walked to the Waiting Room only to find to their shock Monica, David's son and two packed suit cases in the corner.

David and Sarah were speechless. It was Monica who spoke first, "Sorry if this is an interruption but I have a new career opening in Australia and I cannot take Henry with me. I was luckily advised by Caroline, my sister, whom I am visiting the past week and discussing what to do with Henry. She rushed home to me that you are here in Harlem and possibly at this hotel. I have brought Henry so you can take care of him to enable me pursue this opportunity. These are his stuff including birth documents," she said as she grabbed her handbag, kissed Henry who did not show any emotions or cry for being left with these "strangers" David, still speechless could not believe it but saw Monica leave and disappeared out of the hotel door. Sarah smiled at little Henry, picked him up and called someone at the reception to help bring the two suitcases to their room.

"It was your status and wealth she was interested in and not you or a child from you. Even if she had had this marriage, divorce would have overrun your wealth along the line," Sarah cuddled Henry, who smiled at the unknown man, unknown father, and the generous woman and to a new temporary home of a hotel.

CHAPTER FOUR

Happiness

Chika Unigwe

Shylock was a man of very few words and then only when a nod or a shaking of the head would not suffice. Prosperous did not know anyone else less inclined to use their tongue. She told Agu this the first time Shylock came to their house, the friend of a friend and so recently arrived from Nigeria that Prosperous swore that as soon as he walked in, her homesickness lifted because he smelt of home. She did not tell Agu that she thought Shylock looked like him: same high forehead, same roast coffee complexion, they could have been brothers.

"He has a lazy tongue," Agu said. Prosperous said she did not trust a man who would not talk in the company of other men.

"Maybe he's shy."

She said she had thought that too at first when he answered her "Would you like a beer?" with a nod. But the longer he sat there, in their sitting room, nodding and shaking his head to questions, listening to the other men argue and talk but contributing nothing, as if he were a sponge absorbing their voices, she began to feel that her initial assessment of him was wrong.

"He's not shy. He's sly. I could tell from the minute he walked through that door."

"I can tell you from what I've heard that he's a man of action."

She could no longer talk to Agu of Shylock, could not tell Agu that she no longer thought of him as sly. But that was not the only thing she could not talk to Agu about. Prosperous hoped

Shylock would not come today. Yet, she wanted him to come, to bring his silent self and sit in their sitting room and nod his head. She was dicing okra in the kitchen, picking them one at a time from the strainer beside her, and then placing them, dripping wet, on the chopping board. She wanted to see him. She did not want to see him. He would come. He would not come. He would. He wouldn't. If the next okra she picked out was good, he'd come. If it wasn't, even if it was just the tapered end that was bad, it would be fate's message to her that he would not come. She shut her eyes and picked one. It was green, firm – though not as firm as she would have liked *okra*, almost the colour of home. She worked meticulously, first slicing the okra into circles, then semi circles, then quartered. Agu, her husband, stood in a corner of the kitchen, watching her work. He was in her way, but she could not tell him to move. Today was not the day to antagonize him.

Soon, their house would be full of people, men, fellow Nigerians, swelling up their small sitting room with their voices and their presence and their opinions about politics and religion and life. Their wives would be in the kitchen with Prosperous, their own voices muted, less enthusiastic, discussing the insufficiencies of their present lives, the children with them. Prosperous often thought that men adapted better to change, that they were better disposed to find happiness away from the familiar. Agu never complained of homesickness. He did not feel it the way Prosperous did, like a lump in her throat as if she was about to cry. He and his friends did not sit around, the way the women did, complaining that they could not buy *achi* anywhere to thicken *egusi* soup; that the prepackaged *ogbono* from the Tropical Store could not replace the fresh one from back home; that they would give anything for the taste of *moimoi* wrapped in banana leaves which was impossible to find here. Men were like children. They were easily satisfied. They sat in front of the TV watching football and clips of P Square dancing *azonto*, and they ate the egusi not thickened with achi, and they did not even notice, and they argued in loud voices not curled at the edges with nostalgia. They carried on with life, working in bread factories and tomato farms and chicken farms even though they were far better qualified for other things, even though back home, they had held more challenging jobs, owned their own businesses, and had not sought this life so far removed from what they were used to. She could not decide if that made them fearless. If she were a man, she thought, she would have been able to find happiness in little things. She would have had a life of contentment. She would not have gone out to seek it. She would not be needing now to keep Agu sweet.

"You are so blessed," Prosperous said to Agu without thinking, without even looking up from the last of the okra she was dicing.

"What?" He sounded angry. He always sounded angry these days.

"Nothing." She wiped the slime off the knife with a dish towel, moved the diced vegetable from the chopping board into a pot already simmering on the fire. She lowered the fire under the pot. That was the okra soup done. She had to start work on the stew for the jollof rice.

It infuriated her, this having to cook every Sunday as if they were having a party, but she could not complain. Why couldn't any of the other men volunteer their own homes? Why did Agu have to take on the role of the chief of the clan? Everyone said how generous he was, opening up his house like that every week, but she was the one who had to do the work. The only person she could complain to was Joke, and Joke wasn't even her friend, just a young woman she cleaned for. She told Joke that she dreaded Sundays. It was not just the cooking, it was the visitors. She did not always feel like entertaining, did not always feel like having too many people in her house. "Sometimes, I just want to spend my weekends in bed, sleeping. Or reading a book. It's been a long time since I read a book."

"Then you must tell them. Tell your husband he is not being considerate expecting you to do this every week. Tell your friends they cannot come. Tell them you want to rest. Every week, doing this, you must rest. Your husband, your friends, tell them. They will understand, no?"

"I can't."

"Why not?"

Because you don't. Because it's against tradition. Because "Y"

40

has a long tail and two branches. That's the response she would have given a fellow Nigerian, the response to questions which deserve no answer because they are foolish. Instead she smiled at Joke and said, "Indeed. Why not?" They were really from different worlds. She went back to scrubbing the tiled floor.

"Don't forget to fry those gizzards we got last week from John."

"They are fried already."

She had been in the kitchen since morning. What did he think she spent all that time doing? Dancing? She badly wanted to go back to bed. She had had a restless night, waking up every hour. Agu did not even stir once. Yet, she had been the one to get out of bed early to start cooking. She felt nauseous.

"Where is it?"

"What?"

She hoped she would have time for a long shower before the visitors began to come. She looked up at the clock behind Agu. The church service would be over soon and they would troop to her house for Sunday dinner. She and Agu, raised Catholic, were yet to find a church where they could follow the Mass in English, and they still retained the Catholic aversion to Pentecostal churches so that they stayed away from the Holy Mountain of the Lord of Lords, the church run by a Nigerian pastor and to which all their friends went. Instead, Prosperous' Sunday mornings were taken up with making sure that the churchgoers did not have to go home and cook.

"Where is what?" She repeated.

"The meat."

She opened a cupboard and brought out a deep bowl full of chicken parts, fried in incandescent gold.

"The gizzards are at the bottom."

She watched him dig one hand into the bowl. It emerged triumphant, clutching a fried gizzard between thumb and first finger. He popped it into his mouth. In a previous life she would have scolded him, slapped his hand with a laugh, told him not to put his unwashed hand into food other people were going to eat. Here, in this country, her life had changed in more ways than one. Maybe men were happier here because they had the upper

41

hand. They were the ones with jobs that paid the house rent. Their power was magnified. Power corrupts.

"Needs more pepper."

She made no response. He would not help her in the kitchen, and she could not ask. Back home in Nigeria, she would not have been doing this, cooking single-handedly, and he would not have been standing there, watching her cook. They would have been comfortably middle-class, lying in bed while the food got made. They would have had a maid to do the cooking. They had led a life like that. That was their life in Jos before the riots, before Agu's supermarket got razed for belonging to a Southerner, before she had to give up her job and they had to flee fearing for their lives. She sighed. She did not like to dwell on the past. That was her problem. She could not stop dwelling on the past, always wanting a return to it.

She turned off the fire under the soup, stirred the pot, and went to take a shower. With some luck, the visitors would not come until she was dressed up. She did not want Shylock to see her before she had a chance to make up properly. All this business with Shylock, it made her feel less homesick but the sneaking around got to her, kept her awake at night. She hadn't planned it, had not even considered herself capable of it, but Agu had changed. Before, when they were back in Nigeria, when they both had jobs they enjoyed, when the balance of power had been less skewed, Agu's love had been a steady, shiny thing. Like hers had been. Now, it was slippery like spit. She could not hold on to it, could not be sure of it. It did not plug the holes in her porous self.

What is it about love that makes people behave like children? She thought. Holding hands. Giggling. Teasing each other. She imagined Shylock in the shower with her, lathering her breasts, holding her nipples between his fingers, squeezing them. She felt a stirring between her legs. She could not remember the last time she slept with Agu. The last time he made her feel this way. She thought of Shylock again and of how Agu said that first time they met him that he was a man of action; she smiled. If only you knew, Agu, she told herself.

42

"What do you love about me?" She had asked Shylock the first time they were together. Four months ago.

"Everything."

"When did you fall in love with me?"

"The very day I saw you."

"Liar!"

"Not." He rolled away from her and lit a cigarette.

She had not planned this. Bumping into him at the Tropical Store agreeing to help him when he asked for a lift home. And then going in when he asked her to, "A drink. To say thank you." When he kissed her, snaking his tongue into her mouth, she had expected her rage to fan out and consume him, but instead she thought, *His tongue is not lazy at all.* Her own hunger had petrified her. He smelt of her memories, when she and Agu lived in Jos. She needed to go back there and so she abandoned herself to them, even imagined for a moment that he was Agu. The Agu of before, not the one he had become in Belgium. Blissful transgression, she thought. Afterwards, when they lay in bed and Shylock traced the map on her back and asked her how she got it, she did not tell him it was Agu who had poured hot water on her for being late with his dinner. The Agu of before would never have done that. It would have been inconceivable to him, and the she of before would not have taken it, but moving here had done things to them. Yet, she could not leave him. Where would she go to if she did? All their savings had been spent first on the passage out to Belgium, and then on settling in, certain that they could recreate their previous life here. Nobody had warned her that the balance of power would tilt so dangerously that she would be in danger of being crushed. She could not return to Nigeria to start all over again. She was not brave enough.

"What did you do in Nigeria?" she asked Shylock, kneading the muscles of his chest.

He had been a craftsman of sorts in Aba. Ariaria market, he said. "I made shoes. Bags. Chanel. Dolce and Gabanna. Louis Vuitton. Gucci. Hilfiger. Prada. All of them."

"How?"

"Just a sample is enough. I got a sample of the original, tore it apart, copied it. Sewed it in my workshop. I was good. One of the best." It did not sound like a boast, just a statement of fact. Prosperous looked at his fingers. They were long and slim. He had women's fingers, she thought, and placed her palm over one hand.

He leaned across from her and reached for a photo album. He showed her pictures. Huge bags with designer logos plastered over them. Shoes with incredible heels. On one, she spied a discreet logo of Tommy Hilfiger.

Once the supplier in charge of the shoe boxes delivered to him a thousand boxes with "Dolche and Cabanna" printed on them. Prosperous laughed. "What did you do then?"

"I shifted them like that. Some of my buyers couldn't spell either."

But then business began to fail. Once yahoo-yahoo boys started making money by defrauding gullible Westerners, and kidnappers started making a killing from their trade, Aba became awash with money. People started earning enough to afford the real thing, imported from Paris and New York and London. Why buy an Aba Gucci if you could buy the genuine article? Shylock sighed. Business became very bad. He had no choice but to leave. His workshop at Ariaria market was piled high with leather waiting to be transformed into shoes when he left.

Many of his fellow shoemakers emigrated to Malaysia, but he was lucky. He found a man who could bring him to Europe. One of his colleagues who went to Malaysia was arrested for carrying drugs. Shylock said his ultimate goal was America, though. "But until then, here will do." And then he told her he loved her. "Besides, I can't imagine not seeing you every day."

"You've known me only three months!" She sucked on his middle finger.

"Marry me," Shylock said. "Leave Agu and marry me." They both laughed at the impossibility of that. Shylock, still struggling to find his feet, get his papers, move on from the single room he was subletting from a Togolese man, could not look after someone else. And she, with which mouth would she tell people that she had left Agu? The generous husband who opened up his home every Sunday for his fellow Nigerians to come and feast.

Besides, she was not looking for love. All she wanted was for something to close up the holes in her. She sometimes felt like a colander, seeping life, so that she was often lethargic. Shylock's presence made her less lethargic, it quietened her need for a past when life was simpler and she did not have to empty dust bins and clean toilets for a living and take the pill on the sly to make sure that she did not give her husband a child. She wondered now if that had been a wise choice. Agu had wanted a child, and when she asked how they would look after a baby in their small room, − "It's hardly big enough for two!" − Agu had told her that she was speaking like an unbeliever. Did she not know that if God gave them a child, He would also give them the means to look after the child? How much room did a baby need anyway? The very next day, she had called around for a gynecologist and asked to be put on the pill. That was her first secret from Agu, and it had only bothered her for a short while, listening to Agu cajole heaven every time they slept together to "fill her womb with a child." She had not minded when he stopped making love to her, when he started coming home at night after work and going straight to bed. It was around the time he gave her her first beating. Afterwards he had cried and said he was sorry, it was the exhaustion, it made him short-tempered. But her love for him halved, then quartered, then became something that was hardly there. She did not know if it was possible to exhume a love that was dead.

She got out of the shower and wondered what she would tell Shylock if he came. How she would tell him. She thought about it and she knew that there was no way she could tell him. Not today. Maybe not ever. She would have to tell Agu, only not just yet. She sat in front of the mirror and admired her breasts, how full they'd become, how beautiful, like the ones of the women she envied. She thought of the holes in her body, of the big baby-shaped one in her womb, of how having a baby, even in their small flat, would not be such a bad thing.

That night, after the visitors had come and gone, she lay in bed and she remembered how the doctor had told her only a few days ago that it was only in one percent of the cases that women on the pill got pregnant. "Maybe you should play the lottery," he had said. She did not laugh at his joke.

"How can this happen?"

"It's not the pill's fault. Sometimes women are careless with taking it." He had looked like he was accusing her, and she had felt the need to defend herself. She had been careful, she said. "I never missed a day."

"With these new pills, it's not enough to take them every day. You have to take them at the same time each day. You want to keep the baby?"

She had not thought that she would want to. But at that moment, sitting in the doctor's office, she knew that she would. She imagined that baby growing in her and filling up all the holes in her so that she never, ever felt homesick again.

In bed, lying beside Agu, Prosperous supposed it was fortuitous that Shylock and Agu looked alike. She moved closer to her husband and with her fingers, began to work on him.

CHAPTER FIVE

Tunnels and Hidden Passes

Ogochukwu Promise

When our mother summons you to her bedroom on the night of your thirty-fourth birthday, as soon as your birthday party is over and tells you she is inviting you to breakfast the morning after, you need to be wary. If she sits, shifts and indicates with her well-manicured fingers, a spot on which she wants you to sit on her bed and with a dandy smile, pleasant voice, her eyes guiding your faltering steps and with her right hand gently touching your back, she says, "Can we talk?" hey, girl, you are in for it! I do not envy you at all.

So you sit and look at her quizzically as she picks up your hand, placing it on hers for trust. She calls your full name: Dakore Omanufeme.

You raise your long neck, the one with multiple folds from the goddess of beauty herself, the same neck that receives everyone's praise, a neck like the gazelle's and an angelic face that reminds them of your mother's. Yes, no other than your mother's, for she was once a beauty queen. Still is, actually. And you mustn't forget that. You, her favourite daughter of all people!

"You know why I have called you?" she says, for she is never one to mince words or hide them in floral garments.

You nod, not quite sure if it is the same reason mothers wake daughters in the dead of night to try and make them see the fast-ticking clock and listen to what Cleo calls menopausal musings. But our mother is looking at your cute face. And it does not seem as if she is interested in the "fast-ticking-clock talk" any more than you are. She takes her time and then says, "When am I meeting him?" Eh, could it be that she is, after all! Just maybe.

You try to take it all in, you even try to push it all away, but you are unable to leave the matter curiously unresolved. Besides, you are flummoxed indeed, yes you are, despite all the warnings Cleo gave you, notifying you that *it* was coming. But didn't she say that mother's style is strangely unconventional, a bit bitter-sweet at the beginning but really sweet in the long run and didn't you wave it all off, refusing even to ponder it. So you sit up, at the same time you shake your head and shrug, not knowing what response will be good enough.

"But there is someone at the door, right? Only you have not let him in! Talk to me, am I no longer your mother!"

"Actually, there is someone!" you ponder it then.

"I know, but he needs to come in and see us ASAP. Look, here are," she pulls out a trunk from under her bed, "some of the things I have bought for your wedding. This is pure silk, for your bridal train, a bit of gabardine for the cape of their gowns. And this satin to blend with the frills. We shall visit Stanley Bridal to pick out a suitable wedding gown for you. About him, you must think ahead, you know, as you do in your architectural drawings. The future is key, complex as it maybe, you have a mind that is good enough to bring your architectural masterpieces on. So should you bring on your expectations regarding family life, okay."

"Mother!" you blurt out, stopping her, "It isn't that I don't want to marry, but I need my space. And, and, and the man I am dating at the moment is rather controlling, grasping indeed, wants to know everything and even thinks he can make pertinent decisions for me," you try to stop yourself, but it is all pouring out. And the knowing smile on mother's face tells you she likes the fact that you have opened up. Now she will step in to fix things. She always does, don't we know it, even though we are so ungrateful. That, we know quite well, though we never admit it especially as she never accuses us, but carries on with her job of taking us through all the *passes* around the *tunnels* of life.

Oh, no, she is saying what you least expect, "You are lucky, my daughter, a man that is greedy for you sees you in him, that is why he sometimes gets overprotective. It is a flaw, yes, but what the heck! Don't we all have flaws? I call this one a happy flaw. Thank God you did not say he has an overwhelming ego and can't manage his emotions, especially anger! Right?" There is a bit of panic in her voice as she is hoping, willing you in fact to shake your head and relieve her of a mortal fear of spouse battering, that which we knew killed her sister in the hand of that megalomaniac who kicked her child out of her and ran to the police, turned himself in, and everyone said the part where he turned himself in, weeping like a child, was the best thing he ever did.

And I am thinking, this mother of ours, have we really ever heard her husband, our father, so much as shout at her? She must be damn lucky, that's why she thinks everybody should be. Only once when we were children, we heard what sounded like a shouting match happening in their bedroom. But by the time we stuck our ears to their door we heard only loud music, blasting away. And when they came out, they were hugging and kissing as usual. Later, when it was time for our annual holiday, Mother told us the decision rested squarely on her wonderful husband's shoulders. But when we asked Father what his decision was, he simply turned to our mother for her preferred holiday destination. Her preferences, he told us, were his habits.

It was when Cleo was getting married that we heard so much of the handout Mother called her *hidden passes*. Her voice still rings out, reaching me, "Just as you succeed in your career by having sense, skill, soul and sweetness, so should you walk down that aisle armed with those same tools. Give a man his due respect and you will see how well you will turn out, for he will love you for it. Even if he himself does not have a name for the way he feels, totally love-struck and loving it, will he be. Trust me."

And Cleo had laughed a girlish laugh throwing her head back to let her tiny braids fall to her back.

To which Mother had added her boisterous laughter as though she too was a girl, Cleo's friend and confidant with whom she then felt girlie-girlie. "Just go right on, don't quiver. Empower him with your faith in his capabilities and he will go over the top. Applaud every little good in him and his winning spirit buoys, leaving his flaws behind. Let your integrity build a wedge around him, then rule his world and make him feel he rules the world."

"How?" Cleo had asked, studying her mentor's face decidedly. The smile on her face still broadening.

Mother winked, her femininity quite apparent. "Be his home," Mother had said with a tone that suggested she should be lascivious with him and only him. And I wondered if I really saw that or if it was just in my imagination. She caressed Cleo's back reassuringly. I who leaned against the wall watching, listening, dusted it all up and stored them in my heart.

Cleo left, her steps no longer as heavy as I used to know them, but light, very light as though she was riding the airspace and well aware of it. When I visited with them, I saw that she and her husband laughed a lot, rolling over each other. And it wasn't because she helped to knot his tie or because he swept her off her feet often especially when she clinched deals for the bank where she was appointed as its chief executive officer. But there was a connection, a deep knowledge they had of each other and they had a talk pattern that resonates.

II

There are so many beautiful things out there. So many we hardly see even in our homes. So many still we are yet to be thankful for. These thoughts struck me as I kissed my baby's tiny face which was still flush from the strain of labour. She had just been cleaned up, dressed and placed in my rather awkward arms. She was fine-looking and yet so fragile like a newly laid egg. I feared she could break. Her pinkish lips smiled while she slept and her fingers were so tiny, tender and beautiful, I took five of them into my mouth at once and smothered them with kisses.

It was my aunt who thought, when she looked at her own son the moment they brought him to her, "you mean this bundle of joy came from me! I created this one! Yes, indeed, I am God!"

I felt slightly different, awed by this delicate loveliness before me, yes, I placed her little frame against my heart which was beating wildly with joy. I listened to her heartbeat, striking irregular strokes for an unusual song, calling my whole being to dance. I closed my eyes and traced the keyboard to melodies as though on a grand piano, listening to an intricate beat of life that has been given, now living a life all its own. A confluence of excitements trailed by its kind! Perhaps tricky, culminating in its kind!

It has been a bumpy ride, from one form of abstinence to another, from a casual kneeling at the altar of repose, shedding liquid pain, appealing for mercy of the blood shed on Calvary's tortuous paths to crazy moments of celestial dizziness. Longing, hallowed by faith. Smoky love fanned by need. And perhaps refined greed (for why do we keep wanting what we do not have despite all we have). But certainly the sheer tenacity of dreams walking all the year through to their very own realities mattered a lot here. I stopped sometimes and pondered it all, the bank of clouds above me, my daily struggles to become one with joy, taking in every bit of its essence, peeling off many years in pursuit of super-abundant fortune when all the happiness there is, lay replete in the things money cannot buy: an infant's glorious glee, a streak of sunlight's call to friendship as it penetrates the blinds to nudge me awake, the warm air of my husband's deep breathing as he slept soundly in my cleavage, inhaling and exhaling bliss, the thud of rain on my roof and the serenity thereafter. And of course, my baby's seamless growth, as I discover each day that she was gaining weight, her bones firming up, her laughter serenading my life.

Then I thought of that splendid day the blood P-test screamed YES. And I did the spur of the moment spin and catwalk in excitement as my husband broke into a jagged version of Michael Jackson's *Beat It*, actually breakdancing. In that euphoria, we went for an impromptu shopping spree for baby things, and we bought until all our credit cards were exhausted and we had to explain to the driver of the vehicle that brought a truck load of our baby things home, here in Lagos, that he would be paid when we got home. I still remember the knowing smile on his face as he asked, "Is it your first?"

To which we nodded with hilarity as we gave him a bottle of champagne which he said he would take home and drink bit by bit as he could not afford to let it finish in one day for it was his first time of tasting the sparkling wonder, as he called it.

And all through the nine months I dragged myself about doing odd things I never knew I could do. Looking back now, I tell myself it was fun, being beautiful, almost childlike in other ways. I remember the day I insisted on eating sand and even cried for it as my husband pleaded with me, wondering if I was going gaga. His voice of reason downright irritating. But an old woman standing by assured him it was all right and said; "Have you never heard that we are the soil we feed from and the soil is us. Let her feed from the soil from which she came. She will not be harmed, instead, she will be replenished." I ate sand to my fill while my husband watched with a mixture of loving pity and disgust. Afterwards, I went ahead and rubbed my feet with cow dung, the smell of which I developed a special liking for within the first trimester of my pregnancy. By the second trimester I wanted everything that was out of season and I blamed my husband for the dearth of castor oil which I loved to lick and smack my lips, as he said, like a maiden from the interior of the savannah. By the third trimester, all I wanted was for him to display every knowledge he had ever acquired in lovemaking even if he had to hang down from the ceiling. I quite agree with him that it was a period that was oddly pleasant and we were not quite sure how we handled the scary excitement, being so giddy with all manner of passions.

Oh that too! The embarrassment I caused my very polished husband the day I dragged him to the *Oyinbo* market in search of the local palm kernel lotion which was the only lotion my skin agreed with at the time. Every other cream made my skin break out in rashes. If I had followed him into his BMW like the dignified wife he had always wanted me to be, instead of sometimes buying things from hawkers of various wares while seated stately in the car, all would have been superb. But no, I had to hurry out of the car and stop in front of a barrow pusher who was eating African salad with some of it falling back into the enamel plate from his rather big mouth. I neither asked his permission nor washed my hands, but I dipped my right hand in the same plate and scooped as much of the delicacy as my fingers could take, dropping it all into my mouth.

Quite ill at ease, my husband tried to pull me away, his angular frame cringing at the sight, his very light skin, reddish with discomfiture. All of which took no shade off my chocolate hue. But the people asked him to let me be. He smiled nervously as I settled down and ate greedily while the barrow-man gave up his share happily and the seller of the African salad generously gave a second and third helping to me and the child in me. She assured me that there was potash in it so I should not worry about having a runny stomach afterwards. She heaped more of sliced oil-bean, and pumpkin leaves in my plate for protein and diced more onions to keep my heart healthy. Then other women in the market began to donate fruits to me, oranges, banana, pawpaw, pineapple and garden eggs until they filled two baskets which they carried to my husband's car as they prayed for me and wished me safe delivery.

I lapped up the amity, the sweet sweaty hugs of hard-working market women, the thick redolence of vibrant industry, the effusiveness of kindness and the unequalled elegance of good neighbourliness. There was something virginal about the affection that radiated on their faces, in their belly-deep laughter as they teased my husband, showing him where to place his hands as he guided me into the car. Right above my hips, with my left hand held in place on his shoulder, gently but firmly too to keep me from tripping over as I stepped on the part of the red earth made muddy by rain. No one would know that some of them could not afford to eat two times daily. They tied their hunger in their wrapper and proceeded to crush that same hunger with grace and charm. Yes, with a tasteful prettiness that climbed into my mind and followed me home.

What of the day labour started and he had ran about forgetting everything he went to fetch: car keys, the box of baby clothes, a pack of large sanitary pads, and the talculm powder. It was when he got to the hospital he realised he had no shirt and no shoes on. And in the labour room where the doctor and I made the mistake of asking him in, he cried like a baby even though I did not slap him or clasp his wrist till it turned pale like his friend's wife did so that that wrist went numb for days. Several months afterwards, he would smother me with kisses, caressing my shoulders but would not make love to me because he was "still dealing with the trauma of that delivery," he confessed. Then one day, I drew him to myself and showed him how to love me anew with deep respect and admiration. To which he added gratitude as he whispered sweet nothings into my ears once he spotted a window through which he climbed into me, flinging away every fear of another baby bump.

And the first time I suckled my child, the day the heavens laughed aloud and I could swear I touched the frock of God in the aching embrace of baby lips and sore nipple, as her tender fingers went over my full breast, which like the full moon gathered around it all that was beautiful. Even I saw them with my eyes tightly shut, the stars and all that was brilliant indeed came settling down, like rain followed by the rainbow.

And the day I nearly dropped dead from shock. It was my baby and that, that, that I-don't-know-what-to-call-it! It was quite a terrifying day! There, was baby sitting in her pram right there in the courtyard in the open of course, where I spread clothes on the line. I turned only to see a snake actually playing with my baby! Its head tilting sideways as my baby, giggling, stuck those lovely fingers of hers into its jaws, seeking to touch and catch its dodgy tongue. I screamed at once and flung a stone at the wily thing as it scrambled for safety. I made a dash at my baby, who then began to cry in confusion as I was breathing heavily while I fussed over her, checking to be sure she was unhurt even while I hurried to our physician. My husband rang the pest control office especially as two people living across the street had previously reported a case of reptile invasion of their patios. In a jiffy, they had it sorted.

Now she is gaining height and teething and can walk, run a little and call "Ma-Ma! Pa-pa!" as my husband and I rolled on the rugged floor with her, listening to the marvellous melody of our laughter.

III

And when I asked my sister what the secret of their sweetness was, with her husband and lovely baby girl, she simply said, "Don't tell me that Mother hasn't given you the *hidden passes*."

"Will she?"

"Yes, but don't wait till she sits you down. Her method varies. Learn when she hands them out randomly."

Well, didn't I? But when she asks you about Cliff, your mind runs off and brushes through the lives of your friends, the whole lot of them that have left, or are about to leave their men, especially Janet whose spouse has refused to get that much needed training in anger management. And all of her friends, which include you, have marched to him and told him that if he does not stop, you would see to it that he loses her. But as you mother that Cliff, that beau of yours, is not that type of man. Not the goody-goody, is-it-because-I-allow-you-feed-me, alcohol reeking, gum chewing, randy fellow that would tattoo the back of his hand on his wife's face at every provocation.

"Answer me Dakore, I am waiting!" Mother nudges you.

"Oh, rest assured, Mother, Cliff is remarkably composed! And I don't think his ego is that big. It's just that my friends are walking out of their marriages. You know, this thing about not knowing how to balance power, very little happening about right infringements, I simply don't think I can cope just yet."

"And you mustn't, dear. I will cancel the wedding plans then and ask Elle, to take the trousseau we have already collected for you and share it with friends," Mother agreed easily, surprising you.

"I am sorry about that, Mother," you stutter.

"It is all right, child. I am just sorry because you haven't begun to love. But I will wait till you are ready. Then you will come to me on your own and I will pull out this box for your use."

"Really, Mother, you won't summon me about this again?"

"No. But if you ask for my opinion, I will give it. That man that looks out for you, keenly campaigns for your growth, believes in you and seeks to merge his very essence with yours, and is ready to grab you again and again before anyone else does is the man to welcome, keep and cherish. Come to think of it, a lot of men have very little ego unlike you and me."

"Mother!"

"It's true! Why do you think your father, a former President of our great nation, listens to a small woman like me and does my wishes even when he doesn't realise it. And when he does realise it he thinks it does not matter for I am forever at his service anyway, ensuring that our dreams blend and refuse to disentangle," she pushes the trunk back under the bed and rises, kisses you goodnight and does not remind you about the next morning's breakfast.

You look for the feet with which to leave and you find none. You sleep in the family house that night and have the steward serve you breakfast in bed. Cliff rings only once and you hate the fact that you missed his call. You wish he would ring you till your battery runs out, that he would "bug" you even as you used to think when you saw his calls pouring in like those of a stalker. But when they did not come frequently that day, at first you were surprised, then you grew anxious and their dearth offended you. You keep hearing your phone ring only to realise it hasn't rung at all and when it does you sigh for it is not *him*. Then you send him a text, "I am at my parents', drop by if it is convenient!" He replies, "Will do once I clear my desk. Good to know you are good. Love you." It pleases you. You relax a bit.

The day is far spent. You rush to the door at the sound of every passing car and push up the blinds in search of him each time they flirt with the wind. Mother smiles mischievously each time you do that. When she sees that you just might fall from the exhaustion of going up and down, peeping through windows and getting the door when nobody rung the bell, she pities and urges you to ring him. But you will not hear of it. You say you do not want him to think you cannot do without him. You pace the room and decide to go to your office to get swamped with work so you would think less of him. You return to the family house instead of your posh apartment, one of the ones, Father left you.

You give her that what-are-you-talking-about look. She smiles and says, "Ring him."

"And make him feel incredibly important? There is no way I am going to cheapen myself in that manner! If what he wants is to flex muscles just because he went to my apartment and didn't see me, so be it. I won't call him first and have him win this one."

"Win what?" Mother's voice is mellow.

"It's unladylike, Mother, why should I be the one to ring and soothe his pride?" Your blood is boiling. Your heart is yearning for him. You are mad at yourself for feeling the way you do. The way you do not even understand.

"I do not see any competition here, child. What I see is the vanity of your inconsideration. Pick up the phone and put a call to him."

"Please Mother, let me do it my way this time. It is my life after all. He will be here this evening, he should! He usually tires out easily when we have a disagreement. I shall be here waiting!"

Mother shrugs and lets you be.

Cliff does not arrive that day and the next and the next. And when you finally decide in your almighty wisdom to ring him, you could not reach him on the phone. Mother is amused at the nervous wreck you have become. Though she worries about you all the same.

And suddenly the sixth day you get through to his mother who tells you he has been hospitalised. You jump into your car and order your driver to fly to him.

Three weeks later, he is preparing for a talk he is giving young entrepreneurs at Cleveland State University and you send him your thoughts which you put together all through the night. You arrive at his apartment to discuss his speech and Mother calls me aside to ask me if I noted some of what you have been saying: "Is it not my Cliff, their minds will be well fed. You will blow them away and earn the loudest of their ovations as you stand tall there for us!" And your eyes radiate your wishes as you add, "Go, my love, break a leg!"

At another time Mother saw you go up to Cliff after she spotted a frown on your face and a lump of distaste on his, though she carried on as if she saw nothing. You rubbed your cheek on his and said, "Don't you think we'll feel better if we talk about it?"

And he reached out and drew you closer as he responded, "Of course, come on, let's go in and see to it that the sun does not go down on our anger."

Seven months later, you arrive at the house with him so you can discuss your marriage plans in earnest. Across the dining table, Mother asks in that tone of I-will-let-you-also-have-this-all-expenses-paid-wedding-gift, "And where will you love-birds like to have your honeymoon?"

You look at Cliff, "I know my sweetheart loves Paris, San Francisco and California. I will go wherever the owner of the money on my head decides to take me?"

"I will take you only where you want to go, my love," he replies.

Mother nods, her eyes joyous that you now have the *passes*. She raises her glass, "So shall we toast to their happiness!"

We click glasses. And for the first time, I think, "Now Dakore Omanufeme, I envy you."

CHAPTER SIX

Driver

Taiye Selasi

driver [driver]
noun
1. a person who drives a vehicle
2. a factor that causes a particular phenomenon to happen or
develop

I am the full time driver here. I am not going to kill my employers. I
have read that drivers do that now. I will make just a few observations.

First, to state the obvious. My employer is a generous man. He
buys many gifts for many women, none of which is Madam. I
judge not, lest I be judged. This is between him and his God. My
God would smite him right there in the garden. Madam would
weep for her flowers.

Madam says her flowers are the toast of all of Ghana. I would
note that all of us do not, alas, have bread. But her flowers are
spectacular. They line the drive in pots. They burst into flames
of yellow petals. They prettify the concrete walls. I have never
seen such gorgeous flowers until I came to work here – or I had,
but only wild ones, free. Not fed, like at the zoo. Every Madam
walks among these gorgeous flowers in an Angelina *buba* with a
glazed look on her face. She runs her fingers lightly through the
petals as one fingers hair, the wispy hair of women for whom one
buys gold-plated trinkets. I would like to note that, once before, I
passed her bathroom window – which is strangely low and stranger

still, undressed-while she was bathing and I had the thought that Madam might receive more gifts more often were she not to hide her body in that dark green swamp cloth. Madam has contours of a girl I knew in Dansoman and of sculptures sold at Arts Centre and of Bitter Lemon bottles. Slender top and round the rest. A perfect holy roundness that is proof of God's existence and His Goodness furthermore. Her skin is ageless, creaseless, *paint*, her lower back a hiding place. The colour brooks no smile. If you have been to Ghana, you know. If you have never been to Ghana then you might not understand the way the darkest skin can glow as with the purest of all lights.

I slipped across the alley to the quarters that we servants share, a single room with piled up Latex Foam instead of beds. Mamadou, the watchman, says that we should ask for proper beds and Sundays off and cooking gas, but no one does. We huddled in our single room like very sunburned boy scouts with the faded shirts we've washed to dead hanging from the ceiling, and we listen to the crickets or the new cook's ancient iPod, with things that we should ask for piled up, soft, like folded clothes. There used to be some women here, apparently, a laundress and a multi-purpose house girl; where they slept I do not know. When my employer married Madam and she moved here with her mixed-race teenage daughter, called Bianca, all the women were to let go. Madam reasoned. "Don't tempt fate," where fate would seem a proxy for the patent temptability of her generous new husband.

I slipped into this boy-scout room and stood against the concrete wall, my heart attempting to break out from its skin and muscle jail. I was frightened that she'd seen me and would think that I had meant to look, that I had not been idly walking by but lurking, peeping.

On the wall of our room is a sign with rules written out on a torn piece of callboard. There is a similar sign in the hallway that leads to the public toilet inside Accra Mall.

It reads:

1. No washing of kitchen items.
2. No changing of clothes.

3. No buying and selling.
4. No standing on the toilet bowl.
5. No brushing of teeth.
6. No sex.
7. No smoking.

In smaller font, "all offenders will be prosecuted," signed in cheerful colours, "Accra Mall." Our sign is much shorter. ATTENTION is written in red. In black:

1. No stealing.
2. No peeping.
3. No urinating on flowers.

There is no handwritten consequence but I could guess my fate. I am the only servant with real education, which is to contextualize my reasoning skills and not to judge my colleagues. I was offered a seat at the University of Ghana (incidentally, the president's alma mater), which I would have accepted this summer had my dad not fallen ill. It should have been my sister's job to move back home to care for him, but Merriam has children and her husband, Nii, said no. I didn't mind. My dad had worked a thankless job for all my life, the thanklessness of which he only realized when he left. For fifteen years he drove the head of Mensah Mines, "Boss" Mensah, from his home in Trasacco Valley to his mine in Obuasi and back again. Boss adored my father and who doesn't adore a smiley man? A dimpled, demurring, diminutive man? More importantly trusted him. In all those years no missing cash, no leaks of information, no convenient towns down darkened alleys lined by armed Liberians. Boss's children, Barbara (Babs) and Basil (Bossy Jr.), call my father "Eja" (father) having known him most of their lives. Boss's second wife still sends us music playing Christmas cards with yellow packs of Burger Nuts, as if we were kids, starving. Seven hours of driving every single day for fifteen years, the windows up, the airconditioner on, Boss chain smoking in back and when Boss's smiley driver broke the news that he had lung cancer the only thing the Boss had to say was, "Send your boy to me."

My father smiled, and bowed, and coughed, and came back home elated that his good and kind employers would attend to my school fees. My mother ironed my only suit – the shirt of which now hangs here, dead – and told me to "speak properly," although she knew she didn't have to. For my fifteenth birthday my father gave the most amazing gift: his most cherished possession, for which we are named, his Merriam Webster Dictionary. "Knowledge is power," he'd said to me, and kissed me on my forehead, perhaps the only time my father ever kissed me, and the last. To indicate her knowledge of my consummate vocabulary, my mother tugged my tie knot tighter. "Go, my clever Web Star." She said my name the way I love to hear it, as if it were two separate names, as if I were a superhero, an attaché to Spiderman. She also cooked her groundnut soup, which Babs and Bossy Jr. loved and always asked my father for, although their cook could make it. My mother's nephew Kojo drives a taxi. When he came for me, my mother made me sit in back, which Kojo understood.

We drove out to Trasacco Valley day dreaming of eating soup, then gazing at the house with an equal aching appetite.

"This one's mine," said Kojo, slowing. He pointed to a pillared house.

"Then you'll be pleased to know that I have bought the house next door."

We laughed. We rolled across a sleeping policeman. I steadied the pot of groundnut soup. I noticed that my hands were trembling. I breathed, re-tightened my tie. When we reached the Mensahs' tacky palace we stopped and sat in silence, with the growing of the engine and our stomachs growing loud.

"I will wait for you, Webster," Kojo said. His voice was soft and serious. I hadn't imagined he'd leave me there, but nodded and said, "Do."

He didn't wait long. Needless to say, my school fees weren't on offer. Neither were my dad's astounding medical expenses. "I've asked my sister to take you on," said Boss, lips glossed by orange oil. Though he'd told me to come at one o'clock, I'd found him eating lunch. "She has come to her senses, finally and has left the heart of whiteness to get married to a proper man, a Ghanaian friend from Presec. So. We'll see how it goes." He took a bite. "At least the bastard has some cash. That last one, the *obroni*, died a pauper. No excuse for it. Here I am a black man in a racist world and look at me." I looked at him. "While that one, born a white man, dies in debt." A bite. "I told my sister plainly. Look. Nice bastard. Wants to marry you. Say yes. Come home. Enough of this mopey-dopey shit." A bite. "A woman of a certain age must be a bit strategic. With a daughter, too. A pretty girl." He drained his wine. "But stupid. You can guess who paid her school fees eh?," he pointed to his meaty chest. Now they're on the bustard's dime. He laughed. "The girl came, too. Same age as you." He wiped his mouth. "How old are you?"

"I'm eighteen, sah."

He looked at me as if I'd just walked in. "Why does Noor keep sending you those stupid cards?"

"I couldn't say, sah."

"How old is your sister?"

"Twenty four, sah."

"Bloody hell." Boss decried the flagrant waste of blinking singing Christmas cards, the trouble with a Muslim wife with no regard for money. Then he shared his thoughts about helping out of the household help, that is, better not to go get involved and set a bad example. Help one, all ask. No end in sight. A hundred dying grandmas, beating husbands, pregnant mistresses, of course I understood? I did. He rang a bell. He smiled at me, a *kontomire* leaf between his teeth. A houseboy came to fetch me. "Oh! I almost forgot to ask."

I turned to him, prepared to field the question of my father's health. "He's well," I breathed, a reverent murmur. Boss didn't hear. "Can you drive?"

I am a full-time driver now, and this is how we pay for it: my mother working round the clock, the children sending wages. I could have taken another job, a slightly more ennobled job, but nothing that would leave the time that this does for my studies. Driving means waiting and waiting means reading. The money is good and my colleagues are kind. If I were caught peeping I'd lose my job driving. So I stood there and prayed, back to wall, *please make sure she didn't see me, please make sure she didn't see me, in Jesus' name I pray amen,* then I opened my eyes to the cook.

Bulu has been cooking here for seven years, an important fact, as Jean-Louis the junior cook arrived just after I did. I have no idea where Bulu comes from. Bulu is not a local name. But he looks to be ocean-fed, stocky and muscular: central casting Ga. Jean-Louis is younger, maybe twenty, tall, Burkinabe. His shirts remain an optimistic white despite the heat. He also wears a jacket with his name in navy cursive that a girl from Paris gave him while on holiday in Ouaga. Madam hired Jean-Louis to make her meals less fatty; my employer likes his meat with lard and stew submerged in oil. Since moving back to Ghana, she has started drinking heavily and never walks for longer than it takes to reach the car. While my employer keeps himself in shape by riding at the Polo Club and getting up at dawn to golf and jogging through the neighbourhood, Madam seems to move as if through a fog from house to garden to house, with very little action taking place beyond these walls. I have mentioned how I feel about the consequential shape of things. But Madam is less grateful for the graciousness of God. She insisted on a second cook, a Francophone and *skinny* cook, to make her figure less of an inverted question mark.

Bulu takes offense to this, although he never says it; he has simply set his umbrage on our pile of folded clothes. He doesn't speak to Jean-Louis, but took an instant shine to me, perhaps because I never draw attention to his thieving.

The first time, he strolled in with two red-green mangoes and tossed one to me where I lay on my foam. "We're not meant to take any food from the house," I said. I pointed to the cardboard.

"I took these from the tree," he said.

"But isn't that stealing?"

"Stealing from what? The earth?" Bulu laughed, slicing open his mango. The juice dribbled down both his chins.

The second time, I'd driven him to grocery shop, our weekly task. I was reading *Maths: The Basic Skills* while Bulu did his shopping. Madam demands that Bulu shop and only shop at Bekaa-Mart, where expats spend their monthly pay on plastic bags of apples. Madam claims she can't digest untreated local produce after decades out of Ghana; my employer isn't old. He points to use of pesticides, the cost of goods at Bekaa-Mart, the fact that Boss's (wasteful) wife and seedy brother own it. But Madam is insistent. She wants Folger's coffee, Red Delicious, soya milk, spaghetti sauce – genetic engineering.

Bulu appeared with the shopping bags. We loaded them into the boot of the car. He lumbered into the passenger seat. "Where to?" I said. He pointed. Across the street from Bekaa-Mart a group of local women sell fresh produce out of makeshift stalls in the lot of the filling station. I frowned. "For what?"

"*Charlie.* For vegetables.

"You're meant to shop at Bekaa-Mart." "It's too expensive," Bulu said.

"It's not your money. It's not your choice."

"Eh! Madam never notices. The stickman never notices. I have a list of things to buy. I buy what's on the list." I glanced at *Maths: The Basic Skills,* now lying on the dashboard. "What's the difference?" Bulu shrugged. "You understand? I understood. The difference – between what he spent and what she thought he spent on groceries – would be roughly thirty, forty Ghana cedis every week.

This Bulu was standing there looking quite sweet with a frown of concern on his Buddha-fat face. "Why are you crying?"

"I'm not," I objected, but found that I was when I swiped at my cheek. I dried off my face with my navy blue shirtsleeve and hurried back out into none o'clock sun. Her bathroom was empty, the window gone groggy. I went to soap off the car. Second, several weeks ago I dropped off my employer at the Oak Hotel on Spintex Road, on Sunday afternoon. I didn't think too much of it. We've passed this place a million times while driving to and from the house in gated Airport Hills. It looks more like an office park or conference hall this Oak Hotel, with tiny windows, perfect squares, a dull, generic lobby. My employer doesn't go to church, though Madam does and had that day; I'd dropped her off at ten and would return for her at four. The daughter, Bianca, used to go when I first came but promptly stopped and now most of the time lounges at the beach with friends on Sundays. "Wait here, please," he said to me, got out, and strode across the lot, a rather dashing figure in his copied-tailored suit.

My employer is a handsome man, in stellar form at fifty years; he wears his silver beard trimmed low, shoes pointy, collars starched. I would guess by the size of his five-bedroom house that he isn't as rich as his brother-in-law, perhaps on account of his overstretched domestic empire, a classic problem. He runs a waste recycling plant, the first of its kind in the country I'm told; was married two times when he lived in the States and left behind some children. On occasion he will raise his voice on his phone in the back of the car, but it never lasts longs and ends with his chuckling, adjusting his cufflinks while cooing to me, "Please excuse that." A man of careful manners; wears a mask, is what I'm getting at; but clement as employers go, no hauling over coals. He's been in Accra now for seven odd years but still doesn't know how to get around town, how to bob and weave through the narrowest streets of Osu or evade Spintex traffic. 'Webster!' You are a *wizard*." he says, as I bring him more swiftly to this or that meeting, or pick up a box from a jewellers to drop off for this or that East Legon housewife. I suppose his years as a divorcee – which would seem to outnumber his years as a husband have left him with habits that affection and honest intention can't break. I think he cares for Madam, whom he met one night two years ago at Boss's epic yearly bash when she was here for Christmas. I've seen photos of the two of them in swimming suits at White Sands; he is holding her in one of those holds in brides and babies. This must have been that holiday. My employer couldn't stand her now.

Her head is back, her feet are up, her hands conceal her smile. Bianca sits behind them on a beach chair, either scowling at her mother's handsome lover or else squinting at the sun.

A note on Bianca.

"Bia."

Boss was wrong in both regards. Bia isn't pretty. At least, she isn't pretty to me. I know that here in Ghana we're obsessed with skinny mixed-race girls, ascribing as we do some magic powers to their paleness but I'm not that way inclined. I take my berries plump and dark and Bia looks to my eyes like a beggar from

Mauritius. Monochromatic, with wisp legs and wispy strands of squiggly hair, her magic-skin the colour beige of satin sheets and *crème brulee*. Her eyes are pretty, I'll give her that, the same as Madams's wide and sad, slow-blinking as a baby's doll, two perfect Os of silence. The colour is different, light instead of Madam's melt-and-pour dark brown, the glassy gold of a tiger's eye. The problem is her smile. Her brows don't move. Her cheeks don't lift. Her jaw goes stiff. Only the lips move, parted and stretched, as if pulled by a string, to her ears. This is why I'd found her so unnerving when I first arrived and why I still can't meet her eye when meeting her at school.

"My uncle says that you're my age," she'd chirped on my first day of work (that day I never went to sleep, still hopped up on caffeine). Bia goes to Lincoln School, where all the foreign students go, despite her plea to stay abroad for senior year of high school. My employer says that boarding schools in England and New England peddle hash, hegemony and homosexuality. Further, they cost a fortune. Madam imagines that "experiencing Ghana" will encourage her overly Americanized daughter to embrace her African identity. Further it will make a good college essay. Needless to say, I have yet to see anything particularly Ghanaian about Bia's "experience," which mostly involves swimming pools, blow-driers, smart-phones and chauffeured sport utility vehicles. Still, I suppose she was trying to be nice to me. She jumped in the front, where Bulu sits and smiled the small-toothed, flat-eyed smile. "Do you want to go grab some coffee?"

Not knowing how to respond to this, I said, "Yes, ma'am," and started the car.

I wanted to ask her to move to the back, but was struggling with the phrasing.

"You can call me Bia. It's short for Bianca."

"Yes, ma'am," I said, hearing "can," thinking choice.

"Webster! Nooooo! Just Bia!"

"Yes, Bia."

"Dude, I'm not like… *them*. She touched my hand. I shifted gears. Her fingers sort of slipped away. She laughed a short and throaty laugh and fiddled with her hair. "I don't believe in all this twisted slave-becomes-king hierarchical shit." She flicked her abandoned fingers at me, as if I had conceived of the said shit. "It's a holdover from colonization, Webster. That's all it is. Repressed self-hate. *They* had to call their masters 'sir', so they must make you call them 'sir'. The British treated them like shit, so now they treat their staff like shit. My mom, whatever, it's what she knows, but dude, no. I'm not like that. My dad was American. I guess he still is. I mean, I guess you don't lose your nationality when you die. Or maybe you do. That would make war a joke. But that's my point, you know? I am a liberal! I am a pacifist! I went to school in Massa*chu*setts! I don't believe in war. Or 'sir'. I'm normal. I'm like *you*!" She laughed. I tried, but coughed instead. She waited for me to say something. I said:

"Under three things the earth trembles, under four it cannot bear up: a servant who becomes king, a godless fool who gets plenty to eat, a contemptible woman who gets married and a servant who displaces her mistress."

Bia laughed her throaty laugh, a sound of light, bemused contempt. "Hot shit! You know Shakespeare?"

"Yes, Bia," I said. "But that was from the Bible." I pulled into the parking lot of Bekaa-Mart and stopped the car. I looked at her. She looked confused. "Shall I go buy the coffee?"

"Webster! Nooooo!" she cried again, then hugged, or somehow tried to hug me. Without seatbelts on, the best she could do was a cheek pressed against my right shoulder. "It's, like, a thing you *say*, 'get coffee.'" She lifted her cheek. "is there Starbucks in Ghana?" I drove her to Deli France café in Airport Residential. "You have to come inside," she said. I went inside. She ordered in French. The Lebanese man who took her money looked at me in judgment. We sat at the counter with our double espressos. "I know how you feel," she said to me. I don't drink coffee. My heart was racing. I wanted to leave. I nodded. She smiled. "About your father. My uncle told me. My dad and I weren't super close. He left us, like ten years ago, but still it sucks, you know? You know how he met my mother? At Harvard. He's Jewish, so his family freaked. They had to run away together. How romantic, right? Then I was born and things were cool except for he's an alkie so my mom has to ask Uncle Boss to pay, like mortgage and tuition.

Then my dad decides to leave for his young blonde yoga artist chick he met in fucking *rehab*. Like, a cliché much? No, I know. I used to go and stay with them in Santa Fe for Hanukkah and things were cool except she's a bat of a shit fucking hippie. The man gets *liver cancer*, but it's all "no pharmaceuticals," so then of course he wastes away and God, I don't stop talking. Verbal diarrhea much? It's just, the chicks at school are lame, like mice, but fucking *sheltered* and my mom-well, shit. You've seen her. DNR-depressed. I mean, she chose the fucking guy, not me." Her mobile rang. "Shit, this is her." She answered. "I'm at coffee, Mom." The smile. "A friend." She winked at me. "He's no one. You wouldn't know him." She smiled again and touched my hand. Again, I pulled my hand away. But I thought, and still think now, that Bia isn't stupid.

On the Sunday in question, some weeks ago, while Madam sang and fanned herself and emptied her purse in support of her prayers for lost souls and lost kilos, my employer entered the Oak Hotel. The sliding doors slid smoothly shut. I found a spot with decent shade and opened *On the Road*. I didn't even notice when my cousin parked beside me in his newly tricked-out taxi; Kojo had to honk three times. His car was now neon green, with Rasta-themed interior decoration, seat covers of wooden beads, JARASTAFARI decal. "Webster!" he mouthed. We rolled down our windows. The cold air from mine kissed the warm air from his. *No Woman No Cry* drowned the sound of his question. He turned down the music. "You like it?" he called.

"*Too* nice! But how?"

"Jah bless me good!" He held up a small battered baggie of weed. "Webster, we' ll eat like kings one day!"

"The food in prison, you grinning fool. Put that away!" "Who's grinning? Me? *You* driving Mister Daisy!"

It seemed years since I had seen him, since I'd sat in back pretending that my cousin was my driver and my father would recover. I'd heard from my mom (who'd heard from *his* mom) that Kojo had found a second job: selling drugs to tourists at Labadi Beach, on Wednesdays at Kokrobite. I hadn't believed it. The taxi confirmed it. Both on the clock, we both stayed in our cars. We leaned toward each other through our windows, as through cages and we laughed until our jawbones hurt, then sat there, smiling, hurting.

"How is Uncle?" Kojo asked.

"Alive, thanks be to God. In pain."

"*Chale*, why? You should have called your cousin Doctor Koko! My boy there at Labadi, Yaw, his auntie, too, was suffering. Bad. He gave her ganja. Proof! No pain. I have some for Uncle Free Gift. Respeck."

I thanked him. "What are you doing here?"

"You sleep? Bianca dropped just now. Aren't you here to pick her? Eh! Fine girl, oh. Sweet, sweet, sweet. I brought her from Labadi Beach. I don't think she knew that I knew who she was. Girls, they love my taxi, oh!"

I forced a smile. "I sleep for true."

"You working hard. Bless up! *Me ko*." He started his taxi. "*Ye behyia biom*."

He honked three times as he drove away, *No Woman No Cry* blasting, crackly. In the hour that followed I stared at the dull reds and grays of the Oak Hotel lobby. Typically, my employer will ring on the mobile he gave me to say that he's ready to go. I'd drive to the door of wherever he is, as to minimize his time in the heat. I never sit and watch for him. I read until the mobile rings. It was only by chance, as I stared at the door, that I saw them appear in the lobby. She was doing the thing that she does with her hair, pulling it all to one side, twisting it up, letting go. This time, however, she stopped with the twist. My employer kissed Bia on the back of the neck. She smiled that strange smile then she let her hair go. She stepped to the side, out of view. My employer found his phone in a pocket and dialled. The sound of the ring in my lap made me start. The clamshell dropped to the floor by my feet. I fumbled to find it. "I'm here, sah," I said.

"When I call, please answer on the first ring, Webster." "Yes, sah. I'm sor–" But he'd already hung up.

My heartbeat was at talking drum. I started the car. I pulled to the front. I glanced at the lobby as I held his door open, but didn't see Bia and got in the car. I turned on the radio to the BBC World Service, which he usually likes but he said, "Turn that off. I can't hear my thoughts."

That's funny, I thought. *I can.*

I nodded. "Yes, sah."

A third and final observation re: what happened here this morning. I do not mean to say that I did the right thing. But every now and then I'll think of Boss there at his table and his "woman of a certain age" and then of my dad, and the way that he smiles when he first sees my mom in the morning and laughs (though it hurts) at her jokes and the way that she watches him sleep, breathing laboured, a ghost of a man with the weight he has lost and the way that she smiles at him and he clutching her across through her dress and I'll think that we're lucky. Though the roof in our house has a hole, the couch also, though our toilet is a glorified latrine out of doors, though with all of us working we will come up short, I will think that we're loved, that we're lucky. I was thinking of love when I woke up this morning. I dressed and was going to go soap off the car, when again, as had happened, I passed Madam's window and found her just stepping out from her shower.

A note here on the matter of what happened to the driver who was working here before me. When Madam moved in, I once found his groundnuts while cleaning the car, which no one is permitted to drive but my employer. These are the groundnuts you get wrapped in plastic with grilled sweet plantain and the groundnuts with skins on, so salty and dry. As my employer is allergic to nuts, I grew curious: who had been driving when Madam arrived? Boss had referred me a month or so after. I inquired with Bulu, who snorted and laughed. "Poor fellow," he said. "Had a weakness for women." I didn't see how my employer could judge him for that. "Read that you're Bible, eh? Thou shall not covet." Jean-Louis entered and Bulu stopped laughing.

It was only today that I thought of the Poor Fellow, the skins of his groundnuts there under the brakes. I passed by the window and looked up and saw her, but this time she saw me and looked at me, too. Our gazes, like magnets, got stuck to each other; we stared through the glass and we didn't look down. Her eyes, wide and sad, seemed to ask me a question. My eyes, wide and sad, gave an answer. She smiled. She turned from the window, her bottom uncovered, and entered the bedroom and kicked shut the door.

Twenty minutes later she came floating through the garden with her fingers trailing, lazy, through her flowers bowing heads. The massive green *buba* swished-swayed all around her. I froze in a crouch by the Rover's back tires. My hands were still wet when she drifted toward me. I stood up to greet her but couldn't quite speak. I stood with the suds dripping down to the concrete. She walked through the peddle and stopped at my face. "You saw?" she whispered. I nodded, not breathing. She held both my cheeks with her sweet-smelling hands. "You're good at keeping secrets?" I nodded, not breathing. "You think I am beautiful?" There were tears in her eyes. "Will you keep it a secret? If I help with your father?" There were tears in my eyes as her hands touched my waist. Bianca was starting her school day at Lincoln. Bulu was scowling at Jean-Louis's back. Mamadou was sleeping. My employer was golfing. My God would have touched her back , too.

CHAPTER SEVEN

The Woman in the Wood

Irehobhude O. Iyioha

Leonard Gates always shaved slivers off the edges of a plank before whittling away at it. Then he gouged and chiselled, creating contours and mounds until he reached the heart of the lumber. It was how he created his newest masterpiece, Ledie, a one-foot tall woman with eyes the colour of fire. Emilia, his wife of twenty years, knew the rituals. She knew that he gently scoured a block in circular motions, shaved along the cell fibers – carving against the grain only when he could get away with it, before nipping at small crevices and angles with his scalpel to create the profiles he wanted. Whether it was a woman with a body full of turns, a dog gazing into empty space, or a crumpled old man with a chewing-stick hanging from his mouth, he followed the same steps.

Leonard never talked about making objects. That wasn't what he did. He created personalities and gave them names. Although he had a vision for each character, the subject of his vision had no bearing on how he worked: he pierced, cropped and carved until something new fangled was born. It was a methodic process and whether it took days or weeks or even months, had more to do with the subject he was creating than with time. For time was all he now had. After twenty-two years of service, he had quit teaching art at Riverdale's Community School and resigned his seat on the community arts council board. Emilia was by his side when he also made the agonizing decision to end his lifelong romance with St. Peter's Chapel so he could withdraw into an unworldly life lived in small bits. She knew his work and what he had now become. That was why her laughter this morning – only minutes ago – when he said he created Ledie from nothing, hurt as much as it did.

Emilia knew the insides of the little boxes within which he lived his life. He woke at the same time every day – 6.29am – just before his neighbour's lawn sprinkler is turned on. He meditated for fifteen minutes in the same position: his back to the bed, his hands clasping his thighs and his eyes trained on the ceiling. When he was done, he went to the kitchen to make a pot of red hibiscus tea enough for two. He allowed it to simmer for a few minutes, long enough for the aroma to fill the room, long enough he believed – for it to rouse Emilia from sleep, because he believed, liked to think he roused her from sleep. Then at 7am, once he heard the sound of running water in the bathroom, once he'd sighed in acknowledgement of what was looking like another successfully choreographed morning, he made himself and Emilia sandwiches with some stuffing of cheese, olives and papaya.

Emilia rarely questioned the oddities of his life, like the slices of papaya between the bread, his insistence on carving only when a pencil of sunlight was visible in the sky and the regimented days. At nightime, he observed a different ritual: first the stretches, meditations and ablutions, as though in adherence to a religion and then the unsettling silence – like Emilia wasn't even there – as he contemplated the wall opposite the bed. In this way he lived his life in neat little squares, in these cut-up and detached portions, as if it was the only way to make meaning of life.

Leonard had never really wondered about what Emilia thought of their lives. He had no need to. She seemed happy, content maybe and that was enough for him. She sprung out to her bookshop every morning and returned home promptly to eat dinner with him at 7pm. He knew she was sometimes out of breath by the time she got home, sometimes arriving at only a few minutes to the hour. He could never tell whether she had been sprinting to make it home on time; her hair gave nothing away. The coloured curls with grey highlights wove the wind well.

He didn't know, though, that she hated eating dinner at 7pm.

The 7 o'clock hour was when *Clan of Virgins* came on. The *Ladies of Good's Inn* came up after the hour. Between the shows she liked to eat a snack, do things around the house or, if she felt like it, eat a light dinner on the couch in front of the TV. However, she never complained. She laughed easily, in short happy bursts; she laughed at Leonard's jokes, even when he wasn't making one.

But she never laughed about his carvings. His art was his life. His art was the baby in a woman's arms: whether it has ruby cheeks and twinkling eyes or is ashen and looks too much like its balding father, you grab it gently by its little pinkie and coo about rainbows and royalty. Emilia cooed about his work, often with carefully detailed explanations to support her sentiments and he believed strongly in her convictions about his art. When she talked about his work, she had the face that he said he had fallen in love with: the one that settled on a thing and assessed it as if it were a rare elixir. He was convinced that she genuinely cared for his creations, that she treated them with the same measured reverence with which he wielded his scalpel. He held on to the faith that this mutual love and sense of wonder about his work was the bond that kept them close.

It was why Emilia's chuckle over what he said about Ledie this morning startled him. It was not the reaction he expected from Emilia. Something was different this morning. This Saturday morning when his neighbour's lawn sprinkler failed to come on, this day when the sun struggled to break out through overcast clouds: this day brought him feelings of apprehension that he had not known since he walked away from his life as he once knew it.

They were seated on the terrace overlooking the sweep of hedgerows that separated their home from the sidewalk. He had placed Ledie in an upright position on the iron table standing against the far left end of the terrace where he sometimes worked. He looked up at the sky and grunted, baring his teeth in a scowl. He had planned to work today, for though Ledie was fine just the way she was, his purist self wanted a smaller waistline to offset the gargantuan backside. But the sun had failed to come out and it was the first thing he noticed when he reached the terrace. It was never a good sign when the sky was as unyielding as it now was.

"The clouds forbid work," he said as he joined Emilia on the wide bamboo chair on the terrace.

"Hmm," she mumbled, taking a sip of her tea. Its piquant flavour was teasing. With the unmistakable aroma spiraling out easily, its crimson hue and the secret dash of lemon when Leonard wasn't looking, she found it easy to relax with the drink and talk about grey cashmeres in the sky.

"See, see the clouds, see how they're rolling on top of each other to block off the sun? See?"

Following the direction of his finger, Emilia squinted at the sky, and then she sighed softly. Right there in the heart of the sky was a cream-coloured light spreading out softly like buttermilk and illuminating the clouds. The sun had melted into every corner of the sky, blending in smoothly with the clouds. Of course, if she was looking for a single amber ball of fire, then the sun wasn't there. Emilia cleared her throat and murmured incoherently. From the corner of her eyes, she watched Leonard study the sky closely. A minute later, he lowered his gaze and turned to contemplate the statuette standing on the iron table.

She was a powerful sight to behold: her full hair rising tall as if its curly strands were powered by the same current that animated her eyes. Her stomach and waistline spilled over on the sides in ample folds like the hems of a poorly tied wrapper. Her backside, distinctively heavy, stood out like arched elbows; he had fashioned it to look like it could itself carry a person. He topped off all the quirkiness by leaving her naked, her honour protected only by the expensive looking high-heels that cradled her feet.

"All from nothing and yet so different, isn't she?"

Emilia made the strange sound in her throat as she sat upright abruptly. She looked as if his words had jolted her.

She said, "Eh?" before offering a barely audible explanation about her mind momentarily drifting away. He didn't hear what she said and didn't bother to ask. He was rather concerned about her sudden reticence.

"It is different indeed," she said calmly. "To the extent of what it is. But it's like all the others, is it not?"

Leonard should have asked what was wrong and why her mind

was drifting. He should have called her name fondly and asked why she was less of her usual present self, a self that interacted with a focus so intimate, so total, it was uncanny. Emilia had never struck him as a person who left her mind in the distance to sift through yesterday's memories. To be removed, as she now was, from something that was as important to him as his work, itself carried some deeper level of meaning. But Leonard didn't ask why.

She'd have told him if something was wrong. She'd have told him if something had happened at the shop on Friday. She told him things and he never needed to ask. When she first began to want children several years ago, she told him without his prodding. She told him about her dreams, about the babies laughing in her dreams and her water breaking just before she woke up from them. After, he decided they would try in vitro fertilization – a decision he gently dropped on her lap even though there was no sign she'd have trouble getting pregnant naturally and shared her feelings about it with him, especially about his desire to have a baby with specific traits. With a few thousand dollars, Dr. Jamie had offered them the possibility of having a baby with the best chances in life. He would provide them, he promised, a Gates Jr. with hybrid traits carefully mixed and matched so its eyes would hold the calm of Emilia's eyes and have the sea blue of his, its hair would be a longer version of Leonard's golden tufts and its brain, well, according to Leonard, would "of necessity" be designed to be a replica of his.

It was the first time Emilia had objected so strongly to a project that he thought they both cared passionately about. Then and even now, he couldn't understand why she was so upset that he could contemplate having a predesigned baby, let alone one with a brain that had to be like his. It would be a summer of disagreement, and by the end of it, they would fail to agree on what was right for them as a family. Of course, Emilia didn't go ahead with the procedure. Ten years later, neither of them had dared to broach the subject, leaving the issue and all its ugly offspring screened off in the backrooms of their memories.

In a strange way, Emilia's words, "It's like all the others", uttered with the vacant eyes and sallow cheeks, reminded him of that summer. And it worried him.

"Like all the others, Emi?" he asked in a quiet voice.

Emilia cast her eyes over the hedgerows, her eyes lingering on the delightful fusion of flowers on the neighbour's lawn. There were rows of anemone, bloodroot, daffodils, tulips, cornflower and dahlia. She had always loved the glorious exquisiteness of flowers and her neighbour couldn't have been more adept at selecting which flowers to groom. She rarely ever had the time to take on such hobbies. So she was grateful to have these ones to feed her eyes on, to nourish her mind with, and on most days, to enmesh herself into and escape the overly sane plot of her life with Leonard. She spotted an arc of ixoria sprouting around the rows. As they grew, they would be trimmed at every angle, nurtured with sprinklers and by effusive sunrays until their leathery leaves and clusters of tiny flowers looked like a band of stunted militias hedging in and standing guard over the clan.

Emilia dragged her eyes away from the flowers and studied her palms. She didn't look at Ledie as she uttered the words that shattered Leonard's morning.

"You brought the woman out of the wood, Len."

He wanted to believe that he had not heard her exact words. So he didn't immediately reply. When she had made that sound that seemed like a chuckle earlier, he had dismissed it easily even though it troubled him: she was after all drinking a cup of tea. A chuckle or a snort could easily happen over the warm, garnet-red tea. But much as he told himself otherwise, he knew her statement was clear. Emilia had said what he knew he heard.

"I brought the woman out of the wood?"

"Aha, Len. You did."

"I brought the woman out of the wood, Emi?" His frown deepened.

"You did quite expertly."

"What do you mean I brought her out of the wood?"

"She always was in there, wasn't she?"

"Where –"

"I mean, look at her –" and reluctantly she turned her own gaze on Ledie standing boldly on the iron table in the corner. "You brought the best of you to bear on rescuing this one, eh?"

"Rescue?" He pulled back and gazed at her with tortured eyes.

"O, Len. You don't see how they – all of these delightful beings and things – have been there all along?"

Leonard rose and walked a few steps away from her. His shoulders stiff, his jaw line set to a square, he went to a corner of the terrace and looked around. What was this now? He wondered. Where was this coming from? Was she upset about something he had done and wanted to punish him by saying these things? The last time they had such a heated repartee was during that difficult summer, the summer they had now tucked away in the back-pockets of their memories. But the issues were different. This was clearly not about children or about securing their future. This type of conversation about his work was new; it was a pathway they had never treaded. He'd take all of it in his stride and help her – help them both – stir the broken raft of their conversation out onto shore.

So with a straight face he said, "I don't find things and call them art, Emi. You must understand how unsavoury that is now, don't you?"

"O dear, I didn't mean to set you off, Len. Ledie is – eh – gorgeous."

"That's not what you said just now."

"I mean –"

"You said I brought her out of the wood. Like she was in there waiting for me to – to unzip a sack as it were and bring her out."

"I don't think I meant it like that at all." She sighed heavily, crossed her legs and tried smoothing out invisible creases in her skirt with her palms. "I mean I didn't intend my statement to come off that way. But Ledie was in there in the most rustic form, you see. Only gifted hands like yours could give her form. See? See what I mean now?"

Leonard moved further away from her, as if the more she spoke the more he wanted to put some distance between them. Suddenly, he turned and approached the iron table. He looked at Ledie again. She was in every way different from anything he had ever made. Ledie was the one work he couldn't himself define. What was she? Who was she? How would the world see her when he formally unveiled her at Riverdale's prestigious Annual Arts

Fair in a month? He loved the aura of mystery that she exuded. And it was the reason it irked him that his own Emilia couldn't see that this was the most illuminating of his creations yet.

He had always regarded his work as a process of birthing. Although this wasn't something he often dwelt on, he knew it in his gut. It wasn't something he needed to contemplate. He brought pieces of pure pleasure and enigma to life from nothing. He picked up a bland, archetypical lumber, rubbed the dust off it and checked out any crevices. Then, scalpel in hand, he cut and scraped until something fresh emerged. Until he made new life. How could his Emilia not see that? How could she say the life was always there waiting? What did she think Ledie or any of his other creations was? A genie waiting for the bottle's cap to be uncorked?

Leonard shook his head introspectively and then turned to Emilia to say something. The words were right there on his tongue, but he couldn't bring himself to say them. He was more upset than he thought he could be. He took a long look at her before he turned around and walked into the house. He walked past the parlour to the dining area. He stopped before what used to be the wine cabinet and yanked it open. Rather than rows of wine bottles, he came face to face with Emilia's books. All her favourite titles stood side by side with a few of his own. At one end of the shelf were two books on the art of carving, books she had given him as gifts in their first year as a couple. They were books that taught the craft of sculpting. They provided insights and roadmaps to readers as if the craft was something that could be taught. How did one teach the art of creation? How did a person learn to birth life?

He had not touched alcohol in years, not since he gave up the lie that was teaching and his life as it was and began to live ascetically as an artist. It was a decision he made once he was convinced that nothing could be born of imperfection. He gave up the booze along with the divine wine served at the altar. Later, long after this morning would come to an end, he'd feel disappointed about coming here for wine; but right now, his mind was clouded with the anger he was feeling against Emilia. Only she could bring him to this, to a past from which he was fleeing. In a moment of consciousness, he slammed the door shut and walked briskly into the bathroom.

The bathroom was an all-white space, as plain and austere as his carvings were byzantine and multipronged. There were four mirrors on each wall and in each he could see a reflection of himself. He didn't spend a lot of time here. The design was Emilia's. It was a place he could find no part of himself. Leonard glared at the mirror. The lines on his brow and around his lips ran deep. His eyes were somber and drooped a little around the corners. He raised a finger to his face and touched the corner of his right eye. It was a meaningless action. In fact, he was only half aware of doing it because he wasn't there. His mind was on Ledie in all her sublimity. Again and again, he told himself the truth as he knew it: Ledie was unlike his other works, the other women weren't exactly svelte and graceful, but they weren't Ledie. He had made her the way she was because he wanted to be able to relate to her. He didn't need to be pretentious with her. So he made her body as his atypical mind envisioned perfection.

"You could have told me you had a problem with me."

He spun around abruptly to see Emilia standing behind him in the doorway. He had not heard her coming. She was looking at him intently and he could see her eyes looked sore. He wondered fleetingly if she had been crying.

"I don't have a problem with you. Where is this coming from?"

"You designed her to fulfill a fantasy."

"You're wrong, Emi. You don't know what you're talking about."

Emilia passed a hand over her face and shook her head as if in disbelief.

"You control everything. You control our lives. You tried to control the kind of baby we were going to have. Can't you see what you're doing?"

"Is this about the baby?"

"It's— it's not just about the baby. It's so much more. It's about everything and you know it."

She was talking so fast and with hands wildly animated by the rush of blood through her veins. Her voice was coming apart and, even though he didn't understand it, he could hear the raw pain in her voice.

"All I wanted, Emi –" Leonard's voice rose a notch, "– all I ever wanted was to have a child who had the best chances he could get."

"Why would you –"

"Let me finish!" Leonard took a deep breath. "I didn't mean to shut you out of it, if that's what you're thinking."

"You know that's not all, Len."

For a drawn-out moment, Emilia held his gaze, her chest heaving. Then, suddenly, she turned away and headed into the parlour. From the front-view window, she could see Ledie staring out over the hedges with those empty eyes that he had painted a fiery red. As Emilia looked out at her, the years rolled by before her eyes.

She had met Leonard while she was a student of library science at the community college. He had just started his teaching career at the time. They met at a campus café and their casual meeting extended into many dinners. He came across as uncomplicated and rather blasé at the time. Of course he didn't always tell her everything, but it didn't seem like he was hiding much either. In spite of their different backgrounds – she from a world where folklore blends well with alchemy and words with robust meanings are scantily and smartly dressed in proverbs, they got along well and ignored the many glances people threw their way. They also had to overlook the sometimes-barbed comments when Leonard sported her gifts of embroidered kaftans with cinched necklines and blouson sleeves, hiding their unease at the stares behind long, noisy kisses.

They married in the winter of her final year in college. He had already bought this quaint little house with the creaky hardwood floors and lingering smell of red cedar in the heart of Riverdale. After the 45-minute service and the two-hour long dinner, he carried her into the house in her little white dress. That night they made love. He set the pace and chose the places where it happened. They made love in a sequence of settings that left her with questions. The couch felt a bit like the bed; the hardness of the floor in the dining area left her counting the minutes; by the time they were on the kitchen floor with the cold tiles, her heart was beating rapidly. She had never imagined doing it by the window or on the dim terrace, grains of melting snow under their padded slippers, or on the unnecessary ledge protruding from the time-worn terrace before she had it redesigned. She drew the line on the ledge.

She didn't give the experience much thought at the time. He was just a little eccentric. That was all. She had her own foibles. She drove him to the edge in many little ways. Didn't she have a ritual about sex, when and how they did it? Didn't she wash her body after every experience as if to erase the memory of it? How many times had she binged on green smoothies in the desperate bid to stave off unwanted mass? Leonard noticed. Quietly. Over time, he asked less of her in both the bedroom and everywhere else. By the time their summer of disagreement was over, he asked nothing at all. Nothing, except – and this was tacitly – her unwavering approval of his work.

In the last few years, there were times their conversations teetered towards the forbidden. She'd once asked him why he never touched his scalpel during difficult winters or at any other time when the sun was behind clouds.

"The sun always shines, don't you know?" she had said.

Leonard didn't reply.

"You know even when it seems to be hiding from us, it's there for you?"

He had then smiled and said calmly, "You wouldn't understand."

After all these years, nothing had changed. If anything, things were worse. They were now more different than they had ever been.

Emilia wiped a tear off her face as she moved away from the window. Leonard was standing in the dining area quietly looking at her.

"How did we get to this?" he asked.

She licked her lips and looked past him. "We were trying to make a baby – that's how."

Her hands twitched slightly at her sides. The tic came on

whenever she was upset or afraid. She was feeling neither of those emotions right now. What weighed heavily on her mind was an odd mixture, given the present circumstances, of exhaustion and relief.

"You wanted us to make a baby, a perfect baby," she added.

"And that was so wrong?"

"You don't make babies, Len. People don't make babies!"

"So what do they do?" Leonard could hear his own voice ricochet around the room and beyond it and back. "They do nothing and the baby falls out like Ledie? Eh?"

"No, Len! You have it, that's what you do! You just have the baby!"

When she stopped talking, she realized she had been shouting. For a moment, they both stared at each other in silence.

"Emi, listen –"

"I don't want to do this anymore."

"But we are, aren't we?"

"You should've let me carry what was a bit of both of us in its own form."

"It was going to be perfect–"

"You ruined it."

"And just how do you ruin perfection, Emi?"

"You ruined it when you tried to create it!"

Emilia was crying as she rushed past him into their bedroom. She glanced around the room frantically for a split second before she began to pull her clothes down from the hangers. He came after her, and though she knew he was behind her, she shouted her words at him as she threw items of clothing into a small bag.

"You don't design a baby from scratch," she continued. "You don't create a baby with the sun in its hair. You don't get to choose to have a baby with Einstein's brain!"

"I thought we both saw the need…"

"You saw the need! You did! This was you."

"Emi –"

"I never had a say, Len."

"Listen, Emi –"

"Don't you see how it all works?" Her chest heaving, she

stopped pulling the clothes off the hangers for a moment. "You tease the genius out of a gifted child. You nurture it. You don't put it there. It's like Ledie. Just like Ledie." Then she returned to stuffing her clothes into the bag.

There was a fragile pause before he said gravely, "What are you saying, Emilia?" He hadn't called her Emilia in years. While everyone else called her "Emilia", she was always "Emi", his Emi who walked as is if she was stepping on clouds, his Emi with the sylphlike physique that disappeared in his arms; his Emi: the dream he had never had.

"This, this is not about Ledie, is it?"

Emilia sniveled and rubbed her nose.

"What do you see when you look at me?" she asked in a quieter voice.

Leonard said nothing. He heard the question, but it led his thoughts to her body, not as it was but as he had always imagined it could be. Her body had stayed the same all these years.

"What do you want from me that I don't give you?"

Leonard let this one pass too. A lot of things had piled on top of each other over the years; they were now too many to name.

Emilia took in his silence, the discreet way in which his eyelids fluttered, the way in which they blinked away his fragmented thoughts, those broken pieces of himself that he was never going to let her assemble. Emilia took in his demeanour, a patchwork of paradoxes, of love and fear and desire and disillusion. And then a wan smile flitted across her face.

"You can't right the wrong that's us by trying to recreate an illusive dream," she said gravely.

"She's just a woman I made out of wood, Emi," he said in a somber tone before a fleeting sparkle brightened his eyes. "There! I said it the way you want. She's just a woman made from wood."

"Len."

Emilia threw one more blouse in the bag and then zipped it up. She slung the bag over one shoulder as she walked out of the bedroom, past the dining area and into the parlour, with Leonard on her heels. A minute from now, she'd leave her home of twenty years without a goodbye; she'd walk down the streets aware of the eyes on her back, eyes peering from between parted curtains, eyes narrowed to slits, eyes drooping from the weight of the memory of what their owners had just heard. She'd walk away from Riverdale, away from the Don River Valley area that she had come to love, and past Greek town on the Danforth – where she had enjoyed Toronto's exotic *Taste of the Danforth* Greek festival of food with Leonard in the early days. But she'd walk tall, the cool breeze gentle on her lustrous, dusky skin, ignoring the eyes that now had permission to judge her and how different she was from Leonard.

Right now, she opened the parlour door as she quietly said, "That's why this can't work anymore."

Emilia pushed her fingers into her hair and let them settle on the frizzy roots. In that most infinitesimal of moments, she returned to her roots as a girl from somewhere far beyond Riverdale, in a town called Potiskum, far flung beyond the oceans, bordered by states as volatile as itself, where she was raised on a diet of faith and fervency even when there was a fire burning at the door; where she was baptized at a church also named St. Peter's and labelled as God's own while no one told her that ownership comes in many forms and strands; where she played in scorching red sands when blades weren't drawn and with the insouciance of a child who believed the possibilities of living a fairytale life elsewhere.

"Even if for one moment I could become your Ledie," Emilia was saying, "I'd still be something formed by you. I'd still be a Ledie without a soul."

Then she walked out into the street in the crisp morning air, cool breeze on her back and the invisible sun on her face, kind in its warmth even as it gathered strength and drenched the quilted skies with an auric glow.

CHAPTER EIGHT

These Fragments

Yvonne Adhiambo Owuor

Seven fire ants working in tandem carried away the last splinter of a wooden sign that once read, *"Passage de la frontièreici"*. A tall, gaunt, midnight-shaded man, with a smooth head, shaven face, high cheekbones and dark brown eyes squinted at daylight's incandescence. Two hours ago he had, with thirty-two other passengers, been off-loaded from an exhaust-pipe-dragging lorry five kilometres away, where a strip of road carved into the forest had come to a sudden stop in front of a hardwood battlement interwoven with thick vines.

They squeeze themselves past the wooded tangle, these passers-through. They cling to verges with their baggage. They stumble towards a misshapen crater, into which rubbish migrates and smoulders inside covert fires and ten marabou storks stare, and fear is corporeal in the averted gazes of people. They lurch toward, but in the last second, skirt around the cavity, and the sun is red in the sky and the world is on fire, certainly in Langoune where morning birds' chirp, caw, coo, and cackle inside green crispate foliage of soaring trees that elevate the Congo basin. The day ruptures over the passengers' target, a derelict clearing-house inside a barbed-wire framed frontier that is still sheltered enough for mysteries to breed undisturbed, protected by furtive rot that also stains skin.

Pockmarked shed: Immigration office.

Its most visible arrow points to a paint-flaked word: "Douanes".

Beneath the sign, a pop-eyed, corpulent, long-nailed female surveys her fresh arriving prey. Her nails beat a tattoo on a reconditioned autopsy table upon which luggage will be laid and picked apart for small valuable things to be confiscated in the name of the state and for the good of its people. A poster depicts several prohibited goods, impressionistic smudges subject to private interpretations: Red blob: *perfumes, gold rings, false teeth, blue candles and foreign currency are forbidden.* A small cracked window permits a glimpse of the Other Side where the grass is, literally, greener. The shack-office is in the scoured, scalded, scarred, scorched, leeward-side of a mountain no-man's plot. But every so often a North-easterly dispenses droplets into this leeward side and keeps it an expectant brown.

The passengers reached the outside fence of the travellers' processing zone, the thin man hobbling in his too-small pair of pink women's plastic sandals. He leaned against the office's entrance, holding onto his waist, faking exhaustion and using the break to further survey his setting, locating people, isolating security types and their assets. A glance had already found two snipers concealed in a high lookout. He marked exits and observed a single, bespectacled senior immigration officer in a black suit, a swollen troll guarding a self-appropriated bridge who, with a silver whistle dangling from a blue string around his neck, also inspected the wanderers. A nondescript gun leaned against the wall. This officer ordered travellers to his stained desk with a neat *breep* of the whistle--chirp of a rather important chick. Each wanderer approached the desk with lowered eyes, papers ready and a rehearsed reason for daring to cross. Another uniformed useful idiot emerged to shriek and wave a black baton: "*Avancez, Avancez. Arrêt!*"

For some reason, an emerald green guest book lay open on a small round table. The man in a dress wondered at its contents as he shuffled forward, furtively loosening a cord around the chicken's neck. He chose one of two queues to wait his turn. On the blemished wall nearest to him, a bloated pimple of a fly crawled across the bulge of the blue-white planet earth, satellite view of cosmic hauteur, plastered on a fraying map.

Caliphora Vomitoria.

Once upon a simple season this man had attended to such insects. He had roamed their worlds by means of potent microscopes. He tightened the yellow-with red-flowers cloth covering his head, remembering that there were no planned victories in war, just lucky breaks quickly exploited. The chicken in his basket began to gargle.

II

Before. Before.

Men recoiling into forested mountain heights, disappearing among a scattered people to whom they once belonged, and who like them, were weary of their war. Explaining himself to himself – *this is why, what, how* in order to ignore murmurs of foreboding that are the character of all ignominious retreats. Nebulous night lights in the sky, and he whispered, "Regrouping" to fourteen adults and seventeen boy-men who had stayed with him in the service of an idea that had long died. They still believed in resurrections.

III

Lingering in their safe mountain. Hiatus. Then three weeks later, a message comes with one of the boy soldiers who had gone to visit their illicit food supplier. It is written in gold ink, etched into a pink, scented card:

"Colonel,
I want your story,
To take to the world.
Show me your face.
I expect your 'yes.'
Now find me."
Safiya Fakhri.
Filmmaker, Critic, Translator. 03/12

On the cover, the thin white outline of a white lily. Someone had found them. The Colonel took the card. He said nothing. But throughout that day, and over the next seven, he bore the message on his body so that even when he rested on the ground, the card's fragrant promise stayed with him. He memorised the name on the card. *Safiya*. A perfumed name became counterpoint to placenessness. A war-emptied man made his first mistake: he decided to go look at the messenger.

Friday at dawn, shape-changing in the mist. The Colonel stripped off his mustard green war costume and stained his skin with the purple juice of the *bâba* plant. A triangular fisherman's hat pressed down his head. In a tattered blue shirt and grey shorts, on a requisitioned black mamba bicycle weighed down with empty bottles, he pedalled down the mountain, knees jutting out, as he howled rude fishermen songs, now a vendor, now a collector of bottles. He rode down the mountain in a white fog that drenched his clothes so that he shivered as he descended into a darkness that still brooded over a disintegrating small town below.

IV

Kalioyolipi. Place of temporary truces. Moonless night static electricity wariness. Prickle of skin. Someone is watching her again. Someone has been watching her for three days. Yesterday, she could not sleep. At 2 a.m., needing the chill of a cold night wind that swept in from the dense forest river, she raced out of her accommodation rondavel engulfed by a sensation of suffocating in a dark, constricted space. Her hut was one of nine in a compound that many years ago, had been set aside for paying foreigners stopping by on their way to the pristine interior where they exercised Government-sanctioned privileges to decimate the land's treasures: hardwoods, elephants, rhinos and gold. Seven years of civil war in the Northwest had reduced that traffic to an intermittent dribble. Safiya Fakhri was the first Euro – paying foreigner in two years and she was welcomed as a herald of longed-for rain. *Vous etesi ci!*" You are here. "*Ils reviennent!*" They are coming back. No one asked where she was from.

Apart from the ghost-like proprietor who floated in and out of sight in a blue sarong, his untended and unintended big afro bobbing, his face dulled by many secret signs of life included an animated forest that was slinking into retrieve territory, hapless bald-headed chicken scratching for succour, four bony cats, all black and orange and all rheumy-eyed, seven brazen goats, a pair of Hadada ibis, unseen barking dogs that once in the afternoon and once after midnight would howl in an eight-minute relay and a vegetable-fuel charged, yellow *tro-tro* whose cap-wearing driver pulled into all the pre-war stops even when no passengers embarked or disembarked. Safiya watched. She saw a gangly form on a bicycle attempt to peddle empty bottles, his voice raw in harsh song. Safiya waited. She recited phrases from the Japanese language book she had crammed in a bid to bore herself into sleep: *O-namaewanandesu ka? – Sumimasen, Tookyooekiwadokodesu ka? – Koko no chizu o kudasai. – Komattana.* Safiya laughed at herself, the sound, a huff like that of a pangolin.

Yesterday Safiya had sobbed. She cried because she had travelled so far to stop from running and because crouched over a plastic pail, she had tried to wash the fecund stench of the African interior out of her thick, black-grey streaked haircut her Argan-oil conditioner had run out. Today her hair hung in lank locks. Today she smoked, sucking in nicotine until its essence penetrated her lungs. She talked to herself. She said she smoked to stop mosquitoes and midgets from flaying her skin. After she finished the cigarette, she retrieved a pair of scissors and a knife to cut off her hair.

Safiya waited.

She saw the cold light of fireflies. She mixed her Japanese with the German she had previously memorised. She said *"gegenschein"* because she enjoyed how it danced in her mouth. She curled her legs in to assume the lotus position. She was still being watched. So she performed. She wept again. She remembered some more Japanese words. They were not in the phrase book. Google had supplied them: *Mise mono janaiyo – Bakayarou – Temae! Jigokuniikwe – Shinjimae – Achikaere…*

Safiya waited. When she called out, her voice was as sharp as new ice: "Why don't you ask what causes a woman to cry in the

density of night, fucker? Show your face, cowardly *putain*. Ask!"
She threw up her middle finger. Pointed it at the night. Swirled
it in an arc. Then Safiya waited. She smoked. She could not sleep
without pills and a border guard had confiscated her collection.

"*Baroness de la drogue?*" An officious and handsome character
had winked as he lined up her nine pill bottles.

She understood enough about these worlds never to argue after
she had crossed into them. She offered a smile.

He had said, "*Substances dopants?*"

She had shrugged. "*Vous pouvez essayer si vous voulez.*" A gamble.
She lost.

"*Je vous en prie.*" Said the man. He had waved her on. He turned
to pour her pill bottles into a grey canvas sack at his feet.

Here she now was. Watching an inner Africa night sky turn
indigo-violet. She half rose intending to check her camera batteries
again. Only then did a shadow shiver into life behind her. Safiya
turned. "Tomorrow," a severe whisper suggested, "very early, go
to the marketplace in the town centre. Wait inside the green music
stall." Then shadow merged into shadow. Safiya inhaled cold air.
She exhaled old, rotten smoke.

V

There, next to a ravaged former military camp that had been
abandoned for seven years was where a rebel Colonel's "siege
and starvation" strategy had stopped. Safiya lurked in a record
stall wearing a white jumpsuit and white high heels, her shorn
black-grey hair drooped on her forehead. Perfumed, she carried
her camera bag. Safiya waited. Beyond curious glances, nobody
offered more than a greeting to her. She waited and waited. She
picked up CDs on display, flicked off dust. She recognised Manu
Dibango and thought to buy it as her reward for waiting. At dusk,
she left. She was the last person to leave the market area. Her high
heels marched on uneven dirt road. *Clop-clop-clop*, they punctuated
rage. In a landscape like this, grief and fear might erupt at any
moment. For those who lived within the shadow of a restless
mountain given to trembling and burping smoke, it was better not

to tap at pent-up things and nobody approached to ask what she had been waiting for.

VI

Cicada-cricket cacophonies in dense, dark, green sultry forest. Tea-coloured river water – black in the night. Canoes made haphazard shapes on the shoreline, while in the distance, on the water, fishing boat lanterns twinkled – lighting up the labour of seven desperate fishermen. Escorted by three boyish guides who carried home-made weapons, a blindfolded, elegant woman lurched like a lost vessel on uneven high heels and shrunk at the screeching of a billion insects. They had walked for more than four hours already, with short breaks in between. They had another two hours and thirty-seven minutes to reach their destination. When they paused for breath, Safiya dragged off her shoes and hammered the remaining portion of heel out. She hurled the stumps into the unknown. "*Casse-toi!*" she screamed. A boy laughed and then they were moving again.

VII

Someone is watching her so she pivots in the direction from which she senses the scrutiny. Whispers. Hissing. Receding footsteps. Sudden warmth and a calloused touch at her right elbow, a man's gentle "*Bienvenue,*" as if she were a dinner guest. Though she does not answer at once, like him, her host, much, much later, she would be doomed to replay their every word to try to retrace holes through which they would fall to find themselves implicated in the brokenness of the world.

VIII

There was white in the dark, and the white was as cold fire on a firefly, and the white swayed under silver streaked black night's clouds until it was a perfumed woman with a dancer's form. Here was its scent, here its lustrous messenger.

He says, "*Bienvenue.*"

Her answer, when it comes after a tiny cough, is a soft, "I work with light."

"Yes."

"For me darkness is excruciating."

Startled. He remembered. This was how people might speak. Playing with words. Wasting them. Grasping for his reply. "Light is not without its shadows." He leads her into a space that smells of cool vacancy. There muffled sound of water. "Bend," he says. "A short crawl, then you can see it."

She is saying, "Shadows. Those are grey acquaintances. I know them." Her hands move towards her blindfold.

He squeezes her arm and she grunts in pain. "The mask... it stays on."

She gasps, "Blindfold."

"Mask." He says.

"How do I see you?"

"You don't. You hear me."

Her hand touches the cloth on her face. "I'll pull this off."

He says, "I'll glue your eyes shut. Here is a chair... to your left." Safiya stumbles against a hard object. "Sit. Sorry for the draft. It is cold, yes? There's a hole." Safiya touches metal, smells stale oil. A refurbished drum, foliage as padding.

Safiya says. "There's no face attached to you."

"No?"

She tilts her head. "You checked my *bona fides*?"

"No time."

"A risk."

"Yes."

"Why am I here?"

"You baited the trap well."

She smiles.

He says."You could also disappear here. Nobody would know." He lets a finger run through her black-grey hair. On him, she detects the smell of old sweat and mud and musk and the forest, its pungent layers. He whispers. "Scared?"

She senses a smile. "No."

He moves away so he can study her from margins. Something niggles. Instinct ill at ease. She is speaking. "My new work," Safiya announces, "indulges my wondering – my thesis was about men like you – I need your voice to add shades to the work."

"Forest elephants," he notes. Then, "Wondering' is a weak motive."

"Yet it can also be an invading entity that must be exorcised by an act of fire. This is mine." She grimaces. "Moreover," She temples her hands, "We are kindred."

"What?"

"Your kind of stain."

He crouches. "Explain."

She replies. "Sins of the revolution. My father was a guerrilla commander for the Ath-Thawra Al-Jazā'iriyya."

"What?"

"La guerre d'Algérie. He blew up people for The People. Later some post-independence GIA idiots blew up three of my uncles at a family function. Can you believe that? My sister and I were at once dispatched to Paris. The mother wanted us unsullied by complicated ideas. She hoped to preserve the family line. It was just the women left, you see.

"But you continuing as you are... not for long!"

"Beh! My sister will survive. She adapts well. She has bred a new generation. Very European – good with amnesia, and thriving in well – governed, antiseptic tins. I couldn't adapt. Memory of my father, hero, aroma of unfinished myths... overwhelming... I *so* hate definite lines."

He asks, "So what causes such a woman to weep in the density of night?"

Gulp of air. "You? It was you?"

An almost smile. "Your summons were for me, no?"

She picks her next words with care. "I hunt for revolutionary images. Most turn out to be mirages disappointingly human. Still, I look. Still I cry because that hope is a roaring pain in the arse." Stillness. She turns. "You won't show me your face?"

"No."

"You have no desire to meet my eyes."

"None." He reminds her. "You can *hear* the story. You can also stop hoping."

The forest is shuffling nearby, rustling its leaves. She says, "I pour stories into facelessness. A witness," she coughs, "I seize one image to offer as a sacrifice to the dread that roams human fears wanting to swallow us up… like anti-matter." She coughs again. "May I smoke?"

"No." A droll. "The story brings you fame, yes?"

She smiles. "Drenches me with accolades, my violet nail polish praised. I become the official world expert of you." Nose twist. "The thought makes a woman giddy." Bites her lower lip. "Your *hobbits* would not let me carry all my tools. "Audio, yes, Camera, no." She slips out a slender silver ten-centimetre object with tiny gem-like green-orange-red-yellow light spots from her pocket. "The recorder miniaturised. Seen this?

He bends to touch it, to be near her. He whistles.

She says. "I'm a *film* maker. Not a radio tart. My main ingredient is light, not sound."

She senses his shrug. Tack change. "There's a two point five-million dollar price attached to your head."

"You want it?"

"I do."

"Make it four. I'll surrender to you."

They laugh. She asks, "May I quote you?"

"Yes."

"But our topic today is 'Crimes against humanity'."

"Yes?"

"You deny it."

"No."

"Anti-humanity. Inhumanity. Are you guilty?"

"It depends."

"On?"

He grimaces. "What it is to be human."

"There are bodies strewn along roads you walk."

"We treat detainees humanely."

"Third party verification?"

"No."

"Geneva Convention?"

"There are greater burdens."

"Worst ghost?"

"Meaninglessness."

"What does 'meaning' mean for you?"

"Victory."

"Over what?"

"This war."

"What's next?"

Staccato delivery. "Bind wounds. Build a gentle home for my people."

"*Your* killed, maimed, tortured, raped, burned, destroyed, sodomised and made-into-petrified-ghosts people?" She smiles with faux sweetness. Her tone is kind. "Your orphans? Do you hear them cry for their mutilated mothers and not their fathers?"

He tried the truth. "Sometimes."

Her voice: low, breathy, woman. "Is *that* 'meaningful'?"

He waits. He thinks. Only after does he ask, "What's more than pain?"

She leans forward. Something ancient groans from inside the forest. Another being rumbles back. She says, "Tell me."

He is frowning. "I think. Desire."

"You kill." She accuses.

The sound of the word "kill" as it enters his ears. Stomach-turning wariness. "Yes." He answers. "I did." He tests an explanation. "Death's not a catastrophe, you understand?" He watches her hands move and write in the air. They cannot be still. To her, "To destroy in order to build again?" Even to his ears, it sounds like an excuse. He is no longer convinced.

As she murmurs, *There's nothing wrong with what already exists,* he watches her. Finding mutability, a changeling's hauntedness. She is another kind of human.

"Denial." She offers.

He snorts, "Denial is for cowards."

"So what?" She frowns. It is a soft frown, as if her face cannot hold such a hard shape. It fades.

He leans over to smell her hair. "We are meeting our goals."

"Ha!" She retorts.

He sighs, "Go away *petite*. Before the night swallows you." He grasps her wrists. Lowering his mouth to taste the perfume there.

She says, "Too late."

He lifts his head. "Atonement?"

"That too."

They are whispering. Tantalising play. Yet something niggles, sending pinpricks into his solar plexus. Now, he says, as if pushed, "This implausible scent, what is it?"

"Something I blended; Oleander base notes.

"Oleander is poison."

"True."

He inhales. *The hint of…*

She says, "I felt you'd like it."

"You understand me." Sarcasm.

She asks, "What's the hardest part of your war?"

"Solitude."

"You are surrounded by people."

"Lonely men."

"Those boys?"

He studies her blindfold, seduced by a mystery he has allowed himself, a materialisation of oleander and jasmine and something like vanilla, the paradox of a muddy black cloth across a woman's brown face, a world behind eyes he will not look at. He props up his chin to say, "The third evil…"

"Yes?" She prompts.

"Death." He hesitates. "It roams trouble-free in the eyes of these children. Seeing this, sometimes I become afraid."

"Of death?"

"Partly."

Safiya feels for and depresses the audio recorder's switch. The man stretches and then cracks his knuckles. He glances at the entryway where light as vague as that on the bodies of fireflies hovers. She is asking him. "What do you want with your war?" and "Do you bear responsibility for the horror you form?"

His explicit, "Yes" drops her jaw. He also asks, "Is this the interview?"

"No," she answers, perplexed by his "Yes." "No, a reconnaissance. I seek the experience – the private story. That alone interests me. How did your war start?"

He moves closer to let the back of his hand stroke her neck. She tilts her head.

"Don't know." He says. His mind searches for beginnings. "I went to Belgium." A frown. "Shouldn't have. Should've apprenticed with the family. Would've been a boat maker by day, and at night chased away night monsters like my father did and grandfather before him." He crouches and draws lines on the ground. "Six years in Europe studying flies. *Drosophilamelanogaster.* Unnatural, yes? A human being wandering in the cosmos of flies? Over 100,000 different fly species. Maybe more. Do you know this?" Safiya's recorder wobbles in her hand. *Flies?* Intense listening. He says, "Returned with a degree and an urge to evolve my country... one insect at a time."

She laughs. He continues, "Senior Government Scientist. My people were so proud of me, so proud. My mother..." Lump in throat. Fleeting aroma of peppered chicken soup, swirling scent of... Homesickness. *Oleander and jasmine and something else like vanilla, but is not vanilla.* A different man. A Senior Government Scientist governing an under equipped overheated lab, surrounded by shelves and shelves of textbooks, the man waiting for test tubes that were never purchased, presiding over circular meetings that were only about what companies linked to which minister would win the tender to order compounds and tables and microscopes, which like the test tubes would never be bought. And people had been impressed by his strategic position, not his credentials or vision or love of flies.

He watches her. He cracks his knuckle. He returns to the story: "Became a professional sniper. Me. Ninety-eight percent first round hitter at 750 metres." He cocks his finger, "*Pttt.* I was that good. Excellent bullet-kill ratios. True cost efficiency. I flew up the ranks. Made Colonel. Me." He remembers. "Power is sweet." He pauses. "But the Government changed. Not unexpected here." Pacing. "The New Dispensation comes for my General and me. We disappear. They hunt for and purge what belongs to us:

families, friends, their extensions. The future murdered."

"Ah!" Safiya exhales. As if she understands. "Ah!"

"Such pain splits the spirit." He speaks in a hurry. "A bad wound that eats that commands us to repair blood with blood." Outside, dull light shimmers through the tall-tree forest canopy. "You understand?"

"Yes." She says and he notes her certainty.

He adds, "In other years we could have been called 'Freedom fighters'."

Safiya says, "My father the Berber – not Arab – would be 'terrorist' today… you, however, officially translate as 'Warlord'."

"Why?"

Half teasing. "You are black African – I presume. You *can't* possibly be professional soldiers."

Thunder. Safiya shivers.

Soft-voiced, he asks, "What happened to your father?"

She lowers her head. "Your third evil. Now I worry about his soul."

"Good. Even the damned need friends."

It starts to rain. They share restiveness. She switches topics again. "Since my eyes cannot see your face, may I use my hands? May I touch your face?" She asks in a voice that is a mere breath.

He does not answer her. They listen to the rain. Sudden forest silence. The Colonel does not tell her that he is retreating; that he has no new ideas, that before her perfume, he had been wondering how to return to the old world of flies with compound eyes.

She says. "They seized your prophet. He was alive when they pulled him out of a culvert. Helped by the 'allies' of course, in exchange for mining concessions and oil drilling privileges, I think. He is now dead. Did you know this? The *hows* and *whens* are, as always, obscured in the telling."

A man's intense exhalation. A dragged out, hurting "Oh. It is confirmed then?"

She ladles out details knowing it would wound him. "His body on display. Shown on news outlets throughout the world. Made the cover of *Time*: 'Desecrated corpse of the year'. The savagery of his people exposed in slashed-up nakedness. He was dead all right. Now buried – an unmarked grave. No ceremony. No site markers. I think all concerned hope he will be erased from memory. What do you think? You must have an opinion. You are their next target."

IX

History books, he had long ago concluded, should be written out only as prayers.

X

After more than half an hour of stillness, she thought he had abandoned her. She lifted her hand towards the blindfold. It is only then that he shifted. It is only then that his voice croaked, "Don't."

XI

He asked, "Do you still want to touch my face?"
She did.

XII

They sat close together on the metal drum, as if it were a cosy sofa. Her feet were curled beneath her body, her head and her upper torso rested against his chest. His arms were tight around her body, pressing her breasts in. He had lowered his head against her hair. The oleander-jasmine-almost-vanilla was right there. Sensation of woman-skin against muddy darkness. Scented softness. He was breathing in homesickness.

Drowsy toned, all of a sudden she says, "Theology of Nearness." Her hands still tingle. Contours of face, contours of space, the place a body occupies, she knew what she would paint with her camera. She would have to stalk him to seize the image. Tingling hands. "A theology of nearness." She repeats.

"What's that?"

She says, "There's a new pope in the world."

Sharp, "What?"

"The other did not die. He resigned. What I wanted to say is that the new pope invokes a theology of nearness."

He has no answer. So she continues, "I think it means to mingle smells with persons, inter piercing of lives." He breathes. She says, "It's not new." She draws shapes in the air with her hands "Suicide bombers do it." He listens. She turns to breathe his breathing. She must find a title for this – something with import. Something like… *gegenschein*."Gegenschein" she mouths, trying not to yawn, savouring the feeling, at last, of approaching sleep. She is receding like the tide. She is waiting for him to falter in this dark, but she cannot stop herself from bestowing an upside down kiss on his mouth.

XIII

She snores as a small cat might. Her mouth is open. She purrs. She half hears his question. She sleeps through the answer she should have given. *None.* He has asked, her, "How much time do I have?"

XIV

He disperses his men. He tears away dreams they have pasted on him. He tells them. *This is no defeat.* He says. *The war has just ended.* It was not fear that made a youth ask, *Colonel-where-do-we-go?* It was not knowing where to go without being told. *Camouflage is an African art.* The Colonel had replied. *Enter life. Merge with it where you find it. Become life. The war has just ended.* They watch the invaders below. Slithering, awkward, sneaking sudden arrivals. Soldiers, commandos of three nations looking for them, not seeing them, never seeing them. Big men carrying guns the size of small huts. *"This is no defeat. The war has just ended."*

XV

He carried out a final raid. He had no choice. A river man's ruined homestead. His nine children, his two wives. He had shown up waving his M24 sniper rifle. He had used his harsh voice, and rasped in the direction of the forest as if there were others waiting to launch themselves upon the space. When the Colonel leaves, he is wearing the second wife's dress and carrying the first wife's travel papers and her basket, which is filled with family groundnuts, and one of their eight red-headed chicken whose throat is tied to prevent its squawking.

XVI

The hen clucks and cackles.

"Papers." The tall man ignores the ice stare of the immigration officer. "Destination?"

A falsetto, "Miyangoroshi."

Cackling chicken.

"Business? And-shut-up-that-idiot-bird."

"Trade." The man coughs. "Medicine." He moves closer, "TB." He whispers. And the chicken clucks and cackles.

The officer recoils, averts his face, nose wrinkling. "Go, go, go." Stamp, stamp. "Stupid, stupid, stupid woman. Disease spreader." Stamp, stamp on travel papers. "Go, go. Infect others. You think I'll allow you back here?"

But, they would catch the gaunt Colonel in the heart of the second town of another country. Men run countries, and men can be bought. A police roadblock. His first captors would be balaclava-clad men with guns, and voices baying in assorted European accents. He would lower the basket to let the chicken escape. He would not fight back. They stripped him of his sidearm, handcuffed and stuffed him into a small blue car. The car flew over roads, crashed through borderlands, driving over red fire ants. A black helicopter hovering like a thundercloud landed. He was hustled into it. He did not fight back. They landed in a field in the capital city where he was handed over to balaclava-clad men with African accents. The men stripped him naked. They shred his woman dress. They laughed at him. They wrapped up his body in tractor chains. They bruised his head until it bled. They tugged at his penis until he screamed. They punched his lips, these swelled and eyes, these shut tight. He did not fight back. They shoved him into a gorilla's cage, which they lifted into the back of a mud-green lorry. They wanted him to be seen by the public who, on cue, jeered and cheered and screamed and banged at his cage and believed their world had been relieved of the devil and they had been saved. He did not fight back. But he did see her.

Safiya filmed everything. Her body was steady, poised like a dancer. Her camera pointed at him. He knew she did not expect that he would lift his bound, bleeding hands to salute her.

XVII

The media sought exceptional superlatives to describe the happening: *Dark-souled pimpernel… Darkest heart… Chameleon warlord of the shadows…* they shared a word: *"Capturé!"* They distributed its triumphant exclamation mark. Much later, Safiya would choose an image for her sacrificial film art – a bleeding, midnight-dark being in a primate's cage, oily tractor chains wrapped around his naked body, his arm raised in supplication.

XVIII

Most of his body was in tatters, but it was flesh. It would heal. His left eye was seeping. That bothered him; he was not comfortable with darkness. Blindness would be difficult. Medical strangers repaired what they could before he was flown to The Hague. He was surprised by how comfortable aeroplanes had become. Landing in the Netherlands, he was driven straight to hospital. Two weeks later, he was escorted into a detention cell in Scheveningen where he experienced a full night's sleep, his first after eleven years of ceaseless movement. Earlier, he had filled out forms. In a section set aside for "next of kin," he had spelled out one name: 'Safiya Fakhri."

In the days that followed, the Colonel glimpsed Charles Taylor doing crunches with his gym instructor. No diplomats came to visit him. He asked for a spiritual advisor, one in a position to take an epistolary piece he was composing to the new pope who apparently enjoyed a good read and sometimes wrote back to members of his flock. He had returned to the flock. Two look-alikes, auburn haired, pale skinned, blue-eyed, stern but determinedly non-judgmental ladies came to see him from the International Committee of the Red Cross. They carried a care package with sandalwood soap. They asked how he was doing. They studied his behaviour twice a week. He was impressed by their courtesy. He was well. He was delighted a psychiatric evaluation had established this. But he confirmed again that he would admit to the "Crimes Against Humanity" attached to his name. He was sure. He had reduced his Defence team to one stout, red-faced, pugnacious Afrikaaner, a genius legalist with odd green eyes, and a bad shave who refused to quit. Still the Colonel was adamant. He would admit to "Crimes Against Humanity" attached to his name. After three unsuccessful months of trying to get the Colonel to reconsider, the Defence lost its inhibitions. It brought him Belgian chocolates (Cote d'Ivoire cocoa), and split its Zimbabwean tobacco with him. The defence pleaded: "Why do this, man? Feck! They can choose to dangle you, hey?" The Colonel's eyes – even his wounded one – watched his defence with new affection. The Defence glared. "Feck! You frustrate me." One visiting day the Colonel told his Defence that having now familiarised himself with the facilities, he could declare with confidence that they met Tony Blair and George Bush's exacting standards. He thought the pair would make ideal additions to the Defence's stable. The Defence's eyes acquired an evangelical light. It whispered that a feckin' defence for George Bush would give muscle to the marrow, feck, unless Bush, like feckin' X. Aurélien *took on guilt and then the Defence would be truly "fecked"*. They laughed. Colonel X. Aurélien *Dikembe and his Defence team*.

XIX

"The Prosecutor v. Xavier Aurélien Dikembe. The Chamber was satisfied beyond reasonable doubt of Xavier Aurélien Dikembe's guilt as an accessory, within the meaning of article 25(3)(d) of the ICC's founding treaty, the Rome Statute, to twelve crimes against humanity (murder) and five war crimes (murder, attacking a civilian population, destruction of property, pillaging and conscripting and enlisting children under the age of fifteen years and using them to participate actively in hostilities) committed in the period between 14 February 2004 and 17 December 2012 during attacks on the villages of..."

She showed up for his sentencing.

Fifty-five years.

He had wanted "Life." But the Defence had succeeded in presenting him as an accessory, a mute jewel hanging on the neck of a now-dead "real" criminal warlord.

XX

She strode into his prison world as "next of kin," red scarf sailing high, and a lemon-green trench coat that covered a black dress, and skimmed the tops of high-heeled brown boots. She entered a high vaulted meeting room and approached the red bench where he waited, legs crossed, as oleander, jasmine and something like vanilla wafted towards him. Looking down at him, she said in French, "They still would have got you, you know. Once you allowed me in." She stoops to study his face up close. "They marred you. It must have hurt. You are still beautiful." She straightens up, loosens her scarf. "You disappeared. Left me sleeping."

At last, he looks at and into her eyes. Pale brown, gold-flecked.

She blinks first.

He says, "Matchless poignancy in a betrayer's kiss." She flinches. "Scent of sweet poisonous oleander."

Safiya focuses on his shiny black shoes. Leather. German. She frowns. "You had time to kill me. You didn't."

Gravel-voiced, "I had resigned from the priesthood of

slaughterers – your bad timing, I suppose." He rubs the scars above his ears. They ache in the cold.

Safiya sits hard on the bench, thirty centimetres from him. She fumbles for a cigarette. A voice crackles over speakers: "No smoking in here, Ma'am." She rolls the cigarette on the table in front of them, shredding it. She lowers her nose into its contents. They sit together in silence. She exhales. Lifts her head and murmurs, "*Kintsukuroi.*" She then shakes off snow dampness from her woollen hat.

He asks, "What really makes a woman weep in the density of night?"

She stops the scattering to lower her head. Snow flurries on the window. At some point she will speak jerking words. "An ordinary family outing. A mama, papa, and two beautiful, beautiful sons." Quick breath intake "The mother who always drove, turns into a familiar bend – too sharp, too fast, too soon. The car takes over. It flies. Soars off the side of a mountain. Bounces on brown rocks. Lands in the middle of an old European Sea." Safiya will slip into silence.

Together, through a large window, they will watch a north wind throw snow about.

She says, "*Kintsukuroi.*" Longing etched into every syllable.

He gets the word wrong. "*Kisukorai*"

She looks up at him, "The fine art of being broken; the finer art of having the fragments repaired by a master joiner and his gold lacquer who therefore renders the object even more beautiful than its original form." She says, "They used the bones and muscles of my husband and children; fragments of body they did not need put me back together again." She shifts to lean against the man staring at falling snow. "Used to work in one of those secret, special security centres. Know them? Programme Officer, Middle-East Desk. Euphemism for 'Arab Behaviour Interpretation.' Weak laugh. "Imagine that."

His mouth twitches.

She says, "After the fall, after the sea swallowed up my belonging, before vomiting me out on the beach, after I woke up in the hospital bed, I craved death." She swallows. "The agency realised this was a strategic opportunity. They offered me a place in an experiment taken from the book of Suicide Bombers and Trojan Horses. I seized it." She props up her chin. "And other artisans entered my body joinery process to add signals, sensors, signs, bar codes, buttons and lights that would ping data to satellites and mother ships and men who lurk in dark places waiting to pounce. My main weapon, like all *mujahidat*," she turns to him, "is intimacy. It is how we distribute our suffering. Told you we were kin." She stares at him. "It packs a high. I got addicted. You were my seventh. If it helps, you are the only survivor of my tracer vocation." She pauses, "Are you warm enough? You look grey. The cold here can be a bastard."

"Yes." He says. He adjusts his blue coat.

She says, "There was a ground blizzard when I drove in."

He says, "One way ticket in. Had to wonder when you did not ask for a way out of the forest. Not once."

"What did you decide?"

"That you had either come to die, or were a Judas goat." Pause. "So what does two point five million give you?"

She grimaces. "Repairs a fallen house." She grins, "Not with gold lacquer." She tugs at the edge of her red scarf. "Retirement. I've forgiven life. When I survived you, it became clear that I am doomed to live."

A dimple appears on his face."Life imprisonment." She turns to him. He looks at her. "That, ma belle, was what *I* desired." Spurious triumph. Oleander-jasmine-something-like-vanilla permeates the space between them, binding them together again.

She asks, "How did you disappear from our hunt?"

He says, "Won't tell you."

Her fingers touch the buttons of his coat sleeves. She asks, "Next of kin?"

"Yes."

"You bait the trap well."

Quiet.

She asks, "How is life?"

He lifts up his spectacles to wipe his seeping eye. "For a war criminal?"She glares. He answers, "I exercise. I eat European food, pasta this and pasta that. I read. They allowed me a microscope. Books." A smile. "I examine the ephemeral cosmos of *Lampyridae*..." He looks at her, "Fireflies."

The winter wind emits a low moan. She says, "No mere flies? Sounds sensible." A window reveals skies obscured by whiteness. Inside the room, they start to smile at each other. Safiya reaches over to pull off X. Aurélien's large black spectacles. She wipes the lenses with her sleeves. She turns and lifts up her left hand, and closing her eyes, she whispers, "May I, at least, touch your face?"

CHAPTER NINE

Feely-Feely

Ama Ata Aidoo

He had thought they understood one another. He had thought he had taken the trouble and the time to make sure of that; that as they were growing up, the boys would be clear about what to expect from him. That in some respects, he would go to any lengths on their behalf while in others an inch would be too long.

Nothing had prepared him for this.

"I can't, you know," Moses repeated for the ninth time that late afternoon.

"But why not?" Cobbie asked, his voice already higher than his father was used to.

"Because, because…," Moses responded, childishly falling on an expression from as far back as primary school which everyone had used to annoy their classmates whenever they didn't feel like answering questions or giving explanations. "Cobbie, listen," he began again, desperately, knowing that they weren't getting anywhere.

"Dad," Cobbie called out, struggling to bring his voice down. "My grades are extremely good. You see, it will not be a problem." All said easily, but carefully too, as though Cobbie was the father, and his father the unreasonable youngster who had to be coaxed to see sense.

"But that's my point," Moses said, rather quickly, as though speed was of the essence.

"Your point?" questioned the son, wanting to laugh at his dear father and his ridiculous self. What was his point?

"Because you did quite well in the exams, I don't have to go and see anyone. If you had not done well, that would have been a problem. A different matter. This one is really straightforward. At least, that's my understanding. It should be quite simple."

"Dad," Cobbie said again, "please listen to me. It is not straightforward and it is not that simple."

"Why not?," Moses pursued, almost foolishly.

"You see," continued Cobbie, "these days, whether you do brilliantly in the exams or fail outright, someone has to see somebody on your behalf…"

"Why?" the question escaped from Moses before he could swallow it.

"Because for every student who doesn't pass too well but is taken, some student who's done very well loses a place. Because as we all know, enrolment into our universities is severely limited."

"But surely, not to people with good grades?," Moses persisted, surprised at himself.

"That doesn't make any difference anymore." This time Cobbie screamed his lungs out.

"But excellent students like you…"

"Dad… Dad… D-a-d?" Cobbie not only refused to swallow the bait, but could not hide his complete and utter despair. He took a breath, and in the next instance seemed to have come to the conclusion that his father, who had never been as clever as other people's fathers, now seemed to have taken complete leave of what little sense he'd ever had. He, Cobbie, needed to be a little more patient with this new being.

"Dad," Cobbie began again. "If the system was open and depended only on grades, of course, there would be no problem. In fact, the choice for the universities is not necessarily between applicants who did well in the exams and those who didn't do that well. Dad, we hear that these days, it's more often a question of who gets in from among so many BRILLIANT candidates."

"Hmm…," his father responded, not only calmly, but with a baffling absent-mindedness.

"Dad," the younger man pressed on, "even if I'd made A-plus grades in all my subjects, you would still have to go and see somebody at the university to secure my place." He ended ferociously and with an attempt at finality.

"Cobbie," the father was pleading now. "If I went to the campus and actually met with some people, I still wouldn't know what to say to them."

"Why not?" the younger man asked, his voice at the point of breaking, but dangerous, like an old car on the brow of a hill, too tired to go forward, with its owner aware that going back was not an option.

"Because it's not in my nature to know what to say, or do, in such circumstances."

"And what is your nature, Old Chap?" He had heard that when the English wanted to put their fathers in their place, they would add "old man," "old chap," or some such appeallation to their questions. But adding that one to that question had been an accident. He had not meant to.

Moses winced. He began to plead openly. "Please, Cobbie, you know I'm an artist, a musician, a composer."

Cobbie laughed. "An artist! A musician!! A composer?!!!" He looked at his father, and the look on his face was nakedly unbelieving. Inside he was thinking: *So artists don't eat? Musicians don't shit? Composers' children have to lose out on life?*

He couldn't stop laughing. His father, in the meantime was thinking of all the crises they'd gone through since the boys were kids. Always over something he hadn't had, or didn't have, or something lacking in his personality, as compared to 'other people's fathers." Now as Moses turned his back on the shards that were the relationship between him and his son, he looked through the nearest window. He could see that the western sky had turned red. More than ten shades of it. He found himself remembering what one of his uncles, a fisherman, had told him one day when he was a kid about how the evening skies always foretold the next day's catch…

Crises? They had gone through quite a few. The boys at nine and seven, declaring to him, that rather than driving them to and from school in his car, with all that smoke pouring out from the exhaust, he should ask the father of one of their friends to give them rides.

"Why?" he had asked them. "Because everybody's father has a better car," they had answered promptly, sounding very clear and convinced.

Then there had been, and remained, the matter of his clothes. For working in his study and being at home he wore *djellabahs* and *djebas*: long loose garments which were comfortable and sensible for this climate; a style much favoured by northern men of all types and classes, but clearly not considered appropriate modes of dressing for an educated, southern gentleman. Not that he wore them on formal occasions. Even then people, including his in-laws, had talked and the children had heard them. He had not minded the talk, telling himself that he was not on this earth to dress to please other people. Until one day, as they were leaving the house to go and do some shopping, Cobbie had asked them why he didn't dress like other people's fathers? He had been so startled by the question that he'd actually tripped on the front doorsteps and nearly fallen. Then the boy had felt so bad, he had started to cry. He'd been seven then. Edum, his younger brother, joined in the wailing, so Moses decided to spare them whatever explanation he had, at least for the time being. About two weeks later, they had had one of those discussions. He had tried to explain why he preferred loose cotton garments, their appropriateness for the tropics and all that. The boys had seemed not to have heard him. And what they had heard they had clearly not understood.

Then there was the day their mother had told Moses, right in front of the boys, that being well-known for his work as a musician was "all fine, but not being able to afford a bicycle for your sons is really disgracefull." "Shame!" She had shouted. That was just before they discovered the illness. She died a year later. And Moses knew that he could only miss her on account of the boys who would grow up without her.

Cobbie was talking. "Dad, I mean… other people's fathers are doctors, engineers, teachers, businessmen. You know, everybody knows what their work is. But you, who here knows what a composer is?" His voice was at once condemmatory and at the same time caressing, as though he was trying to soothe a colicky baby. "Edum and I never had much pocket money. Not even half of what any of our friends seemed to have... Because you didn't seem to ever have much yourself. And now you are refusing to go and use your mouth to secure my place... Just your mouth, Dad."

Cobbie had delivered this last speech first pacing the room, then moving towards the door into the courtyyard, as if he'd meant to go out. There he'd stopped and stood, facing the door. There followed an incredibly long silence. Then, as if cued by a third person, they both turned and faced one another.

"Cobbie," the father began, "it will not just involve my mouth."

"What do you mean?"

"It is also a question of principle."

"Oh yes?"

"Yes."

Cobbie turned to take hold of the doorknob.

"Listen..." said his father.

"I have listened, Dad." Cobbie cut his father short clearly and decisively, "and I'm not going to continue listening to you... In fact, now you listen to me. If you can't go yourself to say something to anybody, then you should find some money, put it in an envelope, and give it to me. I'll do some research and find out the appropriate person to give it to, and how."

"But... but I would be bribing somebody!" The father was truly shocked.

"Of course," said Cobbie.

"But I can't."

"Why not?"

"Because I think it's wrong and I never learned that art."

"No? Well, Dad, the time has come for you to recognise a fact of life. That if bribery is wrong, people still do it and you too must learn to bribe... Yes, my goodie-goodie father, it's time you learnt 'that art'!" Coobie had clearly decided to abandon patience and caution. "In any case, did you hear me a second ago when I suggested that you just find the money, put it into an envelope and I'll find a way to do the rest?"

"I can't," Moses declared miserably.

"If you love me, you would try," Cobbie challenged deliberately. Moses collapsed. He did not fall down. He just shrank instantly, like a deflated balloon. He sat down and put his head in his hands. But Cobbie had not finished with him. "Its being rumoured that the universities' registries are coming out with full lists of enrolments in two weeks. Please, go and see somebody this week. Otherwise my name would not appear on any of them." He finished with an unmistakable finality, opened the door, shut it carefully and softly, with a reverence normally reserved for the very ill, or the recently dead, then he went out.

They say that the next two weeks were pure and simple hell for father and son. They never spoke to one another. Cobbie went on believing that his father "would do something." And initially, so did Moses. But in the end he couldn't bring himself to go to the campus, or put money in an envelope for Cobbie. Then one morning, the dailies came out with the National Lists of Enrolment into State-Accredited Universities (the acronym NALESAU, was wickedly nicknamed THE SAW). Cobbie went through the list for the first choice university. His name was nowhere. Then he went through the lists for his second and third choices. Ditto. He went over all three again. Same result. After the sixth and most thorough scrutiny, he gave up. He had told himself that he was most probably too stressed out to spot his name among all the others. Perhaps there had been a mess up in the lists' alphabetical order, as nearly always happened. So he turned the entire project over to Edum. His brother spent the rest of the day on the job. He even went through the lists of the other universities his brother had not bothered to apply to. But nothing came out of all the effort. By the time they decided to give up on the enterprise completely, it was dark. Cobbie had not eaten the whole day. Later he couldn't remember whether he had even drunk anything. He went to bed anyway.

The next day, Cobbie woke at dawn. He folded all the newspapers neatly and went to stand before the door of his father's bedroom, which Moses shared with their step-mother. He knocked and when he heard 'come in' he opened it, entered the room and without greeting them, dumped the newspapers on the floor by his father's side of the bed. Then he walked out again, shutting the door behind him. If he heard his father calling his name, he didn't acknowledge it with even a second's pause in his stride.

He just walked on and on?

That's what I heard… They say he hadn't spoken to his younger brother either. He kept walking out of the house and into town. And that was the last time anyone saw or heard of him in this country.

In twenty years?

In twenty-eight-and-a-half years to be exact.

And what happened to his father?

They say when he got out of bed that fateful morning, he went straight to the cupboard where he kept his drinks, took a big gulp of some alcohol and could never stop drinking after that… Now we know that Cobbie left the country soon after and went overseas. In his new country, he continued his education, became a doctor, married a daughter of that land, had children, then he became a citizen of that country and even enlisted in the army…

Do you mean that he had gone to fight for his new country?

And why not? Actually he had not had to fight…

But he was certainly at some war front or other,
as an army medic.

And now he is coming back here as that country's ambassador?

You hear right.

Someone whistled sharply.

Yes, yes.

How is that possible?

Why shouldn't that be possible? What century do you think we are living in?

The twenty-first.

Okay, then please, organise the space around you,

Put your bag firmly under your seat and fasten your seat belts…

Did anyone whistle sharply again, anywhere around?

CHAPTER TEN

The Brick

Tsitsi Dangarembga

There is a green plastic plate of gnawed pig's trotters and leftover *sadza* next to Baba Jo's head.

The barmaid is wearing black canvas shoes. The Thomys are without laces but this is the height of fashion. Even though the corn on her little toe grows out of a hole in the cloth, the barmaid feels good.

"Hey!" the barmaid goes. Her name is Clarissa. She shouts at Baba Jo because she feels good.

Baba Jo does not understand what the young woman wants.

"Are you done?" she goes again. She flicks the plate with her thumbnail. Grease globs at the rim. Then it oozes, clinging all the way, past scales of paint, onto the rusty table.

Baba Jo raises his head. Clarissa does not bother to move out of the way quickly enough. The plate empties over Baba Jo's head.

Alois Madya has never liked Clarissa. Baba Jo thinks she's all right, but Alois doesn't. He watches Clarissa shake Baba Jo's shoulder to dislodge bits from his hair. Baba Jo thinks it's a caress and smiles up at Clarissa's breast.

"Hm-hm!" Clarissa snorts quietly through her nose and swaggers off holding the plate, leaving a trotter under the table.

Alois approaches his drinking mate.

He wonders how long it will be until Baba Jo comes round sufficiently to buy him his first drink today. Baba Jo is one of the lucky ones. His daughter is a nurse at the mission hospital by the bald mountain. She does not come home that often but she sends money each month, regularly. And Baba Jo is a judicious drinker. Even when the e-cash beeps into the cell phone his daughter gave him, he sticks to traditional beer, despises the frothy, gaseous beverages that burst and foam to puddles around their bottles and cans.

"Shake-Shake!" Baba Jo says when he is sober enough. "If it is not Shake-Shake, is that drinking?! Never! Not without a beer pot amongst mates. There has never been drinking without any shaking."

And he always drinks the same amount in the same batches: enough to feel sleepy and for the food to soak it up; and then comes the waking and another cycle, until his muscles quiver like gelatine.

Alois likes to catch Baba Jo after the first batch of Shake-Shake and the first plate of strongly salted offal. The contents of the meal change according to the carcasses sweating in the butchery next to the bar at the dusty Business Centre.

Baba Jo is most generous after a plate of pig's trotters. Then he holds the hoof up and laughs and says, "Don't laugh gentlemen! What were you eating when all you managed was those sons of yours – who don't do anything for you! This is what I ate when I decided it was time for a daughter!"

Alois Madya walks over to his companion whose head has sprawled back onto the table. What would it be like to have such a daughter, he wonders. The thought does not upset him this early afternoon, as thinking of his daughter, Kuda, normally does, since today Alois Madya is feeling good.

Ba'Jo turns his head and the grease from the pig's trotters smears his other cheek.

"Ba'Jo, what's up?" Alois greets his friend hopefully.

Other than Clarissa being the first person he met in the bar, Alois is feeling strong. A little while ago, a matter of days, he admitted that he could not drown, neither in his sorrows nor in his drink. The only way to drown that, Alois saw was a deep smooth river piled against granite outcrops, with currents underneath that can drag a man down. He is not one to get on with water spirits. He has respect for those beings that spin into whirlwinds and dive into the caves of a cold, moving world. Alois accepts he is not the kind to visit deep, wet, powerful places. His place is on gravel and dry veld grass, where the water queen sucks dust into storms when she whirls on her travels.

There is, on some days, idle talk of climate change, even here at the Business Centre. From time to time, drinkers look through broken windows and grimy panes at the sky. They, Alois among them, wonder how it can rain without stopping for three weeks and how the drought comes in the wrong season for another three weeks before restless spirits hurl thunderbolts again and the earth starts shaking.

Soil scientists at the Agricultural Research Institute suspect that soon there will be no more dust, no sand, only rock because people are scything out shrubs and going at the sides of mountains with hoes without terracing and the rain is joining forces with the villagers so that it streaks over the earth like a rake and the thin layer of soil, joyful to be moving, rushes down to the river beds.

But Alois Madya, having recently made peace with his life, does not think too long about these things. True, the rain took the new drought-resistant seed that he and Mrs Madya and occasionally Kuda, had sown during the last planting season. True, what the rain left the baboons took. But that trouble with the baboons came before Alois's plan for change, when his idea was not yet formed, when his wife looked at him in a way that murmured, "A man or no man, here in my husband's or there in my father's house, what isn't dying?" As she came scratching and sneezing from harvesting sorghum; and his daughter did not look at him at all when he passed, but giggled with her friends more intensely as days went by and not once could Alois think up anything that should reasonably be said to the young women in answer.

Without his being able to reply, all through the season of praying for rain when the sun shone scorching white light over the earth, all through the season of interceding for sun when the rain finally arrived as though from the age of Noah, the sharpness of his daughter's laugh prodded at Alois's heart every evening as he trudged to the fields down the path his wife laboured up after her day's work there. But as this was the time when all was not well and Alois's plans were not as his plans should have been, he invariably fell asleep in the lookout at the edge of his maize field as soon as his buttocks rested on the plastic sheet, bright yellow, cut from an old seed sack and his spine ridged against a pole.

The baboons waited until he was asleep. Then they stood up to dance in the moonlight, like a band of villagers at a *pungwe* urged on by former guerrillas and under-cover CIO informers, the people everyone knew had absorbed too many deaths and too many kinds of it to ever be sober, whether they drank Baba Jo's Shake-Shake or water or anything else.

In those days, when the baboons loped off with his last few maize cobs, before his plans came right, Alois did not go home when the sun rose. He waited, as a man should, until Mother of his daughter Kuda brought him breakfast.

Ma'Kuda had a strange way of being unseen and seen when she brought the food: the shades of her skin blended into the earth with one step and threw her into relief with another so that she appeared first smaller then larger than anything mortal. When Ma'Kuda stepped forward, as though out of nothing, she loomed over Alois and the wasted field like one of those monsters people googled and pointed at laughing, on the screens of their cell phones.

On better days, Mai Kuda reverted to herself as she approached and became the woman Alois, with a distant flutter of triumph at resisting the huge apparition of her, knew he did not know. She walked slowly. Balanced on her head was a small wicker basket shaped like a pot. It contained a jug of tea and a plateful of sweet potatoes. On the best days there was also sugar and a few slices of bread, occasionally with a scraping of margarine. When she reached Alois, Ma'Kuda knelt and lifted the food out of her basket with slow, joyless movements. She was a wiry woman who did not expect satisfaction from anywhere any more. Accordingly she tried with all her heart to avoid expectation. However, as this attitude was an expectation of sorts, Ma'Kuda lived in a terrible and bitter state of a quandary. Alois did not look at his wife as he took his food. He recounted, between mouthfuls, how in the past night he had joined the dance with a fierce energy that should have intimidated anything or anyone, but the baboons kept on coming. Thus, dancing until he was exhausted, he had managed to save a corner of the field.

Alois seldom received an answer. He looked into his cup and over its rim at the mountains behind the village. He wanted his wife's company but her presence made him jumpy so that he wanted her to leave him alone. He wanted and did not want to be as alone as a mountain. If there was absolutely no response, Madya put his hand in his pocket. It was his habit to move round the small allotment at daybreak, after the baboons left so that there was no danger of angering the invaders, but before his wife arrived with his provisions. On this round, Alois nipped off a couple of ears of grain that the animals had broken and left hanging. Back in the shelter, he sat down and arranged a trouser pocket carefully against its holes. He put the sorghum inside.

"If it's like that, Baba, we can both stay here tonight," his wife said once in that flat voice of hers. Since she generally mouthed formalities that neither of them paid any attention to, her utterances slid out in slow motion, leaving behind the unnecessary words an anxious trace, half aglitter with a wish, like the slime of a snail. On this occasion, Alois was moved to open his pocket and show her the couple of sorghum ears and tell her what he intended to do with them, but he thought about it again and did not.

When Kuda's mother did not bring Alois his breakfast, it was his daughter Kuda who carried the wicker basket from the kitchen rondavel up at the homestead, across the yard and down the slope by the cattle kraal, to the field.

On those days, not a word was said besides the obligatory "good morning" and enquiring how each had slept. Kuda knelt down in front of her father and peeled off the brown paper that covered the basket. She lifted the cover carefully from where it was tucked between the containers and the wickerwork in order to use it again. She set the dish of sweet potatoes down before Alois and removed its lid. She arranged the enamel mug alongside. Finally, she lifted the tea canister out.

When Kuda brought breakfast, the tea still steamed. On some days Alois thought this was because she walked more quickly. He liked to think his daughter was eager to bring her father his food. Another thing he liked to believe was that his daughter got up from her bed a little earlier so that the kettle had ample time to boil, even for twenty minutes as the Ministry of Health taught, to kill carriers of disease. Alois liked to think this was why his daughter's tea steamed fragrantly and the steam whetted his appetite with its scent before it reached his lips, whereas his wife Mai Kuda's tea neither steamed nor sharpened his desire for anything. Pondering this difference, sometimes Madya thought it came of one reason. Sometimes he thought it was the other. On occasion, Alois liked to believe Kuda's tea reached him hotter than his wife's did for both of the reasons. Madya did not tell his daughter tales of his exploits with the baboons. He found it impossible to lie to her, for at the mere thought of it on his part, her smile grew sharper, more jagged and more dazzling like a lightning bolt flung by an irritated goddess. He sometimes wondered what would happen if he showed her the ears of sorghum in his pocket, but he never dared.

When Alois finished eating, one of the women, whichever it was that day, threw the sweet potato peels into the field to rot. She carried the basket and dirty dishes away, with the load tucked under an arm as, its contents devoured, the basket was too light to balance on her head. Full, Alois, waited until the sun changed its position before he stood up. He did not want to bump into his wife or daughter if either delayed on the path talking to a friend. Before the day he considered his affairs carefully, this avoidance of his family had been Alois's main experience with planning. Once, on the way home from the field, the daughter Kuda had met Tabitha, a young woman who, like Clarissa, worked at the bar at the Business Centre. Kuda set the wicker basket down on a boulder by the path, threw her arms around her friend's shoulders and the two young women started speaking, both at once. They laughed at this and carried on a double conversation. They stepped with small lively steps here and there, touched each other's hair and shrilled out laughter, going "He-he!" They held hands as if to shout "our merriment is so great it will make us fall down this slope beneath my father's cattle pen if we do not support each other! See if it doesn't!"

Alois came upon the two young people as he rounded the bend by the *musasa* grove. Kuda's father knew they were not laughing at him, but he could not get the idea out of his head that he was the reason for their hilarity. For Alois knew people in the village did that and imagined so it was with people everywhere: they constantly looked for something to savage with a burst of mirth; and with people like that, it was most pleasing if the something was someone.

In spite of this knowledge, on that day, with something like hope, Madya slipped his hand into his khaki trouser pocket. He grasped an ear of sorghum and started to pull it out. He wanted to tell Kuda why he carried them. Even though the friend Tabitha would hear also, Alois was on the point of speaking, for his flesh did not curl from Tabitha as it did from Clarissa. With Clarissa, his body congealed into itself and each of his hairs quivered like an antenna. So that morning, on a fatherly impulse, Alois made peace with telling his daughter about this part of him that he knew women would laugh at if they saw, for no reason he understood, in the presence of one of those laughing young women.

Kuda watched her father's hand in his pocket and thought of the village drunk. His name is Skoforo. Drink has burnt up Skoforo's brain.

The liquor that has engulfed Skoforo's mind is distilled from tyres generations old. Over many months, the tyres are changed from a new vehicle to an older model. This happens further and further from town, until finally the rubber is useless for transport and skids foolishly over the road, instead of running smoothly to its destination. At this stage the rubber is cut up into flaps and strips of different sizes. These are twisted into sandals, cheap at two dollars a pair: bargains to thin young men in baggy shirts who congregate on the city's margins. The sandals hold out for a few months. The most anyone has ever got out of them is three. In the fourth month, the owner throws them onto one of the dumps that gently leaks up gases. Or else the young man quietly sells his worn out sandals to the distiller. Skoforo begs five rand from the odd big man from the city. When he gets it, he haggles a discount from the distiller, unscrews the lid from his bottle and sips the thinned down futures.

Kuda sometimes goes to the Business Centre to buy a bar of lye soap when her mother has a bank note from a relative. When Kuda runs her mother's errand, she passes Skoforo lolling by the bottle store. When Skoforo sees Kuda, he puts his hands in his trousers pocket. Kuda sees that she is powerful. She can move the drunkard's body.

Now, on the road, Kuda wonders why her father is standing like that with his hand in his pocket and that look in his eyes that is so unfamiliar and curious. Her eyes gleam. Kuda pulls Tabitha away by the arm, without taking leave of her father.

"He-he!" Tabitha laughs in her high pitch as she stumbles behind Kuda up the slope to Kuda's home. "Let's go, Kuda! Someone's coming to see me tomorrow. I want you to plait my hair nicely!"

Alois watches. He sees the girl who brings hot tea, who has not laughed. His heart immediately forgives his daughter.

The two young people look back over their shoulders. Alois stands still. His hand remains in his pocket.

"He-he-he!" Tabitha lets out another high shriek. This time, Kuda laughs also.

Alois is glad he has not told anyone about the two ears of sorghum in his pocket. He decides not to follow his daughter up to the yard. Instead, he goes into the bushes to relieve himself. Urine hissing over the earth is cleansing. His priorities are ordered now. There is no need to wash as he usually does in the morning. He must go to the bar and find Baba Jo as quickly as possible.

The path from his home to the bar runs over a river bed. The place is a stretch of sand now, which has a firm belief in dryness and retains no memory of a stream. On the far side of the river bed, the village headman's family has put up a barbed wire fence. This fence, sagging here and there now after several years, surrounds three big trees. It is the headman's family cemetery. This area where the headman buries his ancestors is holy, therefore the surrounding bush is holy too. No one in the village dares fetch firewood from here. Children do not clamber over the fence to pick the trees clean of *matamba* or *matunduru*.

Alois was frightened here once when he heard rustling in leaves fallen to the gravelly earth from bushes close to the road. His tongue furred like the hide of an animal. Bile bit his stomach with many teeth. Breathing like a marathon runner, although he had merely meandered down the road as usual, Alois kept his eye on a pile of leaves and twigs. Every time the heap shifted, he stood still. Each time he came to a halt, his heart beat faster. When the pile was still, Alois circled it cautiously. A small head with a red crest moved slowly to and fro, like Baba Jo's head on the bar table. When he saw this, Alois jumped back, fearing a snake. As soon as he was still, but watching, a spotted wing swept weakly over the leaves. Alois shook his head and burst out laughing.

It was a guinea fowl. It had come off the worse in a fight with another. Watching the bird hop and flutter, Alois's eye shone with a light it seldom had. The taste of meat was on his tongue. It was flavoured with tomato, onion and garlic, was pungent and strongly salted. The meat's texture would be slightly tough which would make it wonderfully chewy. Alois's stomach gave a grateful rumble. Bending over, he crept forward, hands tense but ready by his sides to catch and wring the bird's neck. "My man, thank you my man! Thank you, Chihwa, you who only eat what is standing up!" Mai Kuda would respond in her flat voice as he handed her the bird. The sound of a villager chopping wood in the distance was the clap of her hands. He saw his wife plucking the bird and cutting up an onion. A trickle of saliva seeped from the corner of his mouth. When she was happy, Mai Kuda's cooking could make a man cry for his mother.

As Alois dreamed of a delicious meal, the guinea fowl raised the hoods of skin that hid its eyes. In spite of its wounds, the bird hobbled, chuck-chucking away from danger.

Alois stopped in his tracks when the bird moved. After a moment he followed the hurt creature slowly. He allowed *nzambara* brambles to snare him so that he paused to disentangle himself. Spear grass pierced and fell through the holes in his trousers. He stooped to pull out the long filaments. Alois was as aware of the thing that alarmed the wounded bird as the fowl itself was. The thing was always there. When he slept at the lookout, it lurched with long herbivorous fangs around the edge of the field. When he drank Mai Kuda's tea, or even Kuda's, it smacked its lips at him. When he walked to the bar, it slouched and when he zig-zagged home, it jumped behind him. When he fell into a stupor, it stretched out its arms and engulfed him. Each time, he told himself he would spin around or open an eye. He told himself he would confront it.

They were small: a man was used to the size of a hens', Alois told himself, to explain why he did not see the guinea fowl's eggs in time. He was surprised but grateful he stepped on only two. All the same, it was a waste whichever way a man looked at it. Alois carefully withdrew his foot from the hollowed out nest and wiped it on the undergrowth. There were speckled grey and white feathers around the nest and a little blood. Twenty-seven eggs nestled in the blood orange yolk that ran from the other two. He thought of settling half a dozen eggs carefully in his pocket. But there was blood on some of them, which made him think better of it. Disappointed, Alois waved away the bush, the fowl and the nest with its eggs with a movement of his hand and resumed his walk to the bar.

The following day Alois was surprised to find his feet turning off the road again once he was past the river. The guinea hen puffed its wings and screeched at him as he approached the bush that hid the nest. That night Alois settled at the lookout as usual. During his round after the baboons disappeared, he snapped off a few hanging ears of sorghum. Later, at the clump of bush after the river, he walked a few steps into the brambles and grass until he approached the nest. Rubbing the sorghum to dislodge the grain, he threw the kernels close to the nest. The hen watched him and he watched her and then they left each other to continue their business. Alois visited the nest every day for some time, on his way to sit with Baba Jo at the rusty table. When the keets hatched, Alois offered his little sacrifice from a greater distance.

A hawk was counting each day, one, two, three and so forth, on its claws and beak and then on pebbles on the ground, up to twenty-seven days after half a dozen guinea hens laid their eggs in the nest and all but one decided they were done with motherhood. The hawk began tightening its high, sharp-eyed circle at around three weeks, a few days before the keets smashed their way through their shells.

This morning that Alois is walking to sit with Baba Jo at the bar where the insufferable Clarissa will serve them, there are only nine keets left in the scrape. Alois drops the grain as usual. He knows soon all the little balls of feather and meat will be taken. Alois realises then he will stop bringing the sorghum and no one will know he did so.

"Look! Sorghum is growing in the bush!" someone will say and invent stories concerning the beneficence of an ancestral spirit or the morals the village girls have discarded.

Thinking of it, Alois decides to get drunk quickly. There is no point in labouring over a life that cannot give anything to anyone, not even a small ear of grain to a family of creatures with beaks and short red helmets.

The latrine, a hovel of clay and straw, with stick figures drawn in lime depicting on the right side a man and on the left a woman, stands between the beer hall and the parking bay at the Business Centre, where trucks to and from Mozambique park.

That girl, Tabitha, is leaning against a truck door. Pulling a length of cloth out of the truck window, she turns to Kuda who stands close by, arms folded across her breasts. The cloth is a dress. Tabitha, shakes it out and holds the garment against her body, laughing. Kuda shrugs her shoulders, an awkward, unwilling movement, as though she would rather not be there.

It is the awkwardness of his daughter's movement, an in between attempt at something, neither weak nor strong, filled with indecision, without the definition in the temperature of her tea, that does for Madya. If she would simply laugh, "I am a whore. That's how I get my clothing and airtime for your cell phone, Baba!" that would not satisfy Madya, but it would silence him with gratitude if not respect, with a sense of acceptable equity. But Madya realises he and his daughter are not there yet and may never arrive. Kuda is stretched between two poles. Perhaps she is waiting for something from someone, an order possibly, that will not be given.

Alois steps over Skoforo, who sprawls at the bar's entrance, and keeps on going towards the parking bay. "Kuda!" he shouts softly. "Kuda, my daughter, you do not listen to me! Get away! Go home now!"

Kuda neither sees her father nor hears him. Tabitha laughs loudly and drapes the dress over her shoulder. The driver gives a long, deep chuckle. Skoforo comes to investigate the noise. He sees Kuda and puts his hand in his trousers. Madya does not notice this. He continues shouting softly, "Why are you standing there like that! I have told you that I do not want you to play with these truck drivers and bar girls!"

The two young women do not see Alois. The truck driver laughs at the drunken man who veers towards the toilet. When Alois comes out, the driver, Tabitha and Kuda have left. Skoforo is back in the bar doorway.

In his seat at the metal table once more, Alois accepts Baba Jo's Shake-Shake. By mid-afternoon, he is drunk enough to go home. This is part of Alois's new plan. He will drink enough to bear the looks his wife and daughter give, but not become so drunk that he rages and flails his arms at Kuda and Mai Kuda. Alois's plan is to contain his despair and not futilely attempt to wash it away in the hours spent at the beer hall. Beginning the next morning, he will also sit in the yard until noon, observing the women as they go about their chores. For he knows women love to be watched by the man of the house even when they pretend to want to be alone and he recognises his deficit in this matter. He will do it again in the evening, watch them come up from the garden with some leaves of sweet cabbage, or go into the bush for kindling. The important thing is that Madya sits properly upright on the mud foundation around his sleeping room and be seen to be seeing what is going on in his home. Once in a while, as he watches, he will throw out a word of encouragement or surprise the women with a joke.

"Mai Kuda! There's this story people are saying about that Government Minister, the one who died."

Mai Kuda will look up in astonishment and for once a spark of interest will flare in her eyes.

Alois will continue, "They say that Minister went to see his mother one day. She was watching the television, but when the Minister walked into the room and saw what the old woman was doing, he began to cry. 'Mai!' he sobs, watching the television, with water running down his cheeks like that. 'Mai, everyone laughs at me!' 'Why do they do that?' the mother asks. She cannot believe that anyone could laugh at her son, the Minister. 'They say I am the ugliest brute that ever lived,' the Minister replies. 'The TV is always showing the ministers, so the people see me and are always laughing!' His mother dries her son's tears and says, 'Don't worry about that, my son!' Just as she turns back to the television the news begins and the same Minister comes on. 'There!' the mother tells her son triumphantly. "Didn't I tell you? You can't be uglier than him my son, the one who has just come onto television!"

Alois can see the little family, all three of them, laughing out in the yard. Nevertheless, as he takes leave of Baba Jo, thanks him for the beer and starts towards home, Alois cannot keep his hopeful mood up. Instead, he is filled with doubt. The two women have no idea how much it takes a man to simply live these days. Day after day he must go on, keep breathing, tasting, hearing, seeing and knowing. He does so everyday, but nobody recognises this feat of endurance. Will they recognise he is doing it for the three of them this afternoon, when he begins his new plan? The frustration stirs up the Shake-Shake in his stomach so that its strength doubles. By the time Alois sinks his feet into the sand of the river bed and pulls them out, he feels more drunk than his plan allows.

Alois Madya feels each step he takes over the stony road. But his feet have grown rubbery and the stones have grown bigger since he walked to the bar. They fool him with their new dimensions and trip him but do not hurt him. Madya tries to remember. Do the boulders do that every time he walks from the bar? He gets up again and again, ranting at the stones that deceive him by shrinking back to their pre-fall size. When they have done this, they mock him with their smallness. Alois tells himself he will not be like the Government Minister: he will not cry. He will make it home without tears even though his daughter does not respect him, and his wife likes him so little she has not taken her daughter to task about the way Kuda behaves. All Mrs Madya has bothered to do is to give her daughter a few half-hearted admonitions: "Hear what your father says, after all he is the man of this house!"

The afternoon air is hot on the short coils of Alois's hair. The shafts drive the heat to the roots and deep into his skull. There it shimmers and scorches like the sun on the hard village ground. The glare blinds him.

In the yard at the Madya home, Kuda is standing by the dish rack. Fingers of pale grass push out of the ground around the girl's feet, nurtured in some fashion by the soapy water and bits of sadza the women throw out of the tub when they have finished washing the dishes. She is bent over another young person. Kuda's fingers work busily and expertly in the other girl's hair.

Madya enters his homestead and sees his daughter. He commands the ground to be still and it obeys him. Alois finds he can plant his feet firmly apart. He nails his centre of gravity to the air. The air holds. Alois does not topple. He stares at his daughter.

"Kuda!" says Alois.

The young woman does not move.

"Kuda!" Alois says again.

When his daughter does not look at him, Madya succeeds in raising his right arm, but the finger at the end of it disobeys him and droops down limply.

Kuda's companion steals a glance around her friend's body and giggles. It is that girl Tabitha. She is wearing the yellow dress.

"*Iwe!*" Kuda reprimands Tabitha with a tug on the extension she is plaiting.

Kuda looks her father over without raising her head.

His trousers are dry. Kuda sighs. She dares not tell him Tabitha will pay her a dollar for doing her hair so that she has a hairstyle worthy of the dress from the flea markets in Mozambique that the lorry driver brought in. Kuda is afraid her father will want the money. If he says, "give it to me," she will have to do so. But she wishes he would take more interest in what she and her mother do to keep the home running. She gives her mother money for food. She is also saving to buy her father something. Perhaps for Christmas. She thinks it should be a cell phone, like Ba'Jo has.

"What are you doing! You're hurting me!" Tabitha complains. She slaps at Kuda's legs too hard for play, too softly to hurt, somewhere in between.

Kuda relents towards her father.

"Good afternoon, Baba" she says. Her eyes are a tight, thin sheet of metal, through which nothing leaks.

"Who is that?" says Madya, although he knows well it is Tabitha.

Kuda does not answer her father, nor does she tell him what she is thinking. She is wondering whether her father is right. Since Tabitha disappeared with the truck driver in the morning and came back demanding and getting a dress, Kuda is not so sure of the young woman she walks with. She has asked Tabitha to bring more young women to have their hair done, from the other side of the Business Centre where Tabitha lives. Tabitha has promised to bring many, but has not brought anyone, not even Clarissa with whom she works. Kuda is thinking about ending the friendship.

Madya approaches his daughter. He picks up a brick when he is halfway there.

"Kuda!" Alois says again. "Everyone knows you do not respect your father. You play with people who laugh at me. You do not respect what I tell you."

"Everyone is asking about this respect," replies Kuda. She remains bent over Tabitha's hair. "They are saying, who can say anyone should be respected? They are even saying there is no use in any of that respect thing, because what is it? Can you taste it? Is it nice? Can you eat it!"

Madya strikes Kuda on the head with the brick. Kuda falls down, struggling feebly. Madya drops to his knees beside her. He brings the brick down on his daughter's head again and again. Tabitha runs to the kitchen rondavel to call Mrs Madya. Mrs Madya comes out and understands what is taking place. She sits down on the raised foundation around the kitchen in silence. Tremors run silently through Mai Kuda's body.

Finally Kuda makes no sound and does not move. Although he promised himself he will not cry, Madya takes his daughter's head onto his lap. He cradles the girl's head and stretches out his legs. Kuda's mother sits silently. Madya cries. He cannot stop.

CHAPTER ELEVEN

Transition to Glory

Chimamanda Ngozi Adichie

Her clothes smell of spices. It is the middle of the rainy season as she cooks jollof rice, the ceiling fan is off, the rains slapped against the closed windows and the aroma from her pot rises in heady wafts and soaks into the living room curtains, into her clothes, into the bedcover in her tiny room. Later, she pulls her blouse over her head before getting into the bath and stops to breathe in curry and magi and thyme. And doing that, she catches her breath, catches a sob in her throat. Yet, she didn't even cook much for Agha. Only once, in fact, the Saturday he came by from the tennis club. But it is the act of trying to catch something, or recapture something, that causes her pain, that causes the choking sounds to come from her. When she lies in bed and waits for sleep, when she tosses and clutches her pillow, she smells on it the scent of spices gone stale; and she gets up and rips off her pillow and her bedcovers.

She rolled her car windows up as she approached the traffic jam at Oshodi. The last time, a hand has snaked into her car and yanked her left earring and necklace off, so swift and slick that she may had doubted it even happened but for her torn, bleeding ear. It happened last week, the jewellery snatching and now she wondered if that young man whose hand had sneaked into her car would have thought twice if he knew who she was. What if she had shouted. "I'm Ozioma, from Ray Power FM." Would he have stared blankly at her before going on to snatch the necklace anyway? She liked to think not; she liked to think that both the "big men" sitting behind their monster cars in the traffic jams of Victoria Island and the alaye boys loitering on these market streets of Oshodi listened to her show. Sometimes she wasn't so sure. Her producer said her audience was more of the former, but then her producer said a lot of things that made her wish she could slap his face.

It was hot in the car, her air conditioner was long broken and her throat was starting to itch from the stuffiness. The traffic jam was chaos: a bus edged so close she thought it would scratch her, a hawker pressed a Celine Dion CD to her window, horns blared, drivers stuck out their heads and cursed. The sweat felt heavy on her neck and she lifted her braids and held them up in a ponytail with an elastic band. She would let them loose when she got to Surulere, to the hotel, because Agha liked them that way. Agha. She didn't want to think about him just yet, in the breathless heat of the car. She liked to keep thoughts of him special aside for when there was nothing else in her mind to taint them, to get in the way. Just as she liked to eat chocomilo sweets before she ate anything so that the bittersweet cocoa taste would melt in her mouth, pure and unspoiled.

She finally drove out of the car melee of Oshodi and rolled her windows down, letting in a breeze that smelled like the flooded roadside purple bougainvillea climbing on its white walls, she pulled the elastic band from her hair and felt the tiny braids graze her neck. She parked and dabbed perfume behind her ears, blended her lipstick, arranged her breasts in her bra.

Agha was in the room, their room, watching CNN. His white T-shirt clung to the slight of his belly, as well as to the bulge of his arms kept youthful with tennis. She looked at him and felt the same thrill as the first day she met him, and she wondered, again, just what it was about this smallish man who walked with his back straight.

"How are you, eh?" he said. She liked it when he said that, the lazy way he spoke and before she could say anything he was touching her braids, pulling her to him.

He had just led her to the bed when his GSM phone rang. He got up and picked it up from the sofa, where he'd thrown down his tennis bag and racket. He looked at the number, hesitated, then placed the phone on the nightstand and let it ring.

"I should have switched it off," he said, and when she asked "Was it your wife?" he didn't answer, he just went on kissing her and she tasted the spring roll he had been eating.

She turns the TV on and a newscaster on NTA 10 is saying that it is the fourth straight day of rain in Lagos. There is footage of cars submerged in brown floods. During the commercial break, a pastor announces a special fellowship on the theme of Noah's Ark, a bible pressed to his chest. She turns the TV off. The rain thumping on the roof is relentless, it pounds inside her head and she wishes she had the flat downstairs. Agha had said he would get her a new flat, a ground floor flat in Abebe Court. "How will I explain being able to afford a place in Abebe Court?" she had asked him, teasing and he said nothing, he only smiled in that quietly knowing way. She remembers that smile now, that in the hotel room, so clearly that she closes her eyes, shakes her head.

She feels faint. She is not sure when she last ate the bread on top of the fridge. Yesterday night? It couldn't have been, because when she picks up the bread, there are ringlets of purple mould all over it. She admires the pretty colours for a while, using a ladle. Her GSM phone starts ringing, and she wonders how that is possible—she switched it off, didn't she?

She looks around her small living room, not sure where the phone is, even though she is not prepared to answer it. *The Guardian* on the table is crumpled, almost into a ball, and she doesn't remember crumpling it; she never crumples newspapers anyway, she saves them and gives them to the mallam on the next street, the one with the tiny kiosk where she buys matches and sugar. He probably sells the newspapers to the *akara* hawkers, who use them to wrap *akara*. But she is not sure; she only knows that the mallam thanks her warmly whenever she gives the newspapers to him. Maybe it is also why he offers to find her a "Water Boy" during water scarcities, those lean boys who take her one hundred naira and come back with her jerry cans mysteriously full, even when the scarcity is all over the whole of Lagos mainland.

She slowly starts to straighten *The Guardian*; the mallam won't like it crumpled. She lays it on the table and is running her hand over it when she sees the face, Agha's face, the obituary announcement. And now she remembers crumpling the paper, she remembers seeing his face fill an entire page, below the words "Transition to Glory," and she remembers the rain hitting her closed windows and she remembers thinking how stupid that sounded – Transition to Glory.

Her phone rang and a strange number appeared and, for a moment, she peered at it and wanted to ignore it, thinking that maybe some stranger who listened to Ray Power FM had gotten hold of her number. Finally, she picked it up. It was Agha.

"Are you using somebody's phone?" she asked.

He told her it was his; he had just bought a new phone to call her. Just her. From the way he said it, the timbre of his voice, she knew she was supposed to be pleased. But she wasn't. Instead, she felt irritation run over her like a cold shiver. He had bought the phone especially for her, a phone he could switch off when his wife was there.

"Can I see you, please?" he asked. They were not supposed to see each other today; he said he would be busy with meetings. Besides, her producer had just annoyed her. She was reading some of her letters that listeners sent in when he called her into his wood-panelled office and told her to ease off on the philosophy and keep it simple. Her listeners didn't care that she thought God was a human construct, or else why did happy people serve a happy God and surly people serve a mean God? Her listeners wanted, instead, to hear her poke fun at Obassanjo and all his sycophants, at the farce called democracy. They like it the most – the phone lines were clogged – when she did her "man-woman-specials", like the one she did today when she poked fun at women who stood on roadsides all over Lagos, as if they were waiting for taxis when they were really waiting for men to give them rides – men who were stupid enough not to realise that the women wanted to save transport money and were not interested in them.

She didn't agree with her producer, of course, she felt her audience, felt that they liked her questioning the deeper things in life in addition to mocking the shallower. So she said to him, "You think everybody is a dunce like you, eh?" And he laughed and asked her to smile, to have a coke, because they both knew she would ease off on the philosophy: many people would give anything for her job. She walked out of the office with her lower lip clenched between her teeth, and now she was even more annoyed that Agha had gotten a phone just for her calls and she wanted to say "no, I can't see you today and go to hell at that", but she said "yes."

He smelled of sweat and "Eternity for Men" when he hugged her at the door of the hotel room. She thought he would grab her and push her to the bed, but he ordered them shredded chicken with rice and after they had eaten, they sat up in bed and drank orange juice and he asked how her day had been. He said her producer was probably right; she had to keep the show simpler. Not many people can handle that first-class brain, he teased.

She knew he never missed listening to her show and she wondered now if his wife listened to it, too, since it was on at the time when he would be at breakfast. His youngest child, Emeka, might be there as well as his daughter Nnennaya, the one who had finished secondary school, whose chirpy photo was on his office desk. And perhaps the first daughter, Adamma, would drive from her flat, on her way to work and join the family for breakfast and they would all listen to her show.

At this thought, she moved away from his embrace, lay face-up on the bed. He didn't ask her what was wrong and she wondered if he knew that she felt as though she had tripped and was now lunging, head first, into a deep hole, a deep hole full of cold water.

"Did you know it's three months into our affair," she said. In her better moods, she liked that word-affair — liked the decadent affectation that clung to it. But now she said it in a tone that taunted him, that taunted everything.

"Did you know it's three months since I found happiness," he said, in that slow, careful way. And she wanted to kick him, because he sounded so predictable. But it made a giddy, sneaky warmth course through her, nonetheless, hearing him say that.

"I have to be in London this week-end," he said, after a while. "I would like you to come with me."

She didn't say anything, just kept looking at the ceiling. He reached out to touch her braids, she moved away and all of a sudden she wanted to shout, crazed loud shouting. She wanted to ask where his wife would be at the week-end. She wanted to ask if he ever was consumed with the same thoughts as she was: thoughts about right and need.

"Come to London with me, please," he said. "We'll stay the week-end and you'll be back in time for your show."

He always spoke to her like that, quiet, courteously. Yet sometimes she wished he would raise his voice, do something, so that it would all seem more real.

She sits on the toilet seat and stares at the newspaper, at the slope of the print. Lovingly remembered by Didi and the children. Didi. She is sure Didi has done all the proper things a wife should do, followed all the traditions. Heavens know, she would not have. She would not even have tolerated a funeral, or joined in the Igbo songs that would ask God to have mercy on him as though he had done something wrong, as though it was not he who needed to have mercy on God. She would not have sat with the visitors who would come in shaking solemn heads and muttering *ndo* in an irritating drone. She would not have worn all-black or all-white for a year. Is Didi wearing white or black she wonders.

Didi. Her name is Ndidiamaka but Agha called her Didi on the few occasions that he slipped and did not say "my wife". Didi. It is a name Ozioma dislikes, a name she would dislike even if it were not his wife's. It makes her think of a supercilious cat, or a furry white dog, or a rabbit. It reminds her of the Ikejianis who lived next door when she was growing up in Nsukka and the green-eyed German Mrs Ikejiani raising rabbits with names like Didi and Fifi in wire-mesh cages in the garage. Mrs Ikejiani talked to the rabbits in German and stroked their fur on the days her husband staggered home late from the staff club and then on Sundays, Mrs Ikejiani selected the fattest of the rabbits for her stew.

Ozioma does not know where to get a rabbit in Lagos, does not even know who to ask about one. She finds her GSM phone under a chair (she does not remember flinging it there) and calls her producer. When she asks him if he knows where she can get a rabbit, he cackles and asks if she is now too big to eat beef and chicken like everyone else. Rabbit *kwa*?

She puts the phone down. There must be rabbits in Nsukka. Mrs Ikejiani went back to Germany years ago, even before she entered the university, but she is sure somebody will have rabbits in Nsukka.

She calls her producer to tell him she is going to Nsukka and he wants to know when she will be back because they start the new season in two weeks. She tells him she will be back in time for the show.

They were on the roof of the London tour bus, red and rickety and when the rain started, he held her tight and kissed her. The guide was dashing down into the bus, the two couples behind them as well. But he kept kissing her, and the rain was warm on her head and it was so unlike him, this public display, and the breath mint she tasted on his tongue was sharp and sweet. Finally, when the rain slowed, he unwrapped her from his arms and helped her up. They got off at the next stop, Trafalgar Square.

A wizened man, Indian-looking, with folded skin the colour of cinnamon, came up to Agha and asked: "You want pigeon on your wife's head?"

He had a crumpled bag in his hand, pigeon food and he offered to pour it on her head so the pigeons would land on her. Nice photos, he said, they make nice photos: for only one pound. Agha laughed and gave the man five pounds, waved him away. "There must be more dignity in farming a piece of land in Bangladesh, abi?" he asked her.

"You don't know he's from Bangladesh," she said and laughed, a laugh that did not need something funny, really, like a drunken laugh.

He sat down on the pavement and pulled her down on his lap, and they sat there, tangled and silly, and he said he had never done this in all his other times in London. He had never come to Trafalgar Square or been on a bus tour; never had the time to talk to a pigeon man; to do the tourism things. He said nothing about the man calling her his wife. She wished he had and so, as they got up and walked along with their hands locked, she asked if his wife would have wanted pigeons on her head.

"I don't know," he said and then changed the subject and asked what she thought of a statue nearby and she wanted to cry. The tears felt so close. She started to run across the wet ground; she hoped that the air would rush past her ears and clear her head, take the tears back. He was chasing her, she heard his heavy breathing behind, and when he caught her wet coat, he held her to him and pressed his lips to her neck.

"You want to give an old man a heart attack, eh?" he said. He held her for a while and then finally they walked to the road and took a cab to an Italian restaurant in Piccadilly. He pretended to speak poor English to the cab driver, and then gave him a huge tip afterwards. He laughed with the hostess at the restaurant. He reached out and took her hand as they were seated, then came back over and kissed her. He seemed a different person, as if something that had fit just right back in Lagos was now a little loose.

A Ghanaian couple on the way came up and introduced themselves: Abena and Djangmah from Accra. They were slightly drunk. "We knew right away that you were real West Africans," they said, with generous laughter. 'We all know how those Londonised West Africans look, and of course those Kenyans and Tanzanians are different from us, talk less of the Jamaicans!"

They assumed she was his wife, and it didn't help when Agha said, 'Ozioma and I live in Lagos.' As though they came together, the two making one.

After the Ghanaian couple left, she asked him. "Is that how you would have introduced your wife?" And because she knew he would shrug and change the subject again, she added, "Tell me about your wife."

"Don't do this", he said, taking her hand. But it annoyed her the way he said that, as if he were a film, as if he were saying what he thought he was supposed to say.

"Tell me," she said. "Tell me about her."

"What is there to tell?"

"Anything, just anything," she said. So he told her about the marriage rites, before the white wedding, when they first did the door knocking and then the bride price and finally the wine-carrying. How her uncles had complained that the cow was small, that the yams were not that big, that the kegs of palm wine were not that many. She didn't ask him to stop, she should have, but she didn't. She should have told him she was only brining his wife up to remind them both that a wife existed, somewhere, rather than to talk about his wife. She should have asked him, didn't he realise that her bringing his wife up was because she was afraid to bring other things up. But she didn't. Instead she imagined that it was to her father's house that he and his people had brought the palm wine and the yams. And when he told her that, during the wine-carrying ceremony, the children in the neighbourhood had stolen a lot of meat, fried beef wrapped in banana leaves and hidden in pans, she even laughed.

Later, as they lay in bed in the Kensington hotel room, she said, almost in a whisper, "I don't know what is happening to me." And he held her close and stroked her braids and she wished he would say something but he didn't. Finally, she asked, "Do you know your name means war? It's a bad sign, being with a man called War."

And he said, with humour, "And do you know yours means gospel? It's a good sign being with a woman called Gospel."

The house in Nsukka looks the same; it has the same smells from her childhood, the smells of cleaning detergent and spices. The dining room curtains are different, though, they are a brighter yellow. Her mother likes cheerful colours: the living room curtains are pink. She thinks she remembers her mother mentioning the new curtains the last time they talked, but she is not sure. Talking to her mother is a monotony of 'I know you have a good job but you need to find a nice young man,' and so sometimes she puts the phone on the table as her mother talks, so she can fold her clothes or stir her stew.

She hugs her mother, says nothing is wrong, she just wanted to come visit for a few days. Her mother's friends are in the living room, fat women, all members of the Legion of Mary, with black scarves tied across their foreheads. They hug her one after another. They say she has lost so much weight and ask if she is all right, if she recently had malaria. She tells them that somebody died.

"*Onye?*" they ask. "Who died?"

She tells them it is the man she was engaged to and she keeps her face blank because she knows her mother is looking at her in bewilderment.

"Ewooooo," the women moan, "your mother did not even tell us you were engaged." She knows her mother has offered endless masses for her to find a husband and she knows her mother's friends have given up on her. Now for her to have come so close to being married – she has their sympathy and more now.

The house help brings her rice and plantain on a plate and she sits at the dining table and stares at the food and listens to her mother's friends talking in the living room. She is sitting on the seat she sat on as a teenager, looking at the same painting of a serene woman-*Tutu* by Ben Enwonwu – that has hung there forever. She is leaning on the same wooden table that she leaned on when she was a seven-year-old with a runny nose, long before she knew that Agha existed, that she would fall for a man with a quiet smile and a careful voice who would die before she had a chance to sort her feelings out, to sort anything out. She wonders if it was all predestined. When she was that child climbing the mango tree right outside this dining room, was Agha already pencilled into her life?

She shakes her head, shakes the tears back and asks her mother's friends if they know where she can get a rabbit and they say, of course, a man in Orba sells them, and they look at her strangely because they are wondering what she wants with, of all things, a rabbit.

The rabbit she gets is grey and its puff of a tail is white. Very neatly, the man in Orba says, feeling the rabbit's thighs. Very meaty.

She doesn't begin, she only asks that the man get her a leash and even though he looks at her oddly – how crazy these young people from Lagos behave nowadays – he gets her a dog leash and she puts it round the rabbit's neck before leaving.

She mostly ignores her mother, watches the days slide past and walks barefoot under the rains. The rains are different here, more fragrant, less angry. The mud stains her feet red and sometimes she stops to make a careful imprint of the rabbit's feet on the path or to pluck a wild grass or to touch an anthill. They take slightly different paths to Odim Hill every day, she and the rabbit and at the top of the hill they drink from a plastic water bottle, she first and then the rabbit, sometimes from the cap of the bottle, other times from the cup of her palm.

"Look," she says to the rabbit. "Look how the hills are laid all around us; I can see God's hand doing it." It is what her mother used to tell her when she was a child, and she would see God's brown hands with clipped nails, laying out the green-covered hills of Nsukka. But that was when God still had some sense, she thinks now, when he laid out those hills.

She lets the rabbit play in the backyard, after the walks. The leash is long, as much freedom as possible, but she holds on to it anyway because anything can happen, the frangipani trees can fall and squash the rabbit, the lean guava trees can rain hard unripe fruit down. She sits under the mango tree, swats at the flies following the fallen mangoes and watches carefully for an accident, ready to pull at the leash. Somebody should have put a leash on Agha; somebody should have pulled his car back before the drunken trailer driver ran into it on Ibadan road.

But then, if what her mother says is right – that it was God's will – then the leash would have broken or that car would have careened into Agha somehow, anyhow. (She had told her mother a sketchy story, and let her assume that Agha had been single and Catholic and a nice young man.) God's will. It really is the same thing as God's fault. Blame God. But she doesn't blame God for doing it, she blames Him for not preventing it. It is a healthier way to think, a more reasonable way, and then she realises that Agha would have liked her thinking that way. She gets up, picks the rabbit up and goes to her room. She lies in bed and remembers how Agha slept with his hands tucked under the pillow, how easy it was for him to fall asleep after he came. She wonders if Didi saved the last pillowcase he slept on, if it still bears the indentation of his head, she would have saved it. She wonders what his bedroom at home looks like, if he used to leave chewed toothpicks on his nightstand like he did those nights in their London hotel room.

She gets up, beginning to cry, and starts to pick up the dark balls of rabbit shit from her bedroom floor.

Ozioma watched him sleep. She was sated, tired, but she could not sleep because it was his first visit to her flat and he would not leave soon – he was supposed to be at the tennis club – and she wanted to remember every minute. His snoring was raspy. She reached out and touched his lips, which were slightly parted. Then she moved closer and placed her cheek next to his. He stirred, mumbled something, and she thought she heard her name. She smelled the spices on his breath, the thyme and curry from the jollof rice she'd cooked; the rice he'd eaten with the same attentiveness that he paid her body. He was so gentle. She liked that he took his time, that he looked in her eyes for long, eloquent moments, that he had a spreading waist. Did it make sense? She wished she could ask somebody, but there was nobody to ask. She couldn't even imagine asking Chikwere. Chikwere was her only friend who knew about Agha. But she didn't like to talk too much about Agha with Chikwere, because she was scared that somehow it would slip out that she could not imagine dating any young man, that she practiced her first name and Agha's last name in front of her bathroom mirror. Chikwere would laugh, she knew; but worse, Chikwere would not understand. And that Chikwere might even tease her and say in Igbo "Nekwanum anya biko," – is he not almost fifty? "Haven't you heard that if you must eat a frog, then eat a bull frog so that when they call you a frog-eater you can answer? If you want to get serious with a man, then, my dear, find a real man!"

She was gently stroking the hair on his arm when he opened his eyes. She said she was sorry she had woken him and he said no, it was fine, and he had a strange expression as he looked around her tiny room, at her dressing table crowded with creams, her mirror plastered with photos, her shelf lined with books.

"What are you thinking?" she asked.

"I shouldn't have come," he said. "Being here, where you live, makes me want something more. It makes me want more than I should."

There was something to the way he said 'live,' the way he stressed it; he had never said anything like that before. At first she was happy that he said that because it meant that his mind was not always as careful as his smile. Then she was angry that he said that because it meant he did not think he should want more.

"I'm driving to Ibadan tomorrow. I would ask you to come with me but its just for a meeting and then I'll be back in the evening. Can I see you when I come back?" he asked.

"No."

He looked at her for a while then got up and started to get dressed. And she wondered why he never asked her to snap out of it, why he was never insistent.

"I'll call you when I get back," he said.

"What if your wife goes to the tennis club one of these days?" she asked.

He said nothing. He placed a small wrapped box on the table before he left, one of the many politely quiet things he did, leaving her presents – and they were always wrapped – this one a necklace and matching earrings.

The people she walks past on Odim Street, before she gets to the hill, no longer try to grasp her hand, not after she sank her teeth into the shoulder of the woman who forced her into an embrace. Now they focus their sympathetic glances on the leash around the rabbit's neck. It is the same look Doctor Nwoye has; her mother brings him often, begs her to talk to him.

The day before she leaves Nsukka, she asks the house help to kill the rabbit and she cooks it herself, makes a stew with tomatoes and onions. She adds no spices, not even salt and the meat is bland and tough and she suffers indigestion through the night.

When her bus stops in Lagos the next day, she takes a taxi but she does not tell the driver to go to Yaba, where she lives. Instead she tells him to go to Victoria Island, where Agha lives, where Agha lived. At the compound gate, a simple gate, not the ostentatious structures lining the rest of the street, the gateman asks her what she wants, eyeing her travelling bag. She tells him to tell madam that Ozioma from Ray Power FM is here. The gateman lights up, clutches her hand, asks her to come in and before he goes to the front door to announce her presence, he points at the black transmitter radio in his booth and tells her he never misses her show.

A maid lets her into a living room with wide spaces and elegant, uncomfortable-looking chairs. Is this what is called Queen Anne furniture, she wonders. She knows the huge photo on the wall is Agha but she avoids looking right at it as she sits on the tip of a sofa.

Didi appears. She is everything Ozioma imagined, light-skinned and manicured, wearing a black *bou-bou* with exquiste embroidery down its front. Didi is looking at her and it is clear – by the sudden moist tension in the air – that Didi knows who she is, what she is, what she was.

"Will you drink orange juice?" Didi asks.

Ozioma stares at her, startled, because it is the last thing she expects. Didi is the kind of woman that she would poke fun at in her show, the kind of woman who goes to Nail Studio twice a week, who receives calls from boutique owners when they get a new shipment from Italy and Dubai.

"Or would you prefer a coke? Malt?" Didi's face is expressionless.

"No," Ozioma finally says when she finds her voice. 'No, thank you.'

Didi sits down. "How dare you come here? How dare you?"

The question does not surprise Ozioma, but Didi's calmness does. And she realises how like Agha Didi is, the same calm smile, the same civil coating over their body movements. The same incredible control. They are both cultured, worldly people, Agha and Didi. Ozioma feels a strange helplessness, weightlessness; she is sure she would float away if she jumped up now, if her feet left the ground. 'Did he tell you about me?' she asks.

Didi is silent for a while. "He was perfect, my husband. He was perfect at lying, he was perfect at everything." A pause, and for the first time, there is a sneer on Didi's face, or maybe the sneer has always been there and lets itself out now. "No, my dear, of course he didn't tell me about you."

"Then how did you know?"

"I assume you expect me to answer your question." Didi shifts on her seat and slowly crosses her legs. "What I find interesting is that my daughter Adamma is a year older than you." Didi is smiling, and even though it is that familiar civil smile, Ozioma sees the rage in it, the stretch of lip over teeth. Suddenly she too is angry, she too feels full of a frothy rage that bubbles up in her, that buoys her up and she shouts, "How do you know how old I am, eh?"

Didi says nothing. Ozioma feels a churning in her stomach, a mish-mash of emotions. There is a long stretch of silence, like a taut string tied from Didi's sofa to hers and then Didi starts to cry. She has her head in her hands and she is sobbing and her shoulders are moving and for a moment Ozioma wonders if Didi is playing a joke, this woman who offered her orange juice instead of calling the gateman to throw her out.

But she knows the tears are real when she hears the familiar choking sounds-the same sounds that have come out of her, the sounds of angry grief, of grieving anger. She wants to go over and touch Didi, sooth her, say, "*ebezi na*", but she decides not to, because she does not trust herself and she does not trust Didi.

She gets up and quietly lets herself out.

CHAPTER TWELVE

The Son

Ivor Agyeman-Duah

Prof Ike is well-known on the University of Ibadan campus. Handsome in his youthfulness, he is the only child of his parents. He is also known among the relatively older generation as the boy who lost his mother when thieves attacked the university bungalow and whose father, was for many years, a well-known professor of medicine. The father, Prof Peter Ike, has given his son the best of education, sending him to boarding school in England – Eton and eventually to Oxford, where he had read literature and obtained a PhD at 29 years-of-age. Many also said the father should have remarried and that his then fourteen year old son should not have been sent to England. They had said, as they can say many things in Ibadan that, it would not only deprive him of comfort but that it would create greater alienation for father and son.

Thus, it came to many people as a surprise when word filtered through that Ike had completed his studies and been hired as a tutor at Oxford and in fact was on holiday with his retired father in Abeokuta. Some of the same people said: "Why should he come to a country that is on the edge, a sign of Jonah in the hands of the "Butcher of Abuja," when others desperately wanted to leave?"

It was only when Ike went to the Faculty of Humanities and finally received his letter of appointment as a senior lecturer in World Literature that they got to accept his real return to Nigeria. In the farewell party for his father on campus two years before, the State Governor, as guest speaker extolled the achievements

147

and patriotism of Prof Peter Ike for his contribution to teaching and as a renowned sickle cell specialist who put the country on the map of global scholarship.

The junior Ike's return to the university had attracted some media interest because of his own impressive accomplishments as an Oxford don interested in promoting literature in English and not English Literature which means that, he was interested in World Literatures: in the writers of the Commonwealth, Latin America and even translations of Spanish and Greek literature. He wanted his students to understand Nadine Gordimer, J. P. Clark, Doris Lessing, George Lamming and Gabriel Garcia Marquez who have dazzled the world of African, Caribbean and Latin American literature.

Ike walked around campus with what some perceived as a swagger even in innocently simple but expensive long-sleeve shirts and trousers; black or brown shoes to match. The students liked what he had introduced: a sort of a "tutorial system" with a lot of time given to third-year students. The females, especially, loved the liberal disposition when the classes took place under the dying trees on campus but most especially, the Authors Series which discussed great writers. His knowledge of comparative analysis of English and Afro-Caribbean or African writers' consciously or unconsciously influenced by Charles Dickens, Thomas Hardy and others, made literature and the subtlety of colonial rule fascinating for them. He often asked, "When the Empire writes back, to whose benefit is it?" a question which always threw the class into literary politics.

"But we know the difference between him and others," Shadia, one of the third-year students, had riposted to a known Pan Africanist student who detested what he perceived as Ike's exaggeration. The student had in fact said that "It is not because he is so brilliant but in Europe and especially in the UK, if you study literature, you do so in the context of other literary works. It's a cosmopolitan world we now live in and so what is the big deal in this?"

Abidame, the administrative secretary at the English Department and an alumnus who also studied at the University of

Leeds, has been very amused by some of the students' arguments outside class. She likes Ike for his respectful attitude to all but was also aware that some of the lecturers didn't like him. "Is it this funny 'innovation' of seeing students individually and not drawing the line between a student and the reverence they should show their lecturers?" one lecturer said to the other and to Abidame's hearing.

Abidame was not so sure if Ike, whose office was close by and reading the day's newspapers, heard this. She herself had been a subject of gossip at the Department three years ago. "What is she doing after her Leeds qualification and at 33 years of age when her friends and other colleagues were married and having children?" they said.

Initially she had been angry. Her boyfriend of many years standing had impregnated her friend and married her in the two years she had been abroad studying. He had sent her fake letters and emails to conceal the other relationship and therefore she had had a hard time adjusting when she completed her course and returned home.

On this particular day, Abidame left the office before the official closing time of 5pm as she popped into Ike's office to say, as she often does: "Guy, see you tomorrow and have a blessed night," to which the always smiling Ike, with cup in hand after a sip responded: "Good night my dear girl." A jokingly girlish identity to which she had equally protested reminding him that they are at least of the same age. "I will not mind if you call me a boy," he has always said in return.

She had to pick up Akoto her sister at the taxi station – Peterson's Junction which by some contoured means leads to the Ibadan Highway. She was not so sure if her sister was already there and whether their mission to the Ibadan Art Gallery was worth it. She has called her phone without response and sent an SMS message.

Their father, Arnold Oyoman, before he died bought, on a visit to Lagos, two art works from an Igbo author and playwright who does abstract painting and signs off as OP. Their insurance broker father developed interest as an art collector and got to know OP. It was whilst using OP's visitor's toilet on a visit to her home that he discovered some of these paintings stacked in one of the drawers. Exotic paintings crumpled in drawers? He was particularly and instantly attracted to two of them – oil paintings on canvass of convoluted rocks beneath hills and emerging gigantic colonial buildings. First instincts – Abeokuta!! And he was right as OP had captured this mental image on her first visit to this historic town in the western region that had produced anti-colonial leaders, presidents and playwrights.

Embarrassed, she had accepted $400 for the two paintings. After Oyoman left, she started combing the whole house for others she had created out of boredom and to ease stress. Unfortunately, when Oyoman was moving to their new mansion in Abeokuta, the two works, intended for the dining hall, got lost. Either accidently or most probably, the removal boys stole them.

"It is very difficult if you do not understand or value something to appreciate its value," Akoto told Abidame on the morning before their arranged visit to the gallery which had suddenly emerged as a spot to buy Nigerian and African art work – paintings and sculpture and even some Ashanti goldweights. The gallery site, a former slum and hang-out of drug addicts, is a regenerated strategic site and a recreation ground courtesy of a British woman and her Nigerian husband. They bought the land, transformed it into what it had become an adjoining coffee shop. Suddenly, it's a new middle-class haven – an enclave for diplomatic art and a bookshop. Some of the art works, it was said, were bought from peasant artists on the streets and sculptors in the villages at cheap prices and sold in dollars. Other works were commissioned or stolen and sold to the curators.

Abidame was in a hurry and midway to catch up with Akoto when she realized she had left her purse and other materials for their meeting at the office. She speedily drove back and realized on getting there that Ike's light was still on. *Still reading or listening to the BBC World Service as he does sometimes* she thought. As she approached with the intention of putting the light off, she heard a moaning voice. After about a minute, she involuntarily opened the door only to find a shirtless Ike on top of Shadia, the best female defender of the "tutorial system." She quickly shut the door, her heart beating in irregular rhythm; she picked the purse and other materials, descended to the car park and drove off to meet Akoto.

Abidame could not help but discuss the encounter with Akoto when she finally picked her up. Her countenance had changed to a disturbed and angry look that Akoto found unsettling. As she drove and she was still talking about it, Akoto asked: "But you said you only entered and was shocked with disbelief so where did you get all these details from?" Abidame realized her betrayal of emotions. After a fruitless check of the many items, which Abidame did not pay attention to, and a short meeting with the curator about their search, they finally went home.

The following day, Ike did not come to work. *Maybe out of embarrassement*, Abidame thought. She then remembered that Fridays were his off days. When he did come early Monday on morning, he shyly said to her: "So sorry about Thursday incident. Never a pre-meditated thing," as he barely looked at Abidame who could also hardly look back.

Ike would be travelling unexpectedly to the University of Edinburgh to give a series of lectures. The days off could help the embarrassing situation. When in the course of the day, he informed Abidame of this, she said to herself, "It means he will miss my birthday party." "Happy birthday to you in advance. Since I will not be here on the 5th, which is in fact the day I get back to Ibadan, can I invite you to my bungalow for dinner on the 6th at 7pm?," he requested not so sure whether he meant to help erase the incident from her mind or because for a little while now he wanted an opportunity to invite her out.

Abidame who was not expecting this had intuitively said, "OK," but she realized she was more excited about this than the Department's party for her. She started thinking about the meaning of the invitation: to keep her mouth shut about what she had discovered which was becoming secondary to her now or something lovely beyond it? When finally, Ike closed his office door and said "good night," it was more formal but he dropped a pink envelope on her desk. When she opened it, it was a birthday card signed with a note: see you on the 6th at 7pm. Abidame realized her feelings were mixed at this point. Ever since she realized that

Ike's PhD dissertation had been on her 'auntie,' Buchi Emecheta's work especially, *The Joys of Motherland*, her intellectual affection for him had mixed with something else.

Two days after and whilst at work, Abidame did not know what overcame her but she sent a mail to all Ike's students announcing the cancellation of the "tutorial classes" and copied him in. It was after she had pressed the "send" button that she realized it was professionally wrong. She wondered whether she should send another mail to withdraw it but thought that would be worse.

Hours later, while still pondering this, she received a response from Ike but not copied to the others.

"That is fine, as I had thought of doing that myself. All the best…" With a big relief Abidame had read and enjoyed this one-liner a thousand and one times.

II

Akoto incessantly teased Abidame that she was in love, which she regularly denied. As she lay on her bigger sister's bed she suggested that for the evening's dinner, she wears a light pink dress in an indirect response to Ike's pink birthday card. As they laughed over it, Mum Isabella, their sixty-six year old widowed mother, in the next room heard their conversation and in fact, previous conversations on Ike – what they called "girl-talk."

"Pink is better," she said to break their conversation and to make them aware she was listening. Since Abidame returned from abroad, their Mum had tried to persuade her to look for another guy fearful really of age catching up with her daughter. Her wish had been that Abidame gets married before Akoto does to Bankole, with whom Akoto has had a steady relationship for over eight years.

"Eavesdropping is not good oh maama!," Akoto retorted, to which their mother burst into prolonged laughter.

In the end, Abidame settled on the long pink dress with matching shoes, the necessary lipstick and sprayed on drops of perfume. When Akoto told her she looked like Cinderella on the night of merry and confusion, she could not help laughing and she retorted "this is a dinner invitation and nothing more." Akoto replied, "even so make it more than a dinner invitation… and remember, sister to take the appropriate emergency sleepover dress in case you do not come back since today is a Friday…"

On the other side, Ike had been looking over his window since 6.50pm and did so again at 7.11pm and saw Abidame's car lights approaching the house. He was at the door to meet and kiss her cheek and take her in. She was completely overwhelmed with the artistic décor: wall-to-wall shelves with neatly arranged books, African artworks from the Congo, Benin and folklore materials. Ike asked her to sit and offered her a glass of choice South African white wine and engageed her in conversation about his art collection including the paintings of Ablade Glover, El Anatsui and of Congolese and Rwandan artists some of which, depict post-conflict work.

"Let us have dinner now," Ike said as he held her hand to the antique table from the chair she sat in.

"Well, thanks so much for inviting me to dinner and to appreciate your beautiful home and art collection," Abidame had said in response as she looked at the neatly sliced avocado salad, the jollof rice, the fish gravy, the pepper soup close to it whilst listening to the stimulating jazz music of the South African muscian, Louis Mhlanga.

"Did you cook all this?," she asked.

"Yes. And for your birthday!" As he poured wine into her glass he told her funny stories of wines including a wine festival in the vineyards of Sienna in Italy about which Wole Soyinka had written a commemorative play: *From Zia With Love* in 1992.

After dinner, Ike went into his study and brought her birthday present. Wrapped in brown paper, Abidame knew at once it was art work. Uncovered, the painting immediately shocked her. "Naked on these Hills" and "I Come to You" were both signed by OP.

"But these are my father's lost art works," she held them with trembling hands.

"Really?… I bought them in a London gallery for $4,000. The sale catalogue history says, originally from Nigeria. I am sure its sale history is distorted because the creation date is back-dated to

153

give it antique status by those who stole it from Nigeria. Maybe someone stole them and sold them to some tourists and the history of the paintings got exaggerated. I realized immediately I saw them that they were art work about Yoruba traditional architecture."

"They are and…" before she could complete her sentence, her phone registered an SMS message. She knew who sent it: her sister, Akoto and read it: "How is it going sister? See you tomorrow," singned off with a smiley face but Abidame did not reply.

"That was my sister. I did not realize it's past 11pm. Perhaps I need to get back home…"

"I want us to watch this old movie, *Guess Who's Coming to Dinner* that I bought in London," Ike interrupted as he smiled at her and said simultaneously as his hand reached out and drew her closer to his body and to his lips, he said: "a very beautiful and cultured lady." She smiled at the compliment and the next she realised they were in deep embrace, enveloped in his arms and they were kissing on the antique sofa, the same type he had at the office.

When she woke up it was almost mid-day and in Ike's dressing gown, she knew the sequences of the night's dinner, movie and how rightly her sister Akoto has always predicted things about her.

Weeks after this fateful dinner, it became obvious at the Department and around campus that, Prof Ike and Abidame were in a deep relationship. Her car was not only frequently found parked at his bungalow but also occasionally used by Ike and sometimes by Abidame as he sits in the front seat. On Fridays, they would pack their luggage and head off to Abidame's father's huge farm house in Otta. They had gone there a number of times with Akoto and her boyfriend, Bankole and invited a couple of other people for drinks and real organic cuisine. Though Abidame has always looked forward to these farm visits, she became apprehensive because of the bouts of malaria she suffered after such visits.

When they returned from it happily after spending their first Christmas season together and returned to Ibadan on January 3, Abidame suffered a severe feverish condition while also running very high temperatures. She ended up at the Ibadan University Hospital. On the third day of her admission as she lay in bed being given the best of attention, she was in great pain, she opened her eyes to welcome Ike and to say thank you for the flowers and fruits he had brought her.

"It's a bit disturbing but all the tests for malaria and other suspected ailments have proved negative," Ike said to Akoto, who had also come over to see her sister.

"I am sure she will be well. It could be too much stress," Akoto responded in turn.

As they talked about other social issues with Abidame sleeping, Ike felt uneasy when Mum Isabella came. A few minutes later, he begged their permission to leave as he had to teach a class.

"I hope you are not running off because I am here?"

"Not at all Maama, only I have to teach this afternoon," he said.

Abidame's eyes opened again and as Ike left, Akoto assumed a more humorous role.

"Sister, they have done all the tests and there was nothing positive," she whispered something into her sister's ears. Abidame gave a painful but broad laughter and responded, "Go away... I can't be pregnant... All my biological instincts and logic indicate otherwise..." which led to a chorus of laughter from the mother and her two daughters.

Yet, on the fourth day when the doctor did further tests and came back to Abidame, smiling at first, he sat down and removed his stethoscope and glasses, and then his face turned into a grimace and making her feel a sense of trepidation.

"I hope you are prepared for this; because you are three months pregnant. Congratulations!" Instantly a wave euphoria replaced Abidame's feverish condition as she looked at the doctor shyly.

"But I still pass..."

"It happens for some even in six months..."

"Thank you."

"Now that we know, we will discharge you tomorrow and take it up from there," he said, smiling at she whose sense of the world has changed. As he leaving, Ike was entering.

"Congratulations again, Prof Ike," the doctor said, to which

Ike, confused and innocent of what he was being congratulated for, could not respond appropriately. He sought the meaning from a suddenly spirited Abidame and when she told him the good news he collapsed onto the bed with joy. A new conversation that was futuristic began: marriage rites, family, and a new life. Akoto and their mother found Abidame with Ike. He shyly lifted himself from the bed. When Abidame finally explained the circumstances to them, it became an inpromptu celebration.

Akoto's joy hit the roof as she paced within the small room as if she knew all along, perhaps she did with a certain clairvoyance, where it would lead.

"Our elders say that… the Ike lineage will grow," she continued her chanting as tears of joy certainly rolled down her cheeks. She started to pack her sister's items into the bigger suitcase for the next day's return home.

"The Ike lineage will grow!!" Ike reminisced on this reality that only an only child will know.

In the evening of this happy day, as he lay on his sofa thinking and drinking wine, Ike called his father in Abeokuta, interrupting him from his regular listening of the BBC World Service to relay the news. Professor Peter Ike had liked Abidame the very first time he met her. He jokingly told her she looks like his late wife and sometimes too she looks like her boyfriend – meaning his son. She jokingly responded in all coyness saying; "its an unusual confluence of likes then," as she tried whenever possible to avoid looking at the nobility of the man's face.

"Eh! I am so happy to hear this good news, the father said. Abibame will make a good wife. The lineage will be replicated," he said, before adding, "Tell her I will see her at the appropriate time… I hope you also know the implication of this beginning."

"I do, Dad."

CHAPTER THIRTEEN

New Mom

Tope Folarin

The most confusing period of my childhood began when my schizophrenic mother left us and returned to Nigeria. Her sickness had come on so quickly – had wreaked so much havoc in our lives – that my brother and I weren't really traumatized by her departure. When she left, we simply felt wounded and relieved. I was only six-years-old and my brother was five. I had just started the first grade, and I was having a hard time understanding how a family could be a family without both a father and mother.

In her absence my father assumed the guise of a superhero. He kept hunger at bay by working longer hours as a mechanic at various shops across northern Utah. He fought off the forces of sadness by laughing at everything, no matter how bleak or obscene. He vanquished our fears by telling Tayo and me that he would always be there for us, no matter what. And he taught us the meaning of kindness by never once uttering a negative word about our mother.

For many days we lived this way, my father laughing, dancing, working, teasing, praying. He told us that Mom was receiving special care in Nigeria and that she was getting better every day. Tayo and I imagined tall, good-looking doctors standing over her with notepads and clipboards, almost like the doctors we'd seen on TV (unlike the doctors on Dad's favorite show, *M*A*S*H*, our imaginary doctors were black and they spoke Yoruba to each other as they attended to Mom).

In the weeks following Mom's departure though, my brother and I began to notice a change in Dad. He seemed less confident than he'd been before. He maintained his habit of chasing us around our little apartment before leaving for work each morning, but now instead of tickling us at the end he hugged each of us fiercely and he didn't let go until we tapped him on the shoulder and called his name. He still told us he loved us at least twice a day, but the way he said it sometimes made us feel as if he were saying it for the last time.

Sometimes, when we stood by his bedroom door, we heard him praying quietly, insistently, begging God to make Mom right.

One night, after Mom had been gone a month or so, my father tucked Tayo and me in and closed the door without saying a word to us. After a few minutes we heard him sniffling in the living room. Tayo got up and walked to the door and I followed. When we reached the living room we saw Dad sitting on the couch with his head in his hands. Tayo tapped his shoulder and Dad looked up at us. His eyes were red and his moustache was wet. He shook his head slowly. I suddenly felt very queasy. "Mom isn't coming back," he said. I looked down at his feet. He'd been wearing the same pair of socks for four days; I knew this because his big toes were sticking through each one. "She is just too sick. This country's no good for her."

We tried to get more information from him, but Dad began to speak in riddles, as he often did when he didn't feel like giving us any more information. When we asked him why America was no good for her, he told us that we had eyes at the front of our heads for a reason. When we asked him what he meant by that, he told us to go back to sleep.

Tayo and I returned to our bedroom and sat on our beds.

"How can Mom still be sick?" Tayo asked. "She's been gone forever."

"Yeah," I agreed.

Tayo kicked the air and his foot fell back to the side of his bed with a soft thud.

"I'm scared," Tayo said.

I just nodded.

In the days that followed, Dad stopped playing with us and he sent us to bed early each night. Afterwards, he would stay up and yell at the telephone – we knew he was talking to someone in Nigeria whenever he did that. We could never make out what he was saying, but we wondered if he was speaking to Mom. We wondered if Mom was trying to convince Dad that she needed to come back. If Dad was telling her to give America one last chance.

In time, Mom's absence became the most prominent aspect of our lives. Dad stopped talking about her and he encouraged us to do the same, but we could tell that he missed her. Sometimes he'd slip up and tell us to ask Mom what she was preparing for dinner. Other times, when we passed by his bedroom on the way to the bathroom, we saw him fingering some of the items she'd left behind. Her purse. Her records. Her colourful head wraps. Her purple flip-flops.

Tayo and I continued to speak about Mom, but we always whispered when we did so, like she was a secret that only he and I shared. Like her life was a story we had made up.

One spring morning, maybe six or seven months after Mom returned to Nigeria, my father strode into our bedroom while Tayo and I were getting dressed for school. He sat on Tayo's bed, which was closest to the door.

"Come here," he said.

I joined Tayo and my father on the bed.

"I know you guys miss Mom very much. And I know you guys want to talk to her. But she can't talk to you now. And it's possible you won't talk to her for a very long time."

"What do you mean?" asked Tayo.

"Let me finish," Dad said. He smiled and then he coughed. He took off his glasses and rubbed his eyes.

"You guys are both young, but there are certain things that you need to know. Life doesn't always go the way you want it to, but God always has a plan for us. And it's not our job to question His plan. Do you understand?"

"Yes, sah," we both said.

"Good. Things are going to change from now on. And it may be difficult in the beginning. But everything is going to work out."

With that, Dad reached into the front pocket of his overalls and pulled out a small picture. He gave it to me. The woman in the picture was beautiful – she had a round nose, deep dimples and bronze skin.

I did not know who she was.

"This is your new mother," my father said, solemnly. "I am going to Nigeria to pick her up next month. She is from Lagos, like me and she's ready to meet you guys."

We couldn't believe it. We hadn't expected anything like this.

"Who is she?" I asked. "And what about –"

"Everything is going to be fine. Don't worry. Finish getting dressed."

He got up and left the room.

Tayo began to cry. I moved closer to him and rubbed his back. And then I began to cry as well.

Dad flew to Nigeria two weeks later. He left a picture of our new mom for us and I spent hours after school looking at it. I tried my best to see this stranger as a member of our family, but it was hard. I couldn't imagine her preparing *moin moin* the way my mother had when she felt like cooking. I couldn't imagine feeling as safe in her arms as I'd felt in my mother's arms, even when I knew she was only holding me so she could pinch me up and down my back and legs.

I missed Mom, but I was still scared of her. This was the only reason I was willing to give my new mom a chance.

My brother and I stayed with an older white couple while Dad was gone. They lived in a large red brick house on the other side of town. Dad dropped us off on his way to the airport and after introducing us to them he rushed back to the car and waved goodbye before revving the engine and speeding off. Tayo and I stood on their porch waving even after his car had disappeared from view.

The old lady stood there with us, her hands on our shoulders. I'd never seen her in my life. She was taller than Dad and I remember being fascinated by her long, silvery hair. She was the first old person I'd seen with long hair. I'd always thought that people couldn't grow long hair after a certain age.

She gave Tayo and me a hug after Dad disappeared, then she stepped back and stared at us for a moment.

"Welcome to my home," she said. "You can call me Missy."

She smiled and then she turned around and walked into her house. Tayo rubbed his arms behind her back, like he was trying to rub her hug away. I glared at him and he stopped.

I'd never lived in a white person's house before and everything I saw inside assumed a special meaning. In the corner of their living room a tall grandfather clock stood staring at me. I heard it ticking under its breath. There were pictures all over the walls and the people in them looked so happy that I wanted to step into the pictures and sit with them, so I could smile at whatever they were smiling at. Tayo rushed across the room and picked up a small globe that was sitting on a side table next to their dark leather couch. He stared at it as if he expected the miniature people inside to wave at him. I glared at him again but then I looked up to see Missy smiling as she whooshed by me. She took the globe from his hands and showed him how, by shaking it for just a few seconds, he could initiate a small, furious snowstorm, a beautiful blizzard encased in glass. I was jealous as I stood there by myself, watching Tayo shook the globe again and again as Missy nodded her approval. Yet I was happy, too, because I could still smell her. Her scent had remained with me after she rushed by to show Tayo the secret of the globe. She smelled like something soft, like my mother's favourite perfume.

That night, after a dinner of fried fish and rice, the old man showed us our room. I could just make out the fading striped wallpaper in the dim light. The dry carpet scratched my bare feet. The beds were small and thin. Tayo and I stared up at the man and he smiled. He had a thick white moustache and he was missing a few teeth.

"You think you guys will be OK here by yourself?" he asked.

We nodded.

"Let me know if you need anything. You can call me Mr. Devlin." He rubbed my head. "We're happy to have you. Your father's a good man," he said. Then he closed the door behind him.

Tayo and I didn't say a word until we had changed into our pyjamas and I flipped off the light.

"When do you think Daddy's coming back?" he asked.

"I don't know."

"Soon?"

"I don't know."

"Do you think he'll come back with Mom?"

"I don't know."

"What will happen to Mom if he comes back with a new mom?"

"I don't know."

"Why don't you know anything?"

"I don't know."

"Tunde!"

I laughed.

"I hope he comes back with Mom, but I like it here," he said.

I paused for a moment.

"Me too."

A few days after we'd moved in with the old couple, I mentioned to them – over a big dinner of turkey, stuffing and green beans – food that I'd only seen on the television before then – that I loved to read books about karate. Missy leaned over her plate and asked me if I had ever been to a karate class. I told her my father believed that karate was violent, that he had told me he would never allow me to learn. She smiled widely at me. The next day she picked me up from school and took me straight to a karate studio and for two hours I kicked, punched, screeched and had a wonderful time. She took me to karate class every day after that and when I wasn't practicing kicks and punches around their house, Tayo and I played together in their den, which had a massive TV with dozens of Disney movies stacked in neat piles on top.

It seemed like Missy and Mr. Devlin loved us from the moment we arrived. They took us to movies and puppet shows and bought candy for us. They taught us nursery rhymes and fed us strange foods that we learned to love. We went to church with them on Sundays and they held our hands as we sat on the hard pews. Missy hugged and kissed us more than our parents ever did and

I sometimes wondered if she were actually my grandmother, if maybe we had other white relatives that my father had never told us about.

As our days became weeks Tayo and I missed Dad more than we could have imagined, especially when we didn't hear from him. But we couldn't believe that we were living such joy-filled, impossible lives.

After we'd been living with them for about a month, though, Missy and Mr. Devlin began to treat us differently. They began to send us straight to bed after dinner without reading to us. They began to ask us odd questions.

"Did your Daddy tell you when he was coming back?" Mr. Devlin asked, his bushy eyebrows making him seem for all the world like a cartoon character come to life.

"Did your Daddy say anything about what he was planning to do in Africa?" Missy asked, peering at us like one of those angry witches from our favorite Disney movies.

I nodded emphatically at this question and showed them the picture of our new mom. Missy looked at it for a long time before placing the small picture back in my hand.

"Who is this?" she said.

"That's our new mom," said Tayo.

Missy's eyes grew wide. She touched Mr. Devlin's side and they stepped away from our bedroom. They began to whisper to each other. I could not hear much, but I heard Missy say "no divorce" and "good woman." After a few minutes they came back. Missy smiled kindly at me.

"I'm afraid that your father lied to us," she said. "He lied to us about what he was doing in Africa. He lied about how long he would be there. I'm afraid that you and your brother can't live here anymore."

The following morning, Missy woke us up early and drove us to a tall white building a few blocks away. She held our hands as we walked inside and asked us to sit on the couch near the door. She went to speak with a short lady with black hair who was standing behind a big wooden desk on the other side of the room. She occasionally pointed to us as she spoke with the lady, and then she walked back to us, kissed each of us on the forehead, and left. She drove away.

The short lady with black hair was nice, she allowed us to play with the toys that were scattered about the room. Tayo and I couldn't answer any of the questions she asked us. That evening she drove us to another house and introduced us to a younger white couple. The woman with the black hair told us that they were our foster parents, that they would take care of us until our Daddy came back.

II

Dad returned from Nigeria two days after we moved in with our foster parents. He simply showed up one afternoon after school and picked us up.

"Daddy, what about our foster parents?" I asked as we entered the car.

"Don't worry about them," he replied, gruffly. "I am your father, not them."

We drove in silence for a few minutes and then Tayo spoke up from the backseat.

"Is our new mom at home?"

"No."

"Is she coming to join us soon?"

"No."

"What about Mom? Is she coming back?"

"No, and please don't ask me any more questions about her. Don't worry about her. Kick her out of your memory."

Dad looked angry, so we listened to him.

Things went back to normal. Dad never told us why he was late in returning from Nigeria and he didn't mention anything about our new mom again.

My father changed jobs a few weeks later and then he changed jobs again. We saw him even less than before, but he began to talk to us for long periods of time at random moments; sometimes after we'd finished our dinner, sometimes before he left for work, sometimes after he'd tucked us in.

"I have big dreams for both of you," he'd say. "You guys are the only reason I am still in this country. I should have left a long time ago, because I don't have any opportunities here. No one takes me seriously. But whenever I think of leaving I ask myself what both of you would be like if you were to grow up in Nigeria. Here you can become leaders. I don't know what would happen there."

We always nodded, but I can't say that I really understood what he was talking about. My father claimed that I had been to Nigeria before, but I had no memory of the trip and Tayo had never even left Utah. Nigeria, to me, to us, was merely a chorus of scratchy voices over the telephone, a collection of foods and customs that our friends had never heard of. It was a place where everyone was black, where our cousins spoke a language we couldn't fully comprehend, where our mother lived.

But somehow I knew that my father was right. And I was glad we were living in America. In Utah. I never wanted to be anywhere else.

After Dad tucked us in, Tayo and I would stay up and read to each other. We waited until we saw the thin patch of light beneath our door go dark, until we heard Dad's soft snores rattling down the hallway. Then Tayo would reach under his bed, pull out our emergency flashlight and walk over to the single, tall bookshelf on the other side of our room.

We had dozens of books. My father never bought us toys and he always claimed that he was too broke to buy us new clothes, but somehow we each received at least three new books each month. Most of our books were non-fiction – short biographies, children's encyclopaedias, textbooks – because Dad was convinced that novels were for entertainment purposes only and he always told us that we would have time for entertainment when we were old enough to make our own decisions. So Tayo and I would huddle in a single bed, his or mine, with a biography of George Washington, or a book about the invention of the telephone, and each of us would read a page and hand the flashlight over.

We eventually grew tired of these books, though, so we began to make up our own stories. Actually, Tayo made them up. Even though Tayo was a year younger than me, even though he looked up to me and followed me in every other part of our lives, he was a much better storyteller than I was. He was almost as good as Mom.

He always began:

"Once upon a time…"

"There was…"

"There was a large elephant with a long purple nose and polka-dot underwear…"

"That liked to run…"

"That liked to run all over the valleys and desert and the elephant had many friends, giraffes and leopards and a cranky orangutan that always wore a pair of bifocals like Dad's…"

We'd continue in this manner, sometimes for hours at a time, until Tayo fell asleep. Then I'd pull the flashlight from his hands, place it back under his bed and snuggle in next to him until I fell asleep as well.

One Saturday morning, as Tayo and I were playing basketball on the concrete courts behind our apartment building, laughing, shouting and leaping, Tayo stopped dribbling and looked up at me, his eyes shining and hopeful.

"Don't you wish Mom would come back?" he asked.

I didn't know what to say. I took my status as the elder brother seriously and I knew that Tayo would probably mimic whatever I said. I wasn't sure if it would be OK for me to tell him the truth, or if I was supposed to say what Dad would say in this situation. I chose something in the middle.

"Sometimes," I said.

"I do all the time," Tayo said. "I want her to come back now."

And a part of me agreed with him. I wanted her to come back, I wanted everything to be the way it had been before she got sick. Before she left us.

But the other part…

Looking back, I think I was open to the idea of a new mom because there was a part of me that was ready to consign my mother to memory. I wanted to install a false version of her in my mind. I wanted to forgive her by forgetting her cruelty, the pinching, the slapping, the screaming. I wanted to forgive her by forgetting her.

But now, Mom, I remember your hugs. They were warm and tight. When you wrapped your arms around me I always felt as if I were home. And your food was delicious, even when you stopped cooking, even when you would only warm up a few pieces of frozen chicken in the oven and open up cans of beans and corn for dinner, your food tasted as if you'd spent hours preparing it.

And your smiles, I will always remember your smiles. They were rare and lovely, like priceless coins from an ancient kingdom.

III

Our new mom finally arrived in August of 1991, almost three years after our mother returned to Nigeria and a few months after that we moved from Bountiful to nearby Middleton. Tayo and I didn't know who she was – we'd never even seen a picture of her. My father flew back to Nigeria right after I completed second grade and this time he dropped Tayo and me off with the foster family we'd been staying with before. They took us in without any questions and Dad promised them he would be back in a month. When he returned – this time after only a couple weeks – he informed us that we had to prepare for the arrival of our new mother. We excitedly cleaned everything – our walls, our floors, our tables, our clothes – and asked him for more details about her. How does she look? "You'll see," he said, preparing our food as Sunny Ade sang sweetly to us from the living room. What does she do, we asked as we did our homework. "She'll tell you," he replied as he cleaned the stove. Will she love us, we asked as he tucked us in. "How couldn't she?" he said before kissing each of us on the forehead and turning off the light. He gave us the same ambiguous responses each time we asked about her and after a few weeks we stopped believing that she was even real. But on the day of her arrival he told us that we would have a new mother by the evening.

"She is a good woman," he said. "Trust me."

There were other questions I wanted to ask. Why did we need someone else? After all, we already had someone special. After months of disorientation we had finally managed to fashion a new family from the wreckage of what had been before. I was beginning to understand that a family could be something more than a group of people who were supposed to stay together despite the pain they caused each other. My brother and I were living in a single parent home and our father was rarely around, but we were as happy as we had ever been.

Why did anything have to change? How did we know this would even work?

And what about our mother, our real mother? I didn't know what I was supposed to do with all the love I had for her, pulsing inside me.

But then I remembered what my father had said when we'd asked about her before – that we had eyes at the front of our heads for a reason. I suddenly understood what he meant: he wanted us to keep looking forward, no matter what, to keep moving, to overcome our pain by acting as if pain was something temporary and easily forgotten. He was my father and I loved and trusted him, so I tried my best to heed his advice. I didn't know how much anguish I would cause myself by doing this.

Much later I would come to understand that the only way my father had survived in the United States, in Utah, was by doing exactly this; staring ahead always, kicking the pain and heartache away. This was how he was able to survive the torment of living in a place that never fully comprehended his presence, that sometimes treated him as if he were someone who would never really matter. This was how he survived the loss of his wife to a disease that prevented her from remembering him and his love for her, for more than a moment at a time. My father bore his burdens well; he was a walking, talking smile. But now, knowing what I know and feeling as I do, I can only imagine what was actually happening inside. It makes me wonder how well I know him, if he is actually the person who raised me, who hugs me so warmly when I see him today.

We drove to the airport in Salt Lake City that evening and Dad told Tayo and me to wait in the car. After he'd walked a few feet he turned around and looked down at me in the passenger's side seat. "You're going to have to move to the back," he said, and I saw something like sadness glimmering from his eyes. I moved as quickly as I could, but he ignored the smile I flashed at him after I'd settled in the backseat. He stood there looking at Tayo and me for a few minutes, but even as he looked at us it seemed like he was staring at something far away, something we would never see no matter how long and hard we tried. Then he shook his head slowly and his eyes began to well up with tears. He turned around and walked away.

Twenty minutes later we saw Dad approaching with a tall woman beside him and a young child walking slightly in front of them. The woman was carrying another child.

Tayo and I stared at each other. We were shocked. Dad hadn't mentioned anything about kids. When the woman arrived at my window she reached down from the sky and took my hand into hers. She stared deep into my eyes. Her eyes were large, brown and oval. I saw something like love flickering faintly from them. She smiled. I smiled back.

"Hello," she said. "It is wonderful to meet you."

The two children scampered into the back seat with us. They were wearing clothes just like ours, T-shirts and whitewashed jeans. They didn't acknowledge our presence. The older one looked sullenly ahead and the younger one tucked himself into a ball and began to suck his thumb. Dad settled into the driver's seat and appraised us in the rear-view mirror.

"How is my new family doing!" he boomed and he started the car. As we drove out of the parking lot he slipped his right hand into the left hand of the woman.

Our New Mom seemed surprised when we arrived at our apartment. She placed her bags down at the threshold and looked left and right as if she was searching for something. She looked at Dad.

"Where..." she began, and then she walked over to the sink and grabbed a pair of bright yellow cleaning gloves from the middle of the drain board. She wiped her face with her forearm and pulled on the gloves. Then she reached into the cabinet, pulled out a bucket and filled it with soap and water. We were all watching her as she placed the bucket on the floor and got on her hands and knees.

"Join me," she said, simply.

We were bewildered. The little one continued to suck his thumb. Dad looked deflated, as if her words had deprived him of air.

Now she scrubbed the floor with a sponge I'd never seen before and my eyes opened to a different apartment. The floor resembled a painting I had once seen on television, on a show hosted by a man who violently attacked a blank canvas with vibrant colours, as if he were at war with it. When the host finished, Dad scoffed at the finished product, those intersecting jagged lines of colour. "That isn't art," he said. Our floor looked exactly the same. It wasn't art. Our walls were even worse – handprints, bug corpses, the remains of bug corpses, stains of indeterminate origin – maybe it *was* art. A portrait of our poverty.

Tayo walked to the sink and retrieved another sponge and he bent down to work. Soon the older one bent down too and then I joined them. Only Dad and the little one stood together and as I glanced up at them I noticed, for the first time, how similar they looked. Dad was short and thick, like the little one and their faces held the same features in the same proportion. They were both frowning now and Dad's frown, spreading slowly over the lower half of his face, was a larger copy of the little one's frown. Dad stared at us.

"Do we have to do this now? You just arrived! Change your clothes! Go take a shower! I have already prepared a meal for you. And we have already cleaned the house! We can clean some more in the morning!"

New Mom looked up.

"I will not be showering in this filthy apartment. Come and help us clean. Or if you are too tired you can go lie down and I will tell you when we are finished so we can eat together."

She returned to her cleaning and the rest of us looked at Dad to see what he would do. He sheepishly reached over our heads for a rag and went to work on the walls.

We cleaned for about two hours, and at the end our apartment looked better. But not quite clean. I felt ashamed of our apartment for the first time and I wondered how it appeared to my new brothers, fresh from their trip across the sea. New Mom rose to her feet and smiled broadly.

"Now we can eat," she said, and she turned to the stove. She laughed when she saw what was inside the pots.

"Let me work on this for a moment. I will tell you when I'm finished," she said.

The rest of us moved to the living room. A few minutes later I smelled the mingling aromas of tomatoes and onions and peppers. We sat there staring awkwardly at each other for half an hour until New Mom called for us.

There were six steaming plates of fufu and chicken stew on the table. We sat and my father asked us to hold hands. New Mom was sitting next to me and she squeezed my hand every few seconds as Dad prayed. When he finished she winked at me. And we dug in. The food was beautiful and tasty. We all smacked loudly, and then we all went to bed.

That night I felt the older one pressing his knees into my back as I tried to rock myself to sleep. At dinner Dad had informed Tayo and me that we would have to share our beds with our new brothers until he could afford to buy new beds. When we arrived at our bedroom the little one plopped onto the bottom bunk of the bunk bed I shared with Tayo and when I tried to get in with him he began to scream. Dad and New Mom rushed in and Dad shook his head after the little one pointed a miniature accusatory finger at me.

"You have already started trouble?" he said, and when I protested he yelled over me:

"They have just arrived after flying for *godknowshowmany* miles and now you want to prevent them from sleeping? What is wrong with you?" I looked around to see who he was talking to. My father was still staring at me when I glanced at him once more. I was confused. My father had never spoken to me this way before.

The little one fell asleep shortly after Dad and New Mom left and Tayo crawled into bed with him. The little one turned around and hugged Tayo tight around the neck. I climbed up to the top bunk and the older one followed me. We soon began a war for space.

We traded subtle elbows and knee jabs until he fell asleep against my back. I tried, inch by inch, to push him out of the bed, but I became tired myself and I fell asleep too.

New Mom woke me up the following morning and I saw her face up close for the first time. She had large, open, even features. Her slim nose was framed by ample cheeks and her hairline was beginning to leak into the top part of her forehead. I woke up my brother and stepbrothers and we all squeezed around our small breakfast table and introduced ourselves to each other. I learned that the little one was called Ade and the older one was called Femi. Femi resembled his mother more than Ade, but they both had her nose and small ears and when they smiled it was hard to tell them apart. For some reason I was surprised that they spoke English so well. Dad must have been listening in on my thoughts because he looked over at me and said, "Yes, they are very smart! You know that in Nigeria the early school system is much better than it is here. Both of them will probably end up skipping some grades. They may be smarter than you!"

At this he laughed and New Mom looked down with embarrassed pride. I scowled at the table.

Our first few days together were consumed with the business of becoming a family. We threw out countless articles of clothing and various knick-knacks. We went to the department store and purchased new drapes, sheets and comforters. New Mom threw out all of our pots. By the evening she had us cleaning again and by the following morning we started to become more comfortable with one another. Mom came up with nicknames for Tayo and I – she called me "thick eyes" because of my glasses and she called Tayo "handsome."

CHAPTER FOURTEEN

... And the dog lay there dying...

Martin Egblewogbe

Seyram's name was on the list. It was actually the first on the list, a stark *1*. Mr. S. Agbemebiese, ahead of ten others on the noticeboard in the coffee room. He reeled when he saw it, by chance, as he raised his head to savour the morning's coffee. His heart hammered in his rib cage, once, twice, and then gave a third smash that rattled his entire frame. His hand rose to his throat, his breath ran out and he tottered to his office, where a letter lay on his desk.

They had been warned that it was on its way, the "retrenchment." The company had to downsize. But how had they chosen the names? And why was his name the first on the list? He ripped open the envelope. "Dear Mr. Agbemebiese, It is my sad duty to inform you that, as a result of the ongoing re-structuring programme, you were one of the persons selected to be released from the obligation of working with D – Ltd. As stipulated in your contract, you have three months from the date of this letter..."

Somewhere in the lines of type it actually said "... appreciate the high quality of your work" and "... stand ready to give you the highest recommendation." The letter took one full page. *But why*, Seyram thought, *when the message was so simple*.

Throughout the day his colleagues eyed him, some with ill-concealed smugness, others with discomfort colouring their actions, creating an edginess that had not previously existed. The receptionist openly sniggered. In the evening Margaret dumped him. It was via a telephone call. Her voice sounded thin. It was impossible, she said. To live like this, a lie. And so on and on. In the end, Seyram cut the call and went outside, standing on his little porch in the deepening darkness. Some stars were out. Some crickets were screaming. In the morning the mirror looked at him while the toothbrush held his hand patiently, waiting for him to focus, focus. Sleep had eluded him throughout the night and the ill-advised downing of a brandy at 2 a.m. had now given him the jitters as well. Water rose to splash against his face and nothing could take his mind off the weightlessness he felt inside as his soul navigated the scorched, blasted landscape of his heart, which was now broken. The water ran down the sinkhole, a hollow tinkling in the pipes. And the blasted WC chortled when Seyram pulled the lever, he would have sworn at it but all was worthless, worthless, now. In the hall the radio was on and a morning show host was trying to be funny and failing. His shoes had smudges of dirt and he could not bring himself to clean them, let alone polish to a shine, it was all pointless anyway, this thing about trying to look good. Breakfast had never been his thing and in this state a fast was in order – it came naturally. And then he was ready to leave for work and his words at the door were, but I love her. And when he shut the door his thoughts were, *Now what am I going to do ?* The twin losses took turns to haunt him. Thankfully, his next-door neighbour was still inside her apartment. A morning exchange of pleasantries while in this mood would be awkward to say the least. But perhaps she had died in the night, one could never tell; he had not heard her screaming her morning prayers to God as was her wont. God would never let her down. She prayed aloud every morning. Except for today. Maybe she had travelled. His mind was wandering.

His car, a cheap blue Kia Pride bought in a moment of foolish exuberance when his salary first guaranteed him a loan, was listing a little to the right. The reason for this was that the pressure in the front tyre was low. But in Ghana the steering wheel is to the left and Seyram, had he been in a brighter state of mind would have thanked Acheampong for bringing balance to his car, many years down the line, such was his wit.

For a minute he thought that the engine would not start, but just when the first expletive left his lips the ignition caught and the engine fired up with a roar and the car shuddered. Still it was only a small relief to a small distress, compared with everything else.

Just as the car started down the drive, Seyram had an awkward sense of looking upon himself from a great height and could not but be filled with great pity. Why, O God! It was a real pain only felt inside a hollowness and yet it was only emotional, he was not loved, it was nothing. In truth, to be rational, it was a small thing. Emotions were worthless in the grand scheme of things. They were to be stamped upon! Crushed! Heartbreak? What was that? And besides, to put things in perspective, what about all the real pain in the world, what about the little children sleeping rough across the world, killed in bombings, cast off by society and such nonsense. And losing a job? Why, it happened all the time, to countless others. It was not on account of competence. The letter had said this, the letter had said that. Yet all his efforts at rationalisation did not lift the dark cloud over his mood.

It was a quiet road out of the suburb. A bumpy, untarred road, sections of which had yawning potholes and running crevices, a road leading from the suburb to the city. Fifteen minutes along this road fringed with scraggly bushes on either side and he would strike the main road into town. The air coming in through the window was keen, had his senses not been numbed he would have found it invigorating. By force of habit his hand reached towards the radio knob – but ahead...

He slowed down. Some way ahead, to the right hand side of the road, lay a dog. It must have been struck by a car earlier on, he thought and brought the Kia to a stop. He got out and went to have a look at it. It was not a large dog. A mongrel, with a smooth brown coat and a white streak on its chest. The dog must have noticed his approach, because it struggled a little bit more strenuously in its attempt to rise from the ground. Its forelimbs flailed and the claws gouged lines in the dirt and scattered little stones about, but its hind legs dangled uselessly at awkward angles and could not provide any support. The dog shook its head from side to side, raised its snout, grimacing in pain with lips flecked with white saliva and lowered its head again and its silence was more potent than a thousand howls.

The dog must have been lying there for quite a while, judging from the agitation of the dirt around where it lay. The ground had been fitfully scratched and the dirt scattered about. The dog itself was covered in dirt. He stepped closer and the dog raised its head once again – its eyes were misted over. This effort seemed too much for it and it dropped its head on its paws. Save for the slow, laboured breathing it could have been presumed dead.

Had it been hit by a car driven by one careless driver speeding along the bumpy road? At dawn? Or the night before, speeding on the unlit track? And did it have an owner, this dog, or was it a stray? This dog, dying here beside the road? Or perhaps it was set upon by men and bludgeoned with cudgels, with a hope of killing it? To cut short the pain that must be paramount, Seyram thought, the suffering of the poor animal had to be stopped. The dog had to be put down. Yet what tools did he have to accomplish this task? Looking around, he saw some pieces of rock – large stones the size of bricks. Cast with force at the base of the skull the spinal cord could perhaps be severed and the dog be at peace. But he doubted this. What if he only succeeded in breaking the spine, inducing paralysis and even more pain? Yet could the dog suffer more pain than it already had, lying there injured for hours? Alternatively he could use his wheel spanner. It had a handle which allowed for greater control and it would be more in delivering a sudden killer blow. As he picked the L-shaped tool from the boot of the Kia, another car drove by. It was a Toyota Highlander, its powerful engine gave a throaty purr. The driver cast an unconcerned glance at the scene and the car disappeared in a thin cloud of dust. But Seyram paused. Had the car passed by two minutes later, he would have been seen killing a dog with a wheel spanner. And him all dressed up for work, in a neat light blue shirt and well pressed black trousers. How could he explain, had he been spotted, hand upraised with an instrument poised to deliver death, how could he explain that his motive was mercy?

But was it? Perhaps there was another way to deliver mercy. He tossed the spanner back into the boot and went to look at the dog again. There was a vet's somewhere on his route to work. He could carry the animal there. Seyram felt ashamed that this had not been his first thought and that he had rather sought to murder the animal. As he approached the dog it put in another great effort and tried to rise, uttering a weak growl as it did so. Well, Seyram thought, this was not a wise course of action. The dog might, in a final act of frenzy, bite him. And what if, just what if, it happened to be rabid? What if it in fact was rabid? Would that be the reason why some men had set upon it with cudgels? But then they would have beaten it to death.

Seyram considered the situation carefully. It was possible that he would cause further injury and pain by attempting to lift the dog into his car. Proper restraints were required and he had none, nor did he have the skill to move an injured animal. In the final analysis, if the right thing was to be done, a professional was required. And so, he had to get the vet. When he made this decision his mind became clear, his thinking more focussed. The dashboard clock read 08:14am when he started the engine again. As he pulled away another car drove past. There were two people in the back and no-one seemed to pay any attention to the scene. And he wondered why he too had not driven by and ignored the dog.

II

The small man in wire-rimmed spectacles looked up from his table. Sunlight streamed through the parted blinds of a window behind him. There was a pile of books on the right hand side of the table, a notebook lay open on the left and a folded newspaper and a steaming mug were in the middle. The smell of hot cocoa filled the small room. The vet cleared his throat. OPEN AT 8.30 AM, the sign on the door said. That was five minutes away, and he wanted his cocoa! He did not care for such early customers, on a Monday too. Still, he had to be nice.

"A dog," said Seyram, "this very minute lies in pain by the roadside, not quite ten minutes drive from here. I did not know what to do." Yes, it is one of those days, thought the vet. A dog in pain, this very minute, he says. The vet opened a ledger and wrote the date at the top of the page. De-worming, vaccinations, name tags, castrations perhaps later in the day. That was a tolerable working day scheme. But to start with this...

"It looked at me," Seyram said.

"Did it catch your eye?" the vet asked.

"The eyes were glazed in pain, it might not have seen me. It moved its head up and down and its mouth was flecked with foam."

Dear God, the vet thought.

"Why was it there? The dog?" The vet took a sip from his mug.

"Must have been run over," Seyram replied. "Its leg was broken, or legs, I couldn't tell. There was some blood."

"Look," the vet said, "You'll make my stomach turn."

"I wanted to kill it," Seyram went on.

"Hmmm – to put it out of its pain? Euthanasia, your God moment." Then the vet drank again, thoughtfully.

"I could only find a large stone – and my wheel spanner. They were crude."

Seyram paused. "I also considered carrying the dog here. But –"

"But?"

"It was in pain. It could have lashed out blindly."

"Indeed. It is an animal after all."

"Can we go there? I am driving. You could help bring it here for treatment – or do it painlessly."

"Kill it?"

"If need be. But preferably to sedate it and bring it here, save its life. You have your case?"

The vet finished his cocoa, rose to his feet, and placed the mug on top of the bookshelf to his right.

"If the dog was badly injured," he said, "It would be dead by the time we got there. If the injury was slight, on the other hand – which it might well be, mind you – it would have limped away before we got there. Animals have a high pain threshold. And they heal quickly. Think of it in the wild. A predator could have attacked it, a tree could have fallen on it to create similar injury.

And who would be there to help, with anaesthesia? Nature is brutal, my friend. It has no sentiments."

"But I do," Seyram replied. "Its the pain, the thought of it. Gets to me. I cannot abide pain, even in others. Even the thought of it is unbearable."

"Not unbearable," the vet said. "It can be borne. In any case, I am alone here this morning. To leave with you would be to vacate my post. And who knows what other cases might be on their way here? What pain those other animals might be feeling? What distress their owners could be in? And then for them to turn up here and I absent? That would not do. You see my point? I must remain here."

"The dog," Seyram muttered and drifted out of the vets' office. It was getting warmer as the sun rose higher in the eastern sky. The traffic on the road in front of the vets' was heaving. He was late for work as well, which fact did not bother him. He was losing his job anyway, his boss might as well cut him some slack.

It did not seem prudent now to return to the site of the accident and murder the dog with whatever tools he could find. And this was more distress for him to bear.

The Kia started at the first turn of the key.

III

Several weeks later the memory of Margaret only caused a slight anxiety and some trouble falling asleep if he thought about her at night. The dryness in the mouth, the insomnia, the feeling of falling, falling and the sense of great loss, all that was gone. Seyram was returning to normal. His neighbour had not travelled after all and neither had she died, but she had a guest staying. And this guest had been able to cause a cessation of the morning shoutings to God. Where Seyram's petitions, pleas and notes slipped under her door: "Dear Sister Abena, please, pray if you must BUT KEEP IT DOWN! You don't have to shout. I am not God and yet I hear you," etc., had all failed, the appearance of the guest had succeeded. For this, Seyram was thankful. A few days before, he had caught a glimpse of the guest in the early evening. He had an afro and was smoking a pipe on the veranda. It was a gloomy morning, rain threatened but the weather forecast said no rain. Seyram tossed an umbrella into the back seat anyway and started the engine. He had taken the car for a thorough maintenance session and the Kia was doing well. He rolled down the driveway and out onto the road, making a mental list of the groceries he needed to get after work. And by force of habit his hand reached towards the radio knob – He trod on the brakes, too hard and the seatbelt bit into his shoulder while the Kia shuddered to a stop in a cloud of dust. What he saw was unbelievable.

A brown dog, with a streak of white in its fur! And though one of its hind legs was twisted and hung loosely, jerking with every step, the dog still made progress, trotting along the road. It was a crooked, lopsided trot, but the dog, taking advantage of the motionless Kia, cut across the road and headed into the scattered bushes at the other side. Seyram watched the dog until it disappeared. A thrill of delight raced through his body and he stilled an overbearing urge to leap out of the car and dance in the middle of the road. He wondered what the dog was doing.

CHAPTER FIFTEEN

The Skull in the Garden

Peggy Appiah

I stood at the door. The house was very quiet behind me and a cool breeze blew. The house work had been done and I was alone to do as I wanted. My father had long gone to work and my mother had just left for the market. The boys were out of the country. I gave a sigh of contentment. Then I wondered what I should do. I had just finished the last book from the library and must go and change them. I shut the door and turned back into the house.

We had just moved into an old house in the Nhyiasu area. It belonged to the colonial era but had been acquired by a local family when the old era was over. My father bought it from the family when the owner died. He had made a wonderful garden, but obviously as he grew older no one had cared for it. Now, it was all overgrown and we should have to re-make it. I looked forward to doing that as I loved gardening. The surrounding fence was festooned in brilliant pink bougainvillea and there were many trees which shaded what had once been lawns but were now overgrown patches of grass.

The house itself had been completely repainted and the old wooden louvres had been replaced by glass ones in new window frames. I loved the place.

I was not sure what I wanted to do as I had to stay in until my mother returned from town. I went up the stone staircase and was going to my room when I suddenly remembered the old cupboard at the end of the passage which still needed clearing out. For some reason it had been neglected by the decorators and the key had been lost. Luckily, we had a box of old keys and one of them fitted the door. Inside were a lot of old cardboard boxes and cockroaches skittered all round. I decided to get rid of the boxes and carried them down to the *bola* or dust bin. Then I fetched a broom and duster and went back upstairs. I would probably need a bucket of water as well but I could get that from the upstairs bathroom.

When I opened the cupboard door again the cockroaches had disappeared. I carefully swept out the cupboard. At the back, almost fitted onto the wall I realized there was an old door. It was difficult to move but in the end I managed to get it out of the store. Behind the wall was filth and I decided to wash it down. I was half way through the job when I realized that in the corner there was a handle. I pulled hard at it and gradually cracks appeared around what seemed to be a cupboard door. The door burst open and there, behind it, were shelves filled with boxes and papers. I almost shook with excitement. After removing and dusting the first box, I went to my room and cleared my working table. Then, bit by bit, I removed the contents of the cupboard. Many of the papers had been partly destroyed by insects but there were some hard covered old exercise books and some of the files seemed intact. I dusted off the last shelf and closed the store door. Then I settled down to sort the papers in my room.

The man who had left the papers there appeared to be called Yao Frempong. Many of the papers were signed with his name. There were endless bills and receipts, what appeared to be documents which seemed to be a kind of diary record of day-to-day events. The writing was very bad and some of the pages were hard to decipher. After weeks of studying them, I was able to read the writing. One of these was the last Will and Testament of Yao Frempong. This made interesting reading. It had been typed on an old-fashioned typewriter with some words written in by hand. The old man had left all his property to his son, Kwame Adjetey Frempong. There was a reference to the rest of the family and the deliberate cutting them out of the Will as they had treated him so badly. I put down the document and sat wondering who this Kwame was; we had bought the property from a Mrs Augustina Manu. She was not referred to in the Will.

I heard the front door bang and went down to meet my mother. She asked me to help with preparing the mid-day meal as she was back late. We were so busy that I did not have time to tell her about the papers.

When finally my mother went to empty the peelings and rubbish into the bin, she called to me. "Wherever did those boxes come from? They look very old," she said. Although my mother had had some schooling she could hardly read. She did not want to look at the papers but asked me to report fully what I found.

My mother, Abena Serwaa and I were very close and devoted to each other. She had been a wonderful mother and insisted that I should complete my schooling. Soon I was to go to university and had decided to study Business Management as did so many of my generation. I was now between school and university. Sometimes I would go and work in my father's office so that I could get some basic business knowledge. I was also about to learn to use a computer before I went to university.

We decided to tell my father what had happened in the evening as he was always in a rush at lunchtime and sometimes did not even turn up. Today he did. He was full of a successful deal he had just done and handed my mother a small packet of money to be spent on provisions. She gave him a hug and I thanked him warmly. Then he left for his office.

I spent the afternoon shut up in my room and read the papers. It was not until later that I read the diary. I was shocked. It appeared that in the last years of his life the old man was too ill to go out much. His sister, Augustina, had moved in to look after him and had nearly starved him to death. She had refused to feed him unless he gave her money. Luckily, he said, she did not know of all his properties, some of which had been leased out for many years. But she managed to lay her hands on most of his current income. His writing became worse and worse. It appeared that his son had travelled overseas and disappeared but he still hoped to hear from him. The boy had gone to finish his studies and should have been done. There was also a married daughter overseas. There was no mention anywhere of a wife so I presumed she must be dead.

When my father returned in the evening I was able to tell him all about the papers. He was amazed as he had not known of Yao Frempong but had only dealt with Augustina Manu. Who then was this Kwame Adjetey Frempong? My father decided to try and find out. The next door neighbours had been in the house. Although in this area of town we did not mix freely with neighbours, we did know the man was a retired civil servant and his wife did a bit of trading and I was not sure what he did now.

When we had finished supper we decided to call on the Nuamahs. It was quite dark outside and my father unlocked the gates. The next house had a watchman, and I am afraid we took advantage of him and did not bother to have one of our own, though I know my father tipped him from time to time.

The Nuamahs asked us in and offered us drinks and we had a general conversation. My father said he had been meaning to call on them but had been very busy. They said they understood and that in fact it had been up to them to make contact.

My father asked them about the history of our house and as to who Yao Frempong was? Mr Nuamah then launched into a long story about the troubles of Yao Frempong and the behaviour of his family. He had seen the children growing up and said that Kwame was a very nice boy and that he could not understand why he had deserted his father and had not ever written to him over the years. Mrs Manu was a very overbearing woman and they had broken off all contact once the old man died. The family had not even bothered to give him a proper funeral and did not put the death in the papers. It was a real shame and a disgrace but then that was the Ashanti family for you. They were only out for what they could get. We went on chatting and before we left I asked if they could tell me where Kwame Frempong was as I had found some papers addressed to him. "Typical," said Mr Nuamah. "Augustina would never have anything to do with him and certainly would never reveal his address. Maybe you could ask her daughter Maggie who is now independent and never got on with her mother."

"Where does she live?" I asked.

"Somewhere in town, I believe, but her cousin Osei Narh who works in the post office could tell you."

"Which branch?" I asked. "Oh! At G in the sorting office," he said.

The very next day when I had changed my books at the library I went to the General Post Office to see Mr Narh. After explaining to him, I got to know Maggie worked in Takoradi and he was kind enough to give me her address.

I went home and wrote to Maggie, explaining that I needed Kwame's address as I had found something of his in the house. She wrote back to say she did not have it herself but she was sure she had seen it in her mother's house and would look when she came up from Takoradi the following week. I only hoped she would not bother to tell her mother.

I was surprised when a week later Maggie turned up at our house. She had found some letters written by Kwame to his father and put away in a drawer in their house. She said she wondered why they had never been delivered. I could see from her face that she blamed her mother. She was just a little older than me and we sat down for a chat. She told me about her work in a Forex Bureau in Takoradi where she was endeavouring to study computers. She had nearly finished and had been promised a promotion when she got her qualification. Then suddenly she said, "Don't tell my mother I have been here. I have brought you the last two letters I found but Mother must not know. She hated even the mention of Kwame, but I was very fond of him as a child, though he was a bit older than me." I thanked her warmly and accompanied her down the road to find a taxi. I gave a sigh of relief and returned to my room to read the letters and to write to Kwame.

The letter came as a surprise. Kwame had written to ask his father why he never replied to his letters, saying he had been writing monthly since he left Ghana. He now had a very good job and hoped to return home when he heard from his father that he would be welcome. He spoke of sending money to his father through the bank. At once I realized that Augustina had stopped all the letters; she had also probably taken all the money. What a woman! She must have some personal contact at the bank, who arranged things for her.

That evening I settled down to write to Kwame. I made a list of all the papers I had found and had a photo-copy made of the Will to send to him. I was not sure if it would still be valid but thought we would probably have a case since it had been hidden. I began to wonder why it was hidden. Obviously, Augustina had not known of the documents. Then I realized that, knowing he was going to die, the old man had made a final effort to hide away the papers. He had probably tried to communicate with his son but did not have a recent address. Also if he had given letters to Augustina to post, she would never have posted them.

I knew I would have to wait at least a month to get a reply to the registered package sent to Kwame and decided to concentrate on the computer. My father had been saving up to buy one for the house and said that as soon as I was qualified he would do so.

I resolved to study Yao Frempong's diary in detail despite the difficult writing. From the very beginning of the diary it was clear that Yao was suspicious of Augustina. He had to do what she said because of her threats of revealing "the secret between us." What that secret was I was to discover much later.

Yao reported that Augustina did not feed him properly. She used to cook his monotonous soup with very little meat or fish in it but plenty of pepper. He began to have stomach troubles and sometimes vomited after eating the soup. He wrote:

"Why is Augustina doing this to me? I depend on her for everything. I beg for bread but she just laughs. Today when I have eaten the soup on my return from office, I was forced to vomit. She said it must be nerves and that I needed a sedative. Perhaps she was right. When I sleep at night I dream dreams and often my wife comes to warn me about Augustina. I miss her so much and wonder what has happened to her. Is heaven real and if so how can she come and see me in my dreams?"

And so it went on from day to day. Sometimes he said that he hardly felt well enough to go to the office. He decided to hand over responsibility to Edward Sarfo his assistant. He just went in the afternoons and answered mail. I wondered what had happened to this Edward Sarfo. It was much later that I found out that he had left the country when Yao Frempong died.

There were constant complaints about the amount of money

that Augustina demanded from him. Again and again he wrote, "If only Kwame were here to help me..." Sometimes, too, he referred to his daughter, Akosua, but because she was with her husband somewhere he did not expect her to return, though he did complain that she, too, never wrote. "What kind of children are they?" What have I done for them to desert me?" he wrote.

After learning from Maggie what had happened to the letters, my heart bled for poor Yao Frempong. If Kwame were to turn up, what would he too, feel about all these revelations. They went on and on. The last few pages, I could hardly read as the writing was so bad. By now he knew that Augustina was killing him and in a way he had ceased to care.

"I am now too weak to go downstairs. I can just get along to my cupboard when Augustina is out. I have hidden my papers there and I have asked Atta to try and find Kwame when I die. I have given him a note for him, saying where the things are hidden. I hope that God will reveal them to him on time. This diary would have to go into the cupboard too. I have kept it hidden in my bed and Augustina rarely changes the sheets nor bothers to clean the room. She has brought me a toilet chair to use when I cannot get to the toilet. She does not even bother to empty that until the smell becomes too strong. I cover it with an old straw hat of mine which keeps the worst stench away. "

The last entry contained the final phrases: "I can see from Augustina's face that the end is near. Today I will put this away too. May God reward her for all her doings. May He bless my children wherever they are. She is coming. I must cease."

Later, I worked out, according to dates that this was written the day before he did get his final dose of "medicine."

II

The postal system has improved recently but I was really surprised when only three weeks after writing to Kwame Frempong I found a letter from England in the post box. It was quite heavy so I hurried home to open it, knowing that he must have answered my letter in detail.

First of all, Kwame thanked me warmly for writing to him and expressed his surprise and joy at the discovery of the documents. He longed, he said, to see them, but was grateful to me for reading the diary and telling him of the period before his father died. He had never been told of his father's death. He had written regularly to him but never received an answer and imagined that he must be angry with him in some way. At the time his father died, his allowance suddenly stopped coming and the bank informed him that his father had decided not to pay for his studies and so delayed in finishing. He had fortunately done well in his exams and now had a very good job. He had accumulated enough money to afford a ticket home and would come as soon as arrangements could be made. He was very angry with his aunt for having deprived him of contact with his father and now realized that it was she who had kept all his letters from his father. He asked permission to come straight to our house on his arrival so that he could see the papers and decide what to do. I put down the letter and looked at the photograph he sent. It showed a strong face with piercing dark eyes.

I looked forward to meeting him. In the meantime, just before the university started, I passed my final test.

My father was delighted and the next evening I found a computer fixed up in my room. My friends all came in to see it and some of them who were already proficient started to teach me the computer games. I had had no idea that it opened so many opportunities. The only disadvantage was that my father started bringing me work to do in the evenings.

A few days before I was due to start at the University of Science and Technology, or UST as it was called, I was working on my computer when I heard the door bell ring. Mother was again out in town so I went down to see who it was. Imagine my surprise and pleasure when I saw Kwame standing there. He looked just as he did in the photo only he was taller than I had imagined.

"Are you Amma Akyeaa?" he asked. "Yes, Kwame," I said and he gave me a broad smile. "May I come in?" he asked.

I opened the door wide and led him into the sitting room. "Do you want a drink?" I asked. "Now I know I am really back in

Ghana," he replied, "Where manners count." I fetched him a soft drink and we sat down to talk. He said he had just arrived from England and had come up on Government Transport. He wondered why we bothered to lock the outside gate as when he was a child everything was open. He admired the newly painted house. Then he looked sad and talked about his childhood in the house.

After a bit I decided I would go and fetch the papers and bring them down to him. I also gave him the two letters he had written to his father and which his father never received. I explained that the envelopes were still sealed when they were given to me.

As he looked at the papers I saw tears well up in his eyes.

"If only, if only I had known," he said, wiping his eyes with his handkerchief. "*Nim saa ka akyere.*" The old saying came to my mind. "It's too late to have regrets," I said. "Let us see what we can do about it all now. I think you should get a lawyer and see if the Will still stands or if any other has been registered." Then I asked him where he was staying. "I don't know" he replied. "I will have to find somewhere to go but after seeing these papers I can't go to my family as Auntie Augustina is the head of it now and I would probably murder her." I thought for a moment. My brother's room was unoccupied and I wondered if my parents would agree to let him stay there. I would have to wait until they arrived. He was really surprised when I suggested it, but he said that there was nothing he would like better. The boy's room was where he had stayed as a small child. He obviously remembered the house well.

While we were waiting, he suggested that we should go into the garden. He was shocked at its conditions as he remembered how his father had tended it when he was a child. "I'll have to help you get it back into shape," he volunteered. "I'm sure my father would be delighted," I replied.

As we went out of the door and wandered round the house, my mother came back from town. It was actually really lunch time and I had prepared everything for the stove.

I introduced Kwame to my mother. She gave him a good looking over. "So you're the young man who should have inherited this house," she said. "Yes" he replied, but "if Amma had never written to me I could not have known it. It will at any rate take a long time to work things out. I have my Aunt to deal with."

Mother asked him to sit down and told me to come into the kitchen and help with the food. It took a very short time to get everything onto the stove and she asked me all about Kwame. "I think he is very nice" I said. "He was weeping over his father's death and feels strongly upset with his Aunt. Do you think he could stay here until he is settled?" My mother laughed and gave me a kiss. "Of course, but be careful dear, he is an attractive young man!" We both laughed and returned to the sitting-room.

"Will you stay with us?" my mother asked.

"Are you sure I would be welcome?" Kwame replied.

"But of course. I will get the room ready. Amma, keep an eye on the food. Your father should be back soon and then we can all eat."

My father took to him at once and gave him a note to one of his best solicitors in town. He asked him to "take on Kwame as a client as the matter affected his own family closely." The lawyer was my father's fellow member of the Rotary Club and he knew that the lawyer would do his best.

It was late before we went to bed that night. Kwame told us about his experiences in England and how much he regretted not having taken action about his father's lack of communication. My father told him in detail how he had bought the property from his aunt and showed him the document which had only her name. She had shown him all the property papers and arranged the transfer of property rights to him. She might have bribed or persuaded the officials to change the papers without checking on the documents. She was a very persuasive person and he did not imagine that she would have had much trouble.

"What will happen if the house papers are proved to be false?" I asked.

"I don't know," said my father. "That will depend on Kwame of course." "Don't worry," Kwame replied. "By all means you will keep the property and if anything I will get a recompense from my aunt. It's not your fault and I shall be eternally grateful for the way that Amma has taken the trouble to contact me and given me all the papers. After all, you could have destroyed the Will." Of course, none of us had even thought of that. But he was right.

Before he settled for the night I gave him the copy of the diary I had made.

The Early the next morning, Kwame went off to contact Mr. Gambrah the lawyer. He took the Will and the diary with him and a few other property papers. He arrived at the chambers of Mr Gambrah before work and when he had not yet arrived. At last a man came slowly up the steps and arrived at the door. "Excuse me, sir but are you Mr Gambrah?" The man looked him over. "And what if I am?" "Please, Sir, I have a letter for Mr Gambrah from Mr Koranteng." Mr Gambrah's expression changed. "Come right in," he said and led the way into an inner office. Kwame handed over the letter.

Mr Gambrah had a good look at him. He liked what he saw. "Sit down," he said, "and tell me all about it."

The story amazed Mr Gambrah. "I think that you and I should go and visit your Aunt Augustina," he said. "But at first don't tell her anything about the papers. Merely report to her that you have just returned home from abroad and were surprised to find other people living in your father's house and your father himself dead. We will see what her reactions are and then we can judge what to do. I shall be free at about four o'clock this afternoon and by then she should be in her house."

For a short time he wandered through town, seeing what he would recognise and passing the Fort and Post Office, the landmarks of Kumasi's commercial centre of Adum. Since he had time he decided to walk home and passed the Kumasi City Council offices and along the Old Bekwai Road. He was hungry by the time he got to the house and we sat at the kitchen table.

III

Auntie Augustina lived in Ashanti New Town, in a large compound house. Mr Gambrah seemed to know where it was and went straight there. He told Kwame to stay in the car and went into the yard and enquired if Auntie was in? They took him upstairs and there he was met by a large overpowering female who greeted him warmly and asked him to sit down.

"To what do I owe this pleasure?" she asked, smiling sweetly. "I have brought you an unexpected visitor, who is staying with the Korantengs in your old house. He is anxious to meet you as he wants to hear about Yao Frempong. He has been abroad for many years and did not know that he was dead."

Auntie Augustina's face fell and she looked anxious. "What is his name?" she asked, "do I know him?" "Yes, you know him, his name is Kwame Frempong."

Auntie Augustina's face darkened and she began to look angry. "That wizard!" she almost shouted. "Has he come back after all these years. He never let us know where he was and nearly killed his father by failing to contact him!" She waited for a reply.

"I will fetch him," said Lawyer Gambrah and before she could say anything more he went down and fetched Kwame.

By the time they returned upstairs, Augustina's face was almost purple with anger. She gave Kwame no time to greet her but started attacking him verbally. "You wizard, you traitor. You deserted your father and never came to see him when he was ill. What do you want now? All his things have been dispensed with as no one knew where you were. Yet you come back expecting a warm welcome. Rubbish!!"

Mr Gambrah tried to calm her down and he made Kwame sit by his side on the sofa. She collapsed into the chair opposite, still muttering to herself.

Mr Gambrah spoke slowly and calmly. "He has come to inherit his father's property. You, on purpose, did not inform him when his father died so that you could take everything. Now you try to blame Kwame for your sins."

"You don't know what you are talking about," shouted Augustina. "He left everything to me, as I had cared for him for so long, since his wife went off and left him."

"Can I see the Will, please," asked Mr. Gambrah.

"What do you want to see the Will for? Is it not sufficient that I was permitted to take over everything. We all presumed that Kwame had died or disappeared. How was I to know that he still existed?"

Kwame sat quietly on the sofa. His face was pale but he was finding it difficult to control his anger. In the end he burst out:

"Auntie, you know quite well that I wrote regularly to my father and that you intercepted all the letters and made quite sure that I did not hear of his death. You even kept the funeral quiet and put nothing in the papers so that I would not hear. How could you have treated me like that? What have I ever done to you to make you behave in such a way? He burst into tears and Mr Gambrah was forced to put his arm round his shoulders and to tell him urgently to control himself.

Auntie Augustina was now out of control herself and shouting furiously she picked up a broom from round the corner and screamed at them to leave her house at once. Mr Gambrah stood up and taking Kwame's arm, walked slowly down the staircase. The yard was full of anxious faces. Maggie, Augustina's daughter, came into the yard and seeing Kwame rushed up to him and hugged him. "I'm so glad you are back," she said.

Everyone watched in amazement. Augustina started down the stairs. She had now collected a long stick and it was only the restraining arms of the on-lookers that saved Mr Gambrah and Kwame from a beating.

They hurriedly left the yard and Maggie climbed in the car with them. As soon as they were out of sight of the house she hugged Kwame again. "Don't you remember me?" she asked. "I am your cousin Maggie. I am so sorry that my mother treated you like that. I am on your side, whatever happens. Do you remember how we played together as children?"

Kwame was completely devastated and angry but he could not ignore Maggie's affection. "Thank you Maggie," he said, "thank you of course I remember and I am most grateful for your support and for your finding of the letters. But aren't you in danger?" Maggie thought for a moment. "I don't think so. My mother would not dare touch me and at any rate, I live on the other side of town and know all the people in the house. It was pure chance that I passed by when I did. If there is anything I can do to help, please call me."

They went straight to Mr Gambrah's office and up the stairs. Mr

Gambrah asked the secretary to make them all coffee. They sat in the office and there was a moment's silence. Then Mr Gambrah spoke. "You can help, Maggie, by writing out a statement about the letters and anything else you remember. Also I would like a list of your uncle's things which are still in your mother's house." Maggie remained silent. She had been so carried away by her emotions that she had not thought of the consequences. Could she really betray her mother?

Mr Gambrah seemed to understand what she was thinking and after much persuasion she wrote down the necessary information. "If there is any trouble," he said, "let me know at once and I will get you police protection." Maggie looked scared, but what could she do? Mr. Gambrah decided to contact the police and ask for a search warrant for them to go through Auntie Augustina's house. Otherwise she would destroy all the evidence. He had very good relations with the police and insisting that there was stolen property there, persuaded them to search the house. Kwame would have to go with them as only he could recognize his father's things and find his own letters as others were bound to be destroyed. Kwame feared it was now too late to try and collect them. Maggie had told him exactly where to look but of course they might have been removed too.

Things moved quickly. It was quite early in the morning when the police arrived to collect Kwame to go to his Auntie Augustina's house. Mr. Gambrah had told the police officer how violent Augustina could be, so he had brought several other policemen with him. When they arrived, smoke was coming out of the courtyard. They went straight in and the police officer, Sergeant Kofi, looked round. There was a large bonfire burning in the middle of the yard and Auntie Augustina was coming down the stairs with an armful of papers.

Before she realized what was happening the policemen had seized the papers from her. Kwame stood by the side of the stairs and looked at the papers. One or two envelopes fell to the ground and he picked them up. They were his letters to his father, some were still sealed but they all had his address on the back. Sergeant Kofi had been properly briefed and knew they were looking for letters among other things. A few papers were already burning on the fire. One of the policemen filled a bucket with water and attempted to put out the fire.

Auntie Augustina was, of course, furious. Sergeant Kofi showed her the search warrant. She stood in the middle of the stairs and refused to let him pass. When she saw Kwame, she tried to run down and attack him. With a policeman on either side she was persuaded to return up the stairs and the others followed. The policemen shut her in the bathroom while they started to search the rooms. Luckily, Auntie Augustina had opened all the rooms and the floors were strewn with different objects. Some were familiar to Kwame and these he put on one side. It was Auntie Augustina's bedroom that he had had the greatest shock. He found a box at the back of a cupboard, a black tin with flowers on top. He thought he recognized it. The key was in the lock and he opened it. Inside was much of what he recognized as his mother's gold jewelery. Her engagement and wedding rings were also there and a little gold box with which Kwame had often played as a child. In another box were his father's gold chain and several gold rings. There were also several small treasures of his mother's and a silver cigarette box which had been his father's. Kwame showed all these to Sergeant Kofi and explained what they were.

There were many items of China and pottery, wooden carvings and brass *kuduo* pots. All of them had belonged to his father. Some things he imagined must have come from the old house but he did not remember them. A face flashed into his mind. It was that of the man who used to work for his father and looked after the house. His name had been Atta Binga and he came from the North. He would have been able to identify everything. Kwame wondered if he was still alive. Some weeks later they found out that when Yao Frempong died, Atta had been sent back to Navorongo in the North with a substantial pension. They were able to track him down and he helped to identify the rest of Yao Frempong's possessions. But all that happened later.

Auntie Augustina was shouting from behind the bathroom door. The police were amazed at her vocabulary and at the insults she shouted at them. By now many of the household had gathered in the yard and the police asked who the most senior person there was. An elderly woman stood out and they all agreed that she should take over as she was a cousin of Augustina's.

Sergeant Kofi warned them all not to enter the rooms upstairs and said he would send someone to guard them.

Auntie Augustina was dragged screaming into the police van and Kwame went back with Sergeant Kofi to the police station. From there they telephoned Lawyer Gambrah to tell him what had happened and he came straight over to the police station. He wrote out a document explaining what had happened and the reason for the search.

Auntie Augustina, when she calmed down a bit, explained that she had been holding these things in trust for her nephew as he was out of the country and had no intention of keeping them. When she tried to say she had no means of contacting Kwame, he produced some of the envelopes with his address at the back. She was retained in custody. After thanking Sergeant Kofi, Kwame went off with Mr Gambrah to his office. They had a long conversation about everything. The police had retained the gold jewellery but the rest had been left in Augustina's house.

I was so pleased to see Kwame again. I had grown very fond of him. He looked utterly exhausted and we made him rest until supper time when he told us everything, including his memory of Atta Binga and how he had looked after Kwame's father.

The next few days were anti-climax. Mr. Gambrah had to sort out the legal side of things and it would all take time. Kwame asked if there was anything he could do for my father. I suggested he remake the garden. At least he felt he was doing something for his keep. He helped my father in every way he could, cleaning the car, polishing his shoes and taking quite a bit of work off mother and my hands. He soon became indispensable.

The time came for my course at the university to start. The first week was spent in getting to know my fellow students and the lecturers. I realized even then that I was missing Kwame and thought a lot about him and his problems.

Kwame had started to straighten up the garden. He seemed to know quite a bit about gardening as he had worked with his father as a child. At the weekend I went out to join him and we worked together. We went to the Parks and Gardens for advice. My father bought us some new tools and we pruned back the bougainvillea along the walls and fence. It was when we were doing this that we came across an old cement trough, about six feet long. Kwame recognized it and said it used to be in front of the house and planted with roses. We decided that when the garden was finished we would move it back and replant it with roses again.

In the evening Kwame and I would sit and gossip. I would tell him all about my day at the university and gradually he began to tell me about his childhood. I suddenly realised that I knew nothing about his mother. He never spoke of her and I wondered what had happened to her.

One evening when we were sitting out on the balcony and there was a full moon, Kwame told me about what happened. Some ten years ago, when he was at school his mother disappeared. His father was very agitated and Aunt Augustina had finally taken over the house, which was one reason why he worked so hard to go overseas.

Apparently his mother, to everyone's surprise, had gone off overseas and another man seemed to be involved. They had found many travel brochures in her drawer and some receipts for her new clothes such as one would need for going overseas. Her suitcase was also missing and much of her jewellery and valuables.

Kwame said that was why he was so amazed to find his mother's jewellery in Aunt Augustina's house. He had always understood that his mother had taken it with her. Perhaps she had used it to bribe Auntie Augustina not to tell where she was going. Kwame himself could not understand the story. His mother had been a quiet and gentle woman and apparently devoted to his father and her family. She never left a note for him and his sister. Perhaps Aunt Augustina had driven her out with her aggressiveness or she just could not bear to stay in the same house with her as she had moved in "to help her brother" while the children were away.

It was from that time that Kwame's father's illness began. He stayed more and more in the house and went straight from there to the office every day, retiring to his room immediately after his evening meal. Kwame moved out to stay with a cousin in town and only visited his father occasionally to see how he was doing.

I thought to myself what a good thing this has been. Perhaps Auntie Augustina might have poisoned him or found some way of destroying him. I asked Kwame if his father had no other children. "I had one sister, Akosua" he said. But she had already left home and got married. She was living somewhere in Africa with her husband and family. He had never been able to contact her though he had asked many times in his letters to his father for her address.

When I had asked Kwame when he last saw his father, tears welled-up in his eyes again. "As soon as I got the necessary qualifications, I went to university in England," he said. "I went to say goodbye and he promised that he would send me money annually to help me through. He gave me a large cheque to go with and to pay the air fare. Then he gave me a warm hug and told me to be careful and bring honour to the family. He said that as soon as he had an address he would send me my sister's. When I looked back briefly from the door, tears were streaming down my father's face. How I wish I had known what I know now."

I felt so sorry for Kwame and realised that I loved him. I wondered what he thought of me, apart from appreciating what I had done for him.

Since Augustina was either in custody or could be out on bail, there was no one around to hold up the process of getting the Will accepted. She had told the authorities that there was no Will and that she supposed the children must be dead. So there was no other Will to contest. They managed to get round the fact that the Will was five or six years old and at any rate the date on it had been smudged and was very unclear. The date of Yao Frempong's death was the nearest they could get to it. Once the papers were through, Kwame started going round to investigate all the other properties with the necessary documents.

In the last years of Yao Frempong's life the buildings and land had been let out on long leases in exchange for lump sums of money. Most of them were for ten years. This applied to properties inside Kumasi. Those in other parts of the country were all different; taken over by the State as rates and taxes had not been paid for a long time. On all of them money was owing or tenants had paid the taxes. Kwame wondered why the people had not been able to find out that his father was dead.

After one expedition, Kwame returned very cheerful and gave my father a large sum of money and insisted he take it. My father was embarrassed but did not want to hurt Kwame, so he took it. Kwame also brought me two pieces of the best cloth, which he said he wanted me to wear to church.

I went to a small Apostolic Church not too far from where we lived. I was a very committed Christian and called it my "power house." When I first took Kwame there he was amazed at the warmth of the atmosphere and at the singing. Kwame said he had no idea that churches could be like that. He had tried out the rather conservative churches in England and in the end joined up with a small university group which was livelier. Soon he was a recognized member of our congregation. My parents were Presbyterian and went to their own church.

We talked quite a lot about our beliefs in the evening and I told Kwame that Christ had told us to forgive seventy times seven, to turn the other cheek and not let the sun go down on our anger. I think this helped him with his feelings about Auntie Augustina.

Gradually the garden came under control. The new grass grew when the rains came and the flowers we had planted grew. "I think it's time we moved that trough" Kwame said one day. He had obtained white paint already, so as soon as it was moved we painted it. It now remained to get soil and collect roses from friends and Parks and Gardens.

When we had finished the painting, we went back to clear up the place where the trough had been standing for many years. I don't, to this day, know what made me say it, but I suddenly blurted out, "We have to dig to see if there is anything buried underneath." Kwame looked at me curiously but did not object. We got a garden fork and spade and started digging. Imagine our excitement when the spade hit something hard. Kwame cleared the spot with his hands to see what it was and suddenly there was a skull, a human skull lying in the earth. "My God!" shouted Kwame, "who is it?" We got a small fork and with our hands began to loosen the earth.

Gradually a whole skeleton appeared. I began to shake and Kwame was crying. "Do you think it is Mother?" he asked. It depends on when the trough was put there," I said.

Kwame tried to pull himself together and thought for a bit. "It had been moved the last time I came back from school and my mother had gone," he said.

"Mother, oh! Mother" Kwame cried, "how I have misjudged you."

"How can we be sure that it is her?" I asked. "I think we should call the police and see if there is any way of identifying the skeleton."

My mother went quickly to the telephone and rang the police station.

"They are coming," she said.

She made some strong black coffee and made us drink it and then went out to look at it. "It's obvious that the trough was moved to hide the grave." She said. "Someone committed murder and wanted to conceal it."

It was Sergeant Kofi who turned up first in a police car.

"How can we find out who it is?" we asked. "Kwame's mother disappeared at about the time the trough was moved so we suspect it might be her."

"Augustina again," said Sergeant Kofi. "But how can we find out, we must do so."

Sergeant Kofi asked to use the phone. "I will get the experts to come and dig it up. Maybe they will find something and they will be able to tell the height and sex of the person and any other details they can. Did your mother have any special feature, like a broken limb, that could be identified?"

Kwame thought hard. It was all so long ago. His mother had a bit of a limp and he thought she had broken her ankle at some time. He could think of nothing else.

It was evening by the time the team arrived but they brought a strong lamp with them. Gradually they cleared the bones and put the skeleton on a stretcher. The doctor who came with them looked carefully at the ankles. The bone in one of them had at one time been broken and reset. The skull had been crooked at the back. Once the skeleton was out of the grave they searched through the earth and dug deep round and below the place. They put what they found on a piece of cloth. Sgt. Kofi watched their work. When they had finished he went to find Kwame who was collapsed in a chair. I was trying to comfort him but it was difficult to know what to say.

Sgt Kofi asked Kwame to come and look at the bits and pieces that had been found around the grave. Most of them were so eroded that it was impossible to identify them. There, was however, the broken frame of some spectacles and a small gold cross on the end of a piece of a gold chain. Kwame picked it up. "We can't find the rest of the chain," Sgt Kofi said.

Kwame gazed at the tiny cross and looked down at the spectacles. "The cross was my mother's," he said. "She always wore it round her neck, whatever else she wore. The spectacles are hers as well." I was standing by. I put my arm round his waist and helped him back into the house.

Sergeant Kofi said, "The person who buried her must have missed the cross. If she was wearing a dress, of course it could have been completely hidden. Maybe the rest of the chain is in the skeleton. "We shall see."

My father returned from work and for the first time I noticed tears in his eyes. He went and sat by Kwame. "Courage!" he said "We will by all means discover who did this dastardly act. But we know Augustina must have known about it and that is why she was able to control your father. I imagine she threatened to tell the police that he had done it. What he must have suffered!"

Kwame started sobbing again and we all spent the evening comforting him.

IV

"When did Atta Binga, your father's house help, leave your father?" I asked Kwame. He sat up straight and a look of almost relief came onto his face. "Of course," he said "Atta had left when I returned from school to find my mother missing. He must have been sent away deliberately because he knew too much. I

201

will go up to Navorongo immediately to see if he is still alive and remembers anything. My father told me he had wanted to go back to his family and he had pensioned him off. I think he sent him money annually but I don't know for how long. I will go tomorrow and if necessary bring Atta down with me." This decision seemed to cheer him up. He went straight up to bed, determined to leave early the next morning.

"Have you got enough money, for yourself and Atta's fare?" asked my father. A look of surprise came on Kwame's face. "What an idiot I am, I thought I had enough to go and come but I forgot all about Atta."

"Never mind!" said my father. I have some cash for you here and will give you a cheque with a letter to the local Bank in case you get held up."

"How can I thank you?! "Kwame said emotionally.

The house felt quite empty without Kwame. Of course we had no word from him until he returned a week later. He did indeed bring Atta Binga with him and the old man appeared to be devoted to him and cared for him like a child. This is what Kwame told us:

He managed to get a bus to Tamale quite quickly and decided to spend the night there. The driver of the bus showed him a small hotel. Before he went he found out what time the bus left for Navrongo in the morning.

Kwame said that despite his worries he slept like a log on the narrow bed. Luckily he had asked the hotel people to wake him up in the morning. It was only just getting light when he left the hotel for the lorry park. He was directed to the place where vehicles left for Navrongo and after a bit of a climb onto a small *tro-tro* which gradually was half-filled with passengers. They left Tamale and made many stops along the road to pick up extra passengers and drop off some. People were very friendly and seeing he was young and did not have much luggage talked to him in broken English. An older man who spoke good English began to talk with him and came and sat next to him. He asked Kwame what he had come to the North for? Kwame told him of Atta Binga, "whom I believe has a farm in Navrongo." This seemed to please the man, who said he came from Navrongo himself

Again God seemed to be on Kwame's side. The man asked some questions about Atta and then said he thought he knew him. He told Kwame he could stay at the Catering Rest House and after asking his name and the name of his father said he would look for Atta for him. Kwame was very relieved. When they arrived in Navrongo the man took Kwame straight to the Rest House. He seemed to know the people there and told them to look after Kwame.

Kwame was given a simple but pleasant room. He realized he was very thirsty and asked for tea. Many years in England had made him a tea drinker and he did not want to touch a drink until his whole problem was solved.

He went to bed early. They brought him more tea in the morning and as he was drinking it and wondering what to do, there was a knock on his door. He ran to open it. There stood an old but strong man whose face filled with joy when he saw Kwame. They embraced and Kwame asked Atta to sit on the chair while he sat on the edge of the bed.

"Where is the friend who brought you?" he asked. Atta smiled. "He go come later. He say make we talk first." Kwame was relieved.

Kwame told Atta everything. Atta went quiet when Kwame spoke of his mother's body but sat listening. Kwame thought it better to tell the old man the truth so as not to confuse him.

By the time he finished, Atta was quite agitated.

"I no kill Missis," he said. "That woman she tell me that if I no go home and be quiet, she go tell the police that I kill Missis. Who would say I speak the truth if tell them it no be true? I fear, Master Kwame, I fear proper. Master he fit to weep and he give me much money and promise more. So I leave in fear and I no go South again since then. I went to see you but they tell me that you sick for overseas and no go come again. Master I sorry too much, please forgive." The old man went down on his knees and Kwame put his arms round to comfort him. When he was back in the chair Kwame patted his knee. "It no be your fault," he found himself saying.

Then Kwame explained why he had come north. They needed the true story. This is what he was told:

One evening Kwame's mother had been working in the garden behind the house. Augustina had asked her brother to do some hammering in of nails with a large hammer in the house. Then, when he went upstairs and it was nearly dark but his mother could still do work in the garden. Augustina went out with her hand covered while holding the hammer and hit his mother over the head, killing her instantly. She dragged the body under the bushes and went to see Yao Frempong. She was very strong. She told him what she had done and that if he said anything she would report to the police that he had killed his wife. His fingerprints were on the hammer – she had made sure of that."

Atta had been sent out at the time but later his master told him all about it. Augustina then got hold of Atta and said that she would accuse him of murder and his master would support her. He had no choice but to leave. However, he helped them dig the grave and put the body inside. Early the next morning, with the help of the watchman next door and someone's garden boy, they moved the trough to the back of the garden and placed it on top of the grave and did not use the trough any more. As soon as the work was done, Atta packed up his things and left for Navrongo. He had been there ever since.

The old man wept again and apologised. No one he said would support an old Northener against that strong woman Augustina. "She be bad woman proper, bad, bad. God no go forgive her. Maybe she kill Master too?" Kwame wondered indeed if that had been the case.

Kwame asked if he could call on Atta's family and if Master had sent him the money he had promised. Atta reported that at first money had come in each year but not for the last five years. There was nothing he could do about it.

Kwame paid a visit to Atta's family. He had six children and the oldest boy was nearly grown up. He gave the wife what money he could spare and told them he had to travel to Kumasi with Atta.

In Kumasi Atta stayed with us. "Are you sure that your father never wrote down what happened?" Lawyer Gambrah asked.

Kwame decided to go through all the papers again. He also went back to the store and opened the cupboard. He felt all round the back and pulled at the wood. There was a wide gap where something might have slipped down. He realized that there might be a way into the store from the room behind. He found that it was the dressing room of his father's and a tall cupboard leant against the wall. It took Atta and his full strength to move it. As they did so some old papers fell to the floor. Kwame seized them. One was a sealed envelope marked "to be opened after my death."

Kwame brought the envelope downstairs and showed it to me. We called in mother and opened it in her presence. It was a full confession of what had happened and was addressed to his children "with deep apologies."

The case was now complete. We rang Lawyer Gambrah and he was delighted. Augustina was out on bail and all Kwame's father's things had been surveyed by Atta. He found a few more but nothing of any importance.

I decided it was about time we informed Maggie of what had happened and went to her office to see her. "She has not been here for a week" said the other secretary. "We got a message that she was ill in hospital and then that she had been taken to her mother's house." I was horrified. Sgt Kofi was about to arrest Augustina who was out on bail and charge her with murder. Had she got rid of Maggie as well?

Kwame and I went to collect Sgt Kofi and begged him to search Augustina's house at once. He could arrest Augustina at the same time. We were all so anxious that the police did not think of stopping me from joining in the search.

Augustina had moved into one of the downstairs rooms as part of the top was still locked up. We asked straight away where Maggie was? She shrugged her shoulders and said she imagined she was in the office. "I think we will search this house first," said Sgt Kofi. Augustina was very angry, but Kofi did not want to arrest her until he had done the search. He locked her in her room while she shouted and banged on the door from inside. Then the police demanded that every room should be opened and searched. Next to the bathroom was a small spare room which had not previously been locked. The door was now firmly fixed. A key that was found fit and we opened it. There on the bed was Maggie.

At first I thought she was dead but she must have been heavily drugged. She looked thin and dehydrated. Her hands were tied.

There was a gag on her mouth. I quickly untied the gag. The arms were more difficult. Sgt. Kofi let me struggle with the knots, sensing, I suppose that I needed to help. Maggie was quite warm and when we turned her on her side she sighed. Thank God she was still alive. But we had to get her to hospital. Sgt. Kofi suggested that we take her to the police hospital. They would be able to find out what she had been drugged with. He had an arrest warrant for the murder of Kwame's mother but of course nothing about Maggie. That could still wait until things had been sorted out.

There was no phone in the house, but Sgt Kofi had a mobile telephone and phoned for another car to pick him and Augustina up and take her to the police station and detain her. All the time she was shouting behind the door.

The doctor came straightaway to look at Maggie and on hearing the story decided to put her on a drip as she did not look as if she had eaten recently. He asked me to sit by her and hold her hand if she showed signs of waking. He cleaned her arms with disinfectant as they had been scratched by the ropes. He also put some kind of grease on the corners of her month as they had been cut by the gag. I was allowed to ring up my mother and tell her what had happened.

"Bring Maggie with you, if they will release her!" she said. I'm sure we can find a bed for her; there is the spare one in your room if you don't mind." How kind and understanding my parents were.

When Maggie gained consciousness I told her what had happened at her house and merely said that her mother had been arrested. She said she was famished and I went out to buy her some *kelewele*, bread and oranges.

"What did your mother give you?" I asked. "I don't know," she replied, "but it was very strong and every time I woke up my mother gave me a glass of water and slipped in some more medicine. I was so drugged I suppose that I did not realize what was happening. She merely told me I had been very ill and the doctor had ordered that I be kept in bed. One day I nearly woke up properly and started shouting. It was then that she gagged me and tied me up. I shall never forgive her."

"She's crazy!" I said. "Don't worry, they will deal with her now that she is in custody." After the food she was immediately sleepy again and soon she fell fast asleep.

V

Of course, by now, everyone in town had heard of the discovery of the body and many excited friends turned up at the house. We told Kwame to keep out of sight. The strain on him would have been too much. We felt bad about keeping Atta away from his family and persuaded an old friend of his to go and explain to the family. He was very grateful, though quite honestly I think he wanted to stay and keep Kwame company. Together they went on working in the garden though there was now little left to do.

Until the holidays came I went daily to the university and was grateful to be fully occupied. I decided that in the holidays I would teach Kwame how to use the computer. I had a small radio which could get the BBC World Service and Kwame was also interested in "News about Britain" and all the international news. We got him all the newspapers; or rather my father brought his back from the office and I just collected all the opposition papers or scandal sheets as we called them.

Soon he was as good as me on the computer and we decided that he should write out his experiences in detail. The evidence might be useful when the case came on. The sad thing was we could not go out together for fear of being recognized. Kumasi is like a village the way news spreads. But interest in the case was waning so Kwame decided to visit the rest of the properties he had not yet checked on, taking the Will and all necessary papers for changing ownership wherever it was registered.

It is difficult to cover everything at once. Maggie moved into the house for a short time until she recovered. Then she went back to her own work in Takoradi. We did not think there was any risk now that Augustina was in jail.

VI

Alone, except for my parents, I thought a lot about what had happened. I missed Kwame terribly and admitted to myself that at least I was very much in love with him. I had not wanted to do so before as I felt it would look as if I was taking advantage of him. Now I felt as if I could never love anyone else.

I think my parents knew well what was happening and Daddy treated Kwame already as a son. I was relieved to know that they would not mind if he married me. But what about Kwame himself? He had treated me all along as a sister and had made no efforts to court me. I knew he was truly grateful but gratitude is no substitute for love. Although I had had a few casual boyfriends I had never loved anyone before and I positively ached for him to return.

A week later, when I was working in the afternoon, the front door bell rang. I got up slowly and looked out of the widow, but whoever it was was on the porch. I went down and called through the door: "Who is it?" "It's me!" said a deep voice. Of course it was Kwame.

I threw open the door and there he stood, changed back to his old self and looking well and cheerful. He stared for a moment and then dropped his case and took me in his arms. There was no doubt about what he felt. He took me to the sitting room and I had to struggle to free myself and collect his case and shut the front door. Then I went back.

My mother and father were out. The strength of our emotions could not be hidden. How many times we said "I love you" and followed with a deep kiss, I do not know. We were oblivious to our surroundings. We lay in each other's arms until at last the front door clicked open. "It must be Mummy," I said. Kwame released me and went out to meet my mother. Without thinking he embraced her too. She looked a bit surprised but pleased and gave him a hug and kiss in return. "You really are our son!" she said.

Mother stayed in the kitchen to do the cooking. We offered to help but looking at us with a smile, she refused. "Go catch up with the news!" she said. How I loved my Mum at that moment, she was so understanding.

We took Kwame's things upstairs and sat in his room while he did indeed tell me how well his visits had gone, only one tenant had caused trouble but with the help of a local lawyer things were straightened out. Now Kwame really was a "man of property."

When he had finished recounting his travels, Kwame stopped and looked me straight in the face. He put his hands on my shoulders. "When are we getting married?" he asked, with a smile in his eyes.

"When are you ready?" I said. "As soon as possible. I can't wait to be your wife. Oh! Kwame so I wondered if you cared for me as much as I did for you?"

Kwame laughed. "I loved you from the first day I saw you," he said.

"Only I was afraid of taking advantage of you. I had nothing and did not know what would happen to me... I could make no promises and did not know my future." I understood perfectly.

We had another shock before that. The police decided that they must dig up Kwame's father's body to see if there were any signs that he had been murdered. It might be too late, but the graveyard where he had been buried was known for preserving the bodies rather a long time.

We persuaded Kwame not to come to the cemetery. The investigations were a bit tricky but in the end they discovered traces of a drug that was known to debilitate and make digestion difficult, finally leading to death.

So it happened that we could bury the two bodies, side by side as they would have wished. No one thought it odd that we should take such a prominent part in the funeral and have the custom at our house, as the body had been found there and the house had been Kwame's father's at the time of his death. This time we announced the funeral in the newspapers. Partly, I suspect, because of the interest in the murder, hundreds of people turned up. We had a joint service in the Methodist Church afterwards. The preacher had obviously known Mr Frempong well and paid a glowing tribute to him. One of the elderly women members also gave a warm tribute to Kwame's mother and spoke with tears running down her face of her horror at the murder.

"Time does not exist." I always think of the poet's words… and at my back I always hear, "Time's winged chariots near. Yonder all before us lie, deserts and vast eternity. The grave's a fine and private place, but none , I think, do there embrace…"

Both Mummy and Daddy were glad about our engagement. One day my mother asked me if I would not like to go and spend some days on the coast to get a change of atmosphere and to have Kwame to myself. Kwame had to go down again to see to one of the properties where repairs needed doing. We decided to go together and to spend a few days by the sea at Cape Coast or Elmina. It would also be easy to take a bus along the Coast to see Maggie.

The rains were stopping but it was still fairly cool and the waves were breaking with full force on the coast. I had never really explored the castles on the coast and Kwame, who seemed to know them well, promised to show me round. We stayed in a small hotel in Cape Coast and explored several of the beaches within reach of the town. Kwame had soon dealt with his business.

This was the first time we had really been alone together. Kwame insisted on our having separate rooms until we married to consummate our relationship. I realized how highly moral he was. Maggie came to join us for the weekend and on Sunday we all went to the local Methodist Church as we did not know the other characters. Everyone stared at us, wondering no doubt who was the handsome young man with two beautiful women!

The sermon was on my favourite subject: "Thou shall love thy neighbour as thyself." I wondered how in fact I did love myself. I knew I loved Kwame. How does one judge oneself?

Kwame was thoughtful when we returned to the hotel. "How can I forgive?" he asked me. "The wound is too deep and the offence too great. I could never forgive Auntie Augustina."

I tried to think of an answer and then said. "But God is good to us. If it had not been Auntie Augustina, you and I would never have met, Kwame and certainly not in a way for you to become so much one of our family." Kwame hugged me. "You are quite right," he said, "I will, at any rate try hard to forgive."

We climbed up onto the walls of Cape Coast Castle and saw the dungeons from which the slaves were shipped to America. How terrible it must have all been. As we went down to the shore, I am sure we both were thinking of those who sailed off to the unknown shores, not realizing what a future was in store for their children and their children's children once they had become accepted in the United States. African Americans had sometimes come up to Kumasi and I had seen how emotional they had become when they looked for their roots.

As we walked along the edge of the waves, I searched for shells and rock pieces. I have always loved shells. I even found a few cowrie shells – once used for money in Ashanti and the fan shaped shells which were used on stool paraphernalia and necklaces or on waist bands. One wave washed up a well-worn bead, large enough not to have been worn away by the sea.

It was dusk when we reached the hotel and I washed all my treasures and laid them out on the window sill to dry.

The time passed only too quickly. We had time to talk of so many things. One day I asked Kwame about his sister Akosua. He looked surprised. He had forgotten about her in the trauma of recent events. Somehow he must find her and let her know what had happened. As soon as we returned to Kumasi we would go to the Registry of Births, Deaths and Marriages and see what we could find.

We telephoned my father and he said we had better return because it was nearly time for the case to come to court. Kwame went to Maggie's office and explained that she would be called as a witness in a property case of his that was coming up.

We sadly took leave of the Coast and made our way to Kumasi. Kwame now had enough money to buy a small car and asked if we would mind keeping it in our yard. "Of course," said Daddy "only there is no room in the garage."

Kwame had made up his mind to sell off one of the large properties on the coast, in Accra, in order to build a small house for himself in Kumasi. His father had had several plots and he decided to see if they had been taken back by the City Council.

Two of them had but there remained, one in the Nhyiaeso area, tucked away among the old houses and used by someone as a farm.

He decided to build on that land and could probably keep some of the plantain and coconuts on the edge of the plot. The building would have to be put up before he made a garden.

We were soon searching for Kwame's sister. She had married a man called Ephraim Amebetor, an Ewe. They had lived in a place called Tsito in the Volta Region. Fortunately, it was not a big town. Kwame decided to go there. He looked through the records of the local newspaper and finally found a not-too-good photograph of Akosua's wedding. At least some of the people standing round the bride and groom might be recognizable.

When Kwame reached Tsito he went first to the local churches and asked the ministers if they knew of the Amebetor family. Luckily they did and Kwame was taken to the village house which he realised was in good condition and even had a bit of a garden round it. The minister went in and presently came out with an elderly woman. Kwame greeted her and the minister explained that Kwame was looking for Ephraim Amebetor who had married a girl from Kumasi and gone overseas. The woman knew at once whom he was talking about.

"He has not been home for many years," she said, but he does write occasionally and has sent me some money."

"Have you got his address?" asked Kwame anxiously.

"I'll look" said the woman. "Do come in and sit down."

"I can't read myself" she said, "but I think there is an address inside." Kwame saw their rather unclear address scrawled on the back of the envelope she brought from the room. The stamp was from Zimbabwe. There were Ghanaians all over Africa so he was not surprised. He could write to the Embassy there. He asked if he might borrow the envelope and promised to return it. The woman shrugged her shoulders. "I have no more use for it," she said. "If you manage to get in touch please tell him that Auntie Amewu would like to hear from him. Tell him too that his brother has died and also his uncle. Tell him to come home with his family. We will find him somewhere to live."

Kwame put the envelope carefully in his brief case and offered the old lady some Cedi notes. She seemed pleased. He had not explained to her why he wanted to know. He did not think it was necessary.

Once back home, with the help of a magnifying glass and some imagination, he worked out the address, but it was two letters he sent off. One went to his sister explaining what had happened and the other to the Ghanaian Embassy, asking them to try and contact the family for him in order to report on two deaths in the family. Realising the importance which Ghanaians gave to funerals in the family, he hoped that this would make them take the trouble to investigate it. He enclosed another note in the Embassy letter addressed to his brother-in-law, just giving the main facts.

Weeks later his sister wrote back that she had tried in vain to get in touch with him, her mother and father, but had never been able to. Now she understood. If Kwame could help her with the return fares, she would return with the children to hear the full story. Kwame at once sent her a cheque for their air passages. He wrote apologising to his brother-in-law and explaining why he had never been able to contact him. Then he waited for them to arrive. In fact they did not turn up until after the case had gone to court. By then everything of his father's was in his hands and he was able to give his sister his mother's jewellery and some other valuables he had found.

Akosua was a very sweet person and very quiet. It took a bit of time to get to know her. We stayed two or three months in Kumasi which gave her three children, now nearly grown-up, a chance to get to know their grandfather's town. They spoke very good English as in Zimbabwe it was the common language as in Ghana and their education had been in English. Kwame grew particularly fond of the oldest boy, Edward and got his sister to promise to send him over to university in Ghana, when the time came.

The time had come. The case was called and finally the day arrived when we all went to court. Two policemen escorted Auntie Augustina into the court. She had lost a lot of weight and was wearing a plain black dress and no earrings or chain which made her look, to us, sort of half-dressed as she had always displayed her jewellery.

The charges were: "You are accused of the willful murder of Madam Rose Amankwah Frempong and of her secret burial in the garden of her husband Yao Frempong. You are also accused of the drugging and the slow murder of her husband, Yao Kusi Frempong, in the same house and the attempted murder of your daughter Margaret Akuamoah Manu by binding and gagging her for five days without food. Since there are three charges we will hear the first case of murder first. I now call upon the lawyer for the complainant to make his case."

Mr Gambrah stood up and explained the case in detail. He left nothing out. When he had finished there were murmurings. The judge ordered that the witnesses be called so that the case could be proved.

Auntie Augustina was obviously restless. When she saw Atta Binga stand up, her face fell. He gave a very clear account of what had happened. The judge asked him how it was that he had not gone to the police. Atta said, somewhat emotionally: "Master, I no fit to go for police. They go kill me proper. Who would believe poor boy from the North when his Ashanti master say he kill the woman himself?" The judge had no answer for this and there was a murmur of agreement from the audience.

Next, Augustina's lawyer was called and asked if he wanted to say anything. He was an elderly man with grey hair and did not look too happy. Augustina touched his arm, indicating she wanted to reply and he told the judge that his client wanted to question the witness. Augustina asked many questions, accusing Atta of the hidden murder of "Auntie Rose" because he did not like the way she ordered him about. Had he not been found with the hammer which killed the woman and she went on and on. But she made a great mistake. The judge put it to her that if she knew it was Atta, why on earth did she not go straight to the police. "My husband begged me not to!" she said.

No one believed her. She had, of course, pleaded "not guilty."

The next witness to be called was Kwame. He told of the discovery of the body, of the identification of the gold cross and spectacles and also of his mother's broken ankle. He ended with a sob after describing the skeleton. I was called to confirm the story.

Auntie Augustina stood up again saying, "I am sorry, My Lord that I lied a little. I did not want to reveal that it was really my brother who murdured his wife. They had been quarreling for a long time and he felt bitter about her. Daily I could hear them wrangling in the sitting room or kitchen. She had a great command of the Ashanti language and knew how to curse him."

At this point Mr Nuamah shook Mr. Gambrah's arm. "It's not true," he said, let me give evidence." So soon Mr Nuamah was called. He said that he lived next door to the murdered couple for many years and had never heard them quarrelling. Indeed, they were one of the most devoted couples he had known. It was slander to say these things of them, he said.

"What proof have you that Mr Frempong killed his wife?" he asked. "I have to this day, the hammer which he used to do the job and which had his fingerprints on it. Luckily, no one has touched it afterwards and I had with a cloth. The head of the hammer was covered in blood."

Again the judge asked "And why did you not report your brother?" "How could I," she replied. "How could a sister betray her brother? But I decided to stay with him to make sure he never did such a thing again. From that day he was a little mentally disturbed..." Augustina spoke in Ashanti Twi.

The judge listened to what she was saying but no one believed her. It seemed obvious she was lying.

"So you blackmailed your brother to keep quiet and took over his affairs. Is that not true?"said the judge. "Think more carefully how you act and speak."

Augustina had no reply. At this point Mr. Gambrah asked permission to report what had happened to Auntie Rose's possessions. They had indeed vanished from her room but recently when Auntie Augustina's house was searched, the jewellery and some other valuables belonging to Auntie Rose were found in Augustina's house, together with many items from Yao Frempong's house.

"I think we will talk about that when we come to the second charge" said the judge. "Let us adjourn for a bit to enable me to consider the evidence which has been presented so we can continue tomorrow." In the meantime, the jury went to discuss their verdict.

When we got home my mother had a late lunch ready for us. "When I saw Auntie Augustina there, looking so different, I suddenly remembered what she was like. I was quite fond of her and Maggie was devoted to me. Her father was a nice man..." Kwame remembered.

"How did he die?" I asked. "I can't remember but I have a feeling he had a car accident or something happened to him on the coast. I think I remember Maggie was weeping bitterly. You will have to ask her."

Later, when I had a chance, I asked Maggie what had happened to her father. She said he had indeed died outside Kumasi and she remembered them bringing his body home but she could not remember anything else.

"Then your mother could not have killed him?" I asked. Maggie said she had been wondering about this, but it was too late to find out now.

Kwame and I went out into the garden and wandered round. A coconut fell from one of the trees and only just missed us. We went down to where the grave had been. The roses we had planted as a memorial to his mother was just coming into flower. We moved to say a prayer for her and his father. Then we returned to the house.

The decision was unanimous at the court.

Augustina tried to struggle to her feet and looked very angry, but the policemen on either side held her down and tried to calm her. The second case of "slow murder of her brother through drugging" was the next to be heard. The names of the drugs used were rather complicated and a doctor came to give evidence and explain the effect of the drugs over a long period.

"What have you to say?" the judge asked Augustina.

"It's all lies," she said. "I told you that my brother was very upset after he had killed my sister-in-law and I had to find some way to calm him down. I asked for advice from friends and those were the drugs that were recommended to me. At any time that I stopped using them he became abusive and violent. They seemed to calm him. I had no idea that they were dangerous and no one warned me about them. I thought that his illness was what he was dying of."

"Why did you not call a doctor?" asked the judge. "I did not see the point. Things were under control," replied Augustina.

"Why did you not call in the family and send for his son and daughter?" she was asked.

"I did not know where they were and they had stopped communicating." She said.

At this point Maggie and later Kwame gave evidence of the receipt of regular letters. Since Augustina could not read she had only bothered to open those which were fat with enough money in them. Two of Kwame's cheques had been paid into the bank and there was a record of them.

When all the evidence were made public, Augustina became confused and refused to answer any more questions. "I did what I thought was best for my brother," was the last thing she said.

The judge then directed the jury and told them that he could prove no definite intent to murder, though that had been the result. It was rather that Augustina, through either carelessness or intent had brought about his gradual death.

The jury decided to say "carelessness leading to death of Yao Frempong," rather than giving another verdict of willful murder.

The last case was Maggie's. It was narrated that when her mother found out about the letters, her mother was furious and threatened her with disinheritance and worse if she mentioned a word of it. As the case progressed, Augustina, however had realised that Maggie would be forced to give evidence. Therefore, when she came up on a visit from Takoradi, Augustina seized Maggie, drugged her and locked her up. The effect of the drug was strong.

The jury gave the verdict of willful attempted murder. By now Augustina was out of control. She stood up in court and shouted insults at the top of her voice, accusing everyone of manufacturing a case against her. She was finally convicted of the murder of Rose Frempong and Yao and attempted murder of Maggie. She could say nothing at the court for the life imprisonment sentence and twenty years for the attempted murder.

Maggie was soon in a fit state to return to Takoradi. She

promised to keep in touch and I phoned her every few days to check up on her. The police allowed Kwame to collect his father's things. We did not know where to put them until Kwame's new house was finished.

Akosua and the three boys arrived at this point and our minds were occupied with looking after her and the children. Kwame and Akosua were delighted to meet again. We wanted to get married but for the appeal in court. Kwame concentrated on finishing the house and I started making curtains, purchasing bed sheets and other necessities.

In England Kwame had worked for an Insurance company. He had, of course written to report of what had happened. He had been given six months leave, which showed how highly they regarded him. Now, he had to write to the company explaining he had to stay in Ghana to look after the family property. He had asked for a reference so that he could get a local job. He was sent one and in addition a severance pay. He found an insurance company eventually in Kumasi that was impressed with his qualifications.

Augustina's appeal at court failed.

Kwame had acquired a car. He decided to teach me to drive as well and at weekends we drove out of town. After a month I went for my driving test and passed without difficulty. I could now drive myself.

Now that all the cases and troubles were over, my parents suggested it was time for Kwame and I to get married. We asked Maggie be our chief bridesmaid and had the honeymoon in Brong Ahafo at a Rest House in a game reserve, a simple place surrounded by forest and sounds of birdsong. I loved the Senegal Kingfisher with its brilliant blue features as they fly in and sit around on the guava, being scolded by the other birds.

Everything in our lives seemed to lead to adventure. At the Rest House and just after the morning of our arrival, I was up early when Kwame was still sleeping as I could not sleep. Except for the chattering of the birds it was very silent. I wandered around the house and as I went along the back I noticed a kind of shaking in the undergrowth. I heard, surprisingly, a chuckle and a large chimpanzee stepped out in front of me. I saw he was friendly. He began to chat at me. He followed me quietly to the front of the house. Then he held out his hand. We shook hands. I suddenly remembered we had some bananas in our room. I went for them and got a gurgle of pleasure from him.

Mr. Boakye the supervisor was up and about. The chimpanzee followed on behind. Boakye burst into laughter. "So Adam has found you!" he said. "He is a good friend of ours and often comes to call. He has stripped all the banana trees of their fruits and we have to build a fence around our garden with plenty of barbed wire on top." Boakye became our good friend and he showed us round the reserve and talked about the animals.

When I returned to the hut Kwame was just waking up. I prepared breakfast and I told him all about Adam and Boakye. We enjoyed the forest too as there were many different kinds of parrots and one day I did indeed see and heard the blue plantain eater. Its drumming call came loud across the trees. Then it flew to one quite near us and I was able to see its beautiful blue feathers, its crest and long wings and tail. What a beautiful bird it was.

A week passed. Adam came to see us daily and one day brought his wife. We had run out of bananas and so Kwame rushed to the town centre to get some more while I decided to wander around. I took a path I had not followed into the dense part of the forest. The trees were full of monkeys and I kept looking up at them and following the movements of birds.

Keeping an eye on the lianas and looking above as I walked, I trod on a patch of mud and before I knew it I was sliding down a small slope and into a small forest pool. I went right under and when I surfaced coughed up black mud. I hung onto the root of a tree and waited to get back my breath. I was in despair. I shouted and shouted but there was no reply except for the excited chattering of the moneys. No one knew where I was. I heard movement in the branches above and when I looked there was Adam's face looking down at me. He was obviously distracted and hung down from a branch and tried to take my hand; then he started shouting and presently another face appeared alongside his. They both hung on the branch which was brought lower by their weight. After I had gone under a couple of times, I managed to grasp both hands and they began to pull me up and swing me towards the bank. I don't know how they did it but I was soon lying flat on my face near the top of the bank. I crawled slowly up it and found myself on flat ground. Adam and his wife fussed around me and wiped my face and hands and my body with leaves. I relied entirely on my friends to lead me home. As I came into the open space I heard Kwame's car coming. I was sitting on the doorstep chaperoned by my two friends.

"What have they done to you? What is the matter?" he cried. "They saved my life!" I replied.

Boakye was totally amazed when he heard the story. He was truly proud of his friends. We gave him money to spend just when we were about to leave.

The time has almost come to say "good-bye." We are now happily settled in our new house. It is furnished and all our wedding presents are in place. I think my parents miss us badly but they will soon have more family work to do. I am pregnant and our first child should arrive soon. I have managed to finish the term at the university but whether I shall finish the course I, Amma Akyeaa Frempong, do not know.

CHAPTER SIXTEEN

Money Matter

Yaba Badoe

Sheba Patterson believed that to be an authentic "roots" sister, she had to be enamoured of Africa, which everyone who knew her, could confirm that she was. Moreover, her fascination with face masks and mud cloth textiles encouraged her to regard the continent she revered as the most satisfying shopping destination in the world.

A glance in her direction confirmed her cultural orientation: nappy hair twirled in chunky twists, a smudge of Egyptian kohl around dark eyes and flowing from an ample frame, voluminous, sensual fabrics that flattered her curves. Indeed, when she strolled through campus, she seemed to sashay, sucking in the air around her. Not that she intended to draw attention to herself. She simply moved in such a way that the easy roll of her hips proclaimed her namesake: Sheba, lover of Solomon, a king wise enough to succumb to the charms of an extremely intelligent woman.

One morning, after a particularly vivid dream in which she had travelled to the birthplace of her ancestors, Ms. Patterson spotted an advertisement on the notice board of the university in Florida where she taught. She smoothed her index finger over the flyer, absorbed its contents and found herself considering the possibility that she might take a sabbatical in an institution of higher learning in West Africa.

Of course, later on, Sheba would insist that she deliberated long and hard before she came to a decision. She weighed up the pros and cons of uprooting herself from her home. She would say that she wondered how in heaven's name she could endure a year away from her boyfriend, Cyrus Lee, when in fact, before her mind fully grasped what she was about to do, her heart thumped in acquiescence. Cyrus or no Cyrus, she found herself yielding to the temptation of prolonged immersion in an environment she pined for. Sheba informed Cyrus Lee of her plans and made the necessary arrangements. Within six months, she was teaching a course in African American women writers at the University of Ghana, Legon.

Sheba had never been happier than during those first weeks. The tree-lined campus with its white, red roofed buildings was attractive. The heat, though occasionally oppressive, brought out the copper highlights in her skin. She glowed with good health and contentment and when she caught sight of her reflection purring back at her in a mirror, she trembled in awe of an inner re-alignment she sensed, but was unable to articulate.

Convinced she had made the right decision, Sheba uprooted herself once again. She moved from the university campus to a one-bedroomed apartment off East Cantonments road, popularly known as Oxford Street – the most exhilarating venue at the centre of the city – and used her hard-earned savings to settle in.

She fashioned curtains from dramatic Woodin prints and ordered a set of cane furniture from a roadside vendor. Then, after decorating her new abode in an elaborate jigsaw of mirrors and textiles, Sheba acquired a car. At last, at ease inside and out, she sprinkled smiles light as stardust on her colleagues. But behind those smiles there lurked a problem. Sheba had not been paid. The necessary letter had been written to the Registrar through the Head of Department, the requisite copy had been sent to the Head of Salaries. First one month, then a second ended without a pay slip in her pigeonhole.

To begin with, Sheba dismissed the delay as the result of the usual teething problems inherent in an unwieldy bureaucracy. After all, her name had just been placed on the university pay roll and it seemed like only yesterday when she'd overcome the stringent requirements and hurdles put in her way to open an account at the Osu branch of Barclays Bank. The long, agonising wait for remuneration could happen, just as easily, back home. This is what she told herself. But when the second month merged in to a third and Christmas, with its enticements of gifts and consumption loomed closer, Sheba began to wonder if what she had shrugged off as mild inefficiency wasn't, in fact, a case of gross ineptitude.

Sheba expressed her grievance to friends and colleagues. Calls were made, another letter was written and to extract what was due to her from the arcane machinery of the nation's premier university, Sheba became a regular visitor to Salaries. She walked down a long corridor, knocked on a gnarled wooden door, and spoke to a dumpy, wizened man hidden behind a desk stacked high with folders and files.

"Ah, it's you again, Ms. Patterson," the man sniffed at her. "Come about your money matter, I suppose. In my humble opinion, I think you should be paying us for the privilege of being here. After all, compared to your illustrious country, Ghana is very poor indeed."

Sheba bristled: "We've been through this before, Mr Addo. It's no good teasing me because I don't think you're funny. The fact is before I came here, I signed a contract. And that contract says that every month I will be paid a salary."

Sheba wanted her money and she intended to get it, even if it meant orchestrating a one-woman sit-in, in the office of the toad-like creature in front of her: Mr Algernon Albert Addo. Known as triple "A" to his friends, Mr Addo had acquired his nickname because of an uncanny ability to ferret out fictitious accounts on the university payroll.

Triple "A" beamed at Sheba, then lowered a wrinkled eyelid in a reptilian wink as he said: "I am on your case, Ms. Patterson. Hand on heart, you will be paid soon."

Sheba nodded and left the room. She acted in good faith, unaware of the labyrinthine nature of the flow of cash within a gigantic institution: the dams and eddies, the many streams and tributaries, which, like the never-ending Tano river, wind from the Brong Ahafo heartland of Ghana to the magical Nzema coast, where oil-slicks appear one day, only to disappear the next. Sheba knew none of this. What she did know was that without a regular salary to augment her savings, she was living beyond her means.

Christmas came in its festive glory and hanging tightly on its coat-tails, Cyrus Lee arrived for the New Year. At the sight of his tall, lanky, Obama-like frame emerging from Kotoka International Airport, Sheba's heart lurched in anticipation of what was to come. Cyrus's wide, sensual mouth was lined with laughter, while the sleek cut of his suit and his hair shaved close to his head, marked him out as stylish, professional.

He complimented Sheba's attachment to the land of her ancestors by being wryly sceptical, almost detached about her explorations. Indeed, he laughed out loud when she mentioned the aggravation she'd endured because of her unpaid salary.

"Welcome to Africa, Sweetie!"

The couple were lying naked in bed at Elmina Beach Hotel, having reacquainted themselves with the nooks and crannies of their bodies; dips and curves only they knew about.

"This ain't no laughing matter, Cyrus Lee. I want my money."

"You and me both! Ever thought that your Mr Addo may be enjoying taking you for a ride?"

"Never!"

"This is the world, Sheba – the real world."

Sheba trailed her thumb down a vein that ran down Cyrus's forearm. Her fingers garlanded his wrist and as she clambered on top of him and rubbed her nose against his, Cyrus said: "If I were you, I'd give your Mr Addo a little sugar to sweeten his pie, a small incentive to make him smile. Believe you me, within an hour tops, you'll have all the money that's owed you. And then some."

"You crazy or something? It's *my* money, Cyrus and I'm not going to give anyone, let alone *him* a back hander to get what's rightfully mine!"

"It's your call, Sheba. If I know you, you always end up doing what you want in the end."

Whether it was Cyrus's brief visit that bolstered her, or their visit to Elmina castle later that morning, Sheba would never know. She had visited Goree Island on her first trip to Senegal, so she appreciated what was in store for her. Nonetheless, a chill entered her bones the moment she stepped into the castle's white forecourt. And wandering through the dungeons, she felt the weight of her ancestry interrupt the flow of blood through her veins. Red corpuscles buckled into the shape of a sickle moon on a cold night. They blocked capillaries and drained lubrication from her joints, so that when she reached the final holding place of her ancestors and stared through the 'Door of No Return' to the sea beyond, Sheba could scarcely move. And yet she knew. She understood where she was coming from and where she was heading.

To say that Sheba thrilled with delight when, on her return to the university, she saw a payslip in her pigeon hole, is not an exaggeration. She danced in jubilation and then called Barclays Bank to make sure that the rightful amount had been deposited in her account.

"These things take time," the manager warned her. She should give it a day or so.

The following week, when Sheba called again, the money had still not arrived.

What would Zora and Maya and Toni do, Sheba wondered, conjuring up the spirits of her favourite writers, the authors she revered and taught in her class. What would they do to get what was owed them? After all, if Peace Corps volunteers were remunerated for services rendered, surely she should be paid for the work she did as well?

Sheba ventured, once again, to the office she had visited so often. This was her tenth visit. She walked along the corridor and after knocking on the second door on the right, walked in without waiting for a response. Mr Algernon Albert Addo was sitting at his desk, his red-rimmed eyes magnified by an ancient pair of green spectacles. He grinned mischievously at the woman before him. "My dear Ms. Patterson," he said, 'to what do I owe the pleasure of your company today?"

"Mr Addo," Sheba began, waving her payslip in the air. "I've been paid. I thank you for everything you've done to make it possible. However, the money owed me by the university hasn't reached my account. Where is it?"

"How should I know?' Mr Addo opened a thick fat ledger that held the intricate details and secrets of his subterranean world. He thumbed through it, flipping over pages and then ran a knotted finger down a list of names, until he found what he was looking for. "You bank at Osu, don't you young lady?"

Sheba rarely tolerated being referred to as a "young lady" at the best of times. Today, she bit her tongue. "Yes."

"At the Ghana Commercial Bank, Osu?"

"I told you four months ago, Mr Addo, my account is at Barclays."

"Well, that explains it." A thin smile greased Mr Addo's lips. "We've made a mistake. I humbly apologise to you for any inconvenience we have unwittingly caused you."

If humility had had anything to do with it, Sheba might not have found it difficult to accept the apology of a bloated, middle-aged man approaching retirement. If Mr Addo had tried to appear sincere, she might have taken Cyrus's advice and discretly offered him an "incentive." But far from looking apologetic, Mr Addo seemed to be gloating at the myriad impediments he had put in Sheba's path. Relishing his power, revelling in it like a bird sipping from a precious pool of rainwater, he smirked while Sheba spluttered, convinced she had given the correct name and address of her bank. Indeed, she knew that she had watched the man write it down in his ledger.

The more he simpered, contradicting his words, the more determined Sheba became not to give in to him. Cyrus's advice be damned! She was her own woman and despite every obstacle placed in her way, she would eventually get her money. She would do everything that was required of her and she would get it.

That very day, she travelled to the Commercial Bank at Osu with a letter from the university. The bank was to return the money paid into a fictitious account in her name to the university forthwith. The day after the cheque had been delivered by courier, Sheba was instructed to go back to Mr Addo's office at two o' clock on Friday afternoon, to pick up her salary.

Everything went according to plan. Thursday arrived and Sheba spoke to Mr Addo, who assured her that he would be waiting for her. If by chance, he wasn't around, his superior – Mr Arnold Abbam (known affectionately as Double 'A' to friends and family) – would hold on to the cheque and make sure she got it.

At two o' clock on Friday, Sheba knocked on Mr Addo's door one last time. He was nowhere to be found.

"It's *Friday*," said a harassed secretary in a yellow dress. On her desk was a tray of typing she seemed determined to finish. Nevertheless, sensing Sheba's dismay, she heaved herself up with a sigh and although heavily pregnant, led Sheba down a corridor to Mr Abbam's office.

Two men were sitting in his waiting room, browsing through the *Daily Graphic* and *The Ghanaian Times* newspapers. They shook their heads when the secretary asked if Mr Abbam was in.

"He's travelled. Boss always travels on Friday," the taller of the two men replied.

Close to tears, Sheba took a deep breath. Then, summoning up the spirits she loved, begging them to bear witness to her predicament, she called them one after the other: those that had stayed behind and those that had been sent away. She needed their presence to make her last stand. "I want my money," said Sheba. "I haven't been paid for four months, yet I come to work every day. God knows how I survived Christmas and the New Year without a pay cheque. Is it fair? Would *you* put up with it? How in kingdom come am I supposed to pay my rent, feed myself, put petrol in my car? Tell me, how am I supposed to live without money?"

The two men and the secretary standing beside them murmured sympathetically. "Oh," they said, their lips pursed in indignant ovals of astonishment. "You see? *Frustration!*"

The taller man clapped his hands. "Look at this poor woman," he tut-tutted. "Woman work hard, yet they pay her no money. Always plenty big frustration here because Madam, they don't pay us either!"

They chipped in a conciliatory chorus, affirming Sheba's tirade with gentle pouts of commiseration and nods of agreement, so that somehow, the stranger in their midst didn't cross the line between righteous anger and incandescent fury. She didn't say: "You people have a long ways to climb before you can get anywhere!"

She didn't kiss her lips and turn her back on them, asserting that they were hurtling recklessly down a path to nowhere. Their eyes held Sheba while their sympathy flowed through her, allowing her to give vent to seething exasperation.

So, when her tirade finally came to an end and the pregnant woman stepped forward with the words: "Madam, we are very sorry for what is happening to you. Please forgive us because we love you." Sheba remembered what she already knew.

At present, she was where she wanted to be for a reason.

She would collect her money on Monday.

CHAPTER SEVENTEEN

Sahara Desert

Ogochukwu Promise

The air was brittle. The day seemed to be panting for breath, thrashing about like a woman in labour. There was something awkward about the cold that assailed me. It seemed to be breathing in an uncanny manner right under my skin. I tried to ignore it as I told myself it was one season I was sure shares affinity with mischief. It seems to enjoy stripping things, stripping trees of their leaves, stripping houses of their roofs and filling everything in its wake with grime so that people's hair, eyebrows and eyelashes turn brown. It is a season that revels in denuding man, beast and the land, draining the skin, the earth, leaving it chalky. Somewhat baked, broken and ugly, certainly, the harmattan wind is rude. I have just discovered that it has cracked my lips as I began smiling at the joke Sisi Vero made.

"Etuk, you are at it again, your head buried in the clouds even when you are driving. One of these days if you don't learn quickly enough how to laugh at banks of clouds, your head is going to explode and come down to earth like rain!"

"At least not in this season, Sisi Vero. There will be no rain this season. My head is safe."

"Nothing is safe anymore, Etuk. The world is upside down. I won't be surprised if it rains in the middle of harmattan."

"Impossible!"

"With climate change, nothing is impossible, my dear. Don't they teach you anything in that school of yours? Thank goodness we are picking up big sister Bena in a matter of minutes only she may infect you with her strong ideologies. Precisely the thing I don't like about professors, even though this one happens to be my sister. I hope I will still be able to laugh with her though. It's been many decades since she left, you know."

"She's here now, we'll see. Her flight must have landed. It's good we are here because she's probably going through immigration already."

"Etuk, you are going to pull up at the arrival section, OK. And pray hard that the whole of me leaves the car in time for you to drive off without being molested by these law enforcement agents. They forget that no matter how hard some of us try, we cannot jump off the car as quickly as they would like us to in order to avoid traffic here. They must recognise that there are very foggy human elephants like myself around. And this dry gust isn't helping matters, waiting as it is with its claws to tear into our flesh like a cannibal."

But this particular harmattan wind did serve as a distraction as it was accompanied by its evil mate, a mild whirlwind which lifted some lady's flared skirt, revealing her very white lacy panties, a delight to watch, even as she struggled to hold her skirt down. The wind turned on her bag, snatching it away from her and flinging it up in the air. It twirled up there for a while until its zipper snapped letting out all its contents, which scattered in the wind, defying the help several compassionate ones offered her, stripping some of their handkerchiefs, scarves and others of their ties, only to curl around their neck.

Sisi Vero was laughing through visible tears. As usual, there was a carelessness about her that made her wet-eyed laughter quite pronounced in a way that contrasted beautifully with the pity she expressed as she called at the young lady who stood half-naked. Petrified. "Aw, aw child, I am probably the only one who could have helped you. I am gross enough to withstand this terrible wind but the trouble is how to hobble out of here to your rescue."

Would Sisi Vero ever stop being amusing! I laughed. From the side mirror, I saw Sisi Vero laugh too. I think she liked the fact that I was in improved spirits. I knew I liked it too, having the feeling of something being loosened in me, especially after being tickled by those tracery panties. It must have been a wobbly nut in my head perhaps. In my heart, most unlikely.

All too soon, we found that we were already at the arrival section of the Murtala Muhammed Airport, Lagos, Nigeria. In front of me was the sign: No stopping. No parking. No waiting.

A gentleman wearing a reflective jacket on a black shirt and pants, with a motor radio strapped to his black belt announced, "Keep moving. No waiting. No horning. No standing. No looking. No chatting."

Sisi Vero who had flung open the door of our Pajero jeep, did her best to hurry out of the car as I sneezed and coughed. "You heard him, Etuk, no sneezing. No coughing. No breathing!" she teased.

"No laughing!" I said, laughing even louder as I tried hard to keep myself in check.

She knew why I was laughing. She had managed to drag out one of her big thighs, but the other was reluctant to follow her. She laughed too as she tapped my head playfully. Then she grunted as she dragged the stubborn thigh away from the car employing the use of her two mighty hands. The pressure was such that it made her drooping biceps flap noisily, to and fro like a massive pendulum. She was breathing heavily.

I cast a glance at her and shook my head. I was worried about her, about the mass of fat that stalked her. And her round face which seemed to be broadening daily. Above all, I was worried about all the factors that fed that flesh and the clouds that hung over them. I have been with her long enough to know and I have been fascinated about it all long enough to be concerned. I wondered also about her sister, the one we came to the airport to pick up a Professor at Oxford. She has not been home for thirty years. In fact, since she left Nigeria for Oxford, she has not been home. I have only seen her once. I couldn't remember exactly what she looked like. I hoped somehow she was not as big as her younger sister, my madam, who has to struggle always to get out of cars, out of anything at all.

I was relieved when Sisi Vero finally got off, knowing that our car would not be towed away with me in it as it was the last time we were here to pick up a friend of hers. I had left the car outside and gone in with her with a cardboard paper on which was written her friend's name. But those were the days when chaos reigned supreme at this airport, when nobody knew where to park as the parking spaces were few and everybody seemed so much in a hurry that they would be willing to park on top of other cars if they could.

Now the government lays emphasis on maintaining order. They have designated parking spaces and buses to take the newly arrived to the parking lots where their cars and taxis are patiently waiting. It was to this parking lot that I drove. I paid the toll and found a space to ease the Pajero into. I put on Wiz Kid's music, relaxed my seat, put up my feet on the dashboard and laughed again at Sisi Vero's reference to herself as a huge elephant. I wondered if she would have laughed had I called her that. Not likely, for it would have been discourteous. But one never knew with Sisi Vero. She might have laughed it off, especially if there was no offence intended. But then I asked myself, what if someone had called her that? I was sure I would have fought the person quite gallantly even as Sisi Vero would protest, telling me not to be silly. I would stop at nothing to defend her, not necessarily in order to continue to earn her favour but because it would certainly be the right thing to do. Would it?

Truth be told, Sisi Vero is indeed a large woman. I chuckled to myself. She is one of those women who would make you wonder how many times she had been in and out of the fattening room, peculiar to the Cross River people of Southern Nigeria. As a matter of fact, I first saw her when she was going into the fattening room as Uncle Bero's young bride. She was an adolescent then, smallish, newly married. I watched her take jaunty steps into that place where our women traditionally would be kept either soon after they had just been put to bed or right after their bride price had been paid as some would have it. I was far younger and believed then that Sisi Vero was stepping right into a place of enjoyment. A paradise of sorts. A mud-hut full of laughing women. Full of meat. Meat from guinea fowl, which was hard to come by. I never stopped imagining what it would be like to take a piece of all that meat, throw it into my mouth and just hold it there for as many days as I could, savouring its fullness and the reality of its grand taste. The sheer realisation of owning it would be worth hoping for. I waited desperately for a chance to taste a piece of all that cow meat, bush meat of the antelope, grasscutter, fox, leopard. And of course, there was pork, snake, snail, even good old dog meat, which was tasty. Goat meat which was used to make spicy pepper soup, laced with fresh herbs and scent leaves, the aroma of which made my mouth water. Cow meat which was so red and dense with fat you knew it was to be used for a feast fit only for a queen. I did not think then that even the Queen of England, whom we had heard about in fairy tales and dreamt of had access to so much meat.

When I was a child, I used to be one of those who would hang around, waiting to be sent on errands by these very privileged women, who served in those special fattening rooms, hoping for a chance to be invited to lick the spoon used in making delicious broths for one of those about-to-befattened queens. Anyone who would give you a spoon to lick was kind. My mother did, when she made stews at home. Sometimes, she would even generously give me the whole pot to lick and wash up after she had taken out all the soup in it, dished them into enamel plates for our outsized family – eleven children from the womb of one courageous woman! Courageous, that was how she used to describe herself. But each time she went to assist in the fattening of any queen-to-be, she lacked the courage to sneak out meat, any kind of meat to me, no matter how many times I ran errands for her and for the other servers.

It never ceased to amaze me how a newly married little girl would have so many grown women serve her as though she was a queen. Before cock crow, they would take her into a thatched cubicle, to keep her away from the prying eyes of men who couldn't help their curiosity. There they would bathe her and polish her skin with the sweet smelling oil of the palm nuts. Her food would be cooked by a succession of seasoned chefs.

Even though nobody ever mentioned it, at least not to the

hearing of wide-eyed errand people like me who were prone to fall to the charms of the devil in their senseless pursuit of adventure, it would appear that the queen-to-be also ate other types of food at night and was delighted in other very special ways. I stumbled upon this knowledge one nightfall when I could not sleep because my stomach was rumbling, shouting loud at me in strangely familiar tongues to pacify it with food or I would not catch a wink. I braved the night to go close to the fattening room where my mother was serving the queen-to-be.

As I drew close, I saw a man go into the fattening room. I thought the women did not know as they were probably fast asleep. I crept closer, wondering if I shouldn't raise the alarm, especially as I heard creepy movements in the room. A while later the sound of a creaking bed, exuding from that room, in a discordant pattern that confounded me. Then I heard some sort of groaning, muffled cries not of someone being hurt, but strangely of people eating some delicious meal that made them smack their lips, eating and quietly singing distant songs. It was a night of odd feelings as it did seem also as if the song was coming from my chest, hitting hard at it. I could sense as well some heat around my navel, no, below it, further down. As something stood turgid right there between my legs. Alarmed by it, I screamed, pointing not at it, but at the room. "Someone is there! I swear by the gods, I saw someone go in there!"

But the embattled women, I discovered, keeping sentry outside the door of the fattening room, gave me a chase instead. They got hold of me and wrung my ears until they nearly fell off. Even my so-called courageous mother could not save me. She joined them in beating me into silence for upsetting the peace of the night and acting as though I was not well brought up to know that the affairs of the adults were theirs alone. There were things that must not be interrupted, not even by hunger or its neighbour, anger. My mother pretended not to notice until one of the women shouted, "Adiagha, watch that son of yours! Already it appears he has one of his legs in the very house of the evil spirit!"

My mother dragged me home, beat me some more and locked me in, crying hopelessly about how I seemed to have sworn to bring her nothing but disgrace, she who has loved me from the very beginning. She who gave me everything she could afford including soup. Yes, I remembered those soup pots where I poked my fingers again and again each time the opportunity presented itself, licking the sweetness each soup pot hid in its very deep reserves.

I had not known then that it was Uncle Bero who went into the fattening room. That he was the only male who had the right to do so. That the queen-to-be was his heartthrob, a lawful one at that.

But time has gone by. I have grown now, I believe. At least I am no longer that lad who yearned for meat, any kind of meat. Rather than bring more disgrace to my mother, I quickly packed my bag as she instructed and followed Sisi Vero. It turned out that the very queen-to-be I tried to protect by drawing attention to the man who went into her room was no other than Sisi Vero. Then we simply knew her as Vero. She was just too young to be called Sisi Vero. But she matured rather rapidly after she left the fattening room. And she had her four children in quick succession as though she was racing against time. With each childbirth, she was taken back to her husband's ancestral home where her mother-in-law doted on her and did nothing short of putting her repeatedly in the fattening room, only for her to emerge translucent and become pregnant again. The cycle continued till Uncle Bero passed away, the year their fifth child was born. It was the seventh year of their marriage.

When Sisi Vero was able to speak of it, she said, "As if he knew he would not stay long, he made sure he did all his duties by me. We had all the children we wanted and plenty of happiness rolled into seven years. I would have blamed him for not staying to keep me company, but I know him better, if he could he would have. I know he is everywhere now, in a higher place, watching over me and loving me still. I know we will never leave each other."

And Sisi Vero stayed faithful to that belief. To everything they worked on together and that included me. I was one of their works. When I arrived in Lagos with them, they put me in school. Now as an undergraduate, living off-campus, I chose to drive Sisi Vero about when I was not studying. That way, I showed my gratitude for all she had done for me, standing by me when her brothers-in-law opposed my entrance into their home, supporting me still even after her husband's demise. The least I could do was to be there for her, sense and fulfil her needs the way she did everybody else's.

The long van that brought fresh arrivals from the arrival wing of the airport to the parking lot has just pulled up close by. I saw Sisi Vero before she saw me. I hurried to take the carry-on bag she was reaching up for. The van was still rolling forward and she was having difficulty maintaining her balance. "Stop the van, driver, so I can get off," she shouted.

"Get off if you want to get off! We are in a hurry here! Why waste our time," the conductor yelled back at her.

"Perhaps if you take a good look at me you will know why you need to pull up to enable me get off!" Sisi Vero was laughing at herself as usual.

"Madam, it is not anybody's fault that your mouth decided to eat all the food your eyes saw without thinking of leaving even a morsel of fufu for anyone! Must all the food the world produced be stored in you?" the conductor flung at her.

"Ah, it is not true, my sister is here. Ask her if I eat alone. I just have a body that speaks well of food," she was laughing, panting and sweating.

The driver pulled up as some of the passengers who were laughing urged him to.

The one she called her sister was frowning, "What set of impertinent people are these!" she said in a sleek foreign accent. I noticed that her lips were quite thick, her face oval.

"Eee eh, see Oyibo grammarian white-black woman! You better push your grammar aside and do something quickly about your mother before you lose her to heart attack! This fat of hers is too much oo!" the conductor shouted as the van sped away.

"Goodness me! What is this? Did you hear him call my kid sister my mother!" she spoke to no one in particular after they alighted. "And why do they use the word fat? How can they be calling someone fat! Quite uncivilised!" Then she turned to Sisi Vero and very sternly said, "Seriously Vero, you are going to have to register in a gym right away!"

"Ah, ah, not here now, big sister? At least let us get home first," she responded jokingly.

"And who is this character who is grinning as he eavesdrops on our conversation, hugging my carry-on?"

"Forgive my manners. This is Etuk. He is part of the family. Etuk, this is my sister Bena. Where did you park?"

"Pleased to meet you, Prof," I began.

"Yes, my pleasure too," she said, "we need to get going. I am quite tired."

"That's the car, over here," I pointed. "Is there still more luggage?" I asked, surprised that someone who has been away for so long would return with just a carry-on. A woman for that matter.

"Vero, please tell the chauffeur that there are no more bags and we need to leave right now. My feet are hurting from such a long journey."

I stopped short at the word "chauffeur," but as Sisi Vero laughed it off explaining that I was a student at the University of Lagos, I put the carry-on in the boot and decided that I was not hurt in the least.

"Young man," she called as I got behind the wheels, "what are you studying?"

"Philosophy," I said proudly.

The dignity of her raised shoulders was intimidating as she said, "You should come over to Oxford and get an excellent education."

My face lit up at the prospect. But it fell when I thought of leaving Sisi Vero who was saying, "Etuk deserves the best education he can get. I can't tell you how many times I have dreamt of him winning a scholarship."

"We'll see," she said as I pulled out of the driveway, coursing through a long stretch of even roads lined by lush vegetation, flowers and architectural masterpieces that have sprung up along the airport road.

"Hmm, the ambiance here has greatly improved," the Professor mused.

"Haven't I been telling you all this while to come back home. We have lovely things around here too."

"I see that. Every city has its peculiar loveliness. I am fond of Oxford's exquisitely planned, patterned buildings and intricate network of roads. Their grandeur, I believe, is deepened in their quaintness. And their rather awakward narrow roads which irritates some people! But their sheer space management holds charm for me. At the same time, these broad roads I see here are quite fascinating. Compelling."

I was not conscious of the fact that my face was gleaming until I heard Sisi Vero, "Big sister, see how Etuk is completely taken in by the pictures you present of your foreign abode. I am sure his spirit has already relocated there. Etuk, take it easy. And when your body does get there reuniting with your mind, don't stay forever like some people we know."

And I was thinking, *"How on earth can this be possible! And even if it ever will be, dear Sisi Vero, it is going to be very difficult to leave you. Oh, look at you Sisi, ever ready to dream for others and support them. And no one would know what you've been through since Uncle Bero's passing, raising your kids all alone. You began with a small stall in front of your house and grew it into a big supermarket. You refused all those men who wanted to help you but not without first taking whatever sweetness Uncle Bero left in you. How would anybody have known how tough it was, going this journey alone, especially as they see you make fun of everything."*

"Etuk's brain is quite active. It goes everywhere. He's a young man you'd love to help," Sisi Vero went on.

"You must know, Vero, that people have to help themselves first and be disposed to receiving help. Does this young man think constructively? Does he have employable skills? Has he consistently shown willingness to learn and taken steps to grow? Some people may forgive ignorance, which I don't have sentiments for, but the refusal to act on knowledge gained is, for me, inexcusable. So if this Etuk fellow hasn't developed himself and made himself eligible for higher goals, I am afraid I cannot help, however well you praise him for serving you."

"May I say something here, Prof?" I said as I turned the corner, quite peeved.

"Sure, but please still keep an eye on your driving."

"I will. I just wanted to say that I am an A grade student, have been since I was freshman and looking to graduating with a first class. My essays have been published in the university's magazine. Twice I have got the Vice Chancellor's commendation for my temperament for natural leadership and ability to get things done. I am good with hardware, software, can cook, drive, fix just about anything."

"We will discuss the potential of an overseas graduate education for you. I am not making any promises because I expect you to shop around and get good deals for yourself."

By then, I had a smile on my face, an unsure one, though, as I couldn't tell where I stood with this Professor. I knew though that one thing I certainly had was a feeling of awe as I thought about how complex she must be, how advanced living in glowing Oxford must have made her, how hard it must be to please her. I must admit that I also became a bit indignant at myself for wanting to please, always wanting to please. I had earlier, in private sessions I had with myself, cautioned my mind against unconscious tendencies to gratify others which I knew always made me feel somewhat less deserving. And I thought I shouldn't do that to myself. But it is a reflex action I am still working hard to keep in check. The fact that it seemed to have overtaken me a while ago dampened my mood a bit even though I blamed my mood change on the traffic which was building gradually as we approached the ever rowdy and notorious Oshodi. That part of town that continues to resist cleaning, where violence occasionally erupts despite a police presence as though it protests every attempt to sanitise and modernise it. I knew I wasn't altogether settled. I had been driving for less than twenty kilometres from the airport and knew with the cluster of cars ahead that it promised to be a long way home. After all, Lagos traffic they say, defies logic.

Indeed so many drivers were starting to lose their mind as they often do in the Lagos traffic. Mad drivers suddenly jilting their lanes to compete for space with those in other lanes. The tussle for supremacy of driving skills. Someone shouting obscenities at a driver with braided hair with his head popping out of his side window.

The abused one yelled back at him, wound down her car window and showed him her five left fingers spread abusively at him. She stuck out her tongue at him too and wound up hurriedly as he rolled saliva in his mouth ready to spit at her.

I shook my head and decided it was much saner to keep listening to Sisi Vero and her sister whose ambivalent responses left me nonplussed.

"You haven't changed much," Sisi Vero commented, "always wanting people to stand up for themselves. And look at you, you look so well. I know you won't say the same thing for me. I have seen how you have been casting glances at my incredible love handles. You must be wondering how I seem to sit tight letting the world pass me by."

"I am glad you know I don't approve of your looks. And I don't want any excuses."

"I wasn't going to offer any. I can't say this is the best I can do in memory of Bero. But the truth is each time I thought of the hard work required to get me into shape, I just curl up in bed and cuddle the pillows to think hard about it. Then I realise that I dream quite often of hitting my target and that act of dreaming, I must tell you, is quite comforting."

"Yea, yea, dream on until you wake up dead from cardiac arrest. But you must know that I can't stand obesity. It doesn't matter if it is a product of grief and comfort eating. Nobody should allow food or anything for that matter to misuse them. What is this? Do you really intend to commit suicide and don't want anyone to know about it? Come on!"

"I definitely won't leave this world alive anyway. Really, I have often fantasized about reuniting with Bero, only I need to be here a little longer to see the kids through their schooling. Now, don't look at me like that, it's only a joke. But seriously, sometimes I have nightmares too, of Bero chasing me away from graves, screaming that I haven't done justice to his memory. And I scream right back telling him to watch out for part two of my makeover since he doesn't seem to like this massive mammal I have become!"

"And have you truly done justice to his memory or even his love, your love? Just because you haven't remarried or let any man come close to you might make you think you are some superhero.

I'll tell you who the superhero is, the Vero who astounds herself by living all her best dreams. That's the Vero I am hoping to see."

"I hear you, big sister. But let us get home first, so I can treat you to something you won't complain about, if only this traffic which is getting intense will let us."

"Hmmm." She seemed to relax for the first time into her seat, "I can't wait to eat the ever delicious *afang* soup with fufu, the way only you can make it."

"For a prodigal sister like you, I should rejoice that you can still summon the taste of our very best native cooking. I wish we were heading straight to Uyo. I have a mind to recommend you to a full month's confinement in the fattening room. It is something that will do good to this your bony frame. You know…"

It happened too quickly. I did not know how it came about. I just saw the Toyota Prado in front of me stall. The Honda Element beside me skidded as two armed boys dived at it. Another three flew across the culvert ahead and surrounded the Prado, their handguns poised to kill. Sudden pandemonium!

"What is going on here?" the Professor asked.

I could have sworn it was members of the Boko Haram movement as some of them had their heads covered. A drop of urine escaped me at the thought of them.

"Who are these people? What do they want?"

"Please Prof, don't say a word. This is not Oxford. These people hate books. Please, please, don't let them kill us!"

"Mr Man, calm down. What is this about? Is this what I think it is!" Her tone was getting jittery.

I saw the Professor discreetly take a telephone out of her bag and perhaps videoing the confrontation. I thought it was very dangerous and even deadly if the guys saw what she was doing. I wanted to ask her to stop but I addressed Sisi Vero instead, "Sisi Vero, please talk to her!" I urged desperately. I was shivering inwardly. I couldn't think properly, but I kept a straight face hoping that since they hadn't come to our car, we might have the slim chance of escaping their vultures' eyes.

Sisi Vero's hands were moving as she spoke under her breath, "Oh my God, not today, not when my sister is in the car! No, she only just came back, God please!" Then she turned to her sister, "I am sorry about this. Stay focussed, okay. Don't aggravate them. Give me some of your money and jewellery!" She took them along with hers and discreetly slid them into a small sack bag which she normally would wear above or inside her undergarments. I have, by mistake, seen that sack bag once. Brown. With a zipper and a rope at both edges which she tied around her waist. It would appear as if the bag itself found a home at her pelvic region, perhaps right atop her pubic hair, I imagined. It was there I sensed she slid the precious items. I hoped the predators did not see her do that. I feared for her life. And ours. And I wondered how I could save her. How I could save the situation.

Strangely, there was now so much space in front of me which I did not quite know what to do with. Those who were honking horns had stopped. I thought of accelerating, but it was clear I couldn't do much as some people in front had left the discomfort of their cars and ran in different directions. The bad boys didn't give all of them a chase. They simply went into some of the abandoned cars and took what pleased them. They still hadn't come to us. I started to think then that they were simply armed robbers, not the dreadful Boko Haram.

Sisi Vero kept saying, "Do only what you have to do! Nothing aggravating please!"

I let the car roll a bit. Then I slammed the brakes as someone tapped at my car window. My heart flipped. I dared not look at him. I did not want whoever it was to think I saw him.

"Will you wind down!" he commanded. His face was uncovered. So was his head. I felt he was looking straight into my eyes, "God," I prayed silently, *"do not let him recognise me!"* Then I thought, *"how could he? But you never can tell."*

"Good idiot! Now move over, let me drive!"

I swallowed hard. More urine escaped me.

He changed his mind, "Stupid traffic. Declare what you have, you all! You, open the door!"

I stiffened. But it was the Professor he was addressing. I wondered where she hid her phone. I prayed for her to forget her knowledge. I could feel my blood pumping excessively. I thought it was the Professor's heart I heard thumping away. Or was it mine? Or perhaps Sisi Vero's.

The door to where the Professor sat, flung open.

"Where is the money? Your jewellery, everything of value you have? Hurry before I waste you!"

"There, in this wallet, take what you need and go away please," the Professor's voice held a tapestry of terror which she tried quite hard to contain.

"Take it from her!" he ordered one of his boys.

The boy's guffaw hit my ears as he said, "Boss. It's iron money! Pounds Sterling! Lots of it! Let's go, we made a good catch!"

I prayed and hoped that would be our relief.

"Don't be silly!" the boss said, reinstituting our nightmare. "No ambition. Check the fat one. Her purse had better be fat too!"

Butterflies in my stomach. I realised it was my heart that was thumping. I knew Sisi Vero had taken out her gold. I knew where she hid them. I knew the bad boys knew where business women in transit hide their fortunes. Butterflies filled my stomach, fluttering.

It was their boss who went over to Sisi Vero. I caught sight of him, a smooth-faced bulky teenager. "Don't play games with me, woman! Surrender those things or I blast your head now!" he bawled.

"Here is my bag. I am just a poor widow," Sisi Vero's voice came in gasps.

"You are poor and you have the flesh belonging to a thousand people! Don't waste my time. I am a busy man!" He ransacked the bag. Not satisfied with what he saw, he bellowed, "You mean none of you women have gold?"

"Since my husband died..." she began.

"Shut up! Untie your wrapper! I want to see and take what you hid there!"

"Who, me?"

"Who else, fatty. Bring it all out! Trust me, you don't want me to go there!" He raised his gun, which looked sophisticated, imposing. I thought I saw fire threatening to go out from it. By this time, the bad boss had his hand below Sisi Vero's stomach. Ugly hand. Intrepid. Probing. Angry, in fact.

I shut my eyes, paralysed with fear.

"My son," came Sisi Vero's unsteady voice, "Will you really go down that winding, deserted road? It's been a long, long time that path was closed. It is a Sahara Desert! Think of the risk of wading through your grandmother's Sahara Desert! We are Africans, my child! But if you must, well then why don't you do me the favour of shooting me first. I need to be home with that long dead husband of mine!"

The cold defiance in her voice terrified me. It was like an uncoiling of a string of madness lodged in the trauma of her story. The recklessness about it assailed me. My eyes flew open in consternation.

He let his hand go further, but then thought better of it. His eyes met mine. I looked away. I heard the gun shot long after it hit someone. I ducked instinctively as did everyone in the car. But the gun wasn't aimed at us. I looked up in time to see who fired the gun, a policeman on a power bike. I had been too scared to see him arrive with other police bikes in tow. A lot of the robbers were taken unawares too. Unnerved, some opened fire, shooting into the air as they took to their heels. Suddenly, the police were everywhere apprehending some of the fleeing rogues.

More gunshots by the police! A couple of them picked up the teenage boss who accosted us. His right hand where he was shot was bleeding. His gun had fallen to the ground.

"Thank you, Prof, for the initial video you posted which went viral. I hope no one is hurt?" the policeman was courteous.

The Prof nodded at the concerned police as my eyes popped out in wonder and appreciation.

But the frantic cries of the teenage boss astonished me more. As they handcuffed him and dragged him away, he yelled, directing attention to Sisi Vero, "Grandma, speak to them please! I am sorry. It is the work of the devil! Please, tell them I didn't go to your Sahara Desert! Please take back everything! Don't keep silent, don't let them take me away!" Strangely, all the power he had wielded earlier had evaporated. In its place, intense terror lodged in his eyes.

Sisi Vero opened her mouth, but no sound came out. She bent

forward and grabbed her face in her palms, muttering, "Son, go with them. May God grant you the contrition you need!"

Her sister placed a hand on her shoulder. I turned to look at the Prof, the smile that played on her thick lips was rosy as we drove home covered in weighty silence.

CHAPTER EIGHTEEN

Back Home

Monica Arac de Nyeko

The night has been calm, perhaps too calm for your liking. Day is peeling herself away from the dark, shifting the minutes forward. You are worn out with the fear of return. It's been a long time. Nothing has changed. You have not seen your relations for many years. You are not sure who is dead and who still lives. You stopped taking count. The numbers were too high. Bad news never stopped coming. Sometimes you tried to think of the good memories. They were few and could not make you laugh anymore.

You have gotten yourself in the seat by the bus window. You want to see the green and plant it into your mind. Those will be memories of the road you will never use again. You have been saving money for over two years from your pay at Britannia, the Indian biscuit factory. You knew that one day you would have to make this decision to travel up north. Your bag is under the bus boot and is filled with everything you could get your hands on. There is salt. There is soap. With the war, they have become impossible to get. There is the much-loved dried tilapia. The most needed clothes are also stuffed into your travelling bag. There is something for everybody. They are expecting you. You sent word two weeks ago that you were coming back home to them.

This night as you packed your bags to return to the place from which you once fled, you should have been eaten-up with excitement. You have missed home. The laughter with the other village girls as you flirted with the dry season. The baths in the river when she let her banks burst. The cold rights when the moon was high and you trapped *ngwen*. The sunflower stems in the weeded fields searching for a smile in the sun's face. The lustful nights at the *aguma* dances. Revered Janani's Sunday worship drumbeat the next day, summoning the brethren to the word.

You still remember a little how it used to be. Perhaps ten years back. The road from Pugak all the way to Agoro carried great legends and folktales of once upon a time. There was no pain in belonging. No pity in people's eyes when you said you come from the Acoli tribe. Your relations, uncles and aunts, grandparents and great grandparents called you *nyarwa* – our daughter and their eyes lit up at the sight of the brand-new Bata sandals you pulled out from the paper bags. The second-hand clothes delighted their eyes. Those were all fruits of your monthly labour at Wii Gweng P7 School where you were a teacher. It all seems like a tale of yore now. Those things that seemed natural only a while ago. Those thoughts that made you smile and stare into the morning with a steady, unruffled gaze. Those moments which nurtured your longings and hatched your hopes.

The morning gains peace. The bus park is buzzing with life every passing minute. Everyone you see outside has their head held high. They have so much life in them. They never dread the cry of the owl that brings terrible news. They lived according to undeclared codes: "everyone for themselves-and God for us all." This is Kampala. Welcome to the city of seven hills. Like these drivers, who for a day's wage and a few more shillings, honk, call and encourage passengers to enter their vehicles till their voices go hoarse and their ears deafen from the sound of their own tunes.

"Come to my bus. Oh, look how beautiful it is. Express. Express service, via Masindi. I take you direct, no breakdown, for only 10,000 shillings! Hey, hey, hey, beautiful, enter. Don't go there…"

You wonder why the drivers choose to work on their route. Delivering passengers to those places whose music harps with refrains off smoking barrels. Places where foliage stinks of deserted reason. Most of them are so young and full of life. They probably have children who are barely two-years-old. Why should they risk all that? But they are just like you. Making decisions with questions unanswered. Living life as it ought to be lived. Taking two steps back, one forward, two back and then hearing the sound of breaking... *pooom* and the other cringing sound of trying to cling to things collapsing under the weight of the current.

Yes, current. As it commands you on and slouches upon you its weight, you sense mirth at the end of this day. You will see Akena at last. He never forgave you for leaving Mucwini like a bullet darting from a gun. You coiled into his arms that night after choir practice. You asked him to walk you home even when the moon was high and you would have been okay by yourself. You let his warmth into you as you held him so close and called his name. When you left, you turned him into a promise of loneliness, like his name, Akena – "Alone". You wrapped him into a wish, surrendering to solitude. His eyes were fixed on the road. Just as it had taken you away from him, he trusted it to bring you back. That bus to the city of seven hills too. The one that spat gravel into his eyes and disappeared behind a cloud of dust chanting, two steps back, one forward, two back... *pooom pooom pooom...*

The days came and went thereafter with no assurance of your return. That feeling, which Akena had the day that you left grew bigger and bigger. He began to think that perhaps he should have held you tighter and given you an embrace so warm, like a promise that actually becomes fulfilled. Perhaps he should have seen that moment as only a memory of *yaa*-dark – the colour of your face.

The freedom fighters – men with guns under their arms – came from the forests in the weeks, months, maybe years following that day at the bus park and that *yaa* memory. They got Akena seated by the roadside. His hair was matted into a lock, which mimicked the knotting thoughts in his head. He was seated by that same road which beckons travellers to Kampala with its meandering charm, as if the only reason it was paved was to seduce and steal warmth from the embrace of the youth and lovers. It was a hot day and the sun refused to beat down softer, as if it had quarrelled with its mother. That was also the day that the song in Akena's head brought the lure of surrender with it – too tempting to resist. As steadily as the night descends upon day, the desire to speak the truth possessed him.

"Ai maa doo. Allah! Allah! Allah! Allah!

The sun's gaze weakened upon the day. He told the men what only someone who wanted a bloodstained shroud over his eyes could possibly provoke. That they were a bunch of lousy arse-holes who had given the tribe a savage face. That they were not fighting for anything but their lousy penises which wanted to fuck people's wives and daughters in the name of liberation and freedom. That they had made the otherwise fucked-up government look good. That they should all go and fuck their mothers whose wombs had borne curses upon the Acoli people.

One-two-two-one-two... poom

As his forefathers and those before them beckoned him, as the rat-tat-tat of the barrel sounded a solemn cry into his head, he carried into his final surrender the colour of *yaa*, and your voice, which had whispered to him that night: saying:

"I have to leave. Come with me. We shall be okay in Kampala, where the day never ends and the future is void of tinted pasts."

"Lamunu, I can't, this is home," he said.

"Akena, please!"

"The war will end one day... and when it does, someone has to be here to pick up the pieces."

"Yes, someone; it does not have to be you. Look, everyone is leaving. Some have even gone as far as Kenya and Tanzania. We are only going to Kampala," you said to him, almost shouting.

You hated the way his voice sounded. Like it was his duty to clean up the floor after the whole of Mucwini had shitted upon it.

"Yes, but I..." he started and stopped. He had lost his words.

Both of you sat in a silence as painful as a wound throbbing with pus. The burning upon your chest started as if someone was fanning a fire. He did not have to say it. You sensed it. Your harvest was gone and your *Kraal* was breaking. But you managed to speak to him again with a voice that hid the dryness in your throat.

You said, "Akena, I am sorry! I am not going to sit here and wait to die..."

There was silence again as he let your voice sink deeper into his silence. When he tried again to call your name, his words were long gone; they were headed for the enchanted Karuma waterfalls where only those voices and their fate are sealed to go and to dance to the songs of bewildered spirits.

The bus is filling up fast. It will be on its way soon. Even if your husband, whom you met in Kampala comes home and discovers your absence, you will be miles away. The turn boys are packing things on top and calling out for passengers. Sometimes they want to pack the bus, till people are on top of one another like potato sacks headed for a busy market day. Everyone seems to be engrossed in their own thoughts. You are also trying to capture your demons and think of the good and joy that your return will bring. Amidst your eagerness, there is still doubt in your mind. You are still not very sure that it was the right decision to make to return and if that decision was any good for your two sons seated quietly beside you. Your hands are shaking. Isaac, your five-year-old and eldest son, asks you what is wrong.

"*Gin mo peke*" you say in Acoli and quickly asks him if he wants you to buy him the toffee sweets the eager vendor is displaying at the bus window.

He says no and gets back to playing with his plastic toy.

The bus finally fills up. The journey is going to be long, at least seven hours. Some people are standing. Some people are seated. Some are on the bus floor with hardly any space to move a hand. None of that hassles you. You came in early and got the three seats at the end of the bus where no one would bother you much. The bus starts to drive out of the park very slowly through the park city traffic. The noise of hooting vehicles and drivers cursing goes on for a while. It starts to gradually lessen as the bus leaves the most crowed areas. Your eyes shift from scene to scene and person to person. There are the perfect houses, smartly dressed women and cars that look like they have just landed from Dubai. This is a part of town in which you have not lived. Those you left at home probably think you have been living like the people you are seeing on the streets now. Taking huge strides to air-conditioned offices. Eating lunch from fast-food restaurants, celebrating first-kiss anniversaries and getting entangled in this world of dreams that you only see when you imagine yourself living their perfect lives.

If only you could seduce yourself to sleep, your knee joints would not complain so hard, you imagine. As always, sleep is proud. Your headache wants to start again. The bus gains great speed when it has made its way completely out of the city. You can feel its wheels bumping at your buttocks over every pothole. The further you draw away from the city, the less cosy it looks. The scene rolls past the outskirts of Kampala. Tin-made and half-collapsed mud houses. You feel you know the people living there. You have met them, dined with them and flown with the same current. Low-paying jobs at Indiana factories. Zero medicines and death at Mulago hospital. Owino market with her cheap curry-powder and voodoo merchandise to cure syphilis, AIDS, ditched lovers and those deprived of fortune…

Your sons stare into your eyes from time to time. They are not speaking as much as they usually do. They probably sniff fear in your breath. They have never been to Mucwini. They have only heard of home and of Uncle Sabitti. They were born here in Kampala, where everyone comes to seek refuge from poverty, boredom and their own shadows.

This Kampala. It sounds so different when you hear of it from afar. Before you came, many people said it was huge and you could be anything. You could become a breeze or a beautiful jinni like the ones from the Tanzanian coast, meet a wealthy expatriate at Just Kicking Pub, marry him, have mixed-race kids called Katrina or Foster. People said Kampala was also dangerous. The clock never stops ticking and you could disappear like a sesame pod in grass. They said you had to mind your own business like everyone else or get a broken nose on account of staring at the ladies of the night behind Speak Hotel.

When you came, the city was huge and life was as tough as those frozen cowhides that are stored in the industrial warehouse near Britannia. Kampala had landlords who did not understand the lingo of "Please, Sebo, next month." There were Indian bosses at Britannia who paid you 80 shillings for packing a whole box of biscuits after burning your hands on those hotplates till they looked like soot. Oh, and the doctors who called your headaches and nightmares, "post-traumatic blah blah blah" and said you should get 'psychosocial' something and that will cost 15 US dollars after a discount.

"Excuse me, did you say um… dollars?"

"Yes, madam, owing to the depreciation of the Ugandan shilling…"

You told Kyazze, your husband about it. You begged him to get you some miracle dollars to cure your ailment. He laughed; his nose grew bigger and he simply said, "*Maa ato!*"

Kyazze-bolingo-yasolo. Even if it sounds more Congolese Lingala than Uganda, he says that is what his name is. Everyone calls him Kyazze in short. You used to mind when he shouted at you and called you a good-for-nothing bitch who should get out of his house because he was bored stiff with your missionary style. That was when your desire for him burnt hot like your Ma's charcoal stove. That was also about the time he found you at the street corner when you just arrived in Kampala. He told you that you did not belong there. He did not come from your tribe. You knew people back home would not approve. But who would bother about what tribe the man was from that you coiled up to every night, when you had a roof over your head? Kyazze got you a job in Britannia, where he worked, when no school would take you as a teacher. Those squint-eyed bosses at Britannia were cruel, aye! They cut your pay for resting for a minute from the biscuit-packing stand. Everyone said Indians were like that. That if you had come to Britannia expecting anything less, then you must have a loose nut in your head or something. You reconciled what your fate had chosen and tried to make the best of it. Besides, it was worth it. You hid stolen biscuits from the night shift under your skirt and in your knickers and sold them in the market. Kyazze learnt about this and asked you to give him all those shillings.

"That is not going to happen," you said.

He realized after ten minutes of threats and coaxing that you were firm on this stance. When he didn't have his way with you he interpreted it as a deliberate insult to his shortness. He held your head between his two hands and banged it one, two, three times on the floor. The taste of fresh blood-scarlet, like the memories in your head-filled your mouth and nose as your head rested upon the floor when he finally left you for unconscious. You were not unconscious but you could not move for a while. You had been unconscious only once. That had been the first time and that was many years ago. You cried loudly and the neighbours rushed in, threatening to break down the door if he did not let them in. These days they barely notice.

"Why do you stay unless you like it?" everyone asks you, as if deciding to leave is something as easy as picking which bunch of oranges to buy.

Later, with barely enough strength to shift your legs, you sat yourself up. You hugged your sons that night. They cried with you as you rocked them to and fro. They too had tasted scarlet in their mouths a time too many. They knew how it felt like to have your head on that concrete floor.

"Very soon, very soon, we are going home to Mucwini," you said.

Kyazze works the night shift at Britannia. He does not return home till eight o'clock in the morning. By the time he would come back you would be long gone.

All through this journey the bus has been quiet. Your boys have been asleep. Myron, the youngest, has his head on your lap. As the bus sails away on the tarmac road, you pat his hair and hum the lullaby you sang to him when he was born.

Mama yela
Mama yela
Mama disturbs me
Mama disturbs me

He was born at the time you heard rumours of peace. Everyone danced and partied. The labour pains started as soon as the Radio Uganda announcer finished the sentence. You thought of home. The good memories and what everything would be like. Young boys and girls would dance to *aguma* and *larakaraka* in the night again. There would be cows in the *dwols*. Ai Ma!

Mama yela
Mama yela
The nurse placed your little baby boy into your waiting arms.

You stared into his face. There he was, staring back at you. He waved his little arms in the air, as if knowing his birth coincided with a time of ripening hope.

You bit your lips and held him to your chest. The name you had first heard from a missionary woman came to your mind. She had come to Mucwini to visit the congregation there. In one of her sermons, she said that 'Myron' means 'sweet-scented oil', something like sunflower oil that had been smiled upon by abundant sun. You had been in the sunflower fields yourself before the harvest came and as the preacher spoke, you realized that there was always the lingering concern of low yields with sunflowers. Good seeds were hard to come by and without good seeds the prospect of sweet-scented oil did not mean much. The Greek preacher carried on with her sermon. To her, this was a sermon about goodness and how it was very much like sunflower oil. To you, it was a name you would give your son one day. When Isaac was born, times were tough. Sunflower yields were low and fields were almost devoid of sunflower stems. The sun was dull. No one tilled the land. With Myron, there was sweetness in every scent. There were plenty of good sunflower seeds. The sun promised to shine abundantly, allowing the stems a blossoming elegance. And yet, with sunflowers, you could never tell, even with the best seed. Similarly, the hope that surrounded Myron's birth did not last, like a water bubble.

Mama yela

Mama yela

After hours of travel, you have arrived in Gulu town. Gulu declares the nearing end of your journey. In less than two-and-half hours you will be home. The town, whose charm is wearing out, tilts towards an uncertain edge on the compass searching for past glory. The streets are filled with people crossing verandas of buildings riddled with bullet holes. You went to school here a long time ago when it was not so grey and hushed. That time, the day did not weep upon people here with petals as crimson as henna. Buses did not need armed convoys to escort them to the next destination.

A few people had been speaking to each other, but as the bus hits the road to Kitgum District where home – Mucwini – is, there is silence. It is a muteness that only those who have been close to the periphery can recognize. The bumps on the road make the bus seem like it won't make the next mile. But it gains speed. This is the most dangerous part to cross. It's also the place where the sight of burnt houses and overgrown compounds starts to make concrete acquaintance with the eye. You become aware of the unusually disruptive squeal of this bus. It is strangely loud and attracts unnecessary attention. The driver is focused on his wheels. One mother holds her baby close. A nun's head is cast down in prayer. Her figures pluck at the rosary beads as they disappear inside her palms. You are thinking of Akena. The thinking of him made Kampala bearable. It should make this part of the journey all right then. It doesn't. You hold your boys tight and close your eyes. When you look out again, the dull sun promises a bright smile at the end of this day. Maybe. The bus carries on with its monotonous chant of two steps back, one forward, two back, *poooom, pooom...*

Then it stops. A window opens. The driver shouts to someone outside. His tone is gay. It tempts courage and a few faces turn towards the outside.

"*Gudune anyim tye nining,*" he asks the lone figure at the side of the road. It's a form of necessary courtesy for those who dare travel this route.

The man does not speak. He wears an old baseball shirt and a pair of faded khaki shorts. His hands are in his pockets. He is at ease in this area where there has been no sign of life for the past fifty miles. To the driver's question, he nods and waves, signalling that the route ahead is okay, almost with a complete lack of interest. The driver thanks him and tosses him a few shillings. The man regards the reward for a while and like an afterthought, he thanks the driver and looks away.

The bus hits the road again. You are relieved but your mind is not at ease. Who was the lone man at the roadside? What was he doing in a place where no sign of human habitation has been sighted.

You are gone barely twenty minutes when you feel the falling glass on your skin from the window before you hear the shattering and pounding of ammunition that follows you down, as you duck under these at, grabbing Myron and Isaac with you. The chant of 'Jesus save us' comes from under one seat. The bus is still moving. Your knees are grinding like a stone has been laid between those joints. Your feet have grown weak; they would not lift you up if you tried.

Myron wakes from his sleep. Your grip is not firm enough on him. He slips and stands up.

"Are those balloons, mummy? He asks.

You grab him back down so hard that you hit his head on the steel bus seat. He lets out a small cry and goes quiet. No one gets up till the bus stops moving altogether. Even then you are not sure what will happen next.

It's a while before people are sure that it's safe to get out from under their seats. The bus has stopped in the city centre where it's safe. The city dwellers are rushing towards it and shouting. You cannot hear what they are saying. You lift out Isaac from under the seat. You make a go for Myron. He stills sleeps. You try to lift him again. There is blood.

"Myron, Myron!" you call out.

He does not wake up. You lift his head up and quickly grab him to your chest. You shake him hard and press him to your chest again and rock.

"Myron, Myron, coo," you beseech him.

He is stuck to your chest. His hands and feet are limp. He is cold too. The people shouting from outside the bus gain momentum, while the people inside the bus are hurrying to get out. You squeeze through along with them, making for the door to the outside of the bus, crowded with eager people looking for particular faces. Your eyes cloud and shivering repeatedly, he engulfs and then let's go of you. You want to get Myron some fresh air. You want to shake him till he wakes up from his sleep. You miss a step leading out of the bus. You crash down with him.

"*Maa Do!*" you cry.

People are talking about this unfortunate incident, which is the first ambush in several months. You try to lift Myron. You start to crawl between feet that have formed of fortress. A woman from the crowd bends over to you. She asks you to give her the boy. Other people are working quickly inside the bus to get the injured out. You do not pay the woman any attention. You resume your crawl, but this time you can't even crawl. Myron is getting too heavy for you. The woman repeats her plea.

"He is asleep. All he needs," you say, "is cold water on his face. It gets him out of his sleep."

You press Myron to your chest again. A woman steps forward. She persuades you to hand over Myron. You don't hand him over, but you are too weak to protest.

"I have to get home. I have to go home. The water there is cold enough to wake Myron," you cry.

People are coming from all over town to where the bus is. They want to know if their relatives are inside. A discovery is met by their deafening walls.

"Why did you return to us like this. Why? Why?"

Uncle Sabitti has been waiting for you each day since you sent that letter. He has been coming to town and waiting for the bus every evening. As soon as he arrives at the scene, he walks around searching for you. Isaac is seated beside you. His hands hold yours, urging you to reassure him. The crowd has made a clearing where you are seated. Uncle Sabitti notices you. He comes towards you and kneels beside you. He takes your hand into his then slowly wraps you in an embrace.

"I want to go home. Take me home,' you say.

You start to cry, like those years back when the girls at school called you names and he held you in his arms and told you that you should never worry what those children said to you because they were not good enough to even hold your bag. Now he is whispering to you, almost in the same voice. He is saying he has been waiting for you. Later, maybe he will find the words to let you know the men from the forest with guns under their arms came again and there is no one else at home but him because when they came he had travelled to the city to buy some quinine for his wife.

He rubs your sore back. He senses something has gone terribly wrong with this trip. Isaac holds your hand. He has been crying too. He has your shyness and voice. Uncle Sabitti thinks, with water in his eyes. You are thinking of the last time when your two sons looked so at peace seated quietly beside you. At that time, there had almost been an assurance of sweetness in every scent and some sunflower oil at the end of the day.

CHAPTER NINETEEN

Exchanging the Crown Someday for Exile

Faustin Kagame

Kalira was a beautiful woman, possibly the most beautiful of her time. She was born poor and when of marrying age was promised to a young man of similar social status. Their marriage was celebrated as it should be according to their social standing, the best they could.

Kalira was cherished by her husband and blessed with his love. One day, her husband said to his younger brother, "I would like to find you a spouse in case a disease kills all our cows, leaving us with nothing to pay the dowry."

The younger brother did not share this view, saying, "We own so few cows and you have such a beautiful wife, worthier than our misfortune. If you find me a wife, we will have to share our meagre cattle.

Kalira would have to share the milk that she now drinks alone with my wife. She will wither and her complexion will turn ashy. We will be mocked and people will say that you have married a woman whom we are not able to support. They will even try to take her away from us, pretending that we are not able to give her a decent life," he said.

Thus the brothers agreed together and for a time, day in, day out, they continued to provide for the beautiful and kind Kalira until destiny became a factor.

One day, Prince Rujugira embarked on a hunting expedition in the area where Kalira and her husband lived. During his trip, the

Prince decided to rest under the shade of an acacia tree, not far from the entry to their courtyard. Prince Rujugira was hungry and thirsty but his servant had no more food in reserve.

As a way to forget his fatigue and suppress his appetite, the Prince filled his pipe and gave his servant the order to go and find him fire in the neighbourhood.

At this time, accompanied by his brother, Kalira's husband had left to move their cows to the summer pastures. At the entrance of the compound where Kalira, her husband and brother-in-law lived, the Prince's servant saw young calves jumping about in the courtyard, having knocked over the fence that kept them inside the cowshed. The young woman trying to calm them down was under pressure. When she brought one cow back into the stable, two or three others ran through the opening and played in the open air.

The amused servant watched this game before he decided to help her. After many attempts, the two calmed down the small herd. They put fodder in the mangers and could finally sit down. Kalira asked the traveller where he was coming from? He told her that he was the servant of Prince Rujugira who sent him to fetch fire for his pipe. "Before you leave, let me thank you for your assistance," Kalira said.

The man followed her inside the house. Kalira offered him milk in a jar. Having quenched his thirst, he went back to his master. On seeing him return, the Prince asked him what made him stay away so long.

"What made me stay away so long, my Prince? You might have brought it back with you if you had gone in my place," the servant said.

"So what special thing have you seen?" asked the Prince.

The servant told the Prince how, in the nearby house, he found an exceptionally beautiful and kind young woman. He described her with an enthusiasm that left no detail untouched. The account so affected the Prince that he forgot his hunger and weariness. He sent his servant back to Kalira with the mission of gaining her hospitality so they could take some rest from the hot sun.

"Go back and tell him that I will be pleased to shelter him," the young Kalira answered.

And so Prince Rujugira and Kalira greeted each other, but only through the entrance to the house where Kalira was out of sight in semi-darkness. They talked without seeing each other. While the Prince was desperate to look at her, Kalira wondered what to do. She might have offered milk to anyone else. But to a King's son? Would he accept? Rujugira wanted to see her as much as Kalira hesitated on what was the appropriate thing to do.

Things went on that way as they talked, until Rujugira said: "I would like to say goodbye and thank you. Your company and hospitality have been so overwhelming. I will send you a present. But to this end, you have to show me your face. I must recognise you. You will tell me your name and that of your husband. My messenger must know these details."

"I accept what you want but I also want to ask something," she answered.

Kalira dressed herself the best way she could and stepped out, joining the Prince in the doorway. He stood up and they greeted each other properly. Rujugira kept her in his arms. Each time Kalira went to move out of his hug so as to reach back into the semi-darkness of the house, the Prince held her tighter.

"Stay here so that we could talk to each other face to face and if you go back inside your hut, we will have to go in together," he said.

Finding no words, Kalira finally consented and sat beside the man who enjoyed watching her.

In all his life, his eyes had never captured such a lovely sight. Better, never had his heart felt such love – a real love at first sight. As for Kalira, she guessed the feeling that she caused in the heart of the Prince.

"You see, I did what you asked me to do. I would now like to offer you the milk of my cows. I possess nothing else. If it does not taste good for you, do not feel at all obliged to drink it," she said.

Kalira went back into the hut. She poured out the milk and offered it to the Prince. So as to comfort her and put her at ease, he said to her, "Let us drink from the same pot, you are my equal." Kalira accepted. They handed the milk pot to each other in turns. Rujugira then asked for three servants to be called and sent them to three chiefs in the neighbourhood who were asked to send a portable chair. They carried this message: "The Prince felt sick during the travel and requires assistance." The porters were found and the chair availed. Before the arrival of the porters, Kalira's husband and brother-in-law returned from moving their cattle. As they came near the house, they saw a crowd in front of the entrance. They entered their compound with caution, asking what misfortune or wonder had suddenly happened to them. They were told that Rujugira was there. They bowed to the Prince. They approached Kalira and greeted her. At that precise moment, the porters arrived with the chair Rujugira requested.

"Put the chair down and go into the house. Bring the person that you will find near the fireplace; we will go as soon as the sun gets mild." As they heard these words, Kalira and her husband were shocked. The porters went into the house with the chair. Kalira was carried away, tearful, broken-hearted, imagining how her poor husband must feel.

Rujugira waited to see Kalira on the adjoining hilltop. He spoke to the man from whom he had just taken a wife. "I offer you a herd of two times eight as well as land. Live there and find yourself another woman. I will not bring back that one to you!" The husband refused. Deciding to lodge a complaint, he went to the court the next day at daybreak. The court was located near Kamonyi, where King Mazimhaka, father of the abductor, was presiding.

When the Prince arrived home, he invited all the King's children, brothers and sisters and his friends to celebrate the wedding. When the assembly was complete, Rujugira said, "On this blessed day, I found myself a fiancée very dear to my heart. That is why I gathered you, so that you may be my witnesses and that we rejoice together."

The evening was magnificent. The girls and the women gathered around Kalira and the young boys and the men gathered in the main living room with Rujugira till daybreak. The "unveiling" ceremony was considered to honour his new wife. At the end of the rites, everyone went back home. Rujugira remained alone with his conquest and the wedding concluded.

Some days later, a messenger came to tell Rujugira to be present at the Court of the King. He had been summoned. Rujugira went immediately. He was welcomed by a torrent of reproaches. How dare he behave in this way and abuse his status as Prince to snatch a wife from her legitimate husband?

The Prince begged for mercy from his father. The King spoke to Kalira's husband, who was inconsolable.

"Rather than depriving me of this woman, do offer this man the fiancée that you chose for me, but please let me keep the wife that the gods designated to my heart. I have to add that, to my rival, I offered to give him sixteen cows," the Prince pleaded.

"Can you accept sixteen cows? You will choose a spouse among the girls here present at my court or somewhere else if you know of any. I will marry her to you and give you herds and lands. Thus you will be compensated for the woman that Rujugira took from you," the King said.

Kalira's husband refused categorically, saying, "Sir, keep all these marvels but give me back my wife."

King Mazimhaka began to wonder how it could be that there was a woman for whom grown-up men may quarrel with such passion. He ordered that she be brought. Rujugira asked that she be dressed in new clothes to make her look beautiful and that she be carried to the Court. As soon as the King saw her, he was overwhelmed by her beauty. He had never seen someone like her in his life. To the husband and his son, he said, "The King only may possess such a fiancée, I take her from you two."

Speaking to the King, Kalira's first husband said, "I have no choice then, I leave her to you. But tell me, what will happen to me, what will be my fate?"

"I offer you herds of cows, estates and to organise your wedding, but you did not agree." "Now, I agree."

He was given all of these and he became a Lord.

As for Rujugira, he did not go back with Kalira who joined the King's women's quarters. Aggrieved and tormented, Prince Rujugira stopped eating. He could not sleep for Kalira constantly occupied his mind. He brooded over his pain, over and over. Seeing this, some court nobles approached King Mazimhaka.

"Robbing your son is taboo," they said."Killing him with sadness is horrific."

"I did not want to make anyone jealous that is why I took her from both of them," the King answered unconvincingly.

"This is not fair. One went back home with a spouse, estates and herds. As for Rujugira sorrow is his only companion. Do not torment your child."

The husband gave up.

"Give to the Prince what belongs to him," the nobles implored of the King.

Having no answer, the King followed the advice of the wise men. He sent Kalira back to his son. She went back in a bridal procession and a new wedding was celebrated. There was a deal: Kalira had to pay a "visit" to her father-in-law from time to time. After those visits she came back with plenty of gifts. The King was so overwhelmed that among his kinsmen, Rujugira became his father's favourite. He finally inherited Kalinga the royal drum, becoming the official heir of the Kingdom.

Having shared King Mazimhaka's bed and being married to Rujugira, the future King, Kalira was nicknamed "Rwabami," the Lady-of-Kings. She was overwhelmed beyond belief, receiving more favours than all the court's ladies combined. To Rujugira, she gave a son called Sharangabo, the ancestor of the people called Abasharangabo, a clan that prospers to this day. She also gave him a daughter called Mulikanwa.

Despite the fact that Rujugira was officially promised his father's throne, his sick jealousy forces him into exile. The cause? While the King was away, Rujugira found himself in the royal court ladies quarter. When he tried to leave, a royal bull blocked the passage, refusing to move. Frightened that his father might find him, Rujugira had no other choice but to kill the bull with a spear.

A terrible precedent justified the Prince's fear. Under the same circumstances, King Mazimhaka had killed Prince Musigwa and he became submerged in remorse and grief but inspired to write a memorial poem to the son killed by his own hands, which poem he titled:

No More Will I Love.
No more will I love
My love does not love to be loved
Instead of love, everything, everything slips through my hands
In order to vanish away towards Kamagoma
Loving what may not love you
Like rain watering the forest

Knowing his father's temper, Rujugira rushed home and told Kalira. "There is only one thing we can do. We must take the road to exile."

Kalira quickly took her son Sharangabo and his younger sister Mulikanwa. She collected honey in a calabash as well as tobacco. She took two sticks for working a fire, a pipe with no spout and a small piece of wood and put everything in a basket. She then sent for Ndabaramiye, the faithful servant living in Gihinga near Ruzege (where his descendants still live today). Once in Bihembe near Rugalika, Prince Rujugira said, "I am thirsty." His wife, mocking, said to him,"Already?" But how can water be found in this forest?"

She took the honey from the basket and served him. Rujugira drank and sighed. "A small amount of tobacco would not harm me at all." Kalira took some from the basket and handed it to him. "What will I do without a pipe now? With this piece of wood it will not fit." And so Kalira took the piece of wood, worked it and from it made a beautiful pipe spout. Ndabaramiye took the small sticks for fire-making.

He rubbed with his hands and lit the Prince's pipe. Once the break ended, they walked again. Bound for the east, towards the Bugesera and the Gisaka.

II

At the Royal Court of Rwanda, the King passed away. The ritual of the coronation of the successor of Yuhi IV followed. Karemera Rwaka was to become King. But the name Karemera had never been heard among the royal names. It is Ruganzu Ndoli who brought him back from exile in the Karagwe of the Bahinda where Karamera Ndagara was born to Ruhashyampunzi. The latter had hidden, protected and educated him. As a sign of recognition, Ruganzu promised to include him among the Rwandan royal names. Once installed on the throne, Karemera was struck with blindness. Everybody then shouted: "The drum struck him down. It is proof that the crown was not meant for him!"

The Aides Council convened and concluded that Rujugira had to come back because he was his father's rightful heir. Messengers were sent to bring him back. When the news reached him, he immediately cried out; "Never will I come back. My father killed Musigwa just because he spoke to his wife. And I who killed his bull... are you taking me for an idiot?" The messengers plotted. They decided to kidnap Kalira and bring her back. They successfully led Kalira, Ndabaramiye the servant, and the two children into a trap. They brought them back to Kamonyi, leaving Rujugira alone in exile.

Back in Rwanda, Kalira suffered from the plague. She was offered a place to rest in Kivumu near Mpush (a place that was then so called alluding to "*bihushi*" or plague pustules). She settled there and was treated. After recovering, she came back to Kamonyi and was asked to prepare her best perfumes and send some to Rujugira as a proof of love. Ndabaramiye the faithful servant was sent. He did not forget to cover his clothes with Kalira's perfumes. Rujugira hugged him and cried out.

"This perfume is unique. It belongs to nobody else, it comes from Kalira." Interrupted in the middle of "*Igisoro*," a traditional Rwandan board game, Prince Rujugira stood up and followed the messenger. The grains, known as "*ubusoro*" which were used as pawns in the tactical Igisoro, remained in his hand. Ndabaramiye distracted the Prince, speaking about his wife, leading him up to the ford of Busoro (thus named in the future in remembrance to the grains "*Ubusoro*" that slipped out of the Prince's hand along the way).

Rujugira's suspicions could not resist the ploy. Instead of alerting him, the scheming of his wife and of the envoys simply touched him. She was crying out and wanted to see him again. He threw the rest of the grains into the river. He came back and took up his father's throne under the name of Cyilima. A group of royal traditional guardians known as Abiru came to see Kalira. There was then a ban forbidding anyone who escaped in the company of his wife to come back with her. Either she stayed in exile or she was scarified on return. The royal traditional guardians made Kalira "drink" as people called it then. They made her drink a poisoned beverage.

Informed of the death of his wife and full of sadness, Rujugira exclaimed, "There is no such thing as complete purity !"

King Cyilima II Rujugira, the hero in this story ruled until around 1708. After his death, his body was provisionally buried in a Gaseke, in the region of Rukoma. His temporary burial lasted two centuries up to 1932. The traditions meant that a King with the dynastic name of Cyilima could not be buried except under the reign of a Mutara III Rudahigwa – the seventh generation after Cyilima II Rujugira. Later, in 1969, the body of Cyilima II Rujugira was exhumed and sent to the Central Africa Museum at Tervueren in Belgium, where it underwent scientific tests.

CHAPTER TWENTY

In Astove of the Seychelles

Wendy Day Veevers-Carter

Mark did become more restless and frustrated by the limits Remise imposed, not least on his turtle project and in the end we did leave Remise for a larger island.We turned in the lease of Remise and signed one for 99 years, subject to two review periods for Astove, abandoning our new house and all our work to start again. Because Astove was so far from Mahe, the capital of the Seychelles Islands, we sold the France: it would be cheaper to use others' bottoms than to maintain and crew our own. Instead we had a trimaran built cheaply in Hong Kong to use as a fast boat for emergencies.

Rory was eight, Ming six and Digby just eleven-months-old when we boarded the vessel which would take us, our labourers and all their possessions and ours and livestock to this distant island to the south, hundred miles from Aldabra and closer to Madagascar than to Mahe.

Were we crazy? Looking back, I suppose we were. But we were thoroughly hooked on island life and on the turtle project – and Astove was famous for its turtles. That it was also famous for its mosquitoes deterred us no more than the extra hundreds of miles. Its size (1200 acres instead of 62), its big lagoon and its greater fertility far outweighed its disadvantages in our eyes; furthermore, a "government boat" – the Nordvaer – had began to "service" the outer islands and would provide something like regular if infrequent communication, more reliable than the old sailing schooners.

We even overcame the first serious setback to our plans: a government moratorium on the catching of green turtles in Seychelles waters. Collecting eggs, raising hatchlings, freeing them over the reef – all this was also banned, in spite of the likely conservation benefits, as the government believed any such "management" would provide a loophole for illegal activity. Government control, of course, was light to non-existent in the outer islands, but the law looked like progress on the statute books and international conservation organizations were complimentary. We went back to fishing, copra production and livestock. At least we had more room and better soil, in pockets: Astove had been a productive guano island and there was plenty left.

With the help of our second-hand tractor, landed gingerly over the reef with its wheels in two wobbly pirogues, we were able to collect coconuts husked dans bois by the trailer-full and haul building stone (raised reef rock) from distant parts of the island inherited. Meanwhile, the fishermen fished successfully in waters less exploited than the Amirantes.

We also had a bit of luck. A Kenyan company wanting to offer an air connection to Mahe from East Africa looked at the map. Astove, 500 miles from both Mombasa and Mahe would make a good refueling stop for the small planes they used. Could we provide an airstrip? We could and did. A beacon was brought down and installed and barrels of avgas supplied and we were paid for landing. It was only as a stop-gap until the airport in Mahe was completed for large planes and we weren' t paid much. But the flights meant better communications; things seemed to be going pretty well.

This was also the time of Ian Smith's rebellion in Rhodesia and the Royal Navy ships patrolling the Madagascar Channel used to call in occasionally for some R&R. The children watched their first Zodiacs negotiating the surf on our reef, not always successfully and their first cricket matches. "Have you any old sports equipment we might have?" Mark asked, thinking he'd teach us and all the islanders to play. But he forgot the naval penchant for nicknames; one of the young officers, grining broadly, brought ashore a huge tin full of condoms. Our nanny took advantage of this supply, we later discovered, in her affair with one of the married men.

The East African Marine and Fisheries Research vessel, the Manihine, also started visiting us and the Linblad Explorer on its way to or from Aldabra and the ships of the Mombasa-based Bamburi Cement Company sometimes called in on their way from Mauritius in order to wait at Astove – no port charges – for the right tide in Mombasa. We began to feel we were definitely on the map as we had never been in Remise.

The visitors made it easy for Mark, when two teeth of his flared up and little Ming also had tooth trouble and declared he'd hop on the next boat for Mombasa and go to the dentist. He and Ming left on the Manihine one day in March 1970, the boys and I waving cheerfully from the beach.

Ten days later, the Bamburi Cement boat stopped by and two of its young German officers came ashore. They stood in front of me, stiffly. "We have bad news," they said, and stopped. "How bad?" I asked, thinking of my aging mother. "As bad as it can be," one of them said. "Your husband is dead."

One says some pretty idiotic things at such moments. "Will you have some tea?" I asked.

"We have come to take you to Mombasa. The British High Commissioner is looking after your little girl. You must come with us."

I thought, I can't just leave. The men's rations. How soon will I get back? We have no manager. Who can I leave in charge? And Mark-dead? "Why-how-how did he?" I asked.

"We believe, at the denist," one of them said, and the other, "Yes, it was at the dentist."

"I need two hours. There is much to do."

"You must hurry. We must leave by six, for the tide."

Mark had had what is known as an anaesthetic accident in the dentist's chair. The death certificate read "cardiac arrest." By the time I reached Mombasa, he had already been buried. The first thing Ming asked me was "where is Fafa (as the children called him)?" and I had to say, "He is dead."

Ming seemed almost relieved. "I wondered and wondered but

no one would say anything. I thought he had just gone away and left me." Then she cried.

Adjustments are made very slowly. I kept expecting Mark to appear and explain the mistake.

Of course I had to return to the island. All our people were waiting there and could not be abandoned. Everything we owned was on the island. In any case, after a death you cling to the life you led together. I was even determined to carry on. My mother, who flew out to Mombasa at the news, was astonished at such foolishness. "I am not returning to America without you," she declared; and my position was not a strong one since I had so little money. We compromised. I would find someone in Kenya to act temporarily as manager and he, my mother, and I would return to the island with the children for as long as it would take me to teach him the ropes and hand over. This period seemed very long to my mother, who hated island life as much as I loved it and she was very short with me and the children. When the time came to leave the island, Gigby, aged four, flung himself to the ground and held onto the vegetation, screaming. It was the only life he'd ever known.

We went back to the United States for a while, then returned to Astove where I experimented with several more managers, like-minded people who thought island life ideal – in the abstract. Finally Harry Stickley, a radio ham who had been working on Aldabra, asked to come for the low salary I could offer. I found a small cottage to rent in England, got the children into schools and with Harry's help ran the island by radio. Harry seemed fine with the isolation and the *Eclat* in the ham world his island bulletins gave him; on the other hand the constant stream of complaints and reported confrontation that he passed on about the labourers was worrying.

I decided I had to sort things out in person. At the start of a school holiday I placed the children with various friends, flew to Nairobi, got to Mahe, found a yacht willing to take me as a passenger to Astove, wait for me there for at least two days, then drop me in the Comoros Islands on its way to South Africa. From the Comoros Islands I could fly back to Nairobi, England and the children.

This complex arrangement worked until we ran into the edge of a Mauritius-centred cyclone which cost us four days of battering under bare poles off the coast of northern Madagascar. After that, I was able to spend a few hours on Astove listening to both Harry and the labourers and I still missed the plane connection in the Comoros. Then, once back in England, I got news that "the men" had burned Harry's house down, not with him in it fortunately: the trouble appeared irreversible and everyone was leaving on the *Nordvaer*.

I was still wriggling on the hook of "our island" however, when the government abruptly changed. The new power instituted a policy of get tough with low-income producing expatriates and gave me a year to "invest 10,000 pounds or we cancel your lease." I had already been trying to entice investors, with the aid of the German "island agents" Boehm and Vladi, into some joint enterprise involving tourism or sport fishing but after the coup they got cold feet. "Let's see what happens when things settle down," was the general opinion. All too soon my year ran out.

Meanwhile, there is always a meanwhile, isn't there? A friend I met in East Africa and had even been engaged to when I met Mark wrote me first, a letter of condolence and then gradually, a lot more letters. He was then based in Nepal creating the country's first national park; his marriage, he told me had failed. He was separated from his wife; there were four children, the youngest the same age as Ming. Cautiously, in view of our commitments, we arranged to see each other on his next home leave.

We have now been happily married for twenty-five years, many of them spent in Indonesia, Burma and Bhutan in the course of John's work in nature conservation for the United Nations. Our marriage has weathered the difficulties inherent in all second marriages involving so many people and the children are all now married themselves with children of their own. We have fourteen grandchildren between us, I think mine still look back on the two island homes with affection and pleasure, and each of them has an independent, even entrepreneurial cast of mind, each with his or her own business. Rory's is an internet-based travel programme, Ming's a large flower and design company and Digby is a sculptor and foundry owner in rural Maine. In their way, they lead adventurous lives, but none of them has ever gone so far "out on a limb" as Mark and I did.

CHAPTER TWENTY-ONE

One Good Turn

Nadya Somoe Ngumi

It was getting dark fast. Faster than she knew she could drive back to base camp.

"Oh! Why did I come out this far?" Stephanie chided herself quietly as she steadied her hands on the steering wheel, fighting back a panic attack, at the same time gently easing the 4x4 truck into fourth gear as she hit a smooth patch on the trail.

The wild landscape of the Chalbi Desert in northern Kenya, untouched and barren was raw in its beauty. Here, a few hundred kilometres inland from Lake Turkana, you get to experience and understand what it is to be alone.

Stephanie, busy tracking a rare desert ant, had lost herself in the silence of the wilderness. She had left the camp early that morning, following the rising sun and a trail of soil dug up by the ants and now daylight was fading and a chill in the air announced the beginning of a cold desert night.

She wasn't too sure, but she guessed she had an hour of driving and in the dark at that, before reaching anywhere near civilization.

"Well, at least I got what I came for," she said to herself, a slight hint of pride in her voice. She settled in the driver's seat and tried to reassure herself by carrying on a monologue in a murmur, when an unusual sound broke the silence of the desert. It was like a hum in the distance, punctuated from time to time by shorter louder bursts of sound. Without slowing down, she rolled down her window and cocked her head to hear better. It was coming from behind her. And it was getting louder.

She looked up into the rearview mirror, just in time to see a motorbike with two men on it approaching her.

As they pulled up alongside her, one of the men pulled out a gun and shot twice. Once in the air and once directly at the back door of her vehicle. The effect was exactly what the shooter had hoped for. The sound unnerved Stephanie and she lost control of the vehicle and swerved wildly. In that moment of panic, she slammed on the brakes, grinding to a complete halt in a cloud of dust and gravel. The bike skidded to a stop a few metres ahead.

Stephanie didn't waste a moment, unbuckling her belt and clambering over into the passenger seat. Using the dust swirling around her as a cover, she opened the door, slid out and started to run. A few metres away was a large boulder. It would provide some sort of a hiding place for her.

"Hey! Hey you! Stop!" Shouted one of the men as the dust cloud cleared and they saw her. "Stop!" He roared again. Stephanie stumbled, fear rising in her chest and forced herself to continue moving. The sound of feet pounding the ground behind her grew louder and she was tackled hard from behind and knocked to the ground. Sharp stones and the dry ground grazed her skin as her assailant held her down, and pointed a gun at her.

"Where you run to?" He asked her in broken English, a cruel but triumphant smile distorting his face. He grabbed her by the hair and yanked her to her feet, "You much trouble and you pay." Stephanie winced in pain as he led her back to the vehicle where his companion was waiting. "Look, Dan," he said, pulling her hair again to expose her face to his friend, "Big money," he continued gleefully as he pointed his gun at her face.

"Well, be careful Mus. She won't be much use if you kill her," replied Dan in fluent English, as he stepped forward and pushed his friend away. He moved to take her hands and she cringed, afraid of more physical aggression, but was surprised at how gentle his touch was. In a low voice, as he began to bind her hands, he said, "We just want money. We won't hurt you, don't be afraid, okay?" He then moved away quickly as his companion turned back from inspecting the car.

"What you do lady? Huh? What's this?" Mus asked her, as he shoved her bag of instruments and research in her face.

"I'm a scientist," her voice was barely a whisper, she was shaking so hard she looked like she was shivering. "I study insects... ants."

"Ants!" he burst out laughing. "We have many here. You are welcome. But we want money, now! Where is your bag?" Sneering, he roughly grabbed her and pushed her towards the car. "You people always have money, give it to us now."

"I'm a scientist, I don't have much. I only have a little..." A hard slap cut her sentence off, stinging her cheek and making her eyes water.

"Hey! Be careful!," said Dan as he pulled Mus away, "there's no need to do that. Go get the bike and load it into the car, it's getting dark and we better get going." Mus spat on the ground and gave Stephanie a look of loathing before walking off. "Miss, please. My friend is not a reasonable guy, you need to stop playing games and give..." "But I swear," interjected Stephanie, her eyes wild with fear, "I don't have much on me, only what's in my wallet. You can look, search everything..." Her words trailed off as Mus returned.

"So where is it?" he reiterated his question, rounding on her, "Where!?" Dan moved quickly, standing in front of her, blocking Mus's advance.

"Mus, she's not hiding anything, she cannot be. Let's take everything, her equipment, the car, whatever money she has... let's take it and go." Dan reached forward to clasp Mus's shoulder, to try to calm him down, when Mus swung at him and caught him hard on the side of the head. Stephanie yelped as Dan lost his balance and fell and Mus kicked him viciously as he hit the ground. Dan groaned and curled up, trying to protect himself, as Mus flew into a rage.

Turning from his friend who lay whimpering in the dust, Mus turned and advanced menacingly towards Stephanie. His upper lip was curled, making him look like he had fangs. "Now, you are going to give me money. Do you hear!" Mus's fist connected with her face and pain exploded like fireworks in her head. She could taste blood in her mouth and she struggled to keep from passing out.

"It's all in my purse… all of it," Stephanie choked out. Her mind was going numb, stretches of coherent thought interspersed with moments of sheer confusion. The desert at night really did sound like a lone wolf, howling and wailing.

"Leave her alone." Dan was standing, albeit shakily, pointing his gun at Mus, "We are here for money, not her."

Mus turned around slowly, letting go of Stephanie, who sank slowly to her knees. "You're weak Dan, you can't do anything. I don't need you," Mus said, every syllable dripping with contempt. "I don't need you!" he suddenly yelled again, raising his gun in the same breath.

They both fired and fell to the ground. It was deathly quiet. *"Deathly quiet,"* thought Stephanie, *how appropriate* and she knelt on the ground trying to absorb the shock of what had happened. Then a groan of pain startled her. In the dim light, she could see that Dan was moving whereas Mus lay still, as her mind raced to resolve the situation, although she knew what she was going to do already. Shuddering as she stepped over Mus's body, she went over to Dan , who had been shot in the leg and was writhing in pain.

"Untie me," she said and she knelt over him."I cannot help you with my hands tied." He looked up at her incredulously and fumbled with a pocket knife as he cut her free.

"Why? Why are you doing this?" Dan asked in between grunts of pains as she helped him to his feet.

"You were wrong for doing what you did," she said as she strapped him into the passenger seat, "but if it wasn't for you, I'd probably be dead. One good turn deserves another."

CHAPTER TWENTY-TWO

From Chibok to Sambisa

Ogochukwu Promise

"Good afternoon, Lady Reporter, and welcome to my humble abode."

"Pleased to meet you too."

"You may sit on that wooden stool. Let me wipe it clean for you. It belongs to Mariama, the multi-talented, highly skilled one!" She knocked a few pieces of wood together to form that stool. "It is priceless, you see, the stool, I mean. It reminds me of her. Strong-willed Mariama, yes, she is and believes she can do everything. She makes herself very useful in our home, cleaning, washing, singing and cooking. She is my pearl!"

"You asked to see me. You bear many questions? Sit, yes, sit please. Don't worry, I shall answer you today." She said to the reporter. "I dare to speak having kept quiet all these moons. Never mind that I twiddle my hair which is quite tangled now. Its state of neglect speaks of how I miss Zynab, the quiet one, who never allows my hair to become this unkempt. She used to weave my hair for me every week. Oh, never mind my mindless chatter, these sobs and laughter in-between. You know how things are! They are my children after all, my flesh and blood! So, Lady Reporter, if by airing this, my children could be found, ask away!" she said finally before allowing the reporter any chance to say anything.

"I hope you remember me, Madam?" the reporter finally asked.

"Yes, I remember you, you were here when it first happened. You travelled in the dead of night, your car had an accident on one of the death traps we call roads and you braved it all. You did walk on the paths our missing daughters walked, sat on their damaged iron beds, felt their broken lockers and looked keenly at the caved-in roof. You even searched for something private, a teddy-bear one of them might have held dearly and hugged to sleep that night before the marauders halted their night and carted their dreams away. All that was left was the rude dilapidation of the hostel they lived in, the ravaging of their peace and their aching absence. I could not speak to you then for I was numbed by pain and the fear that my loss would be real if I spoke too soon."

"But so many months have gone by now and I am so sorry not much has happened positively," the reporter said to console her.

"We are now counting in years. It is a long time to sit expectantly by the window and jump each time the breeze raises the curtain of hope. We have worried our souls and wearied friends' ears with our woeful tales. But we are fortunate to have listening ears among our kind. They welcome us again and again as we stop by just to recount our fond memories of how our daughters were before their captors arrived. Asmira, my neighbour, has an inexhaustible river of tears which hurry to meet mine as they flow in continuum into the ocean of our loss. In it, we swim until our eyes ache and beg to look and see all the marvellous people out there bearing placards, chanting, *Bring Back Our Girls!*"

"Often when I look at the sweat running down their faces, I see the sun rise in their eyes and I dare to borrow their eyes with which to see my daughters again even if it is for a second. Then I reach up to pluck my courage where I abandoned it on a greying mango tree. And when I am stable enough, I plough back my hoe between yam ridges seeking to weed sorrow away."

"I have had time to ponder the senselessness in the mother-hen sitting and watching the hawks whisk away her chicks. We have cried to Aso Rock and wondered if rocks do not get too rocky for dirges to penetrate them. Other hapless mothers and I have wondered what would happen if it was an Italian matted floor, outlandish carpet or those luxurious Persian rugs that were pulled away from under their feet at Aso Rock! Would they really have stood by and watched? Yet, Persian rugs, customised or not are not nearly as dear as my two teenage girls snatched away from under my full breasts."

The reporter was wondering where there would be a break for her to ask questions as the mother of these unfortunate children continued to wail in sentences.

"... And then the powerful ones we see but cannot touch the fringe of their garments began to speak grammar. They began the showmanship of the affluent, all those rings on all those fingers while my children remained lost! Oh those golden teeth and plastic smiles on silvery lips as they appeared on TV speaking as though they were no longer human beings like you and me! They began to speak from all the corners of their mouth, including their upper and lower lips about how it was not true that my children were gone! Outraged, I got up to pinch them, scratch their puffy cheeks to see if they would feel any pain. But Hajia Aishatu said they would not feel it since I would only be defacing the surface of my neighbour's TV screen, spoiling it. Then I screamed, frustration fuelling my voice, "If the smallest of your children, just one, goes missing, would you honestly go to sleep? Only to wake up and pussyfoot, waiting and waiting to strike at the right time, which hardly feels right! Meanwhile, the missing ones are sold and resold into harsher slavery in Chad, Yemen, anywhere, as wives to old foxes, as walking dead, wearing booby traps?"

"Then the powerful began to weep on national TV, summoning God to deal with those who torment the innocent in His name. And I thought to myself, "What is happening? Are they coming to their senses! Is this an indication that they now acknowledge my children are indeed missing! Is there any chance that they are beginning to hurt for me, like me? Will they now do something to help the situation!" Mh! Ah! Lady Reporter, don't look at me like that – with deep understanding – it brings tears to my eyes. Mhnn! The following day, they went off to campaign for the juicy political posts in my land! That's where they went to, clad in puffy traditional regalia! I felt so small, Lady Reporter, smaller than an ant and my heart began to palpitate for I was gripped with the worst kind of fear, fear of confirming that these people hardly know I exist. This was the fear I had lived with even before the kidnap of our girls."

The Reporter wondered as she was getting tired of the lamentation, but she continued, "Ah, not again, Lady Reporter. I know it is sudden, but I am shouting again. Yes, let me shout, please, let me shout! "Oooh come now! My tormentors come! Drain me of this blood and all that reminds me of you! Come on now and have a cup of my blood too! You snatchers! You pillagers of lives! Takers of baby food! Stealers of dignity! What are you waiting for?"

"They said I have gone mad. But the people in my vicinity knew better. Now tell me, Lady Reporter, if in one night, they abducted your offspring. Not one but two, and those who could help you were in rallies making outlandish political statements, trailed by their diamond rimmed flowing gowns with no memory of your wailing from last night till this morning, would you not charge at them and risk being called mad? So on that day at the rally, I threw not only caution to the wind but my Abaya as well. I slung at them my slippers and pebbles I picked on the dusty road. I flung all I could see at them, giving them also the length of my tongue.

They seized me. It was the fairest among them they took me to.

"Woman, is there something wrong with you? Why were you hurling stones at your betters?"

"Yes, something is wrong with me! My two girls are among the horde stolen by those dreadful captors!"

"*Eeei yaa*! Are you one of the mothers of the unfortunate children! We are most unhappy about this terrible condition and are doing something about it, okay! Don't worry ee, they will be found. We are doing everything humanly possible to locate and bring them back. Here, take this and manage, they will soon be back, okay?" With abandon, she dipped her smooth hand into a glittering bag. Quickly the hand popped out again clutching crispy notes. She pressed them into my right palm, all of what her hand had come up with, which was much. She took my left palm and used it to cover my right one sealing it with her charming smile.

"I looked. They were strange notes. She told me to hide them so no one would take them away from me. She had indeed been generous, I could see. I had never seen so many of those lovely notes all my life."

"Then I let them fall to the ground, shocking not only her but myself. Yes, I let them fall, Lady Reporter, I could not help myself. I turned and walked away. Someone said there was no sense left in me anymore. But I was thinking, those strange notes, would they bring Mariama or Zynab back? And when they do return after coconut water has bled blood, will my Mariama and Zynab still be my Mariama and Zynab?"

"Several moons later we were told that Bahaa had been found. All the distressed mothers ran to see and welcome her, to touch and embrace her in the hope that it would feel a bit like touching our own lost daughters. It turned out that Bahaa was no longer Bahaa. For her beauty had left her. She said she was among those who escaped from a moving truck. Some were shot. She too. Her wound was so fresh like the unsightly yawning of a common grave. Their molesters thought they had died and did not bother to find out for they believed they were being chased. But we were told that those who could have given the chase were not sufficiently mobilised. We sighed. At least Bahaa was back, half dead, but alive."

"I am wailing again, for my anguish is only just beginning. For Bahaa said she was with my Mariama, the stubborn one and Zynab, the charming innocent one. Bahaa said, she said, ah Lady Reporter! How does a mother affirm that her own daughters were raped till they fainted! That when they regained consciousness, they were raped again and again till they began to learn a new way of life. I knew it. I knew that Zynab would cry non-stop begging death to take her. That Mariama would resist until they knocked her out with the butt of their guns! They knocked my daughter out! They knocked her out! Then, they stretched out her legs, holding her down still even in that state of comatose, to do their grubby deeds, knowing that if any energy was left in her, she would resist them still."

"Bahaa said the men were sullied and more greedy for their maidenheads than they were for the worship of any kind of God at all. They dragged the girls like slaves, made them pregnant again and again and consumed both girls and their babies, leaving behind a haze of ugliness, some of which was etched on Bahaa's face.

"So the gruelling journey they began in Chibok worsened as they got to Sambisa?" you asked.

"Why did that inflame my mood, Lady Reporter? I just found myself spring to my feet with these parting shots: "Have dozens of guerrillas feasted on you before for just five minutes? Well, they have ravaged my Mariama and Zynab for over a year now. They have sucked out my brains. My skull is hollow, my heart numb!""

CHAPTER TWENTY-THREE

It's Something That Happens To Other People

Irehobhude O. Iyioha

The second blast came seconds after the first. Blinded by the grit
and rubble retching up around us, we hurled ourselves towards
the cavern. Some of us made it just in time, squeezing ourselves
through its cavity. When the third hit the sheds a few yards away,
it sent us rolling over one another, bodies on top of bodies, bodies
salted in dust. Then, there was a lull. Ten minutes to steel ourselves
for the next fusillade of explosions. And just over a minute ago,
they came in trios, each triad rattling the stony hedges of this
shelter. I squinted through the swirl of dust hurtling into the
mouth of the cavern, struggling to scan the enclosure for those
I know. Through the serrated cleft close to the embankment, a
sliver of sunlight finds its way in and cleaves the cloud of dust,
illuminating air cluttered with particles of dirt of our collective
fear.

When we first made it here, I thought the cavern's aperture was
just wide enough. I pushed myself in without much trouble except
for a few bruises on my hips and shins, which weren't half as bad
as Ramie's shattered knee. There is a wider opening at the rear,
but I didn't notice it when we rushed in. A couple of people hurled
themselves in from there. I couldn't see their faces, but they were
likely the crew from America.

I edge myself off a body sprawled in the dirt and begin to push
towards the wall. As I approached it, a volley of rocks breaches
the aperture. The dust sprays over my body; when the veil lifts,

I'll see that my skin has taken on an ashen hue from the peppering of earth and debris. I rub my eyes frantically. Maybe the aperture is a tad too wide after all. It only barely shields us from the full glare of the shells. My mouth is filled with sand. I tried keeping it closed, but the shelling, when it starts, loosens the body and leaves everything open and hanging. The taste of dirt is now as familiar as the acrid smell of death that haunts everyone who comes into Douma.

Through the miasma of fumes and smoke, I hear a loud cry. It is a delicate sound, soft at the edges but bleeding at its core. You know it is a child. You know it is Kasim if you have heard him yell. His voice cuts to the bone. I can't see him because he blends easily among the bodies in the dust, all like dough rolled in flour. Perched a few steps away from the butt of the cavern, my fingers digging into its sides, I squint harder in the direction of the sound.

"Raseda!" Kasim calls out again.

"Mama," the girl called Raseda cries in response. "Where my Mama?"

I feel my way along the wall, occasionally pushing along with my back to the wall, edging slowly towards the direction of the cry. It is a slow process and I can't see beyond my feet because the dust and smoke are yet to settle; the deluge of shots from the distance keeps them afloat. If I can reach the entrance, I can scan the immediate vicinity for Raseda's mother. The little girl cries for two: the baby in her mother's womb is due home any day now.

Suddenly, I come around a sharp bend and stumble over a body. There is a loud groan and a burst of obscenity. It is Ramie. Egyptian-Canadian Ramie. I reach down and touch his body. He is lying on his side, the good leg carrying his weight while the other flops slightly towards the back. The fragments of his camera are mixed in the rubble. It came crashing down with him. He too is in Douma to tell the story of this conflict. I know it is Ramie because his crying gives him away. The blood around him is still warm to the touch. He was brought down by the first blast, caught where he was standing yards away from my group and now a hole peers out of his knee cap. Members of his crew managed to pull him to the cavern and during the ten-minute break, a young man called Dillie, who was a medical assistant in his past life, pulled out the splinters embedded in the knee in the dimness of the cavern. I'm not sure how he managed to get the shards out, but he told everyone with as much cheer as he could muster in the circumstances that he had wrapped the knee with a grubby cloth pulled from around Ramie's neck.

"Raseda! Are you okay?"

My voice fills the cavern. With the exception of a couple of sharp bends, the cavern is shaped like a gazebo, though not so fancy. The floor is rugged with debris and stumps of rock jut out unevenly. The third shelling tore off a small chunk of rock near the embankment. When the smoke and dust settle in a short while, we will see that the hole, like a gap tooth, lets some light into this corner of the cavern.

"They see my Mama?"

"Shus-shus, Ras," Kasim consoles.

"Tell them, Kas. Tell them to search Mama under stone."

Raseda's mother was sitting with us near a boulder, answering our endless questions about the Kurds, the Christians of Syria, the children of Syria, the rebels, and the killers called ISIS when the explosions interrupted us, cracking and spinning the boulder into an awning. In the mad rush to reach the cavern, I don't know that she made it in.

"Salami! Salami!" My voice is strained. "Please look out the other end."

Salami has been our cameraman through this journey. The labour brings him little to care for his family; but he is, like me, an odd case: we are Americans in Syria, Americans who wear another cloak and travel incognito as Nigerians. We are Nigerian-Americans sitting on the prickly hyphen that connects Nigeria and Syria and the fluid war-torn hinterlands: we are connected as witnesses to that other bloody insurgence eclipsing sanity in our other homeland.

In a way, the layered heritage is a benefit. We are not high-priced targets. So we are able to say we are volunteer African newsmen in the gap between the Kurds and the shifting states of the Islamic State, in that uninhabited slot where the stories of

African fatalities are abridged, like stories of home-grown Islamic rebels painting city after city in Nigeria with the blood of their inhabitants. It is uninhabited because no one wants the job. To go into the zone of death, not propelled by a gun, is cowardice. If you are captured or killed, even your friends will describe your injuries as self-inflicted. But Salami and I have chosen to come, chosen to be like the Americans and Europeans and others who run beyond yellow lines into burning barns, chosen to take risks because sometimes it takes the goo to ruin your shirt to notice the black bird that hovers above.

The dust settles as I reach Kasim and Reseda. Kasim is leaning over Raseda, holding her head with his arm while her body lolls in the dirt. A gash on the right side of her head bleeds onto her overalls. Her hijab, no longer white, is dislodged, revealing a head jarringly full of hair. I kneel beside Kasim and Raseda. Raseda is ten, but has a mind sharp as a blade. She never misses a thing. She carries the discussions of the women and men about in the warmth of her memory like her mates in quieter places carry pink dolls and purses and baskets of flowers. She questions the fighting, the shelling and the hunger. Her mother, a former Armenian Catholic and nurse became a Muslim when she married Raseda's Sunni doctor father. As the fighting intensified, he sent them on the road to what he thought would be a safe Damascus. Raseda's mother found out she was pregnant along the way.

"Raseda! Are you okay? Let me see —"

I brush the hair off her face and peer at the injury through the films of dust hanging in the slivers of sunlight now slowly kindling the cavern.

"Where my Mama? My Mama be okay?"

"You have to stay still for me, Raseda. Your Mama will be — she will — we're looking for her —"

At the start of their journey, Raseda's mother consoled her with promises of peace in an oasis, the freedom to play in the Barada River free from the shower of bullets, frolicking in the water on sunny weekends, reveling in the gilded glow where buttery sunray melt on the incandescent surface of the water, the sounds of war distant and inconsequential. Now the flames of hope have turned to ashes, you will catch her now and then asking her mother what the Quran says about mothers lying to their kids. Her father joined the rebels in Rastan, near Homs. But since he left, her mother has reconciled with Christianity. It happened in the middle of their journey from Homs to Damascus, soon after the baby announced itself, when she didn't think they would make it.

"Mama fear death and run to the other Prophet."

That's how Raseda puts it. Raseda doesn't understand why, but finds it intriguing. Raseda's mother was going to tell us why before the blast. Salami is still looking out for a sign of her. He is squatting on the rungs leading to the embankment and from there he glances around the vicinity.

"Raseda, are you okay?"

I look closely at the wound. It is an ugly slash that snakes around her eyes, barely missing her eyeball.

"I know it hurts, okay, but I just want to take a proper look."

She lets me feel around the laceration. I reach into my left breast-pocket and pull out the off-white handkerchief that sometimes helps me cope with the dust and smoke. I press it against the injury. It drinks the blood slowly.

"Let me. I help,"Kasim says, reaching for the piece of cloth.

Kasim is almost twelve. Last December he lost his father, his mother, his two-year-old sister and then his hand and innocence to this war. Since December he has been running around with Raseda and her mother, going from shelter to shelter, treading through desolate towns to reach Damascus. He is like Raseda in many ways: his tongue moves and cuts like a knife.

Raseda winces as he presses the cloth against her face. I've never seen him so quiet. He looks up at me with questioning eyes.

"She good, no?"

I nod.

"You survived that, didn't you?" I incline my head towards his right hand.

It is severed from the elbow. The stump is smooth like polished wood. He gives me a brief look and smiles; it is the smile of one who has made peace with a bad tattoo. But when Ramie groans, his eyes glaze over; he looks at Ramie quietly, his expression as unperturbed as the hands of an old nurse who has dressed gashes from shelling all her life. Kasim has lived with this far longer than a child should and no longer knows what silence sounds like. He is used to the blood and gasps of expiration. But Raseda is different. Raseda is special. He knows it. He feels the difference. Between blood and death that are common sight and blood and injury that are a part of you.

And there it is. Kasim's indifference to the bloodshed and yet anguish about Raseda reminds me of why I have come to this place. It is neither the bare fact of war nor its progeny that awakens my consciousness to his condition – to our collective condition, but the capacity of human eyes to tell a story of a place beyond the heart, where the stillness is an unwanted love child of hate and violence. Of everything that is contrary to order. A place where the silence is the final act of defiance, the quietus after a lifetime of disorder and decay. The children I have met here, like Kasim and Reseda, are in that place. The look in Kasim's eyes reflects the darkness that moved me here from my position as lead war correspondent in the *African Herald,* a war correspondent who had never been to the back-turf of any war. I am in that place too. Only I look out of it with eyes trained to comprehend life's paradoxes.

Before I arrived at that place, I had a story. An everyday sort of story. Like yours. Like that of many. It is one in which your life is rather normal. You have two daughters, Maria and Mary, three and five, who are the brightest in their classes. You have a wife who is an accountant, whose beauty is as sublime as pearls of dew on a fresh petal. And these daughters and wife are why you live, why you work, why you don't give everything up to be a happy hipster doing what you love in the arid Northern deserts of Nigeria's Borno. You come home to them every day, to the little arms of the girls holding your neck so tightly your neck is happily strained, to the soft kisses pelted over your face, to the curious fingers weaving your wiry hair into cornrows, hipster cornrows, the type of man-weaves you wear in your hipster dreams.

You arrive to an evening tale of new best friends, of Sadana and Alamadin, the new Fulani kids with the smooth complexion, the long nose gently curved at the tip like a North American's and the hair curled in bold, flamboyant whorls. You listen to their sing-song voices asking why Sadana and Alamadin look like the kids on satellite TV, the kids with an orangey hue to their skin, the kids whose parents are black and white. You listen to them question how Sadana and Alamadin can be Nigerians, Nigerian-Fulanis from the ruthlessly scorching heart of the North and have skin colour so unlike their own raven coloured hue. You look into their big, watery eyes, full of wonder and admiration. You kiss them gently each on their cheeks and tell them about a big world full of people of different strands and textures, of people you hope would someday be kind to them.

They ask you about the bloodshed on the nightly news, about why you ask them to cover their faces when videos of far too many people in tarns of blood are played during the newscast. They ask why you don't move away to drier lands. It is the same question your friends, your American friends, your fellow American friends are always asking you, why you don't move away to safer, quieter places. You struggle into your courage like an undersized shirt and answer with the refrain that is now your mantra: that this, Maiduguri, is your homeland, the home of your fathers and their fathers before them, the heart of Borno, the place where you are supposed to live and die. As you speak, you're aware that the extremists have been spotted around the borders of the city, sniffing around like the long-snouted shrew rat for blood and self-worth. You know they have been to the smaller bordering lands of Chad and Cameroon snorting around for lives to steal; you know they have come back empty-handed.

You want to tell the girls about your own worries, those questions that chip away at the edges of your sanity, questions like *how does my army fight the boogeyman with water guns?* But you remember they don't need to know and they shouldn't really care, for like you the girls are privileged. They too were born abroad. Like you they wield American passports, the blunt gizmo for hacking your way from indigence to Utopia, your hopes fuelled by oversold legends about the possibilities. So, when the war in your neighbour's backyard comes home to you and the warmongers threaten to break down your back door, you will pack yourselves, your wife at your elbow and your children on your backs and take the next flight to a France or London stopover then enroute to America, your other home. America, the concubine you now hold close like that other girl in senior secondary school whom you loved and cuddled when you and your intractable girlfriend had a bitter fight. So you say nothing to the girls. You simply rub their heads as you tuck them into bed, as you put their favourite Fairy Princess books back on the shelves, as you turn off the lights, exorcise the boogeymen under their beds and close the door.

You hear the news about the bloodshed repeated just before your accountant wife switches off the TV. It is a one-sentence recital just before commercials. Not a blow-by-blow inside-out on-the-ground account. A quick recap of world news and right there at the tail, in that space where words often get lost when the programming is hastily cut for commercials; right there is the news: *Bloodshed in Nigeria's North. CNN cannot confirm the number of the dead...* They are next door, the Baga people. Your other people. The news doesn't tell you that the massacre is in the thousands. That the recovery team has lost count. That there are bodies of infants and women and girls and boys lying everywhere. That there are men on top of women, men who died protecting their women and daughters and sons and infants. The news doesn't tell you about numbers. They also don't tell you how those numbers are connected to Askira, Azare, Biu, Hawai, Damboa, Ngadda, Kukawa, Damaturu and the pink hearts ripped from their core.

"Come, Lucie," you say. "We have a long day tomorrow."

And you hold Lucie, your wife, your beautiful accountant wife whose beauty reminds you again of blossoms and mist. You hold her by the waist and lead her to the bedroom. You know you should say a prayer for Baga's dead, for the children, the infants, the girls, the boys and their men and women. But you are tired. It has been a long day and Lucie's delicate hands are crawling over your chest, her body gently edging over yours, her breasts soft against your ribs. They will be fine, you say. Baga will be fine. Askira, Azare, Biu, Hawai, Damboa, Ngadda, Kukawa, Damaturu and the daughters in their midst will be fine. Those brave press crew who travel to war lands will write about this. The world will hear. You too will write about it. The world's eyes will be on it, on them, their dead and the stolen, and it wouldn't happen again. You will say a prayer in the morning. A prayer for their dead. Borno's many dead.

"I say you help!" Kasim's voice is almost a shriek.

I didn't notice he has been repeating the same request: he wants me to place Raseda on his thighs so she is lying down on him rather than in the dirt. I lift her gently onto his body. He wedges his stump between her head and his thigh and with the other hand he cleans the blood and tears in her eye with the most gentle of strokes.

"You beautiful a lot," he says through a toothy smile. She returns his smile, a raw tenderness set in her eyes.

"You also," she replies.

"Even this eye do nothing bad for you. You beautiful. Every time."

"You also," she replies.

A shy look suddenly steals across her face wraith-like. Then she says, "But you will go the dance with Salimatu?"

Salimatu is a neighbourhood girl. I have seen her play with Kasim and Raseda. Her father is fighting on the side of the rebels even though her mother, like Raseda's, supports the government forces and the Alawites. The dance is the bonfire we light every other weekend to celebrate being alive. In the open air, teased and incensed by strong winds, it burns high as we dance around it.

"Life too hard for we, Raseda. Life too short to think about many women."

"What you mean now?"

"Meaning you with me will go the dance tomorrow."

Raseda's face falls. She glances at me, seeking some assurance. I think that there will be a bonfire tomorrow, that there will be a tomorrow for us. I am embarrassed. My silence is a shame.

"And you with me will marry. When your papa come back with the head of the snake," Kasim completes his proposal.

"Mama say the snake save us, we Alawite. So he no bad."

I listen, astounded at how easily the president's identity is inserted into the discussion as the primary agent of their reality and yet they don't call him by name, as if to avoid honouring him beyond necessity.

"It no matter, Raseda. You with me will marry and live in big house with real bed and carpet and many flowers."

Raseda grabs his hand to stop its movement over her face as the disconsolate look spreads over her face. She stares at him quietly for a moment.

"That be love? You talk love with peace? That – uhn-uhn –" she shakes her head slowly, as slow as the pain allows, "– it don't happen to people like us."

That latter bit was my unconscious thought – a thought sown even before I met these two when the news of the massacre in several schools in Maiduguri rend the airwaves that other normal morning with Lucie and our girls. Lucie and I had dressed the girls for school, fed them, packed their lunch bags, planted kisses on their heads and shared our own kiss, a warm and lingering kiss. It was after all our anniversary. We went our separate ways, Lucie to drop the kids at school while I, a little later, went off to the office of the *African Herald*. The office drive would take twenty-five minutes. It was just after 8:40am. There was assembly for the kids at 8am, processions back to class at 8:30am. and lectures starting at 8:45am. The news came up as I drove into the office compound and scouted for a parking spot. A voice on the radio was saying something about the killings spread across six schools. Someone was saying something about shootings, stabbings and beheading of school kids, of teachers, of staff and of parents caught in the crossfire, some of them trapped while they were having their monthly meeting with the principal.

Lami will cover that, I said. He was the reporter for the job. I dwelt on the magnitude of it for a few moments. *I will tie it into my coverage of the US 'counterterrorism operations with the Kurds and the battle in Kobani and the other extremist-occupied territories.* I listened for another minute before turning off the ignition. I began to whistle as I emerged from the car. I entered the building of the *African Herald*, singing. It was a solemn song, but it wasn't sad. I wasn't sad. I was as I know Kasim to be. He is not a sad child. He takes most things in careful measures, angry when he thinks he cannot take it anymore, vocal when he thinks something is plainly stupid. But he is for the most part even-tempered.

He leaves me in awe, though, how he handles the tussle between anxieties about the shelling and fatalities and being enveloped in his affection for little Miss Raseda. To retreat so easily behind that dam and yet let his warmth for Raseda burst forth through all that hurt and bleakness is testimony to the infinite capabilities of the heart. His gentleness seeps through his words and actions. I watch as he considers Raseda's words. Her words have struck an accessible place in his heart. It shows in the way he soaks up her words in silence, in the way water gathers in his eyes, in the way they – like a sponge–squeeze to expel the tears. Slowly, he begins to rub the side of her face again.

"People like us be human also, Raseda. Love be for every people."

"My Mama say we different. Mama – where my Mama?"

Suddenly, she turns to me, frowning. Salami is still trying to see beyond the haze for a glimpse of her mother. There are loud cries in the distance, the usual chorus of pain and expiration, of women and men trapped in the fire. Salami is struggling to see through the pall of dust and smoke. He rubs at his eyes. I can't read his expression now, how much he is thinking of the wisdom of being here. The lull allows us time to think of the present as is, of course, the case when we allow a measure of silence into our moments. But not all silences allow us to observe our lives in seconds. Some forms of silence come at you as reels of the past and as snapshots of a hopeless future. They come to you in these forms as thoughts, useless thoughts. The silence comes to you as noise.

It is the form of silence that engulfed us when the first blast sent us sprinting towards the cavern, when we tumbled over each other, blinded as we were by the dirt, the shrapnel and the blood of the injured. It is that form of silence that comes with reels. It was the type of silence that wrapped itself around me like slough when, blinded too by the blood that day, that beautiful, normal morning in Maiduguri, I ran through the compound of Borno High Grade Academy. I was blinded by the blood of the children flowing like a stream towards the school gates as if protesting their massacre by running away from us. I was blinded by the little bodies, their little parts strewn across the compound like sprinkling of broken candy on a massive red cake. I was blinded by the mix of bodies, of teacher and child, parent and child, stranger and child.

I was blinded when I stumbled upon Lucie, Lucie's body holding Maria's body. I was blinded when a cleaner found my Mary, Mary seated on a chair, Mary's little head resting on her desk like she was taking a quick nap before the next run of classes. And though I was blinded by the splash as I stepped into puddles of blood, I picked up her delicate little body, wrapped my arms around it until it was buried in my chest and felt the ogling hole that peered from the front of her chest to her back through her heart. I can't remember crying – I wasn't conscious of anything, but now I find myself trapped in that moment – the moment when I must have crossed the boundaries into where you find the dam. As I remember Lucie, Maria and Mary and the breach in my little girl's heart, I am strangely consoled by the fact that Maria and Mary would never have to build hedges around their hearts. I don't know what Lucie would have made of this odd thought, but I suppose it helps with my own struggle to retreat from behind the hedges, from that spot beyond my heart.

"Why you cry? Something happen with Mama?"

I brush my hand over Raseda's hair, ignoring my own tears. Rising from my crouch, I approach the rungs to skim the outside plains. The fourth blast shatters a boulder a few blocks away, sending pellets towards us through the opening.

"Animals!" Kasim shouts. "Stupid animals! How the world leave us children to die by this smelling people?"

I rub my eyes desperately. My vision is blurry. I don't know why I'm thinking of Lucie now. I should think of Lucie in this way when I'm dying. Thoughts of Maria and Mary should fill my mind because of Kasim's words. But I think of Lucie, my love. I think of our life together, not in fleeting frames of lived and irrecoverable lives, but in full screens with scenes extended beyond that morning in Maiduguri. I hope to rekindle in the afterlife the type of love that happened to us. There, I will tell her about Kasim and Raseda, about their own kind of love and the kind of peace they envision in a future without a daily staple of blasts rattling their dinner table. The kind of love and peace that happen to others who are unlike them. I will tell Lucie, too, that I now pray every time I hear shelling or news about it, as I prayed at her graveside after it happened to us.

CHAPTER TWENTY-FOUR

The Scent of African Dusk

Benjamin Sehene

And while men had whistled as she swung her hips down the streets, none ever made crude proposals to her. She had that sudden upward curl of the upper lip which portends a rebuff. She never said yes and men hate begging. There were missed occasions, chance encounters, hints, overbearing men with hairy nostrils. But still no flowers ever came. No suicides were scheduled beneath her window.

Hers was an unusual beauty: particularly when viewed at forty-five degrees. She was a highly-strung pale girl who expelled cigarette smoke through her nostrils most convincingly and painted her lips scarlet red.

Her adolescence had flowed by like the mucky waters of the Seine. She had gone to university; she read history, changed her mind and read letters, but never fell in love. Then she had found a job as a receptionist at a commercial firm.

Her friends had got married, given birth to red wrinkled babies and indulged in the aesthetics of interior decoration. But for her, happiness had remained elsewhere: in an instant glimpsed in a distant lighted window, in a toothy smile on a billboard, or in the intimate embrace of a young couple kissing on the métro. Her breasts had softened and her hips had spread out. And thus she had set off alone through the interminable corridors of her twenties and down the red-carpeted stairway to old age.

Then presently, a robust African man with a clipped moustache and a crew cut to boot, hurried along ahead of her, snorting through his whiskers. And their itineraries down that stairway of life might have never converged, if she had not raised her eyes to admire the perfect spiral described by the iron handrail. She had missed a step, lunged forward and slid down a flight of steps to the next landing. The man had stopped and walked back to give her a hand.

"Are you alright?" he had asked as he gave her his two hands. And he could not help but notice her momentarily unveiled long and lovely legs.

"Yes," Isabelle had replied.

For a moment they had recoiled into an embarrased silence while she covered her nudity and put on her shoes.

Then perhaps to put her at ease, the man had asked her if she had not hurt herself. "Fortunately, no," she said. "I was admiring the magnificent spiral formed by the staircase. And it gave me vertigo."

"Yes, isn't it beautiful," the man said. And they both looked up the winding staircase. "It is a pity they don't build like this anymore," he added. "Do you live here?" queried the man stroking his whiskers.

"No, I work here," she answered.

They had then resumed their journey down the stairs. They had exchanged a glance of astounded empathy as a heavyset woman lumbered up the staircase, breathing heavily.

He had held open the front door and motioned her out with a sweeping gesture of his right hand.

"Which way are you going?" he had asked her outside.

"To the métro."

"I could give you a ride."

A uniformed chauffeur had fumbled to open doors for them. In the car they had exchanged telephone numbers. For a moment an instinctive sense of decency had refrained her from unveiling herself to a total stranger, but she had been overcome by an irresistible urge to please this kind moustachioed man. The following week they had dined together at an expensive restaurant, where they were tended to by an army of waiters.

II

The man's name was Francis Lutera. He was a minor diplomat posted in Paris, from some English-speaking African country. His bearing carried distinction and he spoke an accented, stilted French, with an occasional lapse into English. At thirty-three, he was still a bachelor, inspite of his good looks and that structural solidity so appealing to women. Isabelle loved the way his nose gracefully rolled back at the tip and spread out towards his smooth cheeks. The way his skin gathered beneath his eyes when he smiled. His full lips were very becoming. Didn't he look like that musician, what's his name?... Belamonte? Belafonte? Yes, like Harry Belafonte.

At the New Year's gala, they had described concentric circles, spinning like entwined tops around the ballroom floor. At the charity ball a melancholic tango had implored them to bend and spin to its languid rhythm. He in his dinner-jacket, and she in her light evening wear had made such an elegant couple that everyone had found them absolutely charming, well matched. They got married that summer.

III

Then a few months later, Francis was recalled. They had moved into a peeling colonial, iron roofed bungalow with wire netting shutters and dry water taps. For the morning bath, the houseboy would fetch water in plastic jerrycans from a neighbour's downhill and fill the tub, in which Francis and Isabelle would take turns bathing in the same water. In the house there was a tiny grey mouse she nicknamed Mickey, which scared the daylights out of her.

Isabelle had discovered with disappointment that Africa was not just the brilliant blue sky and endless savanna myth of the travel agent but was also the suffocating heat, the pervasive red dust, the invisible mosquitoes whizzing through the dark, and a cacophony of cryptic languages.

Her favourite aspect of Africa, was the dusk. She would sit

in a wicker chair on the verandah, with her legs resting on the balustrade to watch the day die a slow crimson death. A floral scent compounded with the warm humid smell of decay, the smell of African dusk, would hang in the air like an invisible curtain. And the distant hills would become giant sepals upon which reposed the celestial flower. Usually, Juma the houseboy, would serve her a glass of lemon juice. And she would sip it very slowly, its acerbic taste tickling her taste buds.

For a moment the celestial flower would waver over the horizon, then wither away into the interminable eulogy of a frog and the chorus of crickets. The distant hills would become gilted with specks of distant street lights. The electric bulb on the verandah would attract a swarm of mosquitoes, an occasional white moth and motionless, translucent geckos hanging upside down on the celling. The mosquitoes and the white moth would perform loops around the light under the watchful eye of the gecko. Eventually, if one of the mosquitoes settled down for a rest, a gecko would suddenly flick out its tongue and engulf it.

Towards seven o'clock, Isabelle would hear her husband's car struggle up the hill in low gear. She would meet him at the front door and would quickly press her pursed painted lips against his mouth. In the sitting room, where a gilted chandelier whose glass pendants hang like an immobile rainfall above a large zebra-skin drum, Isabelle would leisurely kick off her shoes, cuddle in the corner of a large black chesterfield with buttons like a fat woman's navel, folding one leg under her and begin leafing through an outdated illustrated magazine. While her bespectacled husband in the remains of his business suit, dozed into an open newspaper after a harassed day at the office. On his return from Europe, Francis had been appointed to a high position in the ministry of foreign affairs. He had become distracted, detached and he always seemed to have official business waiting. Sometimes he would spend hours on the telephone. At the dining table he would yawn into his fist, as Juma ladled a spoonful of green peas onto his plate.

IV

Their house was not unlike a public house. There was an incessant stream of guests and relatives: uncles, aunts, cousins, nephews, nephews of nephews, who just showed up unexpected and uninvited. They arrived with their bare feet shod in a thin layer of red dust. Some just dropped in on the occasion of a visit to town. Others came seeking favours from Francis, a job at the ministry, a government scholarship for a son. There were seldom fewer than half a dozen people at the dining table. How could one refuse them? They drank their tea from the saucer, ate with their fingers.

And although Francis despised some of these relatives for their countryside manners, Isabelle received them like her own. They were the numerous brothers and sisters she never had. She would preside over the table talk with diligence, rolling and unrolling hers in her Frenchified English. But at the slightest neglect, the conversation would veer off into vernacular. Immediately, poor, susceptible Isabelle, would rush to recover control of the conversation and steer it back into English, for fear the cryptic mirth be at her expense.

V

That Christmas, Francis took Isabelle to his home village. They drove down suburban roads between green hedges, on to the potholed one way streets of the city centre. They bumped past shabby concrete skyscrapers, past the rusty corrugated iron shacks in the slum. Then the bougainvilleas and flower beds along the curb disintegrated into rugged countryside without transition. Speeding lorries and taxis packed with passengers bumped along, raising clouds of red dust.

After a few hours on the motorway, Francis turned off into a dirt road which cut through scrub and banana plantations and led to a village of ochre coloured houses. There were many children tripping about the dusty compounds. Little boys rolled used car tyres along the road. Chickens went about pecking at the ground.

Francis' widowed mother lived in a large house with a dusty

front yard. She was a tall woman with the stern handsome face that mothers-in-law are often endowed with. It was a delicate matter dealing with her, for she understood neither English nor Isabelle's impatient gesticulations. There were numerous members of the extended family spending Christmas at the house. That night, Francis was separated from Isabelle, who was put up with her two sisters-in-law and four other girls; he was put with his brothers and a cousin. Isabelle shared a bed with one of her sisters-in-law, a big woman who smelt of wood smoke and took up most of the bed. The inevitable, invisible mosquito whizzing through the dark kept her awake much of the night.

Next day dawned with that limpid hue which portends a stifling day. Here and there, bulbous white cloudlets spotted the blue sky and turned it into a colossal fresco stretching from one end of the horizon to the other. Isabelle was given a large tin basin of water and was shown to an iron shack besides the latrine, for her morning bath.

From early morning the men sat in the yard playing cards and drinking a traditional brew made from fermented bananas. While the women went to fetch water in yellow jerrycans from the well, with babies tucked into cotton straps on their back. When they came back, they went about the domestic chores in a noisy joviality. They pounded groundnuts in wooden mortars, peeled green plantains and huge purple sweet potatoes for lunch, then lighted charcoal stoves.

Under the oppressive sun, the village was a watery vista. The air was hot and heavy. Vultures drifted in the sky. Isabelle felt lonely and unwelcome, her offers of help went unacknowledged. The fabric in her armpits formed dark round patches of sweat. She found it repugnant to squat over the putrid, fly infested latrine pit. Afterwards, she felt embarrassed to cross the backyard, walk past the men playing cards in the back yard, on her way from the latrine, as if she was coming from doing something unbearably shameful. She became unnecessarily sensitive to the men's and neighbour's stares. Her back tingled as though it was being walked over by a line of black ants.

VI

Later, the children kicked up dust as they chased chickens to be slaughtered for lunch. One of the chickens ran into the house through the back door. Bursts of tinkles and shrieks could be heard as the children went from room to room. Then the chicken flew out of a window and landed a few metres from where the men were playing cards. Francis was part of the shouting, laughing commotion which ran about the yard like a single, multi-limbed creature.

When the chickens were caught, Isabelle saw Francis fold his shirt sleeves and accept a knife. She saw him as she had never seen him before, a sturdy, rugged man with plastic sandals strapped between his toes. In his printed cotton shirt and faded jeans, he looked so much like any other villager. He was handed the cackling chicken and he walked over to a corner of the yard. He clasped the bird's wings beneath his left foot, the feet beneath his right. Someone challenged him to slaughter the hen in a single slash. And he accepted, then he seized the helpless chicken's head and started plucking off its neck feathers. His face was set in an expression Isabelle had never seen before. Two deep furrows cut down his brow to the top of his nose and he was biting his lower lip. There was something ritualistic in the pervading atmosphere not unlike a sacrifice. A primeval, pagan household ritual expurgated from modern life by the cellophane wrapped supermarket chicken. Francis slit the the chicken's throat, as Isabelle looked away in horror.

But in the ensuing applause and confusion, the chicken had escaped from Francis' grasp. Amid the euphoria, it had gone flapping around the yard, its headless bloody neck splashing blood all over the place.

VII

Lunch was served beneath a crackling iron roof. Naturally, Isabelle declined the offer of chicken stew, shuddering to think that perhaps this was the same bird that had flapped around the yard headless. Then later, a big black fly with hairy legs settled on the edge of her plate, rubbed its head with the fore legs, smoothened its delicate transparent wings with the hind legs, before darting off to re-emerge on the brim of her glass. From then on she had lost appetite to think of whence that fly had come.

"Darling are you alright?" asked Francis when he saw that she was not eating and looked very pale. But she said nothing; what was there to be said.

From then on, everything changed: she no longer saw Francis in the same glowing light she had always seen him; the suave diplomat and high-ranking civil servant. Beneath the veneer, his three-piece suits and English accent disguised another man altogether. A man capable of chopping off a chicken's head without a second thoughts. A rugged man with plastic sandals strapped between his toes, who could spend his days sipping beer and playing cards with his mates without paying the least attention to her. She could not understand this transformation. What could have happened to the man she knew and loved? She could not explain how one could go from socializing on the Parisian cocktail circuit to beheading a chicken in a remote African village? She had the impression of living with two distinct individuals: one with whom she did the local cocktail circuit and the other with whom she spent weekends and holidays in a dusty village in the middle of nowhere.

She felt trapped behind the high concrete wall around their house. In idleness, the heat and dust were overwhelming. And there was nothing to do in the city: the only cinema showed blood-and-guts or Bollywood movies. The museum was a dusty little joke of tiny clay models under glass cases, the local theatre was not even worth mentioning. The bookshops sold third- or forth-hand cheap thrillers by James Hardly Chase and vernacular translations of the Bible. In the city, the well-to-do lived sequestered lives, they seldom went out. They were like foreigners in their own country. They looked to Europe for inspiration. They worshipped their foreign-made cars, punctuated their afternoons with a cup of tea, dressed like Englishmen without the attributes of the dreadful English weather. They professed to revere their country but sent their English-speaking children overseas for studies.

Behind their high concrete walls, they were under siege. They lived in a concrete bubble, occasionally emerging in their air-conditioned Japanese four wheel drive cars to go to the air-conditioned office, to the air-conditioned bar at an international hotel. Their lives were at once barren and repetitive.

VII

One evening Isabelle and Francis were invited to a recently opened casino run by a friend. The casino was an air-conditioned, blinded enclave designed to deceive the impressionable client that he was either in Atlantic City or Las Vegas. The management was exclusively white: stout Israelis in tight tuxedos. There were many familiar faces Isabelle often saw around town, faces whose value derived from their proximity to power or wealth – a cousin to a government official, or the son of a rich businessman and their hangers-on. The conversation, in slanted local English, was facetious and tiresome, its subject the tragic events in a neighbouring country. Certain gruesome atrocities committed by the government militias were enumerated like the fouls of a rival football team. The militia drank the blood of their victims after hacking them to death, someone said. They remained on the grisly subject of atrocities for some time. Apparently the militia had forced women to have sex with AIDS patients at a certain hospital, then set them free to go and infect their men. The tragic events in that country having been exhausted, the talk drifted to armed car thefts in the city and other matters.

Isabelle was disgusted, not just at the lewd jokes, but at the general lack of indignation, at the very idea that a tragedy of such magnitude and still fresh in peoples' minds was already reduced to a handful of locker-room jokes. It was history seen through the eyes of a football fan.

Later they went to the newest discotheque in town, where Isabelle deliberately underestimated the potency of a local brew.

Such that the following day she would wake up late and virtually still drunk. But her mind was made up. She had to go back to Europe…

CHAPTER TWENTY-FIVE

Cordelia Thukudza's List

Ellen Banda-Aaku

The moment Junior lay still and stared up unblinking, Cordelia Thukudza remembered that her husband had died eight years prior, almost to the minute. Back then, on a cold June night, Cordelia had left the living room to get him a blanket because he had said he was cold. When she returned with the fluffy navy blanket in her embrace, he was gone. She did not call anyone right away. Instead she sat with his corpse for an hour before she picked up the phone. She wanted to savour her last few minutes alone with her husband of thirty-five years.

Judge Thukudza died long before Cordelia started to write her lists.

Cordelia's second thought as she knelt by Junior was to wonder what her daughters would have to say about the mess on the kitchen floor. It was a big mess: the muddy footprints from Junior's size 12 Jordan's, her white and blue teapot that lay shattered; her head scarf also lay abandoned on the floor with sugar and blood everywhere. It was just as well one of the girls – she was not sure which – was only coming to check on her at lunch time the following day. Cordelia noted with relief that she had time to clean up, but she needed to write a new list. She could not find her *things-to-do* list. She had emptied out all six kitchen drawers where she kept her lists but she could not find the most recent one. The one she had written first thing that morning. Cordelia then wondered what the newspaper headlines would read. In that moment Cordelia Thukudza had the soundness of mind to realise what had just happened was headline worthy in any part of the world.

And although she was not really important in society, most people would have heard of Cordelia Thukudza, widow of the respected Judge Thukudza, retired head teacher and founder of the highly reputable Kula Secondary School for Girls. She had set up the school to produce elegant, intelligent, well-rounded young women, like herself. She was a mother of two female doctors, twins, identical, if not for a mole on the brow of the elder twin.

Cordelia was not one to break a sweat but as she bent over Junior she realised her black and gold embroidered kaftan was stuck to her back. She wiped her hands on her kaftan then fastened the chain of her wrist watch which had come undone in the scuffle. She looked at her watch. It was ten minutes after nine. It was suddenly quiet, apart from the old fridge in the pantry which purred gently. The dogs had stopped barking and scratching on the kitchen door from outside. Cordelia wondered where Samson, the night watchman was. Probably fast asleep in the small concrete house by the main gate. He had slept through all the commotion which was not a surprise. Of late he had been sleeping a lot, all through his shift from 6pm to 6am and he made no secret of the fact. He was once loyal, still was in that he always turned up for work in his bright yellow rain coat and plastic boots – regardless of the weather – and with his rifle slung over his shoulder and a radio in his bag. But after twenty plus years of service the complacency that comes with familiarity of a job and employer had crept in. Cordelia had refused to fire him despite what her daughters said. She valued him and his loyalty. He was the one person who did not react when she forgot his name, nor did he comment like the twins did on the amount of time and paper she spent writing lists. Samson did not look at her as if she was crazy. He still revered her, he knelt when he spoke to her and he listened intently to what she said without a look of exasperation or bemusement on his face.

The two deaths she had witnessed were not comparable. It was ironic that she was present at the passing of the two men closest to her. Father and son, both having caused her intense pain and pleasure to varying degrees in the course of their lives. The judge was dignified in death; Junior was anything but. He screamed, clutched at his side, gasped and jerked violently, before he lay still. Cordelia watched his spasm as if she was watching a movie. At some point she lost her train of thought and actually wondered who the stranger dying in her kitchen was. She contemplated waking Samson up to tell him a young man had slipped and accidentally stabbed himself in the stomach on the kitchen floor, but before she got up to go outside she remembered who he was. It was Junior. Her Junior.

Blood blotched through his pink T-shirt and curdled around him on the pale grey kitchen tiles. She wondered who the T-shirt belonged to; it definitely wasn't his. It was too tight across his chest and pink was not a colour he would buy. Cordelia thought to reach for his face and shut his eyelids like she had seen done on TV but she changed her mind. Instead she reached over Junior's body to retrieve her cream slipper, it was wedged under him and so she had to crank his head up an inch to retrieve it. Half of the slipper was soggy and stained bright red.

She pondered putting the slipper back on and then changed her mind. She would end up with blood on her feet. She already had too much blood on her hands. She stood up slowly and shuffled to the sink. It was a big kitchen, rectangular shaped with a granite topped island – surrounded with four stools too high for her to perch on in the centre. It was a grey and white and black kitchen, a modern one, too modern. The twins had chosen it to their taste not hers. All the stainless steel appliances and accessories made it feel cold and bare. The twins had not asked for her opinion before they installed the kitchen because it was meant to be a surprise. They asked after it was installed. She was honest and told them it had a morgue-like feel to it. They sulked. Called her ungrateful and insensitive, not with words but with their body language. She told them if they didn't want her opinion they shouldn't have asked.

As she got to the sink, Cordelia caught a glimpse of herself in the display cabinet glass door. Junior had yanked her scarf off her head. Her hair underneath was kinky, grey and tousled like an old floor mop. She had been meaning to dye her hair a deep blue like Sister Mukando's from church. But she couldn't find the piece of paper where she had written down the brand and colour of the dye. She really ought to have transferred the details onto her list, but now even that was lost.

There were dark spots on her face, she moved closer to her reflection in the glass and realised blood had splattered onto her face. Was this really her? She looked very different from the elegant Cordelia Thukudza who always matched her handbag and shoes and was big on posture. She didn't look at her image for long but she did straighten up as she reached the sink. She had to think clearly now. What was she to do next? Who was she to call first? She didn't have any notes to jog her memory. She had not written any because she hadn't thought of what to do when he died. Not that she had planned his death, far from it.

But still, she had often thought of how she would react when Junior died. Or how he would die. The twins thought she was heartless when she told them to prepare for what was coming. "He's your son how can you think that way?" they asked.

But at sixty-five one sees the signs, death was coming to everyone, one day, but of late she knew Junior's death was fast approaching. She knew that sooner than later death would find him. Cordelia told her daughters she was being honest about their younger brother. And indeed she was right. She was vindicated because now he was dead, at a young age, just as she had predicted. What she hadn't envisaged was him dying on her kitchen floor, blood streaming from his gut, him gasping, disbelief in his eyes. She had not thought – despite all his misdemeanours in that past – that he would reach for a knife and wave it in her face. She would never have believed that he was capable of yanking her head scarf off and smacking it across her face. Nor did she know she was capable of feeling such intense humiliation and anger.

The boy had the nerve! After the way she had raised him? He should have known better than to disrespect her. He had never lashed out at her before and she had forgiven him many trespasses in the past. She had tried. God was her witness. She tried very hard to understand his disease. Even when his sisters gave up on him because; *God helps those who help themselves,* and, *rehab is for those who want it, not those who need it,* Cordelia had been supportive of her Junior.

And her hopes were not unfounded. He had showed signs of healing. He had accepted his problem was out of his control. He even sat through prayer sessions where Sister Mukando feverishly begged God to cast out the demons in him. Many times Junior had begged his mother for her forgiveness and apologised for bringing shame on the family.

Cordelia had told him it was not about shame. She said so because Sister Mukando whose husband was also possessed by demons, except his came in a bottle, had said, "never accuse them of bringing shame to the family because it is that shame that ultimately leads them back to the demon."

But Cordelia had lied, because Junior brought shame, on his father and his two sisters. And on her. She had held the family together for many years. It was not without scandal or secrets but she had buried them. She had torn up pictures and burnt letters. She was envied because she had successful children and a successful business. Then things changed. Her Junior changed. Typically, as a mother she had not seen the signs. When a man who was an officer in the courts had visited her home with important news, she could never have imagined what the news was. Cordelia sat and blinked at the skinny man in the oversize grey suit after he had broken the news. Her son was due to appear in court for theft. The court officer said he had come to tell her personally because the judge had been good to him many years ago when he was just a young filing clerk in the court. So he wanted to warn madam that young Junior was embarrassing his late father. Because everyone was talking. Except him. He would never gossip about the Judge's only son. He had come to tell Mrs Judge the truth.

As Cordelia processed her visitor's words she had called the house maid and asked her to offer the man a drink. As the drink was being served, Cordelia held a smile that belied the thoughts whirling through her head. To kick the man out or to thank him? Or to pay him to keep his mouth shut? In the end she thanked him, paid him and told him he was welcome to visit anytime when he had personal information for her. But soon after, Cordelia had also started to change. She started to forget names, faces, appointments, daily chores. Her forgetfulness frustrated her; she had always had a good memory, been meticulous in all she did. So she started to write everything down, so that she would not forget.

Cordelia reached for the tap and opened it. She watched the water rinse the blood off her hands and swirl down the drainage hole the colour of rosé wine. When the water turned clear she bent over and splashed cold water on her face. She giggled; it was very naughty of her to wash her face in the kitchen sink.

Cordelia reached for a kitchen towel and wiped her hands and face. The white towel stained bright red. She noticed her hand was bleeding so she wrapped the towel around her wrist. She started to make her way towards the living room to search one more time through the plastic bags in the living room for her list, but she stopped because Junior lay before her, on his side and it didn't feel right to step over him. As she stared down at him she felt a strong urge to hold and comfort him. She shunted towards him, dragging her foot, the one without the slipper, along. Her foot felt sore and heavy. She leaned against the cupboard, slowly raised her foot and with her towelled hand wiped away the sugar that was gritting her sole. When she straightened up she found herself staring at her reflection again in the glass in the display cabinet. She really had to remember to buy the dye, her hair looked terrible. She looked terrible, aged. It wasn't just her grey hair, it was the loose skin under her chin. She moved in closer. She looked like an old woman children ran away from or threw stones at. She laughed out loud at her reflection.

Cordelia stepped away from her reflection and reprimanded herself; she didn't have time to waste joking around when she had so much to do, starting with making a new list. She knelt over Junior. The pool of blood around him had turned a deep red almost black. The tips of his fingers were turning blue but then she seemed to remember his nails and finger tips had blackened over the past few years, as had his lips. She shuffled close to him and she felt his blood seep through her cotton kaftan at the knees. This time she reached across and closed his eyes. Then she lowered her head and placed her lips on his cheek. It felt cold or was it her lips that were cold? They felt very dry. His black lips were also dry, a bit chapped. With his eyes closed he looked at peace.

She stood up hurriedly. She had to get a jumper for him and some Vaseline for her lips and his. He was probably cold. She started heading out to get him some fresh clothes when she remembered he had moved his belongings – a whole back pack – out a week earlier. As he stormed out Cordelia was struck by sadness, not so much that he was leaving, but that after twenty-eight years of living and with a degree in Chemical Engineering, he could fit all he possessed and valued in one green and black back pack.

He had stormed out after they argued because she told him she had decided to stop giving him a weekly allowance. Initially, she had thought it was a good idea to give him money to support his habit. Just to see him through until he got better. With money he could at least buy clean stuff. At least with money he would not have to share needles so he was less likely to get infected with AIDS. And crucially, if she gave him money she would never again have to endure the humiliation of knowing he had crept into the living room and dipped his hands into her guests handbags, as she showed them her green beans and spinach garden. So she had made an informed decision to give him an allowance, but when the twins found out, they accused her of spoiling him and enabling his habit.

It was soon after that Cordelia noticed the girls whispering around her. The whispering became worse when Cordelia picked the leaves from her potted plant and chopped them into the fish stew she was cooking. It was a mistake, she had been checking the soil moisture of her plants and mixed up her plants and her fresh herbs as she placed them back on her kitchen window sill. Cordelia had meant to reach for the fresh parsley. The girls did not accept that it was a simple mistake. They banned her from cooking. She ignored them and continued to cook even though they took turns delivering lunchboxes of stews, of *nshima* wrapped in cling film, of cassava and sweet potato to her house. She packed their lunch boxes in the freezer and labelled them so she did not eat what they cooked. She wanted to show them that she could look after herself and hoped they would give up on delivering food to her as if she were an invalid. They took her stubbornness as a sign she was losing her mind. She heard them whisper to each other and to the doctor. Cordelia realised they were whispering outside the immediate family when the girls called their Aunt Chisunka. She travelled twenty-two hours from Mporokoso village on the carrier of a bicycle and then a bus and then a pontoon across Kalungwishi River and then an overnight bus ride to Lusaka, to rescue her sister. She arrived, balancing her travel bag on her head and her ever present container of tobacco snuff tucked in her ample bosom. Later that evening she broke the news to the twins that she had not come to nurse her youngest sister but rather to take her back to Mporokoso to see a medicine man. She told her nieces their mother had been cursed by her in-laws for sitting by their relative's dead body for an hour before calling an ambulance. Aunt Chisunka was convinced her sister was suffering from a disease that could not be cured with tablets and injections.

"And it was a double curse because your mother refused to have her head shaved when your father died even though it is a cleansing ritual every widow has to go through." Aunt Chisunka said. "The problem with your mother is that she behaves as if she is a white woman."

The twins were horrified; their mother would not be able to squat over a pit latrine, nor would she survive without her daily dose of Nollywood. They reminded their aunt that their Papa had been dead for many years, why would the Thukudza's curse their mother now? Besides, their mother did not need a medicine man because she was suffering from an age-related disease suffered by many people worldwide. Aunt Chisunka laughed in their faces, "what is an age related disease? I was born eighteen years before your mother but I still remember your names and I don't write everywhere or walk around with bags full of useless paper like a mad woman."

Cordelia listened to them argue through the living room wall and then she entered and startled the three of them. They thought she was sleeping. She reminded the twins that she was the mother and they were the children. And she was capable of looking after herself. She then turned to her elder sister and said, "you are the mad one from smoking your brain with all that *nsonka* you have snuffed up your nose for the past fifty years."

Cordelia then asked the three women to leave her house. She was fed up with everyone making decisions for her and behaving as if she had a big problem. So she was a bit forgetful and she did not want to eat what her daughters cooked for her, that did not make her mad.

She was sane enough to realise that giving Junior an allowance was not working. He had started to come home after days away in clothes she did not recognise. He was becoming more aggressive towards her. So she told him she was not going to give him any more money. He had stormed off with his backpack but a week later he resurfaced. He found her in the kitchen. He arrived with a bright smile, hands in pockets, no backpack. He was wearing jeans and a pink T-shirt. Cordelia stood her ground. She was not giving him any more money. He had to go and seek help. His smile vanished. He said he would not leave until she gave him his allowance. He accused her of making him dependent by giving him money. He called her a heartless old hag. Then he pleaded and cried. He promised if she gave him money one last time he would clean up his act and make her proud of him. She reminded him of the number of times she had heard the story of how he was quitting.

She was standing by the island in the middle of the kitchen, grinding fresh ginger for her tea in a small wooden mortar. He was pacing. After a while she stopped talking and let him rant and plead and cry. She pulled out a tray and laid her favourite white-and-blue tea set. She then turned away to fill the kettle with water. It was when she turned back that she realised his face had changed.

He looked at her as if she were a stranger. When he reached for the knife she realised that he intended to use it. She saw in his eyes that he was not Junior. Not her Junior. The person before her was a young man possessed by demons. He was not her Junior. He was a thief who stole from his own family and could kill his own mother.

She placed the kettle on the granite island. And looked him in the face although she knew he was not seeing. He reached for her head scarf and smacked it hard across her face. A big orange ball of fire lit up in her head. She grabbed hold of his arm. She was surprised at the extent of her strength or rather the lack of his. Perhaps he had not expected her to lunge at him. He looked surprised at the strength of her grip. Then he smiled and challenged her to kill him. It was not her intention. She just wanted to scare sense into him so he could become Junior again, her Junior. But he stepped back and somehow he tripped and lost his balance. And then he fell forward, fast and heavy, all 6 feet 3 inches of him, like a log. He took the tea tray down with him. He landed on the knife. He screamed one long howl of pain and fear. He clutched at the knife in his side and coughed. She dropped to her knees beside him. He gasped and shook so violently his trainers came off his feet. And then he was quiet.

Cordelia looked at the time on the oven timer; it was 9.30pm. Forty minutes had elapsed since Junior had strolled into the kitchen. He was getting cold. She hurried out of the kitchen to her laundry cupboard and picked out the thick navy blanket. It was the same blanket she had rushed to get for her husband the day he passed away. The thought warmed her heart, that the two men closest to her were sharing a blanket in death. She took comfort in the thought. Cordelia hurried back to the kitchen, shook the blanket open and placed it over Junior. Her Junior.

Cordelia stood up and reached for her handbag. She rummaged through it for her phone then she changed her mind. She had so much to do and she couldn't afford to forget. She needed to change her blood soaked kaftan. Then she had to clean up the mess. She also had to call Sister Mukando to ask for the colour of the dye. And she needed to make her cup of tea with fresh ginger before she went to bed. She also wanted to spend some time with her only son before she called anyone.

But first she had to write a list of all the things she had to do.

CHAPTER TWENTY-SIX

The Rhinos' Child

Bridget Pitt

I am not dead.

The thought jolts him into consciousness, bringing a strident tattoo of pain drumming on every nerve. And something else – something heavy pressing him down. A cold, hard, unyielding thing, caging him on the surface of the museum roof – *trapped!*

He jerks his body convulsively, twisting frantically until he manages to wriggle free, skinning his hands on the rough concrete in his panic. Then lies with his cheek against the roof, breathing. The air tastes of blood and each breath brings a kick in the ribs.

He stands unsteadily, buffeted by the wind that is still gusting fiercely, driving fine needles of rain into his skin and soaking through his sodden garments. The sky has a greenish cast, lowering under massed torn clouds; the dull glow of the obscured sun is dipping towards the skyline in the west. He stares at the distant fringe of buildings, their familiar outlines serene in the fading light. *Don't look down,* he tells himself. *Not yet.* If he doesn't look he can pretend that nothing has changed.

But he can't stop his gaze from falling, as if it has been sucked into the chaotic turmoil beneath him and the illusion is abruptly dispelled. Everything below two stories is submerged. He'd imagined that it would be a sea, a silver shimmering sea blotting out the chaos and rage and greed in the world, but it isn't. It's a roiling churning broth, slapping against the buildings, thick with debris: cars, splintered wood, tree branches, twisted metal, boats... as if the city had been swallowed, shredded and regurgitated in disgust.

Is anyone alive out there? Crouching on a rooftop like him, or clinging to some piece of flotsam? It seems impossible that many could have survived. The city had been dying already, the subways and basements under water as the higher swells each year breached the levees; the skyscrapers falling in as their foundations tilted and cracked in the sodden earth. Only the destitute remained, those who'd survived the waves of malaria and cholera, living like rats in the shells of buildings, or in Vegas, the huge shantytown that carpeted what had once been Central Park. Before the latest hurricane, they'd sent helicopters with loud hailers calling all to evacuate the city. For days he has stood on the roof, watching the ragged tide dragging their meagre possessions through the streets, as the helicopters wheeled away, their duty perfunctorily executed.

The sky darkens as the copper disc of the clouded sun slides behind the buildings. A wave of dizzying nausea sweeps over him, buckling his legs so that he sinks down against the parapet. He puts his face on his knees and notices first the blood clouding the puddle at his feet and then the long ragged tear through his trousers into the flesh on his calf. Deep, almost to the bone, pale beads of fat gleaming in the blood. As soon as he sees it, it begins to hurt savagely.

It'll kill me, he thinks. A cut like that… infection, gangrene… the slow, grudging death he'd dreaded. He should be dead already, should have been blown into oblivion, just one more flying fragment. He'd come onto the roof to give himself to the storm, to let it rip through him, tearing out the old sorrows, leaving him clean-boned and bloodless.

But he'd been flung against the turret and trapped by – he peers across – a piece of the water tank by the look of it, pinned by the wind like an insect caught on a windshield. He feels a surge of disgust at his persistence in living, this unseemly clinging to life in this land of dead things. The long dead in the glass cases of the museum, the newly dead bobbing together under the waves, bumping against the plethora of things they'd so treasured when alive. Laz-y-boy recliners. Foot spas. Plastic fish that sing *don't worry, be happy.*

He could just stay on the roof, in the wind and rain. Death would come faster here. But a sudden craving for the warm enfolding stillness of the museum impels him to drag himself up painfully against the parapet and limp to the stairhead, wrench open the door and half fall inside.

It's dark in here, but he knows it well enough. He stumbles down the stairs along a short passage and into the hall of Ornithischian Dinosaurs. A cool spray gusts into his face. In the dim light he sees that several panes of the tall windows have been smashed in and one of the great dinosaur skeletons has crashed onto the floor. He stumbles through the glass and broken bones into the corridor leading to the old "Dinostore" shop where he's set up home. He gropes through his few possessions until his fingers curl onto the flashlight. He switches it on and does a quick sweep – everything seems to be untouched here. His head and leg are throbbing, but he needs to see the animals before he can rest.

He makes his way through the passageways of his expansive home, a building he has not left for twenty-five years. Since *that* day, which still comes to him in the strobe light staccato images of madness recalled, he'd travelled to this country to receive his father's posthumous award for bravery in the service of wildlife conservation. But his mind finally shattered when they called his father's name. He'd crushed the champagne glass in his hand, blood splattering his hired suit and run out, through the cars and people and noise, running until he found himself at the museum, drawn by the billboard of the rhinos displayed outside.

How safe it had felt, then. The great thick walls, the dim light… a place where nothing could ever die because everything was already dead. He'd hidden in storerooms, pretending to be a visitor, scavenging the bins when his money ran out. They threw enough food away every day to sustain a village.

Doc found him and helped him hide. Gave him work sorting collections, fed him when the food ran out. The museum had been closed for years now. For a while they'd kept a "skeleton staff" (how tired that old joke became), but it was only Doc and Sono in the end. They talked about taxonomy, compared the Latin names and Zulu names of the millions of species that once roamed the earth. As if uttering their names could stop them from slipping into the long dark night of extinction.

We must go, Doc said when the helicopters came with loud hailers. Worst hurricane on record… they say the whole island will go.

But Sono couldn't leave. And finally Doc had gone reluctantly. *I'll come back,* he promised.

Did Doc get out? Throughout the night before the hurricane hit the shore, Sono had heard the sounds of gunshots, screaming and sirens, as the rats (human and rodent) had fought over each other to get across the bridges – the tunnels were all flooded. How would an old brittle twig like Doc get through that?

As he heads down the marble staircase to the Hall of African Mammals on the second floor, the oily roil of water gleams in his flashlight. He wades down into it – thigh deep, the currents eddying painfully around the cut in his leg. The elephants have stood their ground, emerging like ancient dreams from the water, but some of the smaller animals have been swept out of their alcoves. Their forms bob against him, glass eyes gleaming in the torch light as he moves it over them.

The solar lamp he'd kept burning in the rhinos' alcove has gone out, but the animals are fine – their alcove is high and the water is just lapping the edge. Mother, father, child: the archetypal family. The hollow promise of a future, belied by the bleak horror that seems to lurk in their eyes as they stand, staring darkly past their horns into the chaos beyond. The small patch of dusty grassland on which they eternally graze is scattered and sodden, as if the rhinos had trampled it in panic in the night. The water must have spilled into the alcove, which is no longer encased in glass. Broken when the last vandals sawed off the horns, despite the sign explaining that they were fibreglass. He and Doc had fashioned new horns from the moulds kept in the back rooms, but the glass was never repaired.

There is an orange smear on the young one's mouth. As Sono leans forward to inspect it, his flashlight catches the gleam of eyes. Real eyes, not glass ones. A scrabble as the thing tries to burrow deeper under the mother rhino's belly, but Sono grasps it and hauls out… a child. Barely recognisable as such – a ragged, feral, filthy, thing, twisting round to bite his hand.

"Hold still!" Sono roars, "or I'll drown you like a rat."

The child freezes and squints up at Sono fearfully. Sono sets him down more gently on the grass fragments at the edge of the alcove. The child shrinks away from him.

"What's your name, boy?" *Is it a boy?*

"Draino."

"Draino? What kind of name is that?"

The boy is silent, staring at his feet.

"How did you get in here?"

Nothing.

"Where's your family, Draino? Your folks know you here?"

The boy waves to the three rhinos.

"Them's my folks."

"They're rhinos, boy. I mean your real family."

The boy sticks out his lower lip and glowers at Sono. He reaches behind him and pats the young rhino on its orange-dusted nose.

"'S my brother. Brother Rhino. I gi'm food."

Sono sees now the empty packet at the young rhino's feet. He picks it up. *Cheezy Kurls* in yellow on the red shiny foil packaging. The inside of the foil is dusted with orange.

"Where you get these?"

The boy hangs his head.

"Man drop 'em. Everyone running and running cos' the Hurricane coming, an' I runned an' runned an' squeezed in the pipe an' I found my family. If that Hurricane come here, my family gon' stick'm with those sharp horns. Gon' stick'm right where it hurts, mister. *Right where it hurts.*"

A sudden animation at the end, piercing the sullen passivity.

Sono considers the boy. A refugee from Vegas no doubt. He and Doc had tried to make the museum impenetrable to intruders, but perhaps there was an air vent somewhere that a small child could enter. He must have gotten in here before the storm. Much good it would do him.

"I can't help you," he says. "I got nothing for you, see? You'll just have to fend for yourself."

The boy nods solemnly, as if Sono has given him a useful instruction.

Sono turns to go, pushing against the water, pulling away from the drag of the boy's eyes on the back of his head. *Haai wena!* His long dead mother scolds. You just going to leave that child? Just leave that boy alone in the dark?

Sono sighs and turns back. The boy watches impassively. Barely six-years-old, by the size of him and already with such low expectations of adults.

"Get on my back," Sono says gruffly. The boy reaches small hands over his shoulders, tucks bony knees around his waist. The feel of him, this small live thing, stirs something in Sono, more like nausea than tenderness... that something so vulnerable could exist in a world so brutal.

He wades back past the ghostly elephants and puts the boy down when he reaches the stairs. Back in the storeroom he switches off the flashlight, switches on the solar lamp and considers. The water tanks and solar panels on the roof are gone, but Doc had filled several water barrels from the tanks. Composting toilet still works, although he'll run out of soil soon. Solar lamps can be charged at the windows in the Dinosaur Hall. Enough food for a week perhaps – cans of beans, corn meal. Gas stove. First aid kit. A self-inflating dinghy with waterproof lockers. He'd watched Doc fussing around, getting all this ready, bringing in supplies or dredging them from storerooms. Seemed too cruel to tell him that he had no intention of surviving the storm.

The boy is eyeing the tins hungrily. Looked like he hadn't ever eaten much, even before the storm. Sono opens a can of beans and passes it to him, with a spoon. He shovels the food into his mouth eagerly but keeps his eyes alert, darting between Sono and the door as if calculating his escape route should Sono try to snatch the food back. Sono watches him, absorbed by the pale streaks appearing in the grime as the juice runs down his chin. A white child, he thinks, still conditioned enough by his homeland to be surprised by impoverished white people, although God knows there are enough of them here.

His leg has been throbbing dully, but a sudden sharp stab of pain reminds him that it needs attention.

"Gotta do something, Draino. You stay here. Finish that food, there's water to drink if you want it."

He gathers dry clothes, a bucket of water, rags and the first aid kit, lights another lamp to take with him and moves to the bathroom down the hall. No running water of course, but he can empty the water down the drain.

He puts a plug in a basin and fills it with water from the bucket, props his leg on an upturned bin and examines the wound: a long ragged gaping tear into his calf, embedded with torn fabric and grit. He cuts his trousers away and picks out the scraps with tweezers. He pours disinfectant into the wound, grimacing against the sting, as rivulets of cloudy liquid and blood run over his foot into the drain below. He pours antibiotic powder onto the serrated flesh, lights a candle, threads a needle, heats it in the flame, holds the lip of the cut together and begins to sew. Each stab of the needle sends a hot shard of pain shooting through his leg and by the time he has managed five crude stitches and covered them with a dressing he is sweating and nauseous.

As he winds the bandage over the dressing, he catches a pale ghost in the mirror – the boy, standing behind, watching. He darts away when Sono sees him.

"Come back!" Sono calls.

He pauses.

"Come here, I won't hurt you, just want to wash your face."

The boy approaches warily. Sono ties off the bandage, takes a clean rag, wets it in the bucket and wipes the boy's face. He jerks back as if the water were acid.

"Hold still, boy. Just want to wipe your face and hands. We have standards in this establishment."

He wipes the cloth gently over the face... cheeks, mouth, eyes screwed shut, ears... such painfully familiar geography. Where were they now, the ones whose faces he'd washed, who'd washed his own as a child? *What good is this*, some part of him snarls. *What good is this pretence that we have hope here? That we are still guests at life's table and not beggars at the window waiting for death?* He wipes the boy's hands brusquely, then peels off his own sodden shirt and trousers and puts on the clean clothes. The boy is staring at his face in the mirror, touching it and then the reflection as if it is a wonder he has never encountered. Perhaps it is.

Back in the Dinostore, he sees that the boy has found the set of plastic animals he'd saved from the store before it was looted. The African Wildlife collection. Set out on the great plains of the carpeted floor: elephants, rhinos, giraffes, sable antelope, springbok, buffalo, lion's, zebra, leopards, crocodiles. Neatly lined up in pairs, as if setting off in search of an Ark to carry them into a future.

"It's alright, you can play with those." Sono says, seeing the boy's fear when his eyes fall on the animals. He kneels down beside them.

"C'm here," he says, "I'll teach you their names."

The boy comes forward.

"Elephant, *indlovu*, the wise one," Sono says. "Giraffe, *indulamithi*, the quiet one; lion, *ingonyama*, the royal one; rhino, *umkhombe*, the strong one..." Sono holds up each animal as he names it then sets it down beside its partner.

"These are their names in isiZulu, the language we speak where I come from in Africa. Once all these animals lived there, near the place I lived when I was a child. But now –"

Sono knocks down the elephants, the sable antelope, the lions, the leopards, the rhinos. 'These ones are all gone. And many others have gone. Many, many others."

The boy stares at the fallen animals.

"Where they go?" he whispers.

"People killed them, boy. People killed them."

He pushes himself up and sets out a bedroll and sleeping bag for the boy. "Time to sleep now. We cannot waste the light."

Sono sleeps fitfully. He'd placed the boy's bedding across the room, but in the night the child brings his sleeping bag over and curls against his back. Sono rolls over to watch him sleep, inhaling the sharp musty odour rising from his small body. His face is silver in the moonlight, his long eyelashes dark against the pale cheeks, a plastic rhino in each hand. *What can he know of rhinos, this boy? What does he see in them?* Through the high window the moon looks down on the world, just as it always has.

The next day Sono heats water on the gas stove, fills the bucket and takes it down to the bathroom. Water and gas are precious, but if he's going to sleep beside this boy something must be done.

He comes back and takes the boy by the hand. As they near the bathroom the child tries to break away, but Sono picks him up and carries him kicking and bucking, uttering a guttural wail of fear and distress.

"I'm not going to hurt you, boy. You just need a bath."

In the bathroom he sits on the closed toilet seat, the boy gripped between his knees, while he chops the grey matted hair that is crawling with lice. The boy keeps up his low keening growl as Sono tears off his clothes, then stands shivering while Sono washes him, his shoulders hunched, shorn head down, as if waiting for an executioner's axe.

"There, that wasn't so bad was it?" Sono asks as he towels him dry.

Sono dresses him in clothes from the Dinostore – shorts and a T-shirt with "I" and a picture of a Tyrannosaurus Rex. Much too big, but at least they're clean.

"Why you called Draino, boy?" he asks as he dresses him.

"They found me in a drain when I was a baby. Pastor John says my Ma 'n' Pa is drain rats. But he wrong. Them rhino's my family."

Sono takes the boy to see the Peoples of Africa on the second floor. The water has subsided, but it is still over his ankles and he carries the child on his back. Doc had assured Sono that the Peoples of Africa are not stuffed, but he can't help wondering. There they are, a family of Batwa pygmies aiming arrows into the trees at birds that will never be shot, masked dancers from Guinea Bissau suspended in mid-leap. The information plaques describe these scenes in the present tense (the men go hunting while the women pound the corn) as if they are contemporary vistas into these lives. As if this static, simplistically narrated, ritualised village life still sustains itself somewhere in the world. As if all the forests the Batwa once roamed have not been razed by loggers and miners, the Batwa driven into refugee camps, the animals slaughtered by poachers or soldiers.

"See boy? This is how people lived once..." Sono makes up stories about the frozen figures. The boy holds on to his shoulders, saying nothing but it feels as if he is listening. Such a still child. Langalihle flits through Sono's memory, chattering like a small bright stream, always asking questions, skipping, dancing... This boy says little, keeps his movements small, everything to stop himself from being noticed. But some stubborn spirit seems coiled inside him. He is not all broken.

They wade through the Hall of African Mammals to the rhinos. The animals watch them from their dim, shadowy alcoves; the elephants charge eagerly towards them, trunks raised.

"Indlovu, the wise one," the boy whispers against his neck.

Sono stops so that the boy can stroke a huge leathery ear, his small hands pale against the wrinkled grey skin.

At the rhino's enclave, he scrambles off Sono's back and scrabbles across to them.

"Look Mama Rhino, look Papa Rhino, look Brother Rhino... ", he croons, showing them the two plastic rhinos that he has been carrying all morning.

"New friends for you."

He whispers into the baby rhino's ear, then holds his own ear against its mouth, and nods. He turns to Sono.

"Rhino family sad down here in the dark. They wan' come live wi'us."

"Forget it, boy."

But half an hour later, they are hauling Brother Rhino up the stairs.

Moving Mama and Papa Rhino is impossible – they are old, heavy models, the skin stretched over wood and wire and plaster. But the young one has been redone with moulded foam. Much lighter, but bulky and still a challenge. They'd floated him out of the gallery into the hall, then Sono cut the old canvas fire hose off the wall and tied one end around the rhino's middle. Now the boy is putting everything into pulling him up the marble steps, eyes screwed up with the effort.

"Pull, boy!" Sono says, when he flags. "That's your brother there. Don't you let your brother go... Family gotta stick together."

They put Brother Rhino by the broken windows in the Ornithischian Dinosaur hall, so that he can gaze out at the ruined city. The small plastic animals are placed in a reverent circle around him.

"Brother Rhino happy now," the boy says, his face transformed by a smile that seems to illuminate him from the inside. Sono finds something like a smile tugging at his own mouth and eyes.

"What 'bout his mom and dad? They gotta be missing their boy."

The child considers this. "They happy," he says at length. "They happy 'cos their boy's happy, 'cos their boy's wi' his brother."

Sono looks at the rhino over the bent head of the boy, whose cropped hair gleams in the evening sun like the winter grasslands of Sono's childhood home. Brother Rhino stares out impassively, but something like a smile seems to flit across his boot-shaped snout.

By the evening of the third day, his leg is hot, swollen and throbbing, with red lines running up towards his groin. He languishes on his bedroll, which he has dragged to the big window by Brother Rhino. The damp heat is stifling and he craves the air gusting through the broken panes. Sometimes it brings the smell of decaying things, but other times a sharp salt breeze from the sea blows clean through his lungs. The boy plays beside him, chattering softly to the plastic animals and Brother Rhino, a tender vibrant noise like the sound of new leaves rustling in a spring wind.

The world warps around Sono as his fever grows. He shouts in the night, converses with his dead father who sits across the room from him in his green Rhino Ranger's uniform, his chest a flower of blood, although he did not die in that uniform. He died in a white T-shirt, because that night he was off-duty.

"I didn't know," Sono cries. 'I didn't know you would investigate the shots. I told the poachers to go that night because you were off-duty. You were off-duty, Baba, why did you come running to save your rhinos, not wearing your bullet-proof vest?'

But his father does not answer, just shakes his head in bewildered disbelief.

"It was for Langalihle, Baba, I needed the money for Langalihle. She had to go to a private hospital, she was dying in that rubbish hospital... one night I found a rat under her bed..."

Sono wakes to find the boy wiping his face with a cloth.

"Hol' still," the boy says. "Jus' washin' your face. We got standards this 'stablishment."

"Who's Langalishy?" he asks later, holding a water bottle so that Sono can drink. 'You bin callin' an' callin' langalishy, langalishy."

"Langalihle. My daughter, my little girl. It means the 'beautiful sun.'"

"Where she?"

"She died many years ago. She got sick, we could not save her. She was the same age as you, I think. How old are you?"

The boy shrugs.

Sono's mother pays a visit, poking him awake with her unforgiving finger. *You got to get that boy out of here*, she says, scowling. *Food's low. You gonna let him watch you die, then starve to death himself?*

"*Eish*, Mama," Sono groans, but drags himself back from the twilight into the harsh glare of the living. He tells the boy where to find Doc's telescope. He scans the city, the brown water flowing sluggishly between the buildings. There is no sign of life. But later in the day, he sees a thread of smoke rising from the balcony of a building down the street. He focuses the telescope on the balcony through the afternoon. Two or three shadowy figures flit against the windows. And once, a figure lifting a small one, a child, holding it up and then hugging it.

Did he see it? He looks and looks, but the figure is gone.

It's not much.

But it's all there is.

Drifting in and out of delirium he instructs the boy on inflating the dinghy, filling the lockers with food and water, the first aid kit, the flashlights and solar lamps, the gas stove. Sometimes the room fills with his relatives, helping to prepare for his father's funeral. 'We must get ready to slaughter the ox,' he tells Draino. 'Go see if the women are done with the *umqombothi*.'

329

"Tomorrow we are going in that boat," he says, when it is ready.

"What about my family?"

"We can't take Mama and Papa Rhino, boy. The boat will sink."

"We take Brother Rhino," the boy says firmly. "You don't let your brother go."

Sono finds the strength to help the boy to drag the dinghy and Brother Rhino down to the second floor and out through the fire exit onto the parapet above the tall pillars fronting the museum. As they push away from the parapet with the oars, Sono is gripped with trepidation. How can he send this child and Brother Rhino into this chaotic, devastated world? How can they leave the sanctuary of the museum? Where elephants still charge and the Batwa still draw their bows and masked dancers still dance for the rain in Guinea Bissau?

But it's too late... the building is receding as the current pulls them away through the debris of a destroyed civilisation. The boy laughs, both amazed and alarmed to be floating. And Sono feels the wind of the outside world on his face and laughs too, the sound foreign to his ears, like a long-locked door creaking open.

Their progress is slow and erratic, one oar each, the boy splashing more than rowing, his own hands seemingly joined to his arms by wet string so that he can barely hold the oar, never mind pull it against the water. Things bump against them, anonymous wood and plastic fragments mostly, but occasionally something recognisable – an office chair, a supermarket trolley, a sign that reads "no dumping." And then, two corpses, mother and child floating together, her pale hands reaching out for redemption too long in coming. Sono pushes them away with his oar before the boy can see.

They drift slowly towards the balcony. When they are closer, he lifts his telescope again. A woman with a child is standing at the railing, peering at him as if trying to identify him. He waves wildly. She waves back tentatively.

"We going to that lady, okay?" He says to the boy. The boy nods, doubtfully.

"It will be fine, I promise. I can't look after you alone any more... I'm... I'm not well, boy... you understand that, don't you?"

The boy's lip trembles; a tear runs down his cheek. He turns to bury his face in Brother Rhino.

"Listen, Draino?"

The boy nods, keeping his face pressed to the rhino's wrinkled hide.

"You need a new name, boy. You can't go into the world with a name like Draino. You want a new name?" The boy nods again.

"I'll give you my name, okay? Not Sono... the name my mother gave me. Themba. It means the one who has hope."

The boy looks up from the rhino.

"Themba..." he repeats.

"You like it?"

He nods, vigorously.

"Why you called Sono?" he asks.

"I gave myself this name. I no longer deserved the name my mother gave me. I gave myself the name of Sonosakhe. The one who lives with his sin."

The boy shakes his head. 'You Themba too. You, me both. An' brother Rhino. All Themba.'

Sono smiles, then sinks back against the dinghy. His arms keep rowing mechanically, quite disconnected from his own volition, sustained it seems by an external force. The water splashes his hands, cool against his burning skin. The sun dances on the water's surface and the buildings. He lifts his face to a sky softened by a spray of silver-tipped clouds. He is back in St Lucia, the lake as it was in his childhood, when the elephants still swam with their trunks up like periscopes and the rhinos still wallowed in cool mud holes. A flock of flamingos stand in the shallows, swallows swoop over their heads. His father smiles at him across the boat.

"Keep rowing, Themba my boy," his father says. "Keep rowing."

CHAPTER TWENTY-SEVEN

Sahara

Shadreck Chikoti

It's either the northern raven or the girl. In the case of the raven, he is resting his hands on the balcony railing and looking down Avenue 6 Drive when the passerine bird, large-bodied, long graduated tail, large dark bill, all-black, not the white-necked pied crow known in these regions, flies by and perches on the balcony, barely a metre away. Their eyes lock in a staring contest that appears to last forever. It has brown irises. After a while, the ancient bird takes off, croaking as it soars away in the air, until it disappears behind the metallic edifice in front.

In the case of the girl and her case is commonplace, an aero-bus slowly docks at the Mandala terminal in Blantyre, and he looks at his clock; the square monitor embedded in his left palm reads 11:40am. It's always 11:40am. He is sitting on the chair in the glassy waiting booth, undecided. The passengers scamper out of the locomotive like rats smoked out of their hole as soon as the doors slide open. He rises and walks towards the bus. He gets in through the front door; presses his palm on the Zooter for identification. There is a green light blinking on the driver's console and the android driver nods for him to get in. He turns towards the isle and notices the bus is empty except for this one seat, occupied by a passenger who is looking down, her black dreadlocks shielding her face as they flow all about her.

She raises her head and their eyes meet. Time stops. There is no sound that he hears except the thumping of his heart. Black glistening dreadlocks flowing about her like river water, enveloping an oval face where eyes as shiny as stars, a turned up nose and thick lips have made their home.

Next, he is sitting with her on the chair and he doesn't know how that has happened. She is on his right, sitting on the window seat. She turns and speaks to him.

"What'chu sitting here for?" Her accent is Southern.

"Eee, you said what?"

"Many vacant seats, what'chu sitting here for?" she gestures with her hand.

His eyes track her hand as it quickly swipes around like a surveillance camcorder, showing him all the empty seats. He stands up to walk away from her, find another seat, dunderhead! But she holds his hand and forcefully pulls him down. He collapses back into the chair, excited with the prospect but also wondering where a girl that pretty got all that energy.

"You sit now bwana. Only joking; don't like jokes? I am Sahara."

"Sahara like…"

"Like the desert," she takes the words out of his mouth.

"Pleased to meet you, I am…"

"Kamoto, I know you bwana. Pleased to meet you too."

He freezes, looks at her with awe. *How did she know his name?* he is wondering.

"Look on floor sir, you dropped your mandible," he gets her joke.

"It's the badge on your shirt, it gave you away."

Dunderhead! She is gazing at him like an artist admiring the finishing of his masterpiece. She is smiling at him; that kind of smile a teacher displays when proving to his class the math wasn't really as hard as they thought. Red dress, pink nails, golden earrings, a glassy necklace that sparkles. He smiles back at her.

"This is me," she says as she presses the red button on the sides. "Do you see that green house, behind those trees? That's where I live." She is standing and ready to go. "Sahara Chaponda, I work at the Great Shopping Mall as a manager. I am human." She is smiling again.

She takes something out of her brown handbag which he notices for the first time.

"Here." An e-business card. Her name flashes and goes on the top of the card. In the picture box, her face beams and disappears, to be replaced by a different one, this time she smiles and the next she frowns, yet another she remains expressionless and so on and so forth. Her contact details are at the bottom.

The bus has docked and she is already at the door.

It's always like that, all the time. He has lost count but this is the third month he's been seeing her and the dream always ends here. She gives him her business card and she vanishes.

His psychiatrist says there is no such thing as paranormal in the multiverse. That belief belongs to the old world; when people believed in UFOs and witchcraft. Humanity can no longer afford a room for unidentified things. We live in a world where not to identify a thing is to put the whole of humanity in danger.

"So, these are just dreams?"

"Yes, they are just dreams?"

"But why are they recurring?"

"The only explanation I have is that these are symptoms of post-traumatic stress disorder. It is not a problem at all. You are trying to deal with your imprisonment issue."

"But that issue is resolved, after all I only stayed in prison for ten days."

"Yes, but how do you feel about the government? Do you harbour feelings of resentment towards the government? It's all connected, Mr Kamoto."

"Don't you think these dreams are pointing to something?"

"No, Mr. Don't even go there. That's superstition and it has no room in this world."

"You know the reason they'd arrested me, don't you?"

"They said you were disrupting public order."

"There was a line in my news article that said, *information from a reliable government agent confirms that there is no hope of finding a cure for the disease in the next ten years.*"

"That would bring fear and panic to the public wondn't it?"

"But look, does this not confirm that there are some things we have no answers for?"

"In the case of the disease, we have a whole lot of information on it, we know what causes it, the part of the body it attacks, how to avoid it and many other things. What we don't have is a one-off cure, that's all."

"What do I do then?"

"The dreams will go, slowly, they will go. Once you are back on your feet and you have forgotten all about the incident, it will go."

"Thank you."

But today he wakes up with a different feeling. He wants to pursue his dreams, like literally, see what happens, there is nothing to lose if it turns out he's been chasing after a hologram.

He knows what his psychiatrist would say, so he doesn't call. He calls his workplace instead, telling the chief editor he is pursuing a story in Blantyre.

He doesn't realize it but the time is eight in the morning. Lilongwe is already awake and bustling: the humming of aero-engines, the honking of vehicles below – he is on the last floor, the siren of an ambulance in the distance and the wind whispering by his window. The sky is a huge blue when he parts the drapes, it stretches as far away as his eyes can afford to see, no clouds. There is a bird high up on the far west, playing freely.

It takes two hours to drive a Gravity Mobile on the Gravity D-Road from Lilongwe to Blantyre. He will make it, he tells himself. The plan is as clear as rain water in his mind. By four in the evening he will be home, making himself a sandwich and tea and watching history on the Telecommunication Curtain.

It is 10:53 when he gets to Blantyre, his old city. He worked here twenty years ago when his career was just beginning, before the trophies had clattered his table, before the jealousies from work mates had crept in, before the responsibilities and promotions had come flooding by and the transfer to the headquarters in Lilongwe.

From afar, the city of Blantyre looks like many pencils of different sizes protruding from the ground with mushroom shaped objects interspaced in the air between them. The words on the entrance arch, the one you find soon after crossing the seventeen kilometres of the artificial lake that surrounds the city reads, WELCOME TO BLANTYRE A CITY BUILT ON IDEAS. And the ideas are the many gravity domes that shield the light from the sun all the time. The ideas are the fact that you can't drive your car on the ground streets as they get crammed all the time, forcing people to pay a lot of money to the government so they can fly their Gravity Mobiles, the ideas are that Blantyre is a city feeding on electricity and solar power.

He parks his Gra-Mob on the tenth floor of a parking carnivore and waits on the extended balcony for an aero-motor-scooter.

It is 11:35 when he dismounts from the scooter at the Mandala terminal. He goes into the glassy booth to wait for the bus. The monitor above his head confirms that the next bus will dock at 11:40. He doesn't want to get excited.

There is no such thing as paranormal in the multiverse.

When the bus docks, he does not wait for the passengers to come out before he leaves the booth and the passengers who come out are fewer than the number of fingers on one hand. It is also a human who is driving not a humanoid and the bus is half full. Men in uniform, obviously going for afternoon shifts, a gentleman in a black suit, two women, one in red hair and the other in golden braids, at the very back; these two are the only women in the whole bus. They are absorbed in a conversation. His eyes rest on them for a brief moment, but none of them looks like his dream girl. He can hear faint echoes of laughter from the one with red and the golden hair at the back, the two women unable to conceal their mirth. He finds a seat. The bus takes off.

There is no such thing as paranormal in the multiverse.

He thinks as he exits at the next terminal. He should have trusted his psychiatrist.

"Mr Kamoto, you should trust me."

"Yes, doctor."

"How old are you?"

"Forty-five."

"Oh, you are so young."

"I am not."

336

"You are; how old do you think I am?"

"Sixty?"

"No, Mr Kamoto, I am a hundred and twelve. Don't get shocked. It's all about being healthy, healthy foods, healthy choices and a lot of discipline."

"Yes."

"Humanity has all it needs to live longer, so if you are wondering, no I am not a clone." Laughter. "This is my fifty-sixth year working as a psychiatrist. You should believe me. You know what these things we call dreams are?"

"No."

"Just a window into our unconscious. It's our own thoughts, our own fears, embedded into the subconscious and manifesting themselves in the form of images and sounds when we sleep. Dreams can be your happy moments but they can also be your worst nightmares which you push away during your conscience zones."

"And we have no control over them?"

"No. No control at all, Mr Kamoto."

"I've been reading."

"Okay, you have been reading?"

"That there are actually some inventions that were inspired by dreams?"

"The Periodic table, Dimitri Mendeleyev, many centuries ago, just like James Watson's DNA's double helix spiral form and the modern idea of Free Space. I know all that. And all this confirms that dreams are our thoughts locked in the subconscious."

"How about premonition dreams, where people dream of events that will occur in the future."

"Coincidence."

"Really?"

"Yes, Mr Kamoto."

The frustration must have numbed his brains for he forgets to refuel his Gra-Mob as he leaves Blantyre and only sees the blinking light when he's driven for an hour. The screen on the console says he should refuel here and now. He is at Ntchewu, a town renowned for its cheap housewares.

He stops the Gra-Mob at a pump and presses a button below his chair to let the fuel attendant android in the cubicle structure in front know he is here. The doors to the cubicle open and a female android walks towards him. He is fumbling with the button that opens the lid on the tank and he does not see the android approach.

When he raises his head to command the android, he is filled with shock. He stays for a moment, transfixed and looking at the machine like he is witnessing the sinking of Atlantis.

Black glistening dreadlocks, shiny eyes, a turned-up nose and thick lips, features that make a perfect human face. Red dress, pink nails, golden earrings, a glassy necklace that sparkles. Sahara!

The Android extends her hand, showing him the screen in her palm. He turns to place his palm on hers so their palm clocks can touch, a routine task for identification.

"Mr Kamoto," he almost jumps out of his chair as the android begins to speak.

"How much should we deduct from your account?" the android is smiling. It is a perfect smile.

"Fill it up please," he stumbles over his words.

When the android is done she comes close to his window.

"I have something for you," she leans closer.

Is he imagining things?

"Please don't get startled. Behave normal. I have something for you."

"What do you have for me?"

He looks into her eyes wondering if he is really talking with an android.

"My master wants you to have something."

"Who is your master?"

"It doesn't matter."

The name on her shirt reads, SAHARA. Sahara's head turns around, 360 degrees.

"There is no one in proximity. Please act normal."

She extends her hand into the car. The arm parts in the middle and the two sections partially flip outwards to reveal a metal cylinder standing in the centre of the arm. There is a tiny card on the top of the cylinder. It is black.

"Please take the black devise. It is a memory card. It has information for you."

He is not thinking. He takes the card quickly and keeps it in his hands.

"Thank you sir, it was good doing business with you," the final line from every fuel attendant android.

He is still looking at her as she walks back to the cubicle with a perfect human body and movement.

What just happened?

There is no such a thing as paranormal in the multiverse?

His apartment is on the eighteenth floor on Avenue 6 Drive. After parking his Mob in the parking hallway below, he takes an elevator to the last floor where his two-roomed flat is.

He feels his pocket to see if he still has the device.

He has a lot of questions like, was the device given to him because it was him or was it meant for anybody? And how come the Android was his dream? He chooses not to ponder over the questions. His more-than-a-decade experience in journalism has taught him that there is more to life than the database can tell. People keep secrets and they do not want the secrets known, part of the reason he was imprisoned.

He has learnt to conceal his sources and to play the authority, that's why people trust him. He told them at the police station, "If I tell you my sources, you will be forced to relieve half of your officers including two who are part of this interrogation."

"Why?"

"Because they are some of my sources," he wasn't lying. They never made further enquiries and released him after the ten recommended days.

He sits on the couch in his house. Takes out the device from his pocket, holds it up against the light of the sun from the window. The device has words written on it; SDXC, 164GB. He knows it's an old electronic data storage card. The Telecommunication Curtain – TC – uses it as a symbol for the save button. Or could the TC have a slot where he can insert it?

He takes the remote on the coffee table in front, presses a button that unrolls the TC. The monitor, which hung on the wall like the old scrolls, unwraps. He rises from the chair to check the plastic bar at the bottom of the TC to see if it has a port for the SDXC card. It doesn't.

He also knows that his pad in his room, as well as the audio side drawers on his bed do not have that kind of port.

He switches on the TC with his remote. There is a blue line that cuts through the middle of the TC horizontally; the blue line grows, spreading with speed on both sides, to fill the whole monitor with a sky blue colour. On his remote he presses the keyboard symbol and the coffee table in front is illuminated; a neon keyboard forms on the glass of the table.

He puts both hands on the keyboard and types: Free Space. There is a circular logo on the top right corner of the screen with the letters FS on it, Free Space but also standing for Fast Search.

An empty rectangular box blinks below the logo. He types the words, "SDXC card" in the blinking box. Pictures of cards, similar to the one in his possession, comes up. At the bottom, there is a small write-up.

SDXC cards are storage devices in the family of SD cards developed in the 21st century. SD, Secure Digital, and SDXC, Secure Digital Extended Capacity, can only work on old machines like computers, tablets and cameras from the 21st century. Their use is considered archaic and extinct but…
Expand Space to read on?

No, there is no need to expand space to read on, he tells himself. He remembers an antique item that he received as a trophy for his feature *Has Science Failed Us All?* published in the *Daily Chronicles*, a paper he works for. He is sure it was a computer.

When he finds it, stacked in the pile of books, cartons, old clothes and other cast-offs, he does not struggle to switch it on and to find a slot for the card. The keyboard and pad are the same as those on the TC.

Open file?
Click
Play video?
Click
Windows Media Player. Loading. 45% 60% 87% 92% 100%
Words form on the black screen, words in white.

This information is meant for you Thokozani Kamoto. Please destroy the card after watching.

The words disappear and are replaced by a picture of a man seated on a chair. He is wearing a white shirt and dark blue trousers. He looks young; he has tiny ears, eyes that bulge a little, a flat nose, puffy cheeks, dark brown skin. His eyes are red and tired.

Kamoto doesn't believe it. He knows the man in the picture. The imprisoned scientist, Kalaile, fondly referred to as "the mad scientist" in the papers. They say he deliberately built androids that were packed with anti-government data, whatever that means.

Sorry to put you in such trouble. But it's all connected. Starting with the antique computer you are using, which is a trophy from our association. The award was suggested by me and I had you in mind for the prize. The dreams, Sahara, the raven, it's all connected. Nothing mystical. As they say, There is nothing paranormal in the multiverse.

Let's start with your dreams. It's really technical. But here is the short of it. I found your database on Free Space. I connected your Artificial Intelligence chip in your brain, which connects to your palm clock, with that of Sahara, an android I built. The dreams were enhanced by a process, including that of the raven. The raven has lived with humans for as long as we have existed, owing its survival to its unselective eating habits. I called this project, Project Raven. It is a project for the survival of humanity. I hope that makes sense to you.

But there is more a scientist can do than to just build androids, isn't there? Which brings us to our subject…

The disease is curable. I have found a cure. I reported this to the council three years ago and they told me in my face that they were not interested in any antidote. Our job is to build humanoids, that's all.

What will happen to all the funding we get from the World Council? What will happen to the millions who work in the departments? They asked.

I want you to write and tell the world that there is a cure. I had to use this antique device because you never know who is monitoring you with all these gadgets at our disposal. Here is the formula which you must publish. You and I can save the world. I know we can.

The computer screen goes blank. Words and symbols appear. Before he could read and make sense of the words and symbols, he sees a green telephone icon blinking on the TC. He folds the computer and hides it under the coffee table. He presses a button on the remote that answers the call. A face appears. A woman in a yellow top and green hair. Oval face with a pointed chin. Thick lips and a long nose. Small but wide eyes. Her eyelids look artificial, long and visible.

"Mr Kamoto."

"Doctor."

"How have you been?"

"Fine, I am fine."

"I was expecting you yesterday."

"Yes."

"What happened?"

"I had an emergency trip to Blantyre. Following a story."

"I see. How are the dreams? Any improvements?"

"I think I am feeling better now."

"Good. I will be expecting you on Monday. Is that fine with you?"

"Yes, doctor, it is fine."

"Later then."

"Later, doctor."

When the face of his psychiatrist disappears on the TC, he sighs, collapses his arms on his sides, reclines his head backwards with his eyes closed before returning to his computer.

CHAPTER TWENTY-EIGHT

The Codicil

Ivor Agyeman-Duah

The taxi driver finally pulled up at our house in Kumasi to take me to the coach station. From there, it would take another five hours to Accra the capital, where the next day, I would fly to the United Kingdom to pursue post-graduate studies at the University of Surrey. But I leave home and family with unease. Father, at seventy-one is suffering from kidney complications. He had lifted himself with great effort to say: "You may not come to meet me again because of this illness," as he shook my hands to my mother's strong protestation.

"You don't have to do that and say such things," her own voice at breaking point.

The day before had been equally troubling. My father was an only child of wealthy parents. His mother, that is, my grandmother, was from the royal house of Kokofu which meant she could have been an influential queen, according to the Asante's matrilineal inheritance. But a trained accountant and later a theologian, my father exchanged royalty for the silver chalice, becoming an Anglican priest. He had his fair share of life's troubles which caused him great depression and sometimes severe mood swings that were uncomfortable for us his children.

Father had five children with Mother, Foriwaa, but we were not his only biological children. He had five others with his first wife, one of them, Jerry, had come to the house before my departure, demanding of the sick man he and his siblings' share of his assets. He arrived drunk and almost slapped Father but for the intervention of those around. Father looked at him without emotion, but my mother was upset and in a loud voice said: "If your mother had remained faithful, there would not have been issues of who gets what."

My Aunt, Konadu, who lived with us after her own husband died, explained what led to this.

Father's first wife, Jerry's mother, left when Father became very depressed after the death of his mother many years ago. Relatives stole his mother's assets including money and a lot of gold. In that state of depression and sometimes hallucination, the first wife lost her love. She sought transfer as a nurse and was posted to a district in northern Ghana. It was from there she instituted divorce proceedings. But she did so also because she became pregnant for another man she met there. It was considered abominable and they say it has a way of negative visitation on children. Whether by coincidence or belief, her five children either took to heavy drinking or engaged in social vices that took them to prison. One died.

As the taxi took me to the station, my mind was crowded with thoughts: the spirituality of Father that meant at least my older brother and I had to be Servants of the Sanctuary at the Anglican Church. Handel's "Messiah" and other hymns were standard listening for us while we were growing up. We knew where he bought some of these and those who did not, he would let them know: from Oxford where he had received a British Council scholarship to do research in 1960 and to fond memories of All Souls College of the Faithful where the first African Fellow, William Abrahams was revered in Africa.

I settled into studies in the beautiful English city of Surrey. I called home irregularly because of the difficulties of trans-telecommunication systems. Seven months after the MSc in Economic History course work, I went to live with a cousin in London to work on my dissertation. From there, I could call home more easily and frequently. I spoke to Mother often and in a particular week that she was most cheerful, I did not know father had been hospitalized. She had prepared herself for a terrible outcome and thought I should not know. Two days after the conversation with her, a midnight call announced the transition.

"We were at the hospital day and night," my brother later told me, as he and other relatives rotated during those last days witnessing the once pleasant frame of my father racked by coughing consistently. His loss of flesh was as if by the hour; his dead mother's name on his lips whenever he could utter anything at all.

"He might have loved his mother a lot," a nurse reportedly said, whereupon she was told that our father was an only child.

On the morning before he passed away, he was calm, to the delight of the surrounding family. Just when my brother stepped out to freshen up and only twenty metres away from him, he gave up the ghost. The blanket was pulled over the corpse. All went home, some in silent tears but the women in loud expressions of immortal loss on how death claims its victims.

On the way home, they met Jerry. Again drunk. They told him. He was temporarily stunned.

"But what did he say of his WILL?" he asked as everybody walked past him. He sat under a near *Nim* tree. Started weeping. For his dead father? Or was he rather weeping for the contents of father's unknown Will?

II

Jerry had been a child of promise, hope and excellence but it had all collapsed with his love of alcohol. When he passed the Common Entrance Examination, (as it was then called) and went to secondary school, Mfantsipim School in Cape Coast, these elements were a signal for good. Jerry had not only passed well but had topped his class of which he was also the youngest. And not just to any secondary school but to Ghana's oldest in the coastal region, which had produced some of the country's leading men of timbre, as they say, including a future United Nations Secretary-General and a Nobel Peace Laureate, Kofi Annan.

By the second year in school, he had become to his siblings, the knowledgeable one to listen to on matters to do with the geography of the coastal area, the cultures and customs of the Fantis: fishermen and their trade songs as they paddle their canoes into the vistas of the Atlantic. After all, he was the only one of them who lived outside of Kumasi at least till the end of term.

When Kwame Grushie, Father's house gardener from the Upper-East region heard some of the stories, he knew they were exaggerated or untrue. Older than Jerry, he was not on the best of terms with him. On a few occasions Jerry's insolence towards him had led to threats to resign from work to go to his hometown. Jerry had a creative way of lying and swaying people to his side, particularly, his mother, who hardly rebuked him even when at the end Jerry was found to have lied.

One afternoon, as Kwame Grushie mended the ragged water-hoses and tended the garden, he heard as Jerry was having lunch in the garden surrounded by his siblings, a new interpretation of the folkloric song, the story of the so-called Ghost Song in the playwright Ama Ata Aidoo's *The Dilemma of a Ghost*. Perhaps Jerry was reading it as a course text. "The ghost exists to this day," he said and asked them to sing the song before he continued. They sang in chorus:

> *One early morning*
> *When the moon was up*
> *Shining as the sun*
> *I went to Elmina Junction*
> *And there and there*
> *I saw a wretched ghost*
> *Going up and down*
> *Singing to himself*
> *"Shall I go*
> *To Cape Coast*
> *Or to Elmina*
> *I don't know*
> *I can't tell*
> *I don't know*
> *I can't tell*

He explained to them as Grushie who busied himself with watering the plants and blossoming roses listened in amusement but making sure he did not betray an impression of eavesdropping or mockery of Jerry's narration.

"Ghosts are spirits of darkness." They listened attentively. "Their world is night. Only ghosts could see fellow ghosts in the afternoon. That is why this ghost of the morning is different and dangerous.

"In fact, it is said that on some mornings he appeared in white over-all and people were alerted, many, including fruit traders on the pavements and roads would stay indoors until he disappeared by way of Elmina or the Cape Coast road. He was and is still known to spread bad luck and illness with his presence."

The maturity of that creativity with Jerry and all its amoral nuances came home to bear. And the times of his secondary school days and his many stories were not good, the 1980s. The brutal socialist military regime in Ghana, at the beginning of the "revolution" killed by firing squad and without trial three former leaders of the country and three high court judges were abducted from their homes together with a retired army officer and murdered by people suspected to be part of the regime. Insecurity was visible and the leader of the military regime, Jerry John Rawlings, had to deal with counter-insurgence just as he coped with a failing economy of commodity price collapse of cocoa, gold, timber and other resources with consequent effects on a dwindling national income. It meant scarcity of imports of many items needed for mining and other industries. There was a shortage of spare parts for vehicles, damaged roads and poor railway infrastructure affected the internal mobility. The telecommunication system was operating below ten per cent capacity with associated unreliable postal services. The situation led to the Structural Adjustment Programme the government had to enter into with the World Bank and the International Monetary Fund, but even that had to go another phase, the Programme to Mitigate the Social Cost of Adjustment.

It was such that when Jerry, like other students who went off to boarding school, there was virtually no communication with family till term ended and the chartered State Transport bus would bring the Kumasi students back home.

Jerry was in his third year when Father went to participate in a national Anglican Synod in Cape Coast. He decided after the Synod to visit Jerry and also take a tour of his own old school, Adisadel College near by. Father had always argued with friends about colonial rule that if the British did nothing at least they planted not just schools, but good ones, along the coast and later in the forest areas, schools which would serve the country well. The Gold Coast, by the time the British left had become independent in 1957 and had one of the best educational systems on the west coast of Africa.

Father had become fonder of Jerry as reports from school and Jerry's academic standing had been good, reminding him of his own days at his son's age. It was, however, with some uneasy countenance that Jerry's House Master welcomed Father when he arrived at the school. After the traditional serving of water in his sitting room, the Master asked the purpose of father's visit. The demeanor of the Master who knew him in previous encounters, changed when Father said, "Well, Synod closed on Sunday and as you know, I can't come this close and not bring Jerry greetings from home with a few 'essential commodities' and letters from his siblings."

The Master welcomed father after the exchange of plensatries and afterwards he had expected that the Master would call one of his children to go and fetch Jerry. Master in the momentary silence that followed asked:

"I presume in that sense that you think Jerry is still a student here ?…"

"But is he not?"

Master was caught in a difficult moment because as a parent himself he had struggled to have to tell father that Jerry had absented himself for two terms and therefore got dismissed the previous year. It was also detected just about that time that he and another student were involved in the theft of two receipts and term report booklets.

As father listened in complete silence, with the packages meant for Jerry on the floor, he could only mutter, "So what is it? I get the school reports and bills and give him money to pay the fees and his allowance for the terms... :" He was stunned and lost for words.

"It's likely he prepared his reports and receipts with the stolen booklets and got them posted from Cape Coast. In fact, we have written about all this to you, but I am sure from what you are saying now you obviously did not receive those letters. Maybe he intercepted them," the Master chipped in.

"It's possible. He has always had a spare key to the post office box."

"I am so sorry to have to tell you this and under such circumstances. Jerry was undoubtedly a brilliant boy but nobody knows what overcame him to take the path he took even after I had personally guided him on some of his transgressions."

Confused, embarassed and sad, it was with some dignity that Father thanked the Master and requested him to give to his children the 'essential commodities' he had brought and which he saw no need to take back to Kumasi.

Father became very depressed and on the journey back came to the conclusion that Grushie's report to him months ago that he had seen Jerry in Kejetia, the central commercial district in Kumasi, was most probably true. He had brushed it aside and attributed the report to Grushie's sometimes drunk moods which made him talkative after bouts of *pito*. But he remembered that on that same day of Grushie's story, he had received a purported letter posted from Jerry from Cape Coast.

III

Could this supposed grief on the announcement of his father's death as he wept under the *Nim* tree be of any deeper meaning for Jerry?

IV

The funeral of father as they say in Kumasi, was well attended. As with such funerals you also see 'ghosts' of people one has not seen for years, even a decade, all coming to show their sympathy. Their mother did not attend either. So even that last traditional respect for a father of showing up was not observed, let alone helping to carry the casket into its final resting place.

For if they were upset with their father for his unknown wealth and for how he intended to distribute possessions, which wealth was not much anyway, it was sometimes difficult to understand why they were also very disrespectful to their mother and hurled insults at her. Was it because of Dorothy, their step-sister, the one their mother had with another man? She who was completely disliked by the rest? Or were they just spoilt children who, having squandered all the opportunities to get good education and a good family reputation could at a point only gauge what was left of another man's toils?

"How can she bear the sins of her mother if that is the motivation for disliking her?" A neighbour who detested their behaviour towards Dorothy once confronted the ganged-up siblings which ended in a huge brawl one day between the neighbour and themselves with one sibling from Jerry's side losing her tooth. The police intervened but later the case was withdrawn to be settlement at home.

If that neighbourhood confrontation did anything, it caused hatred for Dorothy to subside. At 22 years, Dorothy had plans of her own. She had waited till she acquired her United Kingdom visa and ticket and three hours to flight's departure, before informing all that by "God's grace she will be travelling tonight to London."

A week after her travel and the funeral, the court in Kumasi served their mother with an invitation to the hearing, together with her children, of the WILL of her late former husband. On the appointed day, she refused to go to the children's surprise.

The tense courtroom at the end cooled with relief as the contents were read.

"... All ten plots of land at Atasomanso should go to Mercy, my former wife and children, but all other property to my current wife and her children: the two houses, pension, savings, my accountancy firm evaluation, etc and other things in my name..."

But there was a codicil to this which explained that the indenture, site plan and other documentation of the land had been given to Mercy years back.

Jerry and siblings were overjoyed and virtually sang their way home, not forgetting to pass by their favourite bar for drinks.

"At least it's $500,000 we have on our hands now. A plot of land at Atasomanso is currently over $50,000 and it's enough money to solve the many problems," Jerry told the others.

They arrived home late at night but found their mother's bedroom door locked. Persistent knocking was greeted with silence until someone woke up from outside their apartment to say, their mother mother left in the morning as soon as they also went to the court.

"Two of your uncles were here in the morning with one of your aunties. They looked troubled, with your mother sobbing. I hope it's nothing bad and God forbid, family death," the apartment neighbour had said. Their thoughts suddenly shifted to Auntie Martha, their mother's sister who had been down with a massive stroke and didn't seem to be getting any better.

It took two days before they at least knew where she was, not dead or harmed. When they got the call to the St. Theresa's Catholic Mission House, they could hardly fathom its purpose. Apparently, a meeting was to be chaired by the parish priest. Other extended family members were present.

After prayers, the priest went straight to the details. "Your mother has sinned against God and you. You might have heard the court reading of your late father's WILL and the codicil. Your mother sold those lands years ago. If you go to the Lands Commission, you will find sadly that it's not in her or your names…"

Jerry violently got up from his seat but was restrained and he started shouting; "Sold to whom…?" By this time, the other siblings were on their feet and protesting.

"And what was the money used for since it does not show on her nor on us?" another asked.

The land had been used as collateral at the bank by the boyfriend she met in Tamale, Dorothy's policeman father in a business he was engaged in. When the business collapsed and the investment could not be recovered including the bank's equity, the land was sold to recover it.

"I always thought mothers love their children and protect them," Jerry said.

"Not all mothers do," his sister Agnes, added, as they all walked past a mother in tears and into the same world they had dreaded.

Biography of Contributors

Wole Soyinka – is Professor of English Literature, playwright, poet and novelist is also a human rights activist, who was awarded the Nobel Prize in Literature in 1986. From 1958, when he wrote *The Swamp Dwellers* to date, he has written over forty books, which include plays, collections of poetry, novels, autobiographical accounts and essays. Soyinka's novels include: *The Interpreters* and *Season of Anomy*; his plays are*: The Lion and the Jewel, The Trials of Brother Jero, Jero Metamorphosis, A Dance of the Forests, Kongi's Harvest, Madmen and Specialists, Death and the King's Horseman, From Zia with Love*; his poetry collections include: *Mandela's Earth and Other Poems, Samarkand and Other Markets I Have Known*. He has been President of The International Theatre Institute in Paris, President of International Parliament of Writers and NESCO's Ambassador for the Promotion of African Culture, Human Rights and Freedom of Expression. He has taught and given lectures at many universities around the world including Obafemi Awolowo, Ibadan, University of Ghana, Legon, Cambridge, Cornell, Harvard, Princeton, Yale, Columbia, Emory and Loyola Marymount in Los Angeles.

Ben Okri – is a novelist, poet and essayist, he is author of eight novels including the Booker Prize-winning, *The Famished Road, Songs of Enchantment, Tales of Freedom, Starbook, In Arcadia, Astounding the Gods* and the short-story collection, *Stars of the New Curfew*. Okri's poetry, celebrated around the world, includes the collections, *Wild, Mental Fight* and *An African Elegy*. His non-fiction including *Birds of Heaven, A Way of Being Free* and *A Time for New Dreams*, have been translated into more than 20 languages. Born in Nigeria and living in London, he is a Fellow of the Royal Society of Literature and Vice President of the English Centre of PEN International.

Among other awards, Okri has received an OBE, the

Commonwealth Writers Prize for Africa, the Aga Khan Prize for Fiction and the Chianti Rufino-Antico Fattore. He has been presented by the World Economic Forum in Davos with the Crystal award.

Ama Ata Aidoo – is best known as an international award-winning playwright, novelist, poet and university Professor. She was from 2004–2010 Professor in Africana Studies at Brown University and before then – from 1993–1999 served as Visiting Professor, Department of English, Hamilton College, Distinguished Visiting Professor, Department of English, Oberlin College, The Madeleine Haas Russell Visiting Professor of Non-Western and Comparative Studies, Brandeis University, Visiting Professor, English and Theatre Departments, Smith College and others. She also taught at the University of Cape Coast and started her teaching career at the University of Ghana where she had earlier graduated from. Her famous works include *The Dilemma of a Ghost* (1965); *Anowa* (1970); *No Sweetness Here* (1970); *Our Sister Killjoy* (1977); *Someone Talking to Sometime* (1985) which won the Nelson Mandela Prize for Poetry; *Changes: A Love Story* (1991), winner of the Commonwealth Writers Prize for Africa; *An Angry Letter in January* (1992); *The Girl Who Can and Other Stories* (1997); *Diplomatic Pounds and Other Stories* (2012) and editor, *African Love Stories: An Anthology* (2006). In 2012, scholars from around the world honoured her with, *Essays in Honour of Ama Ata Aidoo at 70 – A Reader in African Cultural Studies* edited by Anne V. Adams and in 2014 a documentary film; *The Art of Ama Ata Aidoo* was produced by Yaba Badoe.

Sefi Atta – was born in Lagos, Nigeria, in 1964 and was educated at Birmingham University, England and in the United States. She is also a graduate of the Creative Writing programme at Antioch University, Los Angeles. Atta has won several awards including the 2006 Wole Soyinka Prize for Literature in Africa, the 2005 PEN International David T.K. Wong Prize, the Red Hen Press Short Story Award and the 2009 NOMA Award for Publishing in Africa. A former chartered accountant and CPA, Atta is the author of *Everything Good Will Come* (2005) *Swallow* (2010), *News from Home* (2010) and *A Bit of Difference* (2013). Also a playwright, Atta's radio plays have been broadcast by the BBC and her stage plays have been performed internationally. Her short stories have appeared in literary journals such as the Los Angeles Review, the Mississippi Review and World Literature Today, while her books have been translated into several languages. In 2015, her play, *The Sentence* was published in African Theatre 14: Contemporary Women. A critical study of her works, *Writing Contemporary Nigeria: How Sefi Atta Illuminates African Culture and Tradition* written by Professor Walter Collins, *et al*, has been published by Cambria Press. She divides her time between Nigeria, England and the United States.

Ivor Agyeman-Duah – is the Development Policy Advisor to The Lumina Foundation in Lagos which awards The Wole Soyinka Prize for Literature in Africa and 2014-15 Chair of the Literature Jury of the Millennium Excellence Foundation. Agyeman-Duah was part of the production team for the BBC and PBS *'Into Africa* and *Wonders of the African World* presented by Henry Louis Gates, Jnr. He wrote and produced the acclaimed television documentary, *Yaa Asantewaa: The Heroism of an African Queen* and its sequel, *The Return of a King to Seychelles*. He was chief advisor to the Arts Council of England and Ford Foundation – supported theatrical production, *Yaa Asantewaa Warrior Queen* as well as Co-Editor, with Peggy Appiah and Kwame Anthony Appiah of *Bu Me Be: Proverbs of the Akans* (2007); with Ogochukwu Promise of *Essays in Honour of Wole Soyinka at 80* (2014).

Agyeman-Duah has received fifteen awards, fellowships and grants from around the world including: Distinguished Friend of Oxford Award from the University of Oxford. He is a Member of the Order of Volta, Republic of Ghana and a Fellow of the Phi Beta Delta International Society of the College of Arts and Letters, California State University, Pomona. He has also been a US State Department International Visitor and received the Commonwealth's Thomson Foundation Award, among others. Agyeman-Duah has held fellowships at the W.E.B. Du

Bois Institute for African and African American Research at Harvard University and been a Hilary and Trinity Term Resident Scholar at Exeter College, Oxford and from 2014–2015 was a Research Associate at the African Studies Centre, Oxford. He holds graduate degrees from the London School of Economics and Political Science (LSE), the School of Oriental and African Studies, London (SOAS) and the University of Wales.

Chika Unigwe – was born in Enugu, Enugu State in Nigeria and studied at the University of Nigeria, Nssuka before obtaining a PhD in Literature from the University of Leiden in The Netherlands. She is an award-winning author of three novels, including her debut originally published in Dutch as, *De Feniks*; *On Black Sisters Street* (2009, 2011 Jonathan Cape, UK and Random House, New York) which won the Nigeria Prize for Literature and *Night Dancer* (Jonathan Cape, 2012). In 2004, she received both the BBC and Commonwealth Short Story Awards and in 2004 was short-listed for the Caine Prize and made it to The Top 10 of the Million Writers Award in the same year. In 2005, Unigwe won the Equiano Fiction Contest which among others led to Zukiswa Wanner in *The Guardian* (Britain) rating her one of "top five African writers." In 2014, her novel on Olaudah Equiano, *Black Messiah* was published. Her works have been published in journals including *Wasafiri* and *Moving Worlds* and translated into many languages including, German, Japanese, Hebrew, Italian, Hungarian, Spanish and Dutch.

Ogochukwu Promise – is the Director of The Lumina Foundation, administrators of the Wole Soyinka Prize for Literature in Africa, received the 1999 Cadbury Prize for poetry with her collection, *My Mother's Eyes Speak Volumes*, while her novel, *Surveyor of Dreams* got the 1999 Spectrum Prize for prose, also in the same year. In 2000, she was awarded the Okigbo Poetry Prize for *Canals in Paradox* and again won the Spectrum Prize for Prose in 2000 for her novel, *Deep Blue Woman*. In 2002, she earned the maiden ANA/NDDC Prize with *Half of Memories* as well as The Matatu Prize for children's literature the same year with *The*

Street Beggars. In November 2003, she won the Flora Nwapa Prize for prose with *Fumes and Cymbals* whilst her 2004 *In the Middle of the Night* won the first Pat Utomi Book Prize. Again, *Swollen and Rotten Spaces* and *Naked Among These Hills* were selected for the Flora Nwapa Prize for Literature and one of the three best poetry books in Nigeria respectively. Promise is an Azikiwe Fellow in Communication as well as a Fellow of Stiftung Kulturfonds. She has enjoyed fellowships in the US, Italy and Germany and travelled extensively in Europe, Africa and Asia as a scholar, playwright and a poet. She is also an essayist and wrote, *Creative Writing and the Muse, The Writer as God, Dreams, Shadows and Reality* and *Wild Letters in Harmattan.* She does abstract paintings and has exhibited in Nigeria. She holds a PhD in Communication and Language Arts from the University of Ibadan.

Taiye Selasi – was born in London and raised in Massachusetts. She holds a BA in American Studies from Yale and an MPhil in International Relations from Oxford. '*The Sex Lives of African Girls*' (*Granta*, 2011), Selasi's fiction debut, appeared in *Best American Short Stories 2012.* In 2013, *Granta* named her on its once-every-decade list of Best of Young British Novelists. Selasi's first novel *Ghana Must Go* (Penguin, 2013), a *New York Times* bestseller, was selected as one of the 10 Best Books of 2013 by *The Wall Street Journal* and *The Economist.* The novel has been sold in sixteen countries. Selasi lives in Rome.

Irehobhude O. Iyioha – is an award winning legal scholar, writer and advocate. She studied English and Literature for a year before training as a lawyer in Nigeria, obtained a Masters degree in law from the University of Toronto and holds a PhD in law from the University of British Columbia, Canada. She has held professorial and senior policy positions in Canada including, Adjunct Professor at the University of Alberta's John Dossetor Health Ethics Centre. She is the co-editor of a book on comparative health law and policy, which spells the beginning of what may now be formally termed the 'Nigerian health law and policy' and which is described by reviewers as "bold and path-breaking." Iyioha's fiction has appeared in various publications, including Harvard University's *Transition,* the UK's *Litro Magazine* and the Canadian *Maple Tree Literary Supplement.* She was long listed for the Writers Union of Canada's 22nd Annual Short Prose Competition for the short stories "Brave" and "Trans Atlantic." She has a forthcoming collection of short stories, *A Place Beyond the Heart* and a novel. Iyioha lives in Canada.

Yvonne Adhiambo Owuor – is a Kenyan novelist. Her debut novel *Dust* (Knopf, Granta) received global acclaim and tagged "the most important novel to come out of Africa since *Half of a Yellow Sun,*" by *The Observer Books of the Year.* It was shortlisted for both the Folio Prize and Financial Times/Oppenheimer Emerging Voices Award and won the TBC Jomo Kenyatta Prize for Literature, Kenya's pre-eminent literary prize. Owuor who won the 2003 Caine Prize for African Writing was named Woman of the Year (Culture and the Arts) by *Eve* magazine in Kenya in 2004 for her contribution to the country's literature and arts. She has been a fellow of the Iowa Writing Fellowship, a Resident – Fellow of the Lannan Foundation, past recipient of a Chevening Scholarship and a TEDx Nairobi speaker. Her short stories have been published in international literary magazines, including *McSweeney's* and *Chimurenga Chronic.* She lives in Brisbane, Australia and Nairobi, and was previously the Executive Director of the Zanzibar International Film Festival. She occasionally dips into working and lobbying for the arts and creative enterprises in support of the expansion of the African innovation economy. Her second novel has a working title *The Dragonfly Sea.*

Tsitsi Dangarembga – was born in Mutoko, Zimbabwe, novelist poet, activist and filmmaker, Tsitsi Dangarembga completed her education in her home country, where she worked as a copywriter and started writing seriously as a poet and novelist. Dangarembga wrote her first novel, *Nervous Conditions* at the age of twenty-five. It immediately became a seminal piece of literature and was hailed by Doris Lessing as one of the most important novels of the twentieth century. She published her second novel, *The Book of Not* in 2006 and its successor, *A Mournable Body* is forthcoming. She obtained her Masters in Filmmaking from the German Film and Television Academy in Berlin. She lives in Harare, where she founded the production house Nyerai Films and the International Images Film Festival for Women. She also founded the Institute of Creative Arts for Progress in Africa where she works as Director. Her films and literature have been critically acclaimed and have received international awards. She founded her publishing house, ICAPA Publishing in 2014 with a collection of short stories, *A Family Portrait* that interrogates the many endemic forms of violence in Zimbabwe. She is currently writing *SAI--SAI, WATERMAKER*, a dystrophic speculative fiction for young adults.

Chimamanda Ngozi Adichie – is a best-selling Nigerian author resident in the United States, whose writings have been translated into over thirty languages. She is the author of *Purple Hibiscus* which won the Commonwealth Writers Prize, The Hurston/Wright Legacy Award and was long listed for the Booker Prize and of *Half of a Yellow Sun* which won the Orange Prize, Anisfied-Wolf Book Award for 2007 and has been turned into a major film. Her third novel, *Americanah* published in 2013 received the United States National Book Critics Circle Award and the Chicago Tribune Heartland Prize for fiction the same year. Other awards include the BBC (2002) for her short story "That Harmattan Morning," and the O. Henry Prize for her short story "The American Embassy" in 2003. She won the International Nonino Prize for 2009. *This Thing Around Your Neck* (2009) is her first collection of short stories. She was awarded the MacArthur Fellowship in 2009 and between that time and now has appeared as one of Africa's most influential writers and personalities in the *New African, The Africa Report, Time* and the *New Yorker* List of the Best 20 Writers under 40 among others. She served between 2005-2006 as Hodder Fellow at Princeton University and from 2011-12 was awarded a fellowship by the Radcliffe Institute for Advanced Studies, Harvard University to complete *Americanah*. She holds a Masters in Creative Writing from Johns Hopkins University,

Baltimore and a Master of Arts in Africana Studies from Yale University.

Tope Folarin – was educated at Morehouse College and the University of Oxford where he earned two Master's degrees as a Rhodes Scholar. He won the 2013 Caine Prize for African Writing for his short story "Miracle" from *Transition*. He is the recipient of writing fellowships from the Institute for Policy Studies, Washington, DC and serves on the board of the Hurston/Wright Foundation and Editorial Board of *Transition* magazine. His work has been featured in *Transition* (Fall 2012), in the *Breakthrough Voices* edition of *Virginia Quarterly Review* (Fall 2014), in the recent Contemporary Fiction edition of *Callaloo* magazine (Fall 2014) and in *The Africa Report. A Memory this Size and Others Stories* (New Internationalist); *The Literary Experience Textbook Second Edition'* (Cengage Learning); *Out of Many*: *Multiplicity and Divisions in American Today* (Kendall Hunt); and *Snapshots*-Nouvelles *Voix du Caine Prize* (Editions Zulma) in France are among his various works.

He has earned fellowships from Callaloo Magazine, the Hurston/Wright Foundation, the Yale Writers Conference, the Squaw Valley Writers Conference, and the Kimbilio Fiction Writers' Workshop. Folarin was named in the Africa 39 list of the most promising African writers under 40 in 2014. He is a member of the PEN/Faulkner Writer in Schools Programme.

Martin Egblewogbe – is author of the short-story collection, *Mr. Happy and the Hammer of God and Other Stories* (Ayebia, 2012). His story, "The Gonjon Pin" appeared in the 2014 Caine Prize Anthology. Apart from short stories, Egblewogbe also writes poetry and has co-edited two anthologies, *Look Where You Have Gone To Sit* (Woeli Publications, 2010), and *According to Sources* (Woeli Publications, 2015). He co-founded (with Laban Carrick Hill), The Writers Project of Ghana (WPG), an international literary organization based in Accra, Ghana and the United States to promote literary culture in Africa and around the world. Many leading writers, particularly West Africans have participated in WPG's programmes including its author-reading sessions jointly organised with the German cultural organization, Goethe Institute. Egblewogbe teaches physics at the University of Ghana, Legon.

Peggy Appiah – is the daughter of the former English Chancellor of the Exchequer in post-war Britain, Sir Stafford Cripps. Appiah was also the widow of the Ghanaian statesman Joe Appiah and she lived in Ghana for almost half a century and died at the age of 84. She wrote over thirty novels including: *Smell of Onions, Tales from an Ashanti Father, The Pineapple Child and Other Tales from Ashanti* and *The Gift of Mmotia*. With Kwame Anthony Appiah and Agyeman-Duah, they edited, *Bu Me Be: Proverbs of the Akans* which is one of the largest collections of African proverbs and folklore. Peggy Appiah received many international awards for her writing including Membership of the British Empire (MBE) for promotion of Anglo-Ghanaian relations, the 2005 Literature Prize of the Millennium Excellence Foundation and an honorary Doctorate degree from the Kwame Nkrumah University of Science and Technology. She travelled the world initially with her parents in Europe and Asia where her mother held the Order of the Most Brilliant Star of China.

Yaba Badoe – is an award-winning documentary filmmaker and novelist, Badoe lives in London, graduated from King's College, Cambridge and has an MPhil in Development Studies from the University of Sussex. She worked with BBC radio and television and later as producer and director of Britain's terrestrial channels. Her filmography credits, influenced by the subordination of women in development, neo-liberal and Keynesian approaches to economics, include, *The Witches of Gambaga* (co-produced with Amima Mama) which won the Best Documentary at the Black International Film Festival (2010) and second prize at FESPACO (2011). It has been adapted by Amnesty International-Kenya, The Commission for Human Rights (Ghana) and Netright. *Black and White*, on race and racism in Bristol was done for BBC1; *I Want Your Sex*, an exploration of images and myths surrounding black sexuality in Western Art, film and photography was for Channel 4 and a six-part series, *Voluntary Services Overseas* was for ITV. Most recently, she wrote and directed, *The Art of Ama Ata Aidoo*. Badoe's first novel, *True Murder,* was published by Jonathan Cape in 2009. Her short stories have been published in *Critical Quarterly* and in anthologies including *Ayebia's African Love Stories* edited by Ama Ata Aidoo. A Ghanaian-British, Badoe has taught in Spain and Jamaica and spends time as Visiting Scholar at the Institute of African Studies, University of Ghana.

Monica Arac de Nyeko – is a writer from Uganda who won the Caine Prize (2007) for her story, "Jambula Tree" published in the Ayebia's *African Love Stories Anthology* (2006) edited by the distinguished Ghanaian writer Ama Ata Aidoo. She had previously, in 2004, been shortlisted for the Prize for her story, "Strange Fruit." She is a Member of the Uganda Women Writers Association (FEMRITE). Her works have appeared in several anthologies including, *Words From a Granary* (FEMRITE Publication 2003), *Memories of Sun* (Green Willow Books 2004) and *Seventh Street Alchemy* (Jacana Media 2005).

Faustin Kagame – is a Rwandan writer, literary translator, journalist and media advisor. He has been involved in the recent translation of Rwandan traditional and folkore stories from the nationally spoken language, Kinyanwanda into English. These stories were told in the evenings as bed-time moral tales centuries ago and were forbidden to be translated until recently. Now, they are deemed appropriate to add in their English and French translations to the timelessness of an African heritage and of humanity. Kagame's contribution originally had the title, "The Prince Who Fell in Love With a Beautiful Commoner," which is published in this collection as, "Exchanging the Crown Someday for Exile." Kagame lives in Kigali.

Wendy Day Veevers-Carter – is the daughter of the American author, Clarence Day. Veevers-Carter was born in New York and educated at Radcliffe. Her life adventures in the 1960s became the source of the fascinating book, *Island Home* (1970) about plantation island life in the Remire and Astove of the Seychelles. Others works of hers include, *A Garden Of Ede: Plant-Life in South-East Asia* and *Riches of the Rain Forest.* "In Astove of the Seychelles," her contribution in this anthology, is the epilogue to *Island Home* which is still among the best-writing on island adventure.

Nadya Somoe Ngumi – is a Kenyan short story writer. Her writings have appeared in anthologies and in *The East African.* At twenty-four, she is one of Kenya's new generation of writers. She lives in Nairobi.

Benjamin Sehene – became prominent as a writer after the genocide in his homeland of Rwanda. Of the Tutsi ethnic stock, his family like many others in the 1960s, fled to live in Uganda in 1963. He later migrated to France and studied at the Sorbonne in Paris in the 1980s before going to live in Canada and then back in Paris. A member of PEN International, Sehene eventually returned to post-genocide Rwanda to better understand questions of identity and ethnicity which largely define his many short stories and two of his best known works, *Le Piege ethnique* or *The Ethnic Trap* (1999) and later, *Fire Under the Cassock* (2005) a historical novel of a Hutu Catholic Father, Stanistas who offered protection to Tutsi refugees in his cathedral as a pretext to sexually abuse the women among them and later participate in their massacre.

Ellen Banda-Aaku – is a writer from Zambia. Her first book for children, *Wandi's Little Voice*, won the Macmillan Writer's Prize for Africa in 2004. In 2007 her story, "Sozi's Box" was the overall winner of the Commonwealth Short Story Competition. Her first Novel, *Patchwork*, won the Penguin Prize for African Writing and was short-listed for the Commonwealth Book Prize in 2012 in which same year she was awarded the Zambia Arts Council's Ngoma Chairpersons Award for achievements in Literature. Her short stories have been published in anthologies in Australia, United Kingdom, United States and South Africa. She is a patron of The Pelican Post, a Charity dedicated to distributing fiction books for schools in Africa. In 2014, her novel, *Patchwork,* was translated into German.

Banda-Aaku, who has published a novel and six books for children, is a regular facilitator at the FEMRITE (Uganda Women Writers Association) annual African Women Writers' Residency Programme and has conducted creative writing workshops in Ghana, Malawi, Rwanda, South Africa, Uganda and Zambia. She was a judge on the Macmillan Prize for African Writing in 2006, the Malawi Peer Gynt National Novel Writing Competition in 2013 and the Writivisim Short Story Competition in 2014. She holds an MA in Creative Writing and has been an external examiner on the University of Cape Town's Masters in Creative Writing Programme.

Bridget Pitt – is a Zimbabwe-born South African award-winning novelist and poet. Her fist published writing was for *The Grassroots* newspaper, used by Cape Town black communities as an organizing tool in the anti-apartheid struggles. Her three novels are, *Unbroken Wing, The Unseen Leopard* which was shortlisted for the Commonwealth Writers Prize in 2011 and for the Wole Soyinka Prize for Literature in Africa in 2012, and *Notes from the Lost Property Department* published by Penguin Random House in 2015. Her short stories include: "Next Full Moon We Will Release Juno," which was shortlisted for the 2013 Commonwealth Short Story Prize and published as part of the anthology, *Let's Tell this Story Properly* and "The Infant Odysseus" which was runner-up in the 2015 Short Sharp Award and published in *The Incredible Journey.* Her children's story, *The Night of the Go Away Birds* was awarded first place for the Maskew Miller Pearson Literature Prize. Pitt's poetry published in *The Thinker* magazine and elsewhere include: *Salvation Swimgs Towards Us, The Guardians, The Song of the Gorilla* and *The Mother Gave Us Words.* She has written a book for SANBI on urban nature conservation and is involved in communities initiatives in nature conservation. She lives in Cape Town.

Shadreck Chikoti – a writer from Malawi, he was listed by the CNN among the must-read African authors and selected by Elechi

Amadi among the 39 most promising writers under the age of 40 with the potential and talent to define trends in the development of literature in Africa. He won the 2013 Peer Gynt Literary Award for his speculative novel, *Azotus the Kingdom*. An excerpt from it, "The Occupant," was published by Bloomsbury in the Africa 39 anthology in October 2014. His other published works include, *Free Africa Flee!* (2001)https://en.wikipedia.org/wiki/Shadreck_ Chikoti – cite_note 1 and *MwanawaKamuzu* (2010). His short story, "Beggar Girl," was included in the anthology, *Modern Stories from Malawi* (2003). "The Baobab," for which he won third prize in the 2008 FMB/MAWU Literary Awards, was published in *The Bachelor of Chikanda and OtherStories* (2009).https://en.wikipedia. org/wiki/Shadreck_Chikoti – cite_note-4 "Child of a Hyena," was published in the Caine Prize 2011 anthology, *To See the Mountain and Other Stories*.

Chikoti is also the Director of Pan African Publishers and founder of The Story Club, which gathers writers, critics, and others to share and discuss literature in Malawi.

Acknowledgements

This collection is first published in 2016 by Ayebia Clarke Publishing Limited, specialists in African and Caribbean writing based in Oxfordshire in the UK and for over a decade my regular Publishers. I would like to express my gratitude as always to Nana Ayebia Clarke MBE and her husband David and their team at Ayebia. I would also like to express my appreciation to Nana Akua Agyemang-Badu in Accra, Ghana, for reading through the draft manuscript and making useful suggestions.

My deepest appreciation, however, goes to all the contributors who kindly gave their permission and consent for their stories to be included in this Anthology and responded positively and on time for this publication to happen. Only three stories in this collection have been previously published: Ama Ata Aidoo's second contribution, *Feely, Feely,* first published in *Wasafiri,* Volume 19, Issue 42, 2004 and in *Diplomatic Pounds & Other Stories* (Ayebia: 2012). Taiye Selasi's *Driver,* first published in *Granta,* and *Transition to Glory* by Chimamanda Ngozi Adichie published in the *African Love Stories Anthology* edited by Ama Ata Aidoo (Ayebia: 2006). I am grateful to both Nana Ayebia Clarke and Chimamanda Ngozi Adichie for permission to reproduce these here. Also the adaptation of Wendy Veevers-Carter's Epilogue in Island Home, which appears here as, *In Astove of the Seychelles Islands,* by Calusa Bay Publications of Mahe.

-I A-D.